# The Calendar
# of
# New Beginnings

by

Ava Miles

Copyright April 2016, Ava Miles. All rights reserved. No part of this book may be reproduced or transmitted in any form by any means—graphic, electronic or mechanical—without permission in writing from the author, except by a reviewer who may quote brief passages in a review.

This is a work of fiction. All of the characters, organizations, and events portrayed in this novel are either the products of the author's imagination or are used fictionally.

ISBN-13: 978-1-940565-45-3
www.avamiles.com
Ava Miles

# PRAISE FOR AVA MILES

## NORA ROBERTS LAND
Selected as one of the Best Books of 2013 alongside Nora Roberts' DARK WITCH and Julia Quinn's SUM OF ALL KISSES. USA Today Contributor, Becky Lower, Happily Ever After

"Ava's story is witty and charming." Barbara Freethy #1 NYT bestselling author

## FRENCH ROAST
"An entertaining ride...{and) a full-bodied romance." Readers' Favorite

## THE GRAND OPENING
"Ava Miles is fast becoming one of my favorite light contemporary romance writers." Tome Tender

## THE HOLIDAY SERENADE
"This story is all romance, steam, and humor with a touch of the holiday spirit..." The Book Nympho

## THE TOWN SQUARE
"Ms. Miles' words melted into each page until the world receded around me..." Tome Tender

## COUNTRY HEAVEN
"If ever there was a contemporary romance that rated a 10 on a scale of 1 to 5 for me, this one is it!" The Romance Reviews

## THE PARK OF SUNSET DREAMS
"Ava has done it again. I love the whole community of Dare Valley..." Travel Through The Pages Blog

## THE CHOCOLATE GARDEN
"On par with Nicholas Sparks' love stories." Jennifer's Corner Blog

## *Also by Ava Miles*

**The Dare Valley Series:**
NORA ROBERTS LAND
FRENCH ROAST
THE GRAND OPENING
THE HOLIDAY SERENADE
THE TOWN SQUARE
THE PARK OF SUNSET DREAMS
THE PERFECT INGREDIENT
THE BRIDGE TO A BETTER LIFE
DARING BRIDES
DARE VALLEY MEETS PARIS BILLIONAIRE
THE CALENDAR OF NEW BEGINNINGS

DARING DECLARATIONS: An anthology including THE HOLIDAY SERENADE & THE TOWN SQUARE

**The Dare River Series:**
COUNTRY HEAVEN
COUNTRY HEAVEN SONG BOOK
COUNTRY HEAVEN COOKBOOK
THE CHOCOLATE GARDEN
THE CHOCOLATE GARDEN: A MAGICAL TALE(Children's Book)
FIREFLIES & MAGNOLIAS
THE PROMISE OF RAINBOWS

**Non-fiction:**
THE HAPPINESS CORNER: REFLECTIONS SO FAR

*To Aidan—for changing the course of my life and being an integral part of the new beginning I've been calling in.*

*And to my divine entourage, who supports me so beautifully living this new story.*

# Acknowledgements

Every one of my books is supported by the most amazing people ever:

My Dream Team of Sienna, Jade, Angela, Shannon, Emerald, Em, Hilary, and Alisha.

Lori Antonson of The Axelrod Agency for helping me expand even more globally.

Dr. Michael C. Chappell of Arkansas Ophthalmology Associates, whose work with veterans affected with severe eye trauma brought him to me via the best cheerleaders on the planet, Dr. Tabitha King and Dr. Richa Thapa.

Dr. Katie Defore for more medical brilliance.
Tracy Allan, an incredible global photographer, who gave me remarkable insights.

Jean Warrick, an old family friend from Nebraska, who told my parents she'd posed in Tilden's racy "Better Half" Calendar to raise money for the local hospital, and sent me the calendar, which inspired this book.

To all my supporters—from my beloved readers to my representatives at all my distributors and beyond.

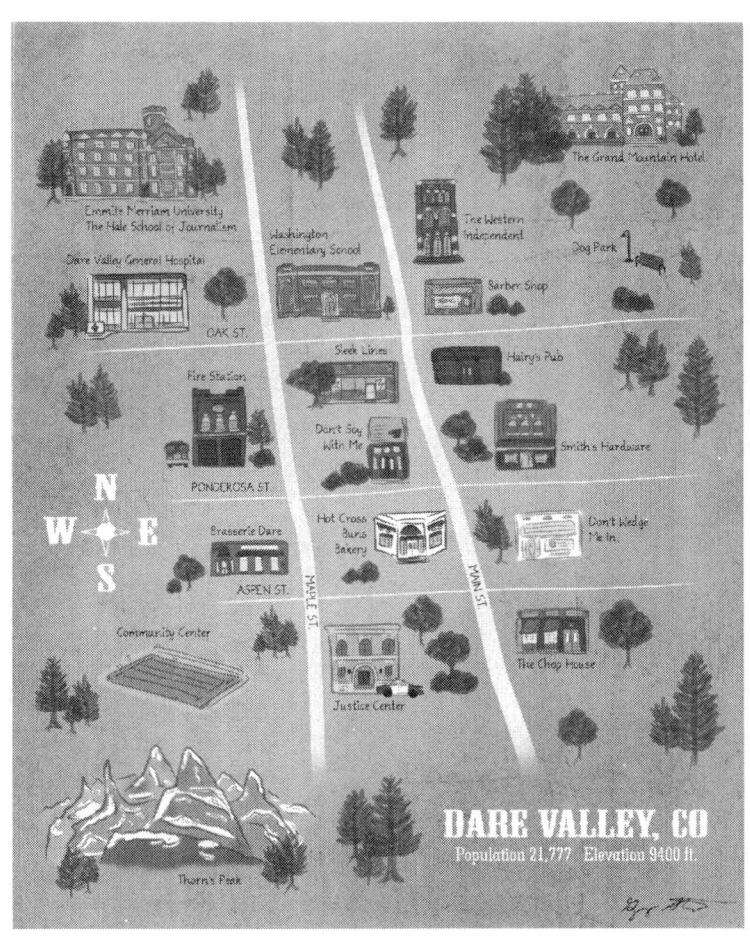

# Chapter 1

Lucy O'Brien had never longed for the small town of Dare Valley while she was globetrotting as a photojournalist in the warring mountains of Afghanistan or the conflict-ridden plains of sub-Saharan Africa. She'd been too eager to explore the world and experience everything it had to offer. And she had. After leaving her hometown for college eighteen years ago with nothing more than a bright blue suitcase, Lucy had seen the full spectrum of life—ancient monuments and natural wonders, horrifying mass graves, and starving children.

But her life had changed dramatically a month ago when she was caught in an attack on a Congolese village. Her injuries had mostly healed, but the vision in her right eye hadn't completely returned. Teaching at Emmits Merriam School of Journalism in Dare Valley for the fall semester would be her holding pattern until it did. Hopefully. As a photographer, she was right-eye dominant, so her whole career hung in the balance.

A thousand memories flittered through her mind as the red Lexus NX Hybrid she'd leased in Denver crested the rise of Sardine Canyon and her hometown came into view. Dare Valley stretched out before her as magical as morning mist on the savannah. The brick and wood-crafted buildings were organized as precisely as the inner workings of a Swiss timepiece. The imposing mountains rose up like sentries guarding the small town. The clouds surrounding the setting sun sunk into the mountains' craggy ridges, softening the scene.

The billboard she passed on her way into town—a new addition since her last visit home, nine months ago for Christmas—made her smile. *Welcome to Dare Valley—A Sweet Home in the Mountains.*

The town was still booming, from everything she could see. Progress had fashioned Dare Valley a new dress, a mix of modern fabric with an old-world hemline. Her dad's Irish bar—the popular Hairy's—was a town icon, but there were newer, trendier places lining Main Street. She passed Sleek Lines, where her mom exercised to Latin music, and Hot Cross Buns Bakery, which had replaced a long-time favorite.

Lucy turned off Main Street onto Ponderosa, crawling along the pavement like she was on a Sunday afternoon drive. In many ways, she was. With only partial vision in her right eye, she was still approved to drive, but she was careful to take it slow. Her brain was still learning how to combine the two very different images her eyes were seeing. Besides, she wanted to absorb everything in sight, hungry for old and new pictures of this place she'd once called home. This place she planned to call home again—although she didn't know for how long. That made everything look and feel different somehow.

The Victorian she'd grown up in was painted yellow now with purple trim, something her parents had debated for a year until her dad finally caved. Harry and Ellen O'Brien might fight over everything from how to load the dishwasher to what kind of vodka her mother put in her cosmopolitans, but her mother usually came out on top.

For the hundredth time, Lucy reminded herself to be patient with her mother. She already knew her mother would use this temporary return to Dare Valley as an opportunity to try and reshape her life. Ellen just couldn't seem to help herself. Lucy understood. While she had gotten her Irish temper from her father, she'd inherited her hard head from her mother.

After all the battles she'd witnessed overseas, she had no desire to dive into a power struggle with her mother over being single at thirty-six. Ellen O'Brien wanted grandchildren from her only child and wasn't shy about saying so. If that wasn't enough pressure, Lucy knew her mother also wanted her to remain in Dare Valley as a permanent professor at the Emmits Merriam School of Journalism. How many times had her mother told her she should stop globetrotting and settle down? More than Lucy could count.

There weren't any parking spaces on the street, so she pulled into her parents' driveway and cut the engine. She took a moment to settle down, her nerves stretched tight from the drive.

Judging from all the cars on their slice of Ponderosa, someone was clearly having a Denver Raiders pre-season game party this Sunday night. One thing Lucy had missed about living in the States was the easy access to American football. She told herself that was another positive about her temporary return home.

No one rushed out of the house to greet her, but while she'd texted her parents before leaving Denver, they were probably watching the game too. They'd made noise about coming to pick her up last night, but that was one battle she had won. She'd needed to drive her long-term rental car to Dare Valley. What she hadn't told them was that she'd wanted to prove to herself she could do normal things like driving.

Her parents didn't know anything about her recent

accident, let alone the doctor's appointment she'd had in Denver this morning. They would freak out if they knew, and since she'd always edited the dangerous stories of her life, she hadn't seen any need to change the status quo. All they knew was she was taking a much-needed break from the unrelenting pressure of her job.

Grabbing her purse, she walked to the front door. The leprechaun doorknocker greeted her, and she touched his rosy-red nose with a smile. She'd loved coming home from school to see that little man winking at her. The door was unlocked like she knew it would be, and she let herself inside.

"Mom. Dad. I'm here." There was an odd scuffle of feet, so she cocked her ears. "Hello?"

A sudden flash off to her left had her head turning.

*"Surprise!"* a chorus erupted.

Lucy jumped a foot as people rushed out from behind the French doors leading to the dining room. If she'd been anywhere other than Dare Valley, she would have dived for cover.

"Holy shit!" she cried out in reflex. Viewing the world with diminished visual acuity was still weird. She fought the urge to close her right eye so she could see perfectly, but that would give her away.

A few people were laughing. Her heart rapped in her chest as she surveyed the crowd. Her parents stood in the center of the Hale family, her longtime friends. Everyone was beaming sunshine at her.

"You guys scared the hell out of me."

"Got ya," her dad said with a wink as mischievous as the leprechaun on the door.

"You sure did," she replied, trying to suck in oxygen. *A surprise party? What were they thinking?* Then again, they didn't know why the timing was terrible, and that was on her.

Her mom charged toward her, wearing a billowy

peasant top and a gypsy-style skirt. Her father was two steps behind, sporting a Raiders T-shirt and cargo shorts. Lucy braced herself for impact.

Her mom's strong arms wrapped around her. "Oh, Lucy! We're so glad you're finally home."

She pressed her head into her mother's hair, inhaling the patchouli smell she wore like a hippie who'd never grown up. "Me too, Mom." And she meant it. Mostly.

"Stop crushing the girl, Ellie," her dad said, hovering. "Hand her over."

"In a minute, you big oaf," she shot back, raising her head and giving him the fish eye. "I gave birth to her."

Harry O'Brien rolled his eyes at his wife like he'd been doing his whole life. "I'm counting to five, woman. One. Two."

The crowd behind them chuckled, and Lucy made a quick scan of them. April Hale, her mom's best friend, was flanked by two of her daughters, Moira and Caroline, near a dessert table loaded with chocolate chip cookies and her mom's lemon squares. Arthur Hale, the man who'd put Dare Valley on the map for outstanding journalism, was leaning on his cane beside the makeshift bar her dad had stocked with everything from beer to her mom's infamous cosmopolitans. His granddaughter, Meredith, and her husband, Tanner, stood next to him. Meredith was Moira and Caroline's cousin.

Her mom cupped her face suddenly, making her look away from the other guests. "We've missed you, Lucy. So much. It's past time you came home for good."

*Oh, heavens. Here she goes.* "I've missed you too, Mom." Lucy finally noticed the light highlights in her mother's hair. "The new look works."

Her mom flicked one of her curls after wiping a stray tear. "I told your father I wanted to go blond to see if they have more fun."

"And do they?" she asked, feeling a bit trapped by her mother's grip.

"I'm working on it," her mom said with a twinkle in her eye. "Now that you're back, we'll work on it together."

That sounded ominous. Lucy had never liked wearing peasant blouses and gypsy skirts. She hoped that wasn't what her mother had in mind.

"Enough, woman," her dad bellowed. "You're hogging our only child. Come here, Lucy Lu."

There was another tug on her arm, and her mother thankfully relinquished her hold. Her dad's big arms brought her to his massive chest. While Lucy had outgrown her mother by four inches while she was in high school, her dad still towered over her at six-foot-six. He might be a little softer around the middle, but he still had the body of a bruiser.

"Ah, Luce," he whispered so only she could hear. "I've missed you so, little one."

For a big man, he'd always been gentle. Sure, he could yell like a warrior or throw a ruffian out of his bar, but he was never like that with her.

"I missed you too, Daddy," she said, smelling the hops and barley he always carried on his skin from all the beers he pulled.

"Let me look at you," he said, pushing her back until she stood an arm's length from him.

Studying her probably wasn't a good idea. She wasn't back to one hundred percent yet, and she didn't want him to have an inkling anything was wrong. Not that there were any visible signs of what had happened to her, especially with her eye.

Maybe it was selfish, but she didn't want to feel the weight of their worry. Besides, if her mom knew, she'd only double her efforts to talk Lucy out of going overseas again. She didn't need her mother exerting that kind of pressure on her when she was this vulnerable.

Her dad's eyes narrowed, like he saw something that concerned him, so she poked him in the stomach to divert him.

"Hey! Can't a girl get a beer around here?" she asked, going for his Achilles. "I haven't had a decent pour since I was home last."

She caught sight of the spread on the dining room table. There was a honey-glazed ham, fresh bread, a fruit and cheese tray, and big green salad in a wooden bowl. Her stomach growled, but while she was hungry enough to eat a bear, there was no way she was choosing food just now. Not when so many people had come here to see her.

The corner of his mouth tipped up, but he didn't take his shrewd eyes off her. "I'll get you a Murphy's right away, kiddo," he said finally, giving her a wink. "Okay, who's next in line?"

"I am," she heard a familiar voice say.

Turning, she felt a smile bloom on her face. Andy Hale, her best friend since kindergarten, was smiling back at her. Together they'd learned how to color inside the lines, climb trees, and ride bikes. They'd stayed close despite how much time she'd spent away.

"Andy Cakes!" she cried, using his nickname, and then they were moving toward each other.

He hugged her tight. "You would ruin a perfectly good homecoming by calling me that."

She knew he didn't mean it. Everyone who truly loved him still called him by his nickname sometimes.

"How could you let my parents throw me a surprise party?" she whispered so only he could hear. "I'm still jet-lagged."

"Like I would say anything," he whispered back. "Everyone knows you don't mess with Ellen O'Brien."

"True that," she said, letting him go and taking a moment to simply stare at him.

He'd been taller than her since the seventh grade,

but not tall enough that she had to crane her neck. That had changed junior year, when he'd sprouted up to six-three. He looked incredible, she had to admit. His short, dark brown hair framed an expressive face anchored by a strong jaw and brow bones. When he wasn't smiling, those angles probably looked harsh to some, but to her, they'd always described the contrast that was Andy Hale. He was as incredibly strong as he was sweet. Always had been.

When they were in high school, she'd felt occasional flashes of attraction to him, but she'd wanted out of Dare Valley too much to let anything interrupt her focus. They'd stayed friends and only friends, and she was grateful she hadn't risked one of the most important relationships in her life.

Lucy had gone off to attend the prestigious School of Visual Arts in New York City, and Andy had gone off to the University of Colorado before finishing his medical degree at their famous School of Medicine in Boulder. He'd met his wife, Kim, through his sister, Natalie, gotten married and had a kid—everything everyone had expected Dr. Andy Hale to do. Then the story had suddenly and heart-wrenchingly changed. Kim had gotten breast cancer and died two years ago, leaving him to raise their son alone.

Few could understand such a tragedy, let alone process it and move forward, and Andy had floundered for a time. Leaving his pressure-ridden job at a leading Denver hospital and returning home to work at the local Dare Valley General had been a good move for him. She was happy to see him looking more relaxed and less grief-stricken than when she'd seen him last.

A brown-haired boy in a yellow shirt and navy shorts ran forward and wrapped his arms around Andy's legs.

Of course, her color vision wasn't back to normal yet either, so perhaps those navy shorts were really black.

She had a hard time distinguishing between similar shades. If the problem stuck, she feared it would hurt her ability to capture important elements like color contrast in her photographs.

Danny Hale had inherited his father's eyes, but his extra-serious gaze was rare for a five-year-old. Having met plenty of other children who had lost their parents young, she understood how tragedy matured a child.

"Danny, do you remember Ms. O'Brien?" Andy asked his son, cupping the back of the little boy's neck in tenderness. "She's the one who takes photos all over the world and sent you the ones of the animals we've only seen in the Denver Zoo."

Not all of her photos were of war and starving children. Sometimes she liked to capture nature's beauty, and she'd thought a little boy who'd lost his mother might like to experience some of life's wonders. It had been her way of helping Andy, whose own devastation over losing Kim was heightened by his son's grief.

"I remember her, Dad," Danny said, climbing around his father's leg like a monkey. "She's the one who took a picture of the baby camel by my bed. Hi, Ms. O'Brien. That's so weird since I call a lady Mrs. O'Brien already."

She shuddered as he pointed to her mom. "Hi, Danny. How about you call me *Miss* Lucy instead? Less confusing that way. You can keep calling my mom Mrs. O'Brien."

"I like your mom," the little boy said, glancing over to where her mother was talking with his grandma and the Hale girls in the dining room. "She's my grandma's best friend. They take me all over town when Dad needs a break."

Andy rolled his eyes.

"Especially for ice cream," Danny said in the high cadence of a little boy. "I like chocolate chip cookie dough. What's your favorite?"

"Mocha almond fudge," Andy replied for her. "She always shared her ice cream with me, and I shared mine with hers."

Memories of them swapping half-eaten ice cream cones filled her mind. Good days. Carefree days. It had been a long time ago. "Butter pecan."

The corners of his eyes deepened as his smile spread. "We're both a couple of nuts. We'll have to take Miss Lucy for ice cream soon. She doesn't get much when she's overseas."

No, she didn't. In some countries, she had to bring her own food, not knowing if there would be a shortage or if the local food would be safe.

"Cool!" Danny said, jumping in the air. "I like Mr. O'Brien too. He gives me free soda at Hairy's."

She could only imagine what Andy thought of that, being a health-conscious doctor and all. "Soda and ice cream are the best," Lucy said, "but my favorite treats are cinnamon rolls."

"From Margie?" Danny asked, letting go of his dad's leg and closing the gap between them. "She makes the best ones since Mrs. Kemstead re... Dad, what did Mrs. Kemstead do?"

"Retired," Andy easily answered.

"Right. Did you know my mom?"

Lucy shot a quick glance at Andy, struggling to hide her surprise at the abrupt question. She'd met Danny a few times since his birth, but it made sense that he wouldn't remember her relationship with his mother.

"Yes, I did," she said, crouching down until she was eye level with the boy. "She was a really nice lady, and she loved you a lot."

She'd spoken to countless children who'd lost loved ones, but it felt jarring to do it in Dare Valley. This was her safe place. Nothing was supposed to go wrong here.

Danny pointed to the ceiling. "She's in heaven now,"

he told her with an earnest shake of his head. "She's an angel and looks after everyone in Dare Valley. But especially me and Dad."

Her chest squeezed. Andy had a heart of gold for telling his son that. "Dare Valley is lucky to have her on their side."

"Yep," he said and then looked back at his dad. "Can Miss Lucy come over and show me her new animal photos sometime?"

"If she has any new ones," Andy said. She looked up to see him studying her with the same intense scrutiny she'd noticed in her father's gaze. "It seems like she's been really busy the past few weeks."

She took her time studying him right back, refusing to be intimidated. Little did he know she'd been convalescing, first in a South African hospital and then in a hotel room near her doctors' offices, waiting to be given travel approval to return home.

"You tell me what day works, and we'll make it happen," she told Danny, rising carefully to her full height, being mindful of the lingering soreness in her back.

"You can come anytime," Andy said. "Danny, how about we find you a healthy snack? Lots of other people are waiting patiently to talk to Miss Lucy, so we shouldn't monopolize her time."

"You're not monopolizing me," Lucy quickly answered. "I've...been looking forward to seeing you." She'd wanted to tell him everything, but to what purpose? He'd only worry, and besides, he'd had a recent scare with his mother's health. The last thing she wanted to do was add more to his plate.

"They *are* monopolizing you," a gravely voice said behind her. "But that's a doctor for you. Always making you wait, even if you're lying on death's doorstep."

She turned around as Arthur Hale tapped his cane on the dark hardwood floor to garner her attention.

"Hello, Mr. Hale."

"I keep telling you not to call me that, girl. Aren't you nearing forty now? High time to give in and call me Arthur. You'd better, or I may bean you with my cane."

"Okay," she said, laughing. "You've convinced me."

"Come over here, Lucy, and give an old man a hug," he said, thrusting his cane to his very pregnant granddaughter.

"Hi, Meredith," Lucy said, watching as the woman handed the cane to her husband. "Hello, Tanner. It's been a while."

Of course, she'd met the warzone correspondent in a few hotspots. Expatriate communities were smaller than a small town like Dare Valley in some ways.

"Good to see you too, Lucy," Tanner said. "I'm going to be sneaking into one of your classes this fall when I'm not teaching myself. I have a feeling I could learn a thing or two."

"Didn't I tell you teaching was a fine idea, Lucy?" Arthur said, ambling forward and hugging her briefly. "Tanner here loves it."

The former correspondent nodded like he still couldn't believe it. "Who knew?"

"I'm glad I could arrange it with the Dean of Journalism last minute after you called me," Arthur continued. "You young people never plan anything anymore."

Lucy hadn't been in much of a position to plan anything. But she was also not very good at sitting still. She'd made a call to Arthur, the one person who could make miracles happen at the last minute, as soon as she realized her right eye needed more time to heal. Though she wasn't eager to start teaching, at least she'd be doing something related to her profession.

"Didn't you just tell me I'm nearing forty?" she asked. "I can't be young *and* old at the same time."

He waved his hand dismissively. "You're still

younger than I am, my dear, and that will never change. All that matters is that you're finally teaching here after all the years I've been asking you. We need more professors who can show these green-behind-the-ears journalists about the proper use of photos to tell a story. No one's better at that than you are, Lucy."

"Amen," Tanner said, and she was humbled by their respect.

"Your last photo on the cover of *Time* magazine of the young Congolese girl dragging an AK-47 up that dusty road to the peacekeepers in exchange for a chicken pretty much did me in," Arthur said. "I might have gotten misty-eyed."

"Me too!" a woman behind her suddenly exclaimed. Lucy turned around to see Moira Hale standing a few yards away. "Sorry, I was eavesdropping," Moira said with a shrug. "I'm a big fan of your work."

"Thank you," she said, giving Andy's sister a warm smile.

"Hard not to be a fan," Arthur said, tapping her to regain her attention. "Tell us how that photo came about."

"Well..." she began, remembering the moment she'd seen the little girl approaching the battalion of UN peacekeepers.

Dressed in what amounted to dirty rags, her bones protruding from her skin, the child had looked to be all of seven. Though Lucy hadn't immediately understood what the little girl wanted, she'd pulled her camera out on instinct.

The girl had spoken in hesitant French, a language Lucy spoke fluently, asking if the peacekeepers would trade her the gun she'd found for a chicken so she and her younger siblings could eat. Their parents were dead, killed by the warring forces destroying the eastern part of the country, and she was responsible for her remaining family. They hadn't eaten a decent meal in weeks.

The commander had sent for a chicken from their compound. Not all of the peacekeepers helped the unfortunate like that. There were simply too many of them. But the girl's request for a weapon-for-food trade had sparked an idea in the commander's mind. Everyone wanted to rid the Congo of the barrage of weapons destroying the country, so perhaps a gun-for-food exchange was the place to start.

Lucy had stayed through the whole process, taking hundreds of photos. When the girl left with the bag holding the dead chicken clutched to her chest, Lucy had turned away and cried.

Only three of those photos had been published, but they told a powerful story.

She tried to hold on to her memory of that story and others like it after everything that had happened.

"Amazing," Moira said when Lucy was finished. The younger woman had edged closer with the telling.

"I owe my start to you, Arthur," Lucy said, carefully hugging the older man who blustered protests in her ear. "If you hadn't agreed to let me intern at *The Western Independent* in high school, where would I be now?"

"Bah!" Arthur exclaimed. "In the same place you are now. Since the moment your daddy put that first Polaroid in your hands, you were destined to take great photos. You have a gift, Lucy."

It humbled her to hear such high praise from one of America's journalistic legends. "Thank you for saying that, Arthur." The name was still uncomfortable on her tongue.

"How about you come down to my office after you settle in?" He held out his hand for his cane, which Tanner extended to him. "I want to talk to you about taking some photos for me and writing an op-ed while you're here."

Arthur's Sunday op-ed was famous among politicians and business leaders, and readers everywhere were compelled by his take on the ever-changing nature of America. Arthur Hale didn't just have his hand on the pulse of the West anymore.

"I'd be honored to write something for you, but as for photos, I can't say there's much to capture in Dare Valley."

"Don't be so sure about that, honey," her mother called out.

She glanced over her shoulder to see what her mother was talking about, but someone grabbed her hand and pressed a cold glass into it. Judging from the shape of the glass, her beer had arrived. "*Finally.* I was wondering where you were, Dad. What's the score?"

"The Raiders just took the lead. Sorry, I got caught up with Blake. I know it's only pre-season and all, but..."

"You have the chance to watch the game with the former Raiders' quarterback," she said knowingly.

"Yeah," her dad said, cheeks reddening. "I try not to freak him out by rolling out player stats. Blake's a great guy. It's good to see him and Natalie back together."

She already knew about that, both from Andy, who was close to his sister, and from her mother, who kept her up to date on everything from the Hales' comings and goings to the town's dynamics. Sometimes Lucy wondered if her mother told those stories as a way of reminding her what she was missing. Since Lucy didn't share the gritty details of what she saw overseas with her parents other than through her photos and articles, she appreciated her mother doing most of the talking. Usually.

Lucy turned to Meredith. "Your baby is due pretty soon, I hear."

"Yes, and we can't wait," she said, rubbing her belly.

"And you look pretty settled for a former war correspondent," Lucy told Tanner.

He nodded. "I'll come by your office at Emmits. We can talk about 'settling' into Dare Valley after leaving the fast lane. It was weird in the beginning."

Her office at Emmits? She'd never had an office before. For that matter, she'd never had a home besides this one. She traveled from assignment to assignment, occasionally stopping for a brief siesta in a short-term rental in London or Rome or Cairo.

She always traveled light, not wanting to be weighed down by stuff. Her mother checked her P.O. box at the Dare Valley Post Office for her, which allowed her to keep her state residence and driver's license, and forwarded any mail to her current address overseas. The system had worked seamlessly for her whole career.

"I'm…ah…not sure I'm staying permanently," she said carefully. "I only have the fall term in mind right now."

Meredith cast Tanner a measured glance, and he rubbed her shoulder as if to assure her everything was all right. Some said the adrenaline from working in war zones never left one's blood. Lucy had been running on it for too many years to know if she was going to be any different.

"You might change your mind, Lucy," Arthur said, tapping his cane on the floor. "While few things are more important than a good story, you still have to live your life."

Hadn't she been doing that? She loved traveling from one place to the next. She lived for it. Now the future had been transformed to one big question mark. Looking away from Arthur, her gaze landed on Andy. He was still studying her. Yeah, he knew something was up with her and this unexpected return home.
She hoped he would give her some time before he asked her what it was.

# Chapter 2

From the time Lucy O'Brien could walk, she'd been an unstoppable force. Andy had seen more than one childhood photo of her dragging him along as he struggled on his then-chubby legs to keep up with her. Over the years, his best friend had talked him into climbing treacherous trees and skiing down death-defying mountain passes.

So her choice of career hadn't surprised him. Of course she'd gone overseas to take photographs of distant places riddled with war and poverty. But that didn't mean he hadn't worried.

He was more than worried now.

She was too skinny for her five-foot-five frame, and her hair didn't possess its natural luster. Being a doctor, he knew what illness looked like. Lucy's body was still mending from some sickness or injury. And she hadn't said a word about it.

Well, that was going to change. When he thought she was ready, he was going to ask what had brought her home to Dare Valley after all these years of insisting it was too small, too provincial. Even her parents weren't buying her bullshit answer that she needed some time off from the fast lane. It wasn't in Lucy's nature to proceed slowly. She was a sports car on a highway filled with sensible vehicles.

"She doesn't look good, does she?" his sister, Moira, whispered to him.

He was so focused on Lucy, he hadn't even noticed his sister's approach. He'd thought she was still on the edges of the group huddled around Lucy. It hadn't surprised him to see Moira listening to his friend with such interest. Few could top Lucy in the story department, and Moira was an amateur photographer, after all.

"Shh," he hissed. "Do you want someone to hear? There's no need to worry her parents more."

Since he was her eldest sibling, Moira usually listened to what he had to say. When she rolled her eyes, he realized he must be off his game.

"Her parents are already worried," she said, tucking her chin-length brown hair behind her ear. "You can see it on their faces."

"Give Lucy some time to tell us what's going on," he whispered back, tugging Moira over to the corner next to a ficus tree. "She just got home."

His sister gave him the kind of look she probably usually reserved for when she had to fire people in her capacity as human resources director at a top Denver engineering firm. Sometimes Moira could be an ass-kicker, and apparently she was about to kick his.

"She doesn't need time," his sister said in an aggrieved tone. "She needs a best friend who's willing to listen. Whatever happened must have been horrible. Especially if she didn't tell you! *You're* her best friend."

He'd already thought of that, and it had dried up all the spit in his mouth.

"Ask her to take a walk with you, Andy. Right now."

"In the middle of her homecoming party?" he asked, aghast. "Ellen would kill me. Slowly."

"No, she won't," Moira informed him with a determined shake of her head. "She and Mom are hoping you two finally hook up and have babies now that you're both back in Dare Valley. Sorry, that was probably a little brusque, but it's true."

Yeah, Moira knew it was hard for him to think about moving on with anyone after losing Kim, let alone with the friend he'd known since babyhood. His stomach wrenched. He'd hoped his mother would understand that, even if Ellen didn't. Not only because Lucy was Lucy, but also because he was taking his time with the whole dating thing.

"Oh, for heaven's sake," Moira said, giving him a push for good measure. "It's not like you have to give in to their fantasies. Just go talk to her."

The more she nudged, the more he wanted to dig his heels in. "Lucy will tell me when she wants to. We respect each other that way." Which was why her silence hurt. He was smart enough to realize how much of her life she censored from their Skype chats and emails, but he'd never thought she'd hold back something important.

"Hogwash, as Uncle Arthur says. Are you afraid to hear what happened?"

"Maybe a little," he admitted softly.

He wasn't sure he could stand any more tragedy, which was why he hadn't asked more questions. He'd fretted over Lucy's sudden announcement that she was coming home. Even then, he'd realized there was something behind it—some dark story. But how was he supposed to help her when he was still shoring up the devastation inside him and trying to start over? He felt guilty—and weak. Lucy deserved better than that from him.

Moira put her hand on his arm. "Imagine how alone she must feel. No one has more respect for Lucy than I do, which is why I just embarrassed myself by having a fan moment. The places she goes and the images she captures... Even I'm not that tough."

He studied her no-nonsense expression. "You're plenty tough." Right now, he was starting to feel a little bullied. Thank God, his mother and two other sisters hadn't jumped on the pile with Moira. Otherwise, he'd be suffocating.

"Be her friend," Moira said with another push. "You can do it, Andy Cakes."

He gritted his teeth. "I hate it when you call me that."

"That's why even Lucy still uses the nickname." She gave him an encouraging smile. "Now, go. I'll keep an eye on Danny."

Since she wasn't going to give him an inch, he rolled his shoulders and prepared himself to face Lucy again. "You're a pest."

"And you're our hero," Moira said, giving him a sporty pat on the behind that made him snarl. "That's why you were born in the number one slot, and I chose number four."

He hated being the eldest sometimes. Everyone expected him to be responsible and supportive, to set a good example. At moments like this, he wished he could give them all the bird.

"Fine, I'm going," he said. "But don't *ever* pat me on the butt again."

Moira was laughing as he set off to talk to Lucy. She was now surrounded by a new crowd—one much less interested in her journalistic endeavors. Andy's two other sisters, Natalie and Caroline, saw him and shifted to include him in the huddle. His mom shot him an eager smile—God help him—as Lucy mentioned having a few appointments to see rental properties in the next couple of days.

"But I thought you would stay with your dad and me," Ellen said, a frown marring her face. "You loved your room growing up."

"Mom, we talked about this," Lucy said diplomatically. "I still love it, but as Arthur pointed out earlier, I'm almost forty. I couldn't possibly live with my parents for more than a few weeks. What *would* people think?" She laughed, playing up the famous O'Brien charm, causing others to laugh with her.

But Ellen was having none of it. "I don't give a fig what people think," she said, folding her arms across her chest.

"Now, Mom," Lucy said, jostling her playfully. "I'll be closer than I have been in years. Trust me. This is going to be the best for everyone."

"You can stay with me, Lucy," April said, glancing at Ellen. "It's only me in that big old house."

Lucy's charming smile faltered, and she looked over at him. He could almost hear her thoughts. They both hated when April and Ellen did their conspiratorial mother thing. They were scary as hell when they combined forces.

"Or you can bunk in Andy's spare bedroom," Caroline said, laughing gaily. "After all, who wouldn't like to have a doctor on duty full-time? And he's the cleanest Hale of us all!"

The people in the huddle continued to sputter laughter, but the light in Lucy's eyes was dimming. It was like watching a cloud pass over Orion in the night sky. His friend needed her freedom, and he could tell she was feeling trapped.

"That's a great—" Ellen started to say.

"I'm not the cleanest Hale anymore," he said, interrupting her. "Danny is pretty good about cleaning up, but he's only five. Some nights, I step on a lone green bean even our new dog won't eat, or one of Danny's many racecars. Those hurt like hell, let me tell you."

"I can personally attest to that," Natalie said,

hopping on one foot, trying to help a brother out.

April and Ellen only narrowed their eyes, more determined than ever.

Oh God, Ellen and April *really* were hoping he and Lucy would do the whole friends-to-lovers thing and get married, providing them with more grandchildren. They were going to be impossible.

"And then there's Danny's bathroom to consider," he said. "If you don't like broken crayons, I suggest you *never* cross the threshold." He made a show of shuddering.

Lucy laughed, but he could tell she was forcing it. She felt as distressed by their mothers' pushing as he did. "Broken crayons in the bathroom? Say it ain't so."

*"So,"* he said, causing Lucy to laugh along with his sisters, feeling the familiar rhythm of their banter return.

"Then I couldn't *possibly* stay with you," she said, a twinkle returning to her eyes.

There was a change in his energy, and Andy realized his heart was beating faster than normal even though he was merely standing. And he couldn't escape the obvious conclusion.

He was attracted to her.

Lucy was beautiful and funny, and she engaged him in a way few people ever had. She faced life head-on and made the best of things, but she called a spade a spade and let people be human. And of all the people who were dear to him, she was the only one who hadn't danced around Kim's death, and how he'd felt in the aftermath.

Before meeting Kim, he'd fought an on-again, off-again crush for his best friend. How could he help it? But he'd always known Lucy had her sights set on a fast-paced life, filled with travel and danger and excitement. That wasn't something Andy had wanted for himself, so he'd never challenged their friendship by trying to add romance to the equation. Then he'd met Kim and fallen harder than he ever expected to fall again.

Jolting back to the present moment, he gave his friend a wry smile and said, "Sorry, Luce, seems like you're on your own then."

"Don't I know it?" she answered, and since he knew her, he heard the lower timbre in her voice.

Was she trying to tell him what he'd already concluded before she'd arrived? That even if they fell for each other, it would never work? She'd laugh if she knew how much he'd thought it through, but that's what he did. Sure, he was supposedly free again—although that moniker felt wrong. His wife had *died*. It's not like he'd been given a choice in the matter.

The truth was, he wasn't sure he could love anyone like he had loved Kim, and he wouldn't sell himself or another woman short. And then there was Lucy's career. She wouldn't stay in Dare Valley forever. It would kill her larger-than-life spirit. And he was no more of a globetrotter now than he'd been when they were younger.

"Your house is fine, Andy," April said in a rare, scolding tone. "My cleaning lady does a great job."

His sisters blinked, as surprised as he was by their mother's reaction.

"I know she does, Mom," he said good-naturedly. "Let's table the cleaning talk for now. Lucy just got home, and she's probably tired."

His friend nodded agreeably. "It was a long couple days of traveling."

When she made a show of yawning, he took her arm. "Come on, sport, let's find you another beer and stretch your legs. Might help your jet lag."

Her smile didn't totally reach her eyes. "A beer and a walk sounds great, Andy Cakes. Those transatlantic flights are pure torture."

"You kids enjoy your walk," Ellen said, shooing them

toward the front door.

Never let it be said Ellen O'Brien didn't appreciate a good strategic retreat.

"We won't be long," Lucy said, hooking her arm through his. "Do you need to tell Danny we're stepping out?"

He spied his son in the corner of the dining room, performing his signature trick. After making fake choking noises, he proudly flourished an uneaten carrot like a magician would display a rabbit. Danny was holding court with Moira, their brother, Matt, and his fiancée, Jane. When Danny threw the carrot up and opened his mouth to catch it like a dolphin, Andy shook his head.

"No, he's fine. My family looks out for him. He won't even know I'm gone."

"I'll have to show him how many grapes I can catch in my mouth later," she said. "That trick won me a hand-carved wooden flute from a snake charmer in Delhi."

"Leave it to you to win a musical instrument by catching fruit," he said dryly, trying not to imagine the snakes.

"Where are you two headed?" his cousin Jill Hale drawled as she rushed over from the dessert table. "Sneaking out?"

One of Jill's twins, Mia, gurgled on the floor, crawling toward them like a small panther. Jill shoved her brownie into her mouth and snatched the little girl up.

"Going for a walk," Andy said with a laugh, remembering the days when he'd had to watch Danny like a hawk. "See you later, cuz."

She made a noise through her full mouth as Mia tugged on her red curls.

"Better make a break for it, or we'll never get out," Andy said, picking up his pace. "Do you want to grab another beer?"

"We'll never make it," Lucy said, shaking her head.

When they reached the front door, he opened it and made a melodramatic sprint down the sidewalk to the street. He did it to make her laugh, but he suddenly realized he was practically dragging her. Immediately stopping, he turned to face her. She was breathing hard, he realized. A short run shouldn't do that to a normal adult system, but it would to an injured one. His gut tightened.

"Let's walk to the park," he said, giving her a moment to catch her breath.

Nodding, Lucy removed her arm from his and took off, saying nothing, which worried him even more. He followed her, walking slowly beside her. When they reached the park, he pointed to the bench by the swings.

"I bring Danny to this park a lot when the weather's nice," he commented when they were seated, surreptitiously scanning her face out of the corner of his eye. "We're only a block away from my house."

Her color was a ghastly gray, and while she wasn't breathing hard now, her pulse was still pounding visibly in her neck.

"Okay, Luce," he said, folding his sweating hands in his lap. "Why don't you tell me what's really going on? You're sick, and you're scaring me."

"I am *not* sick," she immediately shot back, "so you have no reason to be scared. It's the altitude. I appreciate your help in deflecting my mother's efforts to stop me from getting my own place while I'm here, but you didn't have to take me on a walk. I can take care of myself."

He turned to face her again. There was fire in her eyes, and the gray pallor of her face was disappearing. So she wasn't going to tell him after all. At least not willingly.

He nudged her with his shoulder like he used to do

in school when she was angry. "How long have we been friends, Lucy? You need to tell me why you came home."

She crossed her legs and stared straight ahead. "I already told you—and everyone else for that matter. I'm—"

"Don't bullshit me," he said, edging closer until his knee brushed her leg. "I'm a doctor. I'm trained to tell when a body has been injured."

When she remained silent, he proceeded to tick off the signs like he was writing them on a patient's chart at the hospital. "Your clothes are hanging on you from a sudden loss in weight. Your face is pale, your cheeks look hollow, and your rigid posture is a sign you have pain somewhere in the body. And if that's not enough, your heart rate increases from a simple activity like walking. So, let me ask again. How were *you* hurt?"

She rested her chin on her chest mulishly. "Can't we just sit here quietly? Andy, I just traveled for two days. I'm exhausted."

Her voice—usually so strong—quavered. Clearly, she was afraid to tell him. He thought back to how Moira had asked him if he was afraid to hear the truth. He was more than afraid now. He was terrified.

He took his friend's hands in his and shook them so she'd look at him. Her green eyes finally did, and in them he saw a million agonies. He knew that look. He'd seen it in the mirror after Kim had died.

"Lucy," he said softly, looking into her eyes, "talk to me."

She was quiet for a long moment, and then she released a jagged exhale that sounded like it had been wrenched from her body. "Soldiers attacked the Congolese village I was visiting." She gripped his hands so hard he could feel her bones. "They bombed it first—to kill as many people as they could—and then raided it on foot. One of the bombs exploded near me. It knocked me out."

It took him a moment to process her words. A bomb? An attack on a village? Dear God. "Oh, Lucy," he said helplessly, feeling her hands tremble in his.

"I can't be sure if they thought I was dead or if they just left me alone because I'm a white journalist," she continued in a monotone voice indicative of shock. He'd heard that same tone time and again in the emergency room at the hospital. "Sometimes there's a strange code of conduct among soldiers. They don't want to attract international media attention by unwittingly killing a journalist. It happens, of course, but usually it makes the news."

He forced himself to swallow as his mind conjured up a scene out of a movie. Explosions. Smoke. Gunfire. People lying dead on the ground.

"How bad were your injuries?" He didn't ask, *Why didn't you tell us?* He knew.

She finally met his gaze, and he saw the shine of tears in her eyes. Very un-Lucy-like.

"Bad. They medevac'd me to a hospital in South Africa. As you can tell, I'm still recovering my strength, but I'm mostly well. Dammit! I didn't want to worry you. I was hoping you wouldn't notice."

"That would be like not noticing my son had grown horns. I'm trained to notice these things. And you haven't fully recovered."

"I thought I could tough it out," she said, squeezing her eyes shut for a brief moment. "Bluff my way through the homecoming. I couldn't wait any longer. Classes start next week, and I wanted time to acclimate."

More questions were surfacing. "Have you been in South Africa this whole time?"

"Yes."

From her monosyllabic response, he braced himself to extract the details from her. "Tell me about your injuries."

She blew out a breath. "It will only worry you more,

and there's nothing you can do anyway."

"I'm already sick to my stomach," he said more harshly than he meant. "More information will make me feel better. It's the doctor in me. Don't make me beg you."

She flinched at his sincerity and let out a thready breath like she was gathering herself to face some grueling challenge. "I caught some shrapnel...in the back. The wounds still itch like crazy, but they're healing pretty well."

So, she'd been stitched up. Good Lord. But he could feel the weight of the other shoe about to drop. "What else?"

Her whole frame trembled. "They're worried about my right eye. When I landed after the blast, I hit my right temple on the SUV we'd come in. I have something called traumatic optic neuropathy."

*Oh, shit.*

"Andy," she whispered, her sad, vulnerable eyes meeting his. "They're not sure I'll regain my full visual acuity or my color vision. I mean, my vision improved a lot in the week I spent in the hospital. I went from twenty-four hundred to twenty-fifty, which is what my vision is now. At first red and black looked the same to me, but I can make out colors better now. It's just hard to tell between shades within a color palette."

His heart twisted at the bravery she was trying to inject into her voice. "Oh, Lucy."

"They said time will tell, but Andy...there's nothing they can do. Nothing! Can you believe that? No glasses or contact lenses. The only thing that will help is if my brain gets used to combining the two different images from my eyes, and the worst thing is that I can't simply close my bad eye whenever I want to see correctly. It'll only make this whole brain integration thing take longer if the vision in my right eye doesn't return to twenty-twenty."

"Wait!" he said, his mind spinning. "I don't know enough about this condition to understand why they can't correct it." The moment he got home, he'd research the crap out of this thing.

"My doctors could explain it better, but they basically explained it like this. The retina is the camera. Har-de-har-har. Ironic, huh?"

He couldn't even crack a smile.

"The optic nerve is the cable between the nerve and the brain, which renders the retina's images, so to speak. Since my nerve is damaged, it's like the cable connecting the camera and the renderer has been unplugged. My vision isn't correctible like for people who are far- or near-sighted."

His stomach sank. Nerve damage was the worst kind. "They can't operate?"

"No. And there are no eye drops to fix things. That's what makes this so hard. There's *nothing* they can do. It will either return to normal or it won't."

"But you said it's already improved," he said, trying to hold onto some thread of hope.

When she bent over like she'd been kicked in the guts, the only thing he knew to do was grip her hands harder.

"Not enough for someone like me," she whispered. "I'm a right-eye dominant photographer. How am I supposed to take award-winning photos of people when I can't see through my Leica? How am I supposed to show the horrors of battle or the beauty of a sunset after a massacre when I can't make out the contrast of the colors?"

Oh, how he wished he had an answer for her. But he didn't. He wasn't sure how she was supposed to move forward. Photography was her life. If she couldn't see properly...

"What am I going to do if I can't travel anymore and take pictures?" she asked, rocking in place. "It's who I am."

The enormity of her return home finally hit him, and he leaned forward until he could press their temples together. "You took the teaching job at Emmits—"

"The doctors say that if my vision is going to fully return, it'll happen within the next three months. I'll know right about when classes finish," she finished harshly. "The weird thing is my visual acuity could return, but not my color vision or vice versa. The eye is so weird and complex. I had no idea. According to my doctors, it doesn't help that I'm a photographer and a Type A personality. Apparently, this whole brain reconciliation thing is simpler for easygoing people who have less stressful careers."

Andy had always thought the human body was nature's most amazing marvel. But with Kim, he'd seen what could happen when things went badly.

"So, I'm taking a break while all this settles," Lucy said. "I wasn't lying when I said I needed one. I've been in a lot of tough spots, but this shook me. More than I can ever tell you. When I think about what they could have done to me while I was unconscious… I've never been that vulnerable."

"What's the worst-case scenario?" he made himself ask, because he knew Lucy had already gone there.

She took a long, ragged inhale. "My career will be over."

He felt her tremble all the way to her fingertips, and his heart broke for her.

"I don't mean to sound like a crybaby or a drama queen," she said, still huddled against him. "I just can't settle for taking photographs that aren't up to my usual standards."

That couldn't be the outcome. "I've seen people relearn how to do things again after massive strokes. Talk. Walk. Function. It's hard work, but it's possible. Don't you dare stop fighting, Lucy. You'll get through this. I know you will."

A tear dripped down onto his pant leg, and he froze. *She's crying?* Of course she was crying.

"You're right," she said, sniffing now. "If I work hard, I *might* be able to take the kind of pictures I'm used to taking. I just don't want to have to struggle that hard to be myself again, you know?"

When she shifted to sit up straighter on the bench, he found himself unable to do the same. His shoulders felt weighed down by stones.

"I'm lucky really," she said, interjecting that very Lucy-like optimism into her voice again. "It could have been so much worse. Hundreds of people died in that village, and the atrocities committed..."

He gulped. That could have been *her*.

"I'm trying to focus on my blessings, but I have my moments," she continued. "I have excellent medical care, a teaching position at one of the leading journalism schools in the country for as long as I want, and family and friends who care about me."

God, could she be any tougher or more beautiful right now? It almost hurt to look at her. To listen to her.

"You don't have to try to make the best of everything with me, Lucy," he said softly. "You never made me do that about Kim. I know you must be angry. And...don't hit me, okay? You're probably scared too."

Her eyes flickered down before meeting his. "I *am* scared, but that's not anything new. I know how to handle my fears. Am I scared that my visual acuity and color vision may not completely return? Yes. Am I scared I won't be able to take the same photos again? Yes. Am I scared to go overseas again if my sight does return? Yes. But it's only fear, Andy."

*Only* fear? Fear had been his living and breathing roommate since the first moment the doctors had revealed Kim's diagnosis to them. And that fear hadn't left him after her death. No, it had only gotten craftier.

Now he had a freak-out if Danny got a cold. Worse, his sleep had been troubled ever since his mother told him about the benign lump her doctors had found in her breast. Then there was Lucy. He'd always fretted about her safety, and he'd been especially worried over these past few weeks.

When in the hell was the fear ever going to go away?

"I don't know what that means," he said, slumping back against the bench. "From where I'm sitting, fear is pretty much the biggest, baddest bully on the playground."

That prompted a half smile from her. "Don't you remember what I used to do to the biggest, baddest bully on the playground?"

His own mouth twitched. "You punched Jason Adams in the face, then kicked him on the ground." And she'd gotten into big trouble for it—a whole week of after-school detention.

She nodded. "Exactly. Jason never bothered us again, remember? If you don't fight your fears, you'll always be a victim. I'm not a victim. Despite my little pity party."

Even in her worst moment, no one could ever mistake Lucy O'Brien for a victim. She was a tower of strength. "Lucy, about your injuries. Who are you planning to see for them?"

"My doctor in South Africa said the rest of my injuries have healed. I need to recover my strength, but I don't need to see anyone other than an eye trauma specialist. That's why I stayed overnight in Denver. I had an appointment this morning."

"Who is it?" he asked, tapping his foot in eagerness. "I might know him or her."

"It's Dr. Davidson. I like him a lot. He was in an accident himself. Rock climbing. Lost partial feeling in his face when his jaw broke. He's tough and practical."

"I've heard of him. Eric, right?"

She nodded.

"He has a good rep. I think I've met him at a few fundraisers. I wish you would have told me earlier. I would have gone with you today, Lucy." Anger rose up, catching him by surprise. "You don't have to do this alone, dammit! Besides, doctors go the extra mile for other doctors' friends and families." Not that it had saved Kim in the end, but the additional care had mattered to him.

She was quiet for a minute. "That's the other reason I didn't want to tell you, Andy. You don't have to save me. In fact, you can't. I'm not saying this to hurt you, but it has to be said. I'm not Kim."

Something popped in his chest, like her words had physically cracked his ribs. "I know...you aren't."

She rubbed her thumb over his hand. "But I know *you* and all your superhero healing ways. I know you feel like you failed Kim as a doctor for not detecting her breast cancer sooner. I won't let you be hurt if my right eye doesn't return to normal. It won't be anyone's fault."

"I don't see you as a second chance!" He had to press his lips together to keep the angry words from spurting out. "First of all, you're my friend, and that's what friends do. Second, I'm a doctor. Even if it's not my specialty, I can use my contacts to help. I can do some research, ask around. Don't deny me the opportunity to support you."

Turning, she settled back against the bench and crossed her feet again. "I didn't mean to make you angry. I'm not great...at accepting help sometimes."

No shit, he wanted to say. "Good thing I know that about you." He let go of one of her hands to nudge her shoulder, but then he stilled, horrified. "That didn't hurt you, did it?"

She barked out a harsh laugh. "Not really. It only made my kidneys twitch."

Was she kidding? "Let me see your kidneys," he

ordered.

"You can't, moron," she said in an aggrieved tone. "They're internal organs, remember?"

"I know that." He let go of her other hand and reached for her shirt. "Are you sure your doctors said you only need an ophthalmologist? Everything should be looked at."

"Let me rephrase. My *team* of doctors agreed the only doctor I need to see is an ophthalmologist who specializes in eye trauma, and that's Dr. Davidson. And I am *not* showing you my kidneys. I was only kidding anyway. I had a few wounds and a little gash on my back, but they're healing nicely."

He wasn't so sure he bought it. "Don't make me pull out my Dr. Hardcase with you, Luce," he said in a hard tone. "I mean business."

"Don't make *me* call for a police officer and get your ass thrown in jail."

"I want to see your back," he ground out.

She stood. "No. It will only make me uncomfortable. All you need to know is the stitches are out and everything's progressing normally—to use one of your doctor terms."

He stared her down, but she didn't budge. "If something changes—" he started.

"I'll take care of it," she assured him. "Andy, I need you to promise not to tell anyone about this."

Somehow he hadn't seen that coming, although he should have known better. "Dammit, Lucy, your parents deserve to know what happened. They love you! Don't keep something like this from them."

"It's my decision," she said, putting her hands on her hips. "I'll tell them if and when I feel it's right. I don't want them to lose any sleep trying to fix something that can't be changed. Besides, I don't want them playing on the fears I already have about going back overseas."

Standing, he gazed across the park. Decades ago, they used to swing together here. Back then, the worst thing she had to worry about was her braids being pulled by Jason the bully. Times had changed so much, and they kept right on changing. Everyone else seemed to keep up, so why did it feel like such a struggle for him?

"Fine!" he said, kicking at the gravel under his foot. "I'll keep your counsel on one condition. You will keep me up to date on your medical progress."

"What?" she blasted out.

"I'm not asking to go to your appointments with you, but I will if you'll let me." He held up a hand when she opened her mouth to protest. "Please don't shut me out of this, Luce. It would...kill me."

She turned her back to him, and he heard another unmistakable sniff. He took a few deep breaths to calm the messy emotions coursing through his own chest.

"Okay," she said, "but I want your promise you won't boss me around when it comes to medical things."

"I'm not completely sure what you mean by that. I would never do anything that wasn't in your best interest."

"That's what I'm afraid of," she said, looking weary suddenly.

He fought a string of curses. "Fine. I promise I will not do anything without talking to you first," he said, hoping he could keep that promise.

"Or do anything *period*," Lucy said, wrapping her arms around herself like she was suddenly cold. "I'm pretty independent. I don't like being told what to do."

He fought a smile. "Don't I know it? It's one of your most charming and aggravating qualities."

"If I wasn't so tired, I'd throw a handful of gravel at you right now," she said with a trace of humor in her voice.

"It's a good thing I'm adept at ducking," he said,

making a show of his skills. "Just promise me something, okay?"

Her eyes turned wary.

"That you'll remember you have people who love you. There's no reason for you to tough everything out by yourself. You don't need to prove anything to anyone."

She rubbed her forehead wearily. "All right."

He held out his hand to her. "I'm glad you came home, Lucy."

She took it, gripping it firmly. "Me too, Andy Cakes."

# CHAPTER 3

Moira Hale was a little embarrassed of her fangirl moment, but the way Lucy saw the world and photographed it...few people had that kind of gift. Moira had always admired her for her courage and abilities, but the five-year age difference between them had felt a lot larger when they were kids. Now that Lucy was home, for however long, Moira hoped they might become friends. And if she could learn anything about photography from her, she would be in seventh heaven.

She had been watching the door, waiting for Andy and Lucy to walk back in—hoping she was wrong about there being some dire reason for Lucy's return, knowing she was not—but maybe it was time for another drink. Something to pass the time until they returned. She stepped up to the O'Briens' makeshift bar in the dining room of their house and considered her options.

Her phone vibrated in her jeans pocket again, and she almost cursed aloud. Her new boss had no right to hound her like this! Moira reached for something stronger than her earlier Guinness. An Irish whiskey might remove the bad taste in her mouth from her boss's ongoing texts, not to mention her worry about

Lucy.

"You're going for the Knappogue Castle single malt?" her brother, Matt, asked, crowding close. "What's wrong? This isn't just concern about Lucy. You've been checking your phone more than usual."

Before heading to the O'Briens', their family had gotten together at Natalie and Blake's house for an early dinner. She'd stepped out twice to call her boss back.

"No, it's not only Lucy, although I practically had to shove Andy toward her."

"I noticed you giving him a pep talk," Matt said, a half smile on his face. "I knew he was in good hands."

She nodded, pouring herself a hefty shot of whiskey. "The other reason is my boss. She's driving me nuts! I've had a lot of bosses in the past ten years, and not all of them have been a peach to work for. I always end up winning them over in the end. But honestly, Taylor Brennan makes all the others look like cupcakes."

"She still giving you a hard time?" Matt asked, pouring himself a whiskey. "Jane is driving, so I'll join you."

"Yeah," Moira said, taking a measured sip even though all she wanted to do was knock it back. "I think Taylor is trying to push me out. I'm going to have to start looking for a new job."

Her brother put his arm around her. "I was afraid of that. Based on everything you've told me, there isn't anything more you can do."

"No, I think she made up her mind about me in our first meeting," Moira said, taking another sip of the whiskey, remembering the frigid way Taylor had asked her to summarize her hiring suggestions in the company for the last six months. "I hate female bosses who see other women as a threat. It's so freaking old school. A cliché. Shouldn't smart, confident women support one another?"

"She's obviously insecure as hell and doesn't want

anyone else catching on," Matt said with a sigh. "Male managers do it too. Hence the Napoleonic syndrome. I saw it all the time at my old law firm."

Moira was so pissed off she wanted to kick something. "I've made a good name for myself at Peterson Engineering." Heck, she'd been promoted three times in the past five years and now served as the human resources director. "Part of me wants to tough it out just to spite her, but I'm done with all her late-night and weekend texts, last-minute deadline changes, and demands for information she could access on her own."

"She's a bitch," Matt said, and then glanced over his shoulder. He was probably checking for Danny, who was talking to Jane and Caroline in the corner with their mom. "You'll have no trouble getting another job."

"I know," she said, and this time the burn in her throat was from something other than the whiskey. "I'm going to get a forty percent increase on my salary too. I'm ready for six figures."

"You go, girl," Matt said, thrusting out his tumbler. "To bigger and better things."

"What bigger and better things?" Natalie asked, appearing beside them. "Oh, no. Whiskey, Moira? Weren't you going to drive home to Denver tonight?"

She gave her older sister the fish eye as she clinked her glass with Matt's and then took another sip. "Caroline can drive."

Sure, they'd taken her car, but it wouldn't be the first time Caroline had driven it back to Denver. Moira's phone vibrated again, making her see red. She slammed her glass on the table and dug it out of her pocket. Sure enough, Taylor had texted her *again*, asking if she'd received her last four texts—in all caps this time—noting that she needed the references for the computer programmer candidates they were hiring. Like the company would end if Taylor didn't get them on a Sunday night.

Natalie leaned in and peered at the screen. "You weren't kidding about her being a bitch. By bigger and better, did you finally decide to look for another job? I've been hoping you would. That woman has it in for you."

"Yeah, she knows she can't fire me. I have one of the strongest performance ratings in the company. But enough is enough. I can't keep working with someone like that. Excuse me while I call her back and tell her how it's going to be." Maybe it was the whiskey talking, but the words felt right. And it felt liberating to finally walk away.

The mountains seemed to wrap around her when she stepped outside into the O'Briens' backyard. The calm that washed over her told her this was the right thing to do.

Being as diplomatic as possible, she told Taylor that she was leaving Peterson Engineering for personal reasons, and would tender her official notice tomorrow morning. Rather than try to talk her out of it, Taylor said she'd prefer for the notice to be effective immediately. After all, the company would pay out her remaining vacation time.

That slapped Moira back. Taylor wouldn't even give her the professional courtesy of two weeks to transition everything. Well, so be it.

When Moira ended the call, she noted it had only taken two minutes and thirty-eight seconds to change her life. But she felt free. And lighter.

Turning off her cell phone, she went back inside. Matt and Natalie were waiting for her, anxious looks on their faces.

"I quit," she told them, "and Taylor is such a bitch she won't even let me stay around for two weeks to help transition a new person."

"She probably already has someone in mind," Matt said, frowning. "Well, at least you're done with her. You don't want to work with someone like that. How much vacation do you have?"

"Six weeks," she told them. "Plenty of time to find a new job." And the payout would float her financially so she wouldn't have to dip into her savings. Something to be grateful for.

"I'm proud of you for not staying in a miserable position any longer." Natalie gave her a hug. "You're going to find an even better job in no time."

"Damn skippy I will."

Caroline, Jane, and her mom came over, followed by her cousins, Meredith and Jill.

"Looks like there's a celebration, and we're missing out," her mom said, ruffling Danny's hair when he ran over to join them.

"I've had it with my boss," she said, reaching for her whiskey again, "so I just gave my notice, which she accepted. I'm going to find a new job with a *nice* boss."

"Good for you," her mother said, putting her arm around her. "I didn't like how that Taylor woman has been treating you. If I were her mother, I would have sent her to time out. Matt, pour me a little of that whiskey so I can toast Moira's decision."

There was a chorus of agreement from her family. Moira already felt better. She always did when she was with them. When Andy returned with Lucy, she'd have to share her news with him. He was always reminding her life was too short to stay in a bad situation, something Kim's death had taught them all.

"And do you know what?" she said, lifting her glass. "I'm going to take a spa day in Aspen and then spend some time in Dare Valley. Natalie, do you think I could use one of your cars? Caroline, you'll have to drive back without me. Mom, can I stay with you?"

"Of course you can, honey," her mother said in delight. "You deserve some time off in between jobs. Once you've rested, you can look for a new job. Maybe you'll find something in Dare Valley."

Her siblings all looked at her—they were well aware of their mom's hope that all her chickens would come home to roost.

"Who knows?" she said to be agreeable to her mother. The last thing she wanted was to take a pay cut or a title dip, something she'd expect from the smaller job pool in Dare Valley. "There might be something."

Either way, Moira was going to find the best damn job out there.

# Chapter 4

Lucy lurched up in bed when a harsh pounding broke through her consciousness.

*Was someone coming for her?*

Her gaze flew to the door. For a moment, she didn't know where she was. Congo? Her vision was blurry, which only pumped more adrenaline through her system. Then she recognized her old pine dresser, topped with a photo of her and her parents cross-country skiing. A younger George Clooney smiled wickedly at her from the poster her mother had left on her purple walls.

She was in Dare Valley. Recovering from the attack. Right. That was why her vision was wonky.

"Lucy!" her mother called from the other side of the door. "Time to rise and shine."

The jarring wake-up call was another reason she couldn't stay with her parents. Ellen O'Brien did not believe in sleeping. She said people died in bed, so best not spend too much time there. The door cracked open, causing her to jump.

Her mother popped her head through. "April's here, dear, and would love to see you."

Hadn't she seen the woman just last night? "Be right out," she answered with a fake smile.

When the door closed, Lucy flopped back down and settled deeper into the covers. She sucked in calming breaths. The alarm clock was the same one she'd had in high school, and it read 8:27 a.m. She supposed she should be grateful her mom had let her sleep so late. After the party, she'd pretty much passed out at nine o'clock. She'd awoken at three in the morning, but the best way to fight jet leg was to force your body to acclimate to the new time zone. So she'd stayed in bed, thinking way too much about her conversation with Andy, her future, and being home. Somewhere along the line, she'd fallen back asleep.

Lucy grabbed her shaggy white terrycloth robe and crawled out of bed. Shuffling her feet, she stretched as she made her way to the kitchen—her mother's lair. Some women entertained in the parlor, but Ellen O'Brien conducted the orchestra of her life from the kitchen. Most of her childhood memories of her mother were set in this room.

"There you are!" her mother said, hustling across the room and hugging her tight. "I was telling April you got a free pass on sleeping in today because you had a long journey here, but tomorrow, it's back to normal."

Normal. That meant waking up no later than seven a.m. She needed to find her own place—stat.

April Hale was smiling at the mother-daughter reunion over a blue pottery mug that smelled enticingly of coffee. Other delicious food smells like bacon floated through the air, making her feel a little zing of happiness.

"Good morning, April," she said as her mother released her.

"Hi, Lucy. It's good to see you in your mother's kitchen again." She came over and hugged her as well.

Even though Lucy had seen and talked to her last

night, a fresh spurt of happiness filled her as memories flashed through her mind. She remembered eating oatmeal raisin cookies after school on the Hales' Harvest Gold kitchen table as April bandaged her scraped knees or helped her with homework.

April stepped back. "Your hair is as long and fiery as I remember it. The auburn looks so good with your green eyes. Always has."

Her compliment was a little surprising. After all, she almost always saw April on her visits home. Was she simply being extra sweet, or subtly suggesting Lucy needed a haircut? Her last one had been in Beirut, and hadn't that been a trip... She'd gotten as close as she could to the Syrian border without getting into trouble. "Thank you."

Her mom set a cup of steaming coffee in front of her, and she stared at it carefully. Another problem with her injury was that it threw off her depth perception with the objects closest to her, making it hard for her brain to pinpoint exactly where her hand needed to move to grasp them.

"Is that a hawk outside the window?" she asked, making them both turn their heads.

She put her hand toward where she thought the cup was, missed, and moved it a couple inches until she had a good grip on the mug.

"I don't see one," her mother said.

"Me either," April said, "although there are plenty of them around."

"This coffee is delicious," she said, taking a sip, congratulating herself on the misdirection.

"You and your father always did need coffee to function in the morning," her mom said, pinching her cheek. "Although sleeping this late, you'd think you could do without the jolt. You need a haircut."

"I was just thinking that," she responded pleasantly.

"Do I even want to see your toes?" her mom asked,

looking down at her feet.

She covered one foot over the other. "Stop. You know there are no nail salons in the places I visit." Best not mention that hepatitis C was a real risk at most of the salons she could have visited.

"We can get our nails done today," her mom said, checking her own manicure.

It looked like purple to Lucy, but it could have been blue. There was no way to be sure anymore unless she closed her bad eye, and that was the problem. Relenting to temptation would only make the healing process take longer, darn it all to hell.

"I'll make you a hair appointment too, Luce."

It was already starting. "Mom, I can handle my own appointments."

Her mom yanked on a lock of her hair before turning and loading a plate with bacon and scrambled eggs for her. "I'm only trying to be helpful, honey."

"I know." She did. It just annoyed the hell out of her. "Let me do things at my own pace, okay?"

"Fine," her mom said, sharing a glance with April, who was oddly quiet.

Were they wondering why she was back too? God, she hoped they wouldn't ask. She hadn't kept the incident in the Congo to herself only to keep her parents from worrying. Her mother was allergic to what she called 'sad things.' Lucy couldn't count the number of times her mother had pursed her lips and told her not to be a downer. After a while, Lucy had started self-editing everything she told her mom.

Lucy grabbed the fork her mother handed her, and felt for the plate with her free hand. Upon contact, she dug into the eggs, pushing those thoughts aside. "Cheddar cheese and dill eggs. Oh, yum." She couldn't remember the last time she'd had dill. "And apple-smoked bacon...I'm in heaven."

"Hopefully this proves I'm not an ogre."

Her excitement dimmed. "Mom, I don't think you're an ogre. But I'm a grown woman used to running my own life. You wouldn't appreciate it if I tried to rearrange yours. The apple doesn't fall far from the tree."

"Indeed," her mother said, her mouth twisting. "Go ahead and eat. April and I will tell you about our project."

That sounded ominous. If they had a project, Dare Valley had better watch out. When they were young mothers, Ellen and April had organized a breastfeeding fair for women. They'd suggested that women should stop covering themselves in church, restaurants, and local stores. Suffice it to say, the whole town had been scandalized. Her dad might have thrown a blanket over her mom's boob and begged her to stop. Breastfeeding openly was more widespread now, of course—her mother had been ahead of her time.

"It was so nice to see you and Andy together again last night," April said, pouring herself another cup of coffee. She and Ellen stood next to each other, a united front, while Lucy ate off the kitchen island. "Your friendship has certainly stood the test of time. Just like mine with your mother."

The two women put their arms around each other with sisterly affection.

"Yeah, we've done pretty good, Shorty," her mother said, making April laugh.

Was her mother quoting rap lyrics? Lucy didn't want to know.

"Andy is doing better, I suppose," April continued. "Moving back here was the best decision he could have made. He's been able to spend more time with Danny."

According to Andy, that was one of the main reasons he'd made the plunge. He didn't want to miss out on anything as Danny grew up. Moreover, he needed to be mother and father to the little boy, and long hospital hours weren't conducive to quality family time.

"It was good for me too," April continued, "coming back here. I get to be a hands-on grandma and reconnect with all of my old friends."

Lucy watched April and Ellen share a look before they turned their attention on her. She felt as pinned down as a butterfly in a display case.

"Like you get to reconnect with Andy," her mother added, as if April hadn't already laid the groundwork brilliantly.

Lucy took another bite of her steaming eggs. She couldn't talk with her mouth full.

"Danny's growing like a weed," her mother continued. "He's as cute as button and then some."

*Subtle, Mother.* She gulped her coffee next, burning her mouth.

"Just like his father," April said, grabbing the coffee pot and topping off her mug.

"I'm glad to see you're eating so well, Lucy," her mother said, eyeing her plate. "You're too skinny. All that traveling overseas is hard on you."

"I'm fine." Lucy gave her a look before shoveling in more eggs.

"That's a great segue to our project," April said, setting her mug on the island. "We were hoping to get your help. With all your photography experience, this will be a piece of cake."

Lucy's chewing slowed. Why were the hairs on the back of her neck suddenly standing at attention?

"What project?" she asked, seeing no escape.

Her mom rested a hand on her shoulder. *Oh, no. Not the hand-on-the-shoulder move!*

"You know those calendars you take photos for?" April asked. "The ones of the poor kids in Africa?"

"Yes," she said cautiously, gritting her teeth at the description.

"They look great, dear," her mom said, pointing to

the current year calendar hanging on the side of the refrigerator. "But really sad too."

Sad was her mother's code for bad. Ellen O'Brien didn't do sad. Lucy set her fork down. "What do you want me to do?"

April tucked her salt-and-pepper hair behind her ears. "We want you to shoot the photos for a calendar we've organized to raise money for breast cancer awareness and research."

Lucy knew about April's recent scare. And of course there was Kim. "What kind of photos did you have in mind?" Could she even shoot them with her vision being what it was? She hadn't taken a single photo since the accident. Hadn't been able to pick up her Leica.

April shared a look with her mother. "You tell her. It was your idea."

Somehow that kindled fear in her very heart. Her mother was known for her outlandish ideas.

"Have you seen the movie *Calendar Girls*, honey?" her mother asked. "The one with Helen Mirren?"

"I didn't catch that one," she said, trying to remember the last movie she'd seen. "I don't get to see many movies, Mom."

Her mother patted her shoulder. "It's a British film about women raising money for some medical issue—can't remember what kind right now. Doesn't matter. And all the women in the calendar show a little skin. If you know what I mean." The grin on her face told Lucy *exactly* what she meant.

She blinked a couple times. "You want me to shoot photos for a *Playboy*-like calendar?" Her mom had never been shy about her body. In fact, she was infamous around town for her habit of hopping into the backyard hot tub naked in broad daylight. But this...

"No, dear," April said earnestly, patting Lucy's hand. "Nothing like that. Although I have been called Miss April before."

Her mother snorted. Miss April? This was not the kind of information Lucy wanted taking up space in her brain.

"While it might be fun to go for the full monty, your mother and I have decided on something else," April continued. "We'll be naked—like the women in the movie—and cover our...ah...feminine parts with amusing props. Like cantaloupes or something." She made a gesture to her ample chest.

"We're going to need pretty big cantaloupes for you, April," her mom said, starting to laugh.

"Or those small watermelons at the market," April added seriously, shorting out Lucy's brain momentarily.

Mrs. Hale, the woman who used to make cookies for the school bake sale and had taught all her daughters not to let boys touch their private parts, was talking like this?

Lucy felt a headache coming on. She just couldn't get past the naked part—and all the melon talk.

Then her mom walked to the fruit bowl sitting on the counter. "Too bad I don't have a weenie because we have to use this banana for something. Guess I'll have to settle for the avocados since I'm only a B-cup."

Lucy put a hand to her forehead as her mother picked up a pair of avocados and arranged them against her boobs. "Please, Mom. Stop. You're going to give me nightmares."

April chortled. "Hand me those mangoes, Ellen, and I'll show you where to put them."

All hell really had broken loose. Her mom was pressing two avocados to her breasts while April nestled the mangoes against her girls.

"I really am going to need cantaloupes or watermelons," April said, tsking as she set her fruit on the counter. "Mangoes are way too small."

"Ladies, please," Lucy implored, trying to rein them back in. "If you want me to take this seriously, you need to put the fruit down. Now, Mother."

Her mom wiggled her body suggestively before putting the avocados down. "You're so serious sometimes."

"I'm a professional," Lucy said, making them both sputter with laughter. "Let's start over. You're planning to do a calendar to raise money for breast cancer. Obviously, the two of you have volunteered for photos, but a year has twelve months."

Her mom rolled her eyes. "We have other people lined up besides us, Lucy. Everyone has lost someone to cancer. And it's not just women. We have men too. Your father had reservations, but April and I are committed to the idea of an equal opportunity calendar."

She could imagine it now. Old men with hot dogs in front of their family jewels. Her stomach churned from the horror. "You don't mean Andy, do you?" Surely her friend would have told her about this if he'd known. Besides, she couldn't see Andy posing nude with a foot-long in front of his... Oh, she needed to stop that train of thought right this minute.

"Of course not," her mother said. "He's the father of a young son. How would it look if he posed naked with a frankfurter covering his crotch?"

The nightmare just wouldn't stop. "Please. Can we try and keep this...I don't know...somewhat professional? Right now, this whole thing sounds pretty risqué. I've never done anything like this, and even though it's for a good cause, I might not be the right person to help." Besides, she wasn't sure she could even take photos right now.

April's face fell. "It's going to be tasteful, Lucy, I promise you."

Her mother glared at her. "Do you think something like this is beneath you, what with you being a hot-shot photojournalist and all?"

Now that hurt. But there was some truth to it. She

was known for her work. How would it look if she photographed a scantily-clad calendar, even if it did raise money for a worthy cause?

"Do you really think Dare Valley is...liberal enough to support this effort?" Lucy could easily imagine how some would react.

"It's a small community," April said with a sigh. "We expect there will be some resistance, but we're hoping that it won't be an issue considering how many respected citizens have agreed to participate."

"Don't forget the involvement of a famous, well-respected photographer," her mother added, picking up the banana and shaking it in her direction.

Lucy felt a pinch of guilt, which was probably her mother's intention.

"Florence Henklemeyer is going to be fit to be tied over this," her mom continued, waving the banana about like she was Justice with her shining sword. "But after the smear campaign Florence's son pulled on Matt in the mayoral primary, we're looking forward to putting their knickers in a wad."

"Florence went after Jane for being a former poker babe, saying she was indecent," April said, a hard gleam in her eyes. "Your mom and I aren't going to back down to the likes of her. This calendar is nothing to be ashamed of. It's going to help a lot of women get mammograms and other care. After what happened to Kim and my own scare with breast cancer, I want to do something to help."

There was fire in her voice, and it roused the fighter in Lucy. Breast cancer did need to be fought, both through raising awareness and money for research and care.

"Lucy," April said, taking her hand. "We all plan to dedicate our month to the loved one we lost. And I have a name for it. The calendar, I mean."

Lucy nodded, feeling her hand vibrate with emotion.

"I figured that since we've all had to learn to live again after losing someone to cancer, we'll call it The Calendar of New Beginnings."

Lucy had to swallow the lump in her throat. She knew something about new beginnings. "April, it's a beautiful name and a beautiful idea."

"I'm dedicating my month to your grandmother," her mom told her. "My mom was a tough woman, but she loved me and you too, kid. Do you remember how she used to make you ham sandwiches and oatmeal raisin cookies every Tuesday for school lunch? I wish I could still pick up the phone and call her. I even miss playing bridge with her—although she delighted in beating me into the ground."

Her grandmother had been fierce and competitive, but she'd always been kind to Lucy. She had died of lung cancer eight years ago. "Of course I remember, Mom. She was something."

"And my month is dedicated to Kim, of course," April said, pursing her lips as if fighting strong emotion. "I miss that girl. She was a shining light in our family, and for Andy and Danny."

"So will you do it?" her mom asked.

She reached for April's other hand, both of them gazing at her with hope and determination. They would do it without her, she knew. And if she didn't help, she'd feel like crap. Maybe this was her chance to learn how to take photos without her normal vision. If her condition didn't rectify itself, she'd need all the practice she could get to adjust to her new constraints. While she would give it her best, no one would be expecting award-winning photographs for this calendar. That should help her deal with her terror over taking photos again, shouldn't it?

"All right, I'll do it," she announced, "but I want full artistic control."

They shrieked and high-fived each other.

"Hear me well," Lucy said, rubbing her ear. "We are *not* doing cantaloupes."

April grabbed her in a hug. "Don't worry, Lucy. They'll be going out of season soon anyway."

"If you don't like the cantaloupes, Lucy," her mom said, putting her arms around them both, "I've got lots of other ideas."

Lucy could only imagine. "I bet."

"There's only one other thing," April added, giving them all space.

"What?" she asked.

"Everyone has promised to keep the calendar a secret until it's ready for publication."

"Good idea," she agreed.

Her mom cocked a brow. "April isn't sure how Andy will take the news. Her scare...stirred him up...and then there are his memories of Kim."

To her mind, it didn't help Andy the way everyone tried to handle him with kid gloves. "I won't keep my involvement in this calendar a secret from him. He's my best friend."

April's face contorted. "I'm afraid to tell him. He...tried to hide it from me, but I know how much my scare affected him."

Lucy tucked her tongue against her cheek. "He's stronger than you think, and it's not like you can hide this from him forever. The calendar will be published at some point."

"True," her mother remarked. "Maybe you might help April out by telling Andy?"

If she hadn't known April was less devious than her mother, she would have believed they'd planned this trap together.

Her mother batted her eyelashes at her like a silent film ingénue. Lucy mirrored her crazy expression right back. April remained silent, looking back and forth between the two of them.

"Fine," she said finally, seeing no way out. "I'll tell him."

"Good," her mom said, patting her on the arm. "Now, about the poses. Everyone wants to have a say. Since it's so personal and all..."

Lucy suppressed a shudder. "I'll be happy to listen. Within reason. Am I supposed to talk to everyone individually? I'll also have to find a space for the shoot." Could they do it in a couple days? She didn't think so. From her experience, getting a person comfortable enough to show his or her true self in a photo intended for a calendar took hours. The shooting was completely different than the kind she did on the fly in war zones.

"Don't worry about the details too much," her mother said, doing the cha-cha in the kitchen. "We'll have everyone over to brainstorm together."

Her artistic control was flying right out the window. They were going to struggle over this calendar, she had no doubt.

"Maybe I can ask your father to bring home a long-neck from the bar for one of the men," her mom said, guffawing madly. "Why don't you ask him, Lucy?"

She decided leaving the kitchen was her best course of action. "I am not listening to this."

Her mother slapped her butt on her way out. "Better get dressed. It'll be lunchtime before you know it."

As she headed to her old room, Lucy reflected on just how far she was from her normal routine. Somehow she'd agreed to take racy pictures of her mother and her friends for a good cause.

She sure wasn't in Kansas anymore.

# Chapter 5

Andy raced around the kitchen like a Nascar driver in his final lap. He managed to pour dog food in Rufus' bowl, flip his son's eggs, and butter toast in one turn around the island. Too bad no one was waiting at the finish line with an award and a cold beer.

It was just another day in the life of a single dad.

He pulled a yogurt from the fridge and juggled it in the air like a baseball because...he felt a little cuckoo on mornings like this. And it was only Monday.

"Dad!"

Andy almost dropped the yogurt. "Yes?" he hollered back.

Danny's shuffling steps sounded on the stairs, so Andy detoured to the doorway. His son didn't look too happy when he came into view. His lip was stuck out, and he still had bed head.

"Rufus took my navy shoes with the flames again."

Would they ever have another calm morning? Ever since he'd caved and gotten Danny a dog from the pound, there had been nothing but chaos. "Pick out a different pair," he said, peeling open his yogurt.

"No," Danny whined. "I want those."

Somehow he'd ended up with a kid who had a shoe fetish. Kim, who had always been particular about her shoes, would have found it amusing. Andy could care less about footwear so long as they were comfortable. Clearly his son had also gotten up on the wrong side of the bed. He'd gone to bed later than usual because of Lucy's party and eaten more junk food than was normally allowed.

"Is that a whine I hear?" he asked.

"No, Dad," came the immediate response.

"It had better not be because otherwise I'll have to get out the—"

"Whine-O-Meter," Danny finished in a high-pitched voice.

"And then the..."

"Not the Whine-Buster!"

Andy fought a smile. The Whine-Buster was a fancy name for a tickle attack, but the threat had worked like a charm. Danny's pout was history. Andy glanced at the clock in the hall. He had forty minutes to get Danny dressed, fed, driven to school, and then himself off to the hospital. It was going to be tight.

"Rufus!" he called, trying to channel authority.

The golden retriever trotted into view and put his head down on his paws when he sat.

"Bad dog," he said sternly. "You've got to stop taking Danny's shoes."

The dog started whining too, and Andy felt a headache coming on. He needed Jane to work her dog training magic on Rufus. If she could do it for his brother's dog, Henry, she could do it for this guy.

"Go find the shoes," he ordered Rufus.

The smell of overcooked eggs reached his nose, and he nearly cursed. He'd forgotten the eggs! He darted over to the stove. The edges were burned, and the yolks cooked through. Maybe this one time Danny would eat a hard yolk. *Please, God.* He scooped them onto a plate with the toast and added a liberal amount of ketchup to hide the burn. Usually he was light with the condiment, but today he added it liberally. Danny loved it on hot dogs. Maybe it would work with eggs.

"Come and eat, Danny. I'll look for your shoes."

He poured Danny some milk and set his own uneaten yogurt on the table. Danny shuffled into the kitchen. Rufus trailed after him, his head hanging woefully. It was hard to stay mad at a dog that acted so guilty.

"Grab a fork and a spoon. I'll be right back."

Andy flew up the stairs, throwing up bed skirts and searching through closets.

"Dad!" his son called. "My egg is burned, and the yolk's not runny."

So much for the ketchup disguise. "Eat my yogurt then." He could grab one on the way out the door.

After five minutes of crouching down in ways a grown man simply shouldn't, he admitted defeat and chose another pair of shoes with a sense of dread. He hated shoe battles with his son. He jogged down the stairs and froze at the entrance to the kitchen. Bits of toast littered the floor. He narrowed his eyes. Danny pushed his egg around on his plate without looking up. Rufus plopped down on the floor beside the table and let out a whine.

"What happened?" He hated asking questions he could answer himself, but it was a dreaded—and unavoidable—part of parenting.

"Rufus took the toast off my plate," Danny said, making fork tracks in his ketchup.

Andy set the shoes on the kitchen counter, striving for calm. "Rufus doesn't like toast. That's why it's still lying on the floor instead of in his stomach. You threw your toast on the floor because you didn't want it. What have I told you about fibbing to me? Just say you don't want to eat it."

"I'm sorry I fibbed," Danny said in a heavy tone. "I think I'm allergic to toast."

How did kids figure out how to incorporate topics from their parents' careers into their arguments? Allergies, indeed. "I'm the doctor in this family. For the record, you don't have any allergies. And you know grains are good for you." Andy slid his yogurt over to his son. "Try the yogurt."

Danny made gagging sounds. "I hate yogurt. Alice Adams says it tastes like chalk."

"You liked it last week." Great. Now other kids—worse the daughter of his childhood bully, Jason Adams—were influencing his son's eating habits. "It does not taste like chalk."

"It does to me," Danny said, crossing his arms.

Boy, he was in a mood today. Usually, Danny was the sweetest kid ever. Andy tried to remember these moments were blips on the screen. "Fine. You have two minutes to choose something from the refrigerator to eat. Danny, you need to hustle. We're running late."

While Danny studied the contents of their fridge, Andy shoveled in the yogurt. His son picked out sliced cheddar cheese and ham sandwich meat, so he rolled the cheese and meat into pinwheels, handing them to Danny one at a time. As a breakfast, it wasn't the best, but at least it would provide him with a good portion of dairy and protein.

"I'm full," Danny said, rubbing his belly. "See." Then he stuck it out, laughing.

Rufus barked encouragingly, and Danny ran over to hug him. Andy made a couple of extra pinwheels for himself since he knew he'd burn through the yogurt in his rounds.

"Time to get dressed," he said after chewing. "I couldn't find your navy shoes, so you'll have to wear these."

Danny stuck his chin out. "I don't want to wear the

brown ones. We have to keep looking."

"You are so getting the Whine-Buster when we get home." Andy poured his cooling coffee in a to-go container. "We don't have time to keep looking. Let's get you dressed stat."

"But, Dad—"

"No buts, mister. Upstairs."

Danny moved to the stairs like a turtle in a three-legged race. "I don't want to wear the brown shoes."

Cripes, Danny was acting like the world had ended. Andy wanted to pull his hair out. He surveyed the toast bits on the floor. If they had the time, he would make Danny pick up the crumbs. "Life's tough. Be glad you have shoes. Lucy takes pictures of kids who don't have any. You should be grateful."

God. Had those words sailed out of his mouth? His parents had said things like that to him and his sisters, talking about starving kids in Ethiopia before he even knew where that was. He'd hoped to never resort to that schtick.

"I'm sorry for saying that, Danny. I know you want the other shoes. I just can't find them today. Please give me a break and go upstairs so we can get you dressed and off to school. I'm doing my best here. Okay, buddy?"

There. That was more loving.

Danny wrapped his arms around Andy's leg. "I'm sorry too, Dad. I'll wear the brown shoes."

"And brush your teeth," he added, picking him up and hugging him tight.

The love he had for his son burst through like sun from behind the clouds. Who cared if toast bits lined the floor or that his son had whined about a pair of shoes? He was alive and healthy, and in the end, that was all that mattered.

"I love you," he said, cupping Danny's head, feeling the soft hair cradling his skull.

"I love you too, Dad," he answered, squeezing Andy's neck.

"Now let's get ready to blow this joint," he said, taking the stairs two at a time with his son in his arms. "It's going to be a great day."

After seeing Danny off to school, he headed to Dare Valley General. Morning rounds went well. All his patients were improving—a rarity—and their visiting family members were in good spirits. He even discharged Everett Corrigan, who'd been with them over a week with an obstructed bowel. Realizing he'd have time for a lunch break, he texted his brother to see if he wanted to join him for a run. He received Matt's one-word answer—*yes*—as he headed back to his office on the seventh floor to do some paperwork.

Patient files lined the metal holder situated on the corner of his desk. In his Denver hospital, he'd been able to type his notes onto a hand-held device. Dare Valley General wasn't as automated, which was a pain in the butt. He'd brought the innovation up to the hospital board in the hopes they would go for his suggestion. Sometimes it was hard to read his notes, though Joyce Henners, the charge nurse, had become a master at deciphering his handwriting. He completed the charts from his rounds that morning and then sat back in his chair.

Lucy filtered through his mind, and he went online to see if she was on Skype. After talking with her last night about her accident and injuries, he was tempted to call up Dr. Davidson to informally discuss her case out of professional courtesy. Doctors still did that—even with HIPAA. He shook his head, realizing that he was doing precisely what Lucy had asked him not to do.

She had been right to make him promise not to intervene without her blessing. But he couldn't deny he was worried about her. That worry had kept him up for hours after he'd put Danny to bed. Didn't she need extra support after all she'd been through? Her stubborn Irish side really ticked him off sometimes.

He reached for his phone to text her, only to realize he didn't have her number. They always used Skype. She usually picked up a new disposable phone every few weeks since most of the countries she went to had different cellular systems—if only rudimentary ones. Or satellite phones, which were reserved for emergencies—like being injured in a bombing.

He eyed his phone. Should he call her house? Would that be awkward? Ellen O'Brien would love it, as would his mother. Popping open a bottle of water, he concluded he was making too big a deal of it. She was living at her parents' house for the moment. He wanted to talk to her about getting together. It was as simple as that.

And if he knew Lucy, her mother was going to drive her bat-shit crazy if she didn't have frequent breaks from the madness. He picked up the phone and dialed the O'Brien residence.

"Hello," Ellen answered.

"Hi, Ellen," he said in as even a tone as he could muster. "I wasn't sure if Lucy had a cell phone she was using, so I figured I'd try your home phone. Could you put her on for me?"

Brief. Factual. Friendly.

He needed to keep Ellen and his mother from spinning fairy tales about them finding happily ever after together after all this time.

"Well, well, well," Ellen drawled. "Andy Hale. It's been a while since you called this house asking for Lucy."

The first burn of embarrassment heated his cheeks. God, when Ellen said it that way, he felt like he was back in high school. "Indeed it has. Is she around?"

"Sure. I'm trying to talk her into going to the salon to get her nails done."

He knew how well that was likely to go over. Lucy had never been much for girly things, even when it came to summer pool parties or prom.

"Must be a quiet day at the hospital," Ellen continued, her usual chatty self.

"It's been pretty normal," he responded, hoping he wouldn't have to keep up the small talk much longer. "Are you getting Lucy? I only have a short break."

"Sure. Lucy! Andy's on the phone for you."

That woman could puncture an ear drum.

Lucy answered a couple of moments later. "Hello?"

"Hey," Andy replied, sitting back in his chair. "You've survived the morning, I see. No mention of you on the police scanner yet."

"It was touch and go there for a while," she said in a quieter voice. "Give me a moment to get back to my room."

Yeah, Ellen would listen to every word if she could.

"All clear," Lucy said in a brighter voice. "How's it going, Andy Cakes?"

He ignored the endearment. "Fine so far. I realized I didn't have a way to reach you beyond Skype. Have you bought a cell yet?"

"Yeah, in Denver. You ready for it?"

"Shoot."

She dictated the number, and he plugged it into his cell and texted her immediately. A reply text came a second later with a smiley face and a *You know who*. He was smiling as he sent a matching emoticon back to her.

"My mother is trying to convince me to get a manicure and a pedicure," she said in an aggrieved tone. "She refuses to recall how much I hate those kinds of things. I need to get my own place fast."

"When are you looking at places?"

"I have a few lined up for this afternoon. I'm telling myself not to settle for something I don't like just to get out of here. I love my mother, but…"

"I know," he answered because she'd been saying the same thing all her life. "Are you feeling all right? I mean, is there anything you need?"

Silence permeated the line for a moment. "I told you. I'm fine. You went home and worried, didn't you? Please tell me you haven't called my eye doctor in Denver."

It was a low point to realize he was so predictable. He didn't tell her about the research he'd done online. "I managed to talk myself down from doing any such thing, but Lucy, I *am* worried." More so after seeing she was right. There was nothing they could do for traumatic optic neuropathy.

"I won't tell you what to feel, Andy Cakes. I gave up feeling responsible for other people's reactions a long time ago. But there is something I was wrangled into telling you. It's a long story. Do you have any time to get together in the next few days?"

He sat up straighter in his chair. "You have something to tell me? Why do I sense the long shadow of our mothers here?"

She laughed. "Because you're smart. It's nothing to worry about. It's just...weird and a little harebrained...and kinda sweet."

"They picked out a date for us to get married," he said easily, laughing too.

"That would be the day," she responded as easily. "You're right, though, they have grand plans for us. You know how they are."

He glanced down at the family photo on his desk. Kim had her arms around him, and he was holding a newborn Danny. They were gazing at each other, cherishing the miracle they'd made. God, he couldn't imagine ever looking at someone like that again. And making a child with someone again... There was no bigger commitment.

His spirits sank, and he felt sadness pull at him as

he thought about being alone for the rest of his life. Of course, Kim hadn't wanted him to stay alone forever. In the letter she'd written before her death, which she'd instructed him to open one year after her passing, she'd asked him to find love again. *That* was the kind of woman he'd married. The kind of woman he'd lost.

It broke his heart every time he read that letter. He'd showed it to Natalie a couple of months back, right after Blake had returned to her life. He'd made his sister a deal that day. If she'd give Blake a chance, he'd try dating again. It was the hardest thing he'd ever done, but since Kim was the one who'd asked him to find love again, he'd squared his shoulders to begin the quest.

Natalie had fallen back in love with Blake, so at least one of them had found a happy ending. So far, Andy had only gone on a couple of dates. Each one had only made him feel more hopeless about the whole love thing. Truth be told, he really didn't want to date anyone. He wasn't any good at dating, which Kim had known all too well. She was the one who'd needed to make the first move with him. He'd been too intimidated by her to imagine she'd return his interest.

"Our mothers do want us to end up with awesome people," he murmured into the phone, finally looking away from the photo. "We'll just have to get everyone used to seeing us as friends again. It'll only be as hard as we make it." Saying the words made his chest loosen up immediately.

"Exactly! We did it before. We'll do it again. Some people need more hobbies, if you ask me."

He completely agreed. The whole thing was embarrassing. He didn't need his mother and Ellen to get involved in his struggle. Besides, truth be told, he didn't really need matchmaking help. It didn't happen too often, but every now and then he'd received an offer for coffee, or a woman would make a casual mention of bringing by dinner for him since he was all by his lonesome, raising such a sweet little boy. But it was never the right woman, and he didn't know if there could be another right woman.

"How about we meet at Hairy's tonight?" he said. "It will make your dad happy. Plus, I can bring Danny if we go early."

"Yeah. About that. I won't be able to tell you in front of Danny."

"Is it *that* bad?" he asked, leaning forward until his elbows rested on his desk. "You have to tell me now. I can't wait."

"No way," she said with a chuckle. "I've decided the only blessing in this whole situation is seeing your face when I tell you."

That didn't sound good. "When are we meeting then? I get off at five and could meet you at Hairy's by five thirty. Maybe I'll bring one of my siblings to keep an eye Danny so you can tell me the big secret." And since her refusal to tell him said secret was giving him heartburn, he added, "Of course, that's only if you can drag yourself away from the salon. I can't wait to see your nails. What color are you going with?"

"I hate you," she said without heat. "You're a doctor. You're supposed to be compassionate."

My, she didn't know doctors very well, did she? Most of them were complete assholes. He'd always prided himself on not having a God-complex like some of his colleagues.

"I'm only compassionate to those in need," he said, checking the time. "Ellen might try and prod you toward her way of thinking, but she still loves you. Remember that. How's that for a dose of compassion?"

"You're supposed to be compassionate toward me. She wants me to be someone I'm not. I don't know why she keeps trying. I *like* who I am."

"So do I. Look, I need to run. Literally. Matt is meeting me for a run through the park on my lunch hour. I need to finish up some more paperwork before I go."

"Have a great run. See you at five thirty."

After all her time away, darn it if he didn't like the sound of that. "Make sure to wear open-toed shoes so I can admire your nail polish," he joked.

"I'm going to kill you, Andy Cakes," she said in a dark voice. "As revenge, I'm going to come up with an even more colorful description of the plan our mothers have cooked up."

"Do your best. Later, alligator."

"After a while, crocodile," she finished and hung up.

Sitting back in his chair, he wondered again what Ellen and his mother had planned.

Truth be told, it really didn't matter. Nothing could dim his joy that Lucy O'Brien was back in town.

# Chapter 6

By the time Lucy drove down Main Street later that afternoon to meet Andy, she had lost one skirmish and won a much larger battle. While her toenails were a glittery pink, she had a new place to hang her hat while she was in Dare Valley.

After seeing four rental properties, she'd selected a quaint cottage up in the mountains surrounded by lush trees and craggy rock walls. The owner, Mrs. Weidman, an eccentric elderly woman who'd moved in with her son for health reasons, had described her place as a tad too old-fashioned for students at Emmits Merriam. Lucy remembered seeing her at some town functions growing up, but she'd never really known the family.

The house was a decided change from all of the blank, white-wall spaces she'd occupied while traveling overseas. Fully furnished with a Victorian couch—her mother had described it as mustard-colored, but to her it had looked brownish—in the lavender parlor and a brass bed in the light-pink master bedroom, it suited Lucy perfectly. The second bedroom, painted a light blue, would be her home office. In the small cottage, Lucy felt like she was inside a cupcake.

After dropping her mother off at the house for a power-walking date with April, Lucy drove to her father's bar. Dare Valley's stores seemed more prosperous than ever, what with the fresh paint, power-washed brick, and shining windows. People mingled on the street, running errands and sharing gossip. Parking was a pain, so she ended up choosing a spot three blocks away. She almost laughed at herself for being annoyed—parking spaces and paved roads were luxuries in many parts of the world, but it was funny how quickly a person started to take them for granted.

She walked down Main Street to Hairy's. Growing up, this bar had been her second home. She traced the green sign on the door announcing that an Irish band called Maddie's Shillelagh would be playing this Saturday. The door chimed an Irish jig when she opened it.

The hardwood floors, dark mahogany bar, and carved bench seats made her think of the pubs she'd crawled through in Dublin on past vacations. The smell of strong stout and freshly fried fish and chips teased her nose. She could no longer distinguish between the two shades of green on the walls—lime and Kelly—but before she had time to stew over it, a familiar voice called out her name.

Her dad strode toward her in jeans and a black T-shirt with a green logo that read "Irish Superhero."

"Hey everybody! My daughter is back from saving the world!" He grabbed her shoulders and kissed her cheek as the small crowd of regulars cheered from their posts all around the bar. "Welcome home, sweet girl."

She gave him a bright smile. "I was just thinking about all the afternoons I did my homework here."

He grinned back, the laugh lines around his mouth deepening. "Pretty much whenever your mother was taking some class or another."

Yeah, her mother had tried everything from stained

glass to wicker furniture making. Of course, Lucy had also gone over to Andy's house a lot too. Maybe that was why she had the ability to feel at home anywhere—she'd started living a vagabond existence at a young age.

"I've missed this place, Dad," she said, leaning her head against his shoulder after he situated her on a bar stool in the corner. "I've been to lots of pubs around the world, but there's no place to match yours."

He kissed her temple before walking around to the back of the bar. "You're partial, but I'll take the praise. Your mother has been busting my balls for not talking you out of renting Eustace Weidman's cottage."

Eustace was that eighty-seven-year-old lady's first name? She winced. "News travels fast." Not that she was surprised. Her mother had insisted on accompanying her on what she'd described as "rental shopping," and she'd carped all the while about how Lucy should stay at home. "I need my own space, Dad. Surely you understand."

"I know it," he said, building a Guinness for her. "You're like me that way. Now, your mother. She doesn't understand the concept of personal space, God love her."

Lucy's heart swelled as she stroked the bar's wood grain. "You planning on drinking with me? It's my first beer in your place in some time."

He beamed as brightly as his bald head shone under the lights. "How could I refuse?"

After pouring himself a Guinness, he lifted his glass to hers. "Slainte."

"Slainte," she repeated and took a sip. The foam tickled her lips and the dark brew coated her tongue. "Mmm. Delicious."

He wiped the foam from his mouth with the back of his hand. "Nothing like mother's milk, as they say in the old country. Should I ask to see your new toes?"

She shuddered playfully. "Don't encourage Mom. I

decided to pick my battles."

He laughed. "Always were a smarty pants. I also heard you agreed to shoot the photos for this calendar she and April have cooked up," he said, leaning his elbows on the bar.

Since his expression was neutral, she couldn't get a read on him. "What do you think about it?"

"It's like a lot of things your mother has set her sights on over the years," he said with a sigh. "It's for a good cause and comes from a good place. Personally? Well, I figure the photos of your mother are the closest thing I'm going to get to those boudoir photos I've heard about."

Lucy's beer went down the wrong pipe, and she coughed violently. "Oh, gross! Did you have to put that thought in my head?"

"When you've been married forty years, you can judge me for looking for a little marital spice wherever I can find it," he said, reaching across the bar and pounding her back.

The whack of his hand inflamed her lingering soreness, and she made a sound of distress before she could stop herself.

His hand froze immediately, and his clever eyes narrowed. "Are you hurt, young lady?"

She continued to sputter, shaking her head. *Uh-oh*. But he came around the bar and planted himself down on the stool beside her as she coughed into a napkin.

"Don't make me pull up your shirt in the back and embarrass us both," he said, putting his hand on her knee.

He sounded way too much like Andy Hale, and she wasn't sure how to deflect his concern.

"I'm fine," she said, rubbing her chest. "You have a hand like a meat cleaver."

"Bullshit. I know my daughter. You wouldn't return to Dare Valley if something dire hadn't happened."

She clutched the beer in her hand. "I was burned out."

"Don't make me say bullshit again. You've been burned out before. Talk to me."

Since she knew he would only press her until she caved, she decided to share a vague description of the events. "Fine. Something bad happened in a village where I was working, and I needed time to recover."

His mouth pursed, and his ears turned red before her eyes—a sure sign he was more than upset. He was livid. "Recover from what?"

"I wasn't beaten or raped," she said, putting her hand on top of his. "But I was hurt, and I'm recovering. Please don't make me talk about it more, and please don't tell Mom."

He pulled her close and hugged her, and for a moment, she let her arms curl around him.

"You worry me something fierce, young lady," he said, his voice rough. "I remind myself you're your own woman and always will be, but I love you, and your work in all those war zones takes a toll on those who love you too. I don't say it to make you feel guilty. I only say it because...shit...it gives me some bad moments. Okay?"

"I know it does," she said softly, helpless in the face of his show of emotion.

He let her go and picked up his beer, downing half the contents. "I can't promise not to tell your mother."

"But—"

"You know how this works, Luce," he said, setting his beer back on the bar top with a clack. "She's my partner, and you're our kid. I don't keep secrets from Ellie. Not even for you."

No, he never had, and it was something she admired. Most of the time. "I was hoping for a reprieve this one time."

"Not a chance, kid. But I will do my best to get her to

give you some space. If you've come home to heal, we'll do everything we can to support that. You have my word."

"Oh, Daddy," she said, feeling uncharacteristically teary-eyed.

"Don't you dare make me cry, missy," he said, swiping at his eyes. "But you have to promise to tell me if you need help with anything. I won't accept anything but a resounding yes from you there."

As a bargain, it was the best she could hope for. "I promise."

"Good," he said, cracking his neck and standing. "Now, how about some fish and chips?"

Lucy tapped her finger in time with the Irish music playing over the speakers to lighten the moment between them. She'd always known her dad worried about her, but he usually didn't let her see it. "Sounds great."

"This time home will be good for you, Luce. And the calendar will be a fun change." He gave her a wink, shaking off his own emotions. "Then you can decide what the incredible Lucy O'Brien will do next. I can't wait to see what that will be."

She knew how much that cost him to say, fighting his worry and all, so she stood and kissed his cheek. "I love you, Daddy."

He gave her a butterfly kiss like he'd done when she was little. "I love you too, Lucy Lu."

By the time happy hour officially rolled around, the noise level in the bar had risen to concert-level. Lucy found herself wedged against the bar while her dad built beers like a pro with Mike, his main bartender, and reconnected her with his local patrons. Of course, she'd seen many of them during her brief visits home, but those visits had typically been limited to a few days at a time, meaning there was usually only time to connect with family and close friends. It felt good to get reacquainted with a wider net of people. Some of them were long-time Dare Valley residents she had known since she was a little girl. A few of her dad's friends chucked her under the chin, joking that maybe his hair would finally grow back now that she'd returned. Like she'd made it fall out in the first place.

She even chatted with a few people she'd grown up with. Patrick O'Shaughnessy, a fireman, still had a crooked smile and streaky blond hair. He was a couple years younger, but he'd lived on their block and played Ghosts in the Graveyard with her and the other neighborhood kids.

Her dad also introduced her to several newbies, who'd moved to Dare Valley from bigger cities, seeking more time with their families and less time commuting. She'd never remember everyone's names, but it turned out they knew hers. According to the bar patrons, her dad talked about her frequently.

One of the newbies, a young doctor who knew her parents, explained that many of Dare Valley's new arrivals worked in the town's expanding medical industry. Dr. Jeff Geller was easy on the eyes, but his faux hawk—perfectly gelled to a point in the middle of his forehead—made her want to giggle. He'd signed up for a three-year stint at Dare Valley General to lower his student loan payments since it was technically still categorized as a rural hospital.

"Medical practices are popping up everywhere to support our patients," he told her. "You heard General won an award for being a leading regional hospital, right?"

Lucy shook her head, keeping an eye out for Andy and Danny, who were due to arrive any moment now.

"No, I hadn't heard that," she said, soaking in the view of her dad building beers and laughing at something one of his regulars was going on about. She really had missed this place.

"Of course, there's some like your pal, Dr. Andy Hale," Jeff said, giving her a sly smile, "who left because of the insane hours in city hospitals."

"How do you know Andy is my pal?" she asked, her eyes narrowing.

"Your mom talks about you," Jeff said, making her frown.

Was her mom hoping to set her up with this cute, too-young doctor? Sure, her mom might want her to hook up with Andy, but Lucy wouldn't put it past her to consider back-up options. When it came to getting grandchildren, Ellen O'Brien would pull out all the stops.

"What exactly did my mother say about me?" she asked.

"Besides the fact that you're wicked smart, funny, and pretty?"

That line didn't much surprise her. He'd been looking his fill as he sipped his Guinness, and in all honesty, Lucy had been enjoying his eyes on her. Sadly, it had been a while since she'd had a pleasant encounter with male admiration. The last one had been with two frisky chimpanzees in Uganda, who had pounded their massive chests upon seeing her. It had made her chortle to be the subject of that kind of male admiration.

"I'm all that and more," she said, grabbing a handful of her dad's spicy peanuts from the bowl on the bar. "What else did my mom say?"

He brushed closer, like he thought he was scoring points, which was sort of annoying. "Ellen said you have the biggest heart out there and that any man would be lucky to have you."

Lucy tried to appreciate her mother's compliments. She really did. "That's nice of her."

"I have a secret to tell you," he murmured.

She edged back as his breath tickled her ear. She was almost afraid to ask. "What's that?"

"April's recruited me for the calendar. I have some ideas for you to consider."

Great. Dr. Faux Hawk was part of the hot dog crew. "Oh, really?"

His head darted closer, making her think of pigeon feeding in a park. Any earlier excitement she'd felt faded.

"My mom died of breast cancer three years ago," he said quietly.

Great. Just when she was about to kick him to the curb, he had to go all vulnerable on her. "I'm so sorry."

He shrugged, straightening and giving her space again. "Shit happens. I'm just glad to be part of something that helps. Plus, it'll be fun."

Fun might be stretching it, but Jeff had driven home something important. Even though her mom and April had told her everyone doing the calendar had lost someone, Lucy hadn't really registered what that meant. Sure, her mom and April might like to joke about cantaloupes, but there were plenty of deeper emotions behind this enterprise. Lucy knew all about joking up a storm to cover pain. Right then and there, she decided she was going to give everything she could to this calendar.

"I'm glad you're on board, Jeff," she told him with a smile.

Okay, so it sucked that her mother had obviously told everyone she'd agreed to do the calendar before bothering to tell Lucy there *was* a calendar.

"Me too," he said, checking her out again.

She wanted to roll her eyes, but someone grabbed her hand just then, making her jump.

"Hi, Miss Lucy," Danny called out, grinning up at her in his Star Wars shirt and jeans. Could he be any more adorable?

She let a smile spread across her face. "Hi there, Danny Hale. Wanna sit on the bar? My dad always let me when I was your age."

A glance over her shoulder brought Andy into view. He was taller than most of Hairy's patrons and looked well dressed in a dark blue button-down shirt and tan slacks—or at least that's how she read the colors. Her friend had never much gone for the casual look of jeans and a T-shirt. She always looked like a slob next to him, and today she was no different in her worn jeans and ribbed green top.

"Can I, Dad?" Danny asked, and when he nodded, Lucy lifted the little boy up on the bar top.

"Hey, Andy," she said to her friend, a little self-conscious of how Jeff was watching them.

"Hi. You planning on getting my kid to serve beers?" Andy asked, leaning in to kiss her on the cheek.

She could feel everyone in the surrounding area watching them now, including her dad. "Not yet," she answered. "I don't corrupt minors."

"Funny," Andy said, keeping his cool despite all the eager eyes on them. "How's it going, Jeff?"

"Pretty good, man," Jeff responded, shaking his hand. "I'm going to play some pool. Wanna come, Lucy?"

He was sweet. But...he was testing out her feelings by asking her to accompany him. "I have to order my friend a drink." She pointed to Danny. "It was good talking to you, Jeff. I'll see you around."

His eyes held hers for a tad longer than appropriate. "Sure. Come find me if you change your mind. See you later, Andy."

Her friend waggled his eyebrows at her as Jeff walked off. "Some things never change."

She socked him, and her dad, who was still watching them, laughed and turned away. "What *do* you mean?"

"You always stir up male interest wherever you go," he said, shaking his head.

While it was true, she wasn't in the mood to

converse on the subject. "How would you know? I haven't lived here in forever."

He gave her a bland look.

"Can I help being friendly?" Since she wanted to consider that subject good and closed, she turned to Danny. "What would you like to drink, kiddo?"

When the boy opened his mouth, Andy said, "No soda today, Danny. You had your quota for the week at Mrs. O'Brien's party last night."

"But Dad!" Danny cried, swinging his little legs off the bar. "It's a special drink if Ms. Lucy is paying."

Her lips twitched, and Andy shot her a look.

"Not a word," he told her.

"I don't know what you mean," she replied, chuckling under her breath.

Andy wouldn't want her to tell Danny that once upon a time his dad had been her soda partner in crime. Her mom had rationed her intake as a kid since her father would give her endless soda whenever she visited the bar. Somehow, her mother had believed in the evils of excessive sugar in children before it became popular.

That hadn't stopped Lucy. She'd found other ways to get her fix when she wasn't at Hairy's. Andy had let her steal cans from the Hale refrigerator on more than one occasion, and sometimes he'd even sneaked them into her house. She'd drunk soda in her bathroom and thrown the cans in her neighbor's garbage on her way to school. As far as she knew, her mother was still none the wiser.

"Milk or orange juice today, Danny?" Andy asked, making his son frown.

"How about we try a new drink?" Lucy asked, making the kid perk right back up. "Milk *and* orange juice. Maybe it will taste like orange sherbet."

Danny nodded enthusiastically. "Cool."

Lucy asked her father to make two glasses of her concoction. Andy selected a Murphy's. When their drinks came, Lucy eyed the milk/juice glasses with suspicion. This might not have been her best idea, but she liked trying new things.

"Well, no one found a diamond without looking in the rough."

Danny looked at her in confusion. Andy rolled his eyes.

"On three," she told the little boy. "One. Two. Three."

The chalky mixture hit her tongue when she took a sip, and she gagged. "Oh, yuck. It's like drinking paint."

*"Blah!"* Danny shouted dramatically, setting his glass on the bar top and grabbing his neck for effect. "That's the most horrible drink ever!"

Andy signaled to her father, his lips twitching. "Orange juice please for my industrious son. *Straight.*"

"Coming right up," her dad said, his grin as wide as a dinner plate. "Lucy?"

The foulness of the drink saturated her mouth. "I might need a Jameson to wash that down. Neat."

"The only way to drink the water of life," her dad said, all Irish-like. "Coming up."

"Can I have a Jameson too, Dad?" Danny asked hopefully.

"Yes," Andy said, tousling his brown hair. "When you're twenty-one."

His face fell. "But that's *forever*. Mr. O'Brien says it's water."

"Water with alcohol," Andy corrected. "But you *can* have fries with your burger."

"Cool!" Danny said. "Sometimes Dad makes me eat salad. It's horrible—even if all my aunts eat it like candy. Oh, except Aunt Natalie. She likes fries as much as I do."

Should she act horrified in front of Danny in camaraderie? She was tempted, but Andy looked way too serious about the subject, so she kept silent as her dad brought their drinks.

"Speaking of my son's French-fry loving Aunt Natalie, she's meeting us here with Blake and Matt and Jane and Moira," Andy told her. "So you can spill this thing you've had me stewing over all day."

Thinking about Jeff and the other members of the hot dog patrol, her lips twitched. How was Andy going to react to the notion of an equal-opportunity calendar? Personally, she wasn't sure how she felt about taking risqué photos of Jeff considering how he was trying to cozy up to her. Sure as shooting, she wouldn't be taking those photos alone.

"You might have to pry it out of me," she said, sipping her Jameson instead of downing it like she might have if a child wasn't around.

Danny downed his orange juice like he'd been on a fast.

Andy leaned over her, trying to be menacing.

"You couldn't intimidate a fly," she told him, pushing him back.

Danny barked out a laugh and Lucy joined in. Was there anything better than kid giggles? Lucy had learned that one of the major indications a country was in serious trouble was the absence of children laughing.

"You forget," Andy said, putting his hands on his hips like he'd taken a Toughen-Up pill. "I know you can't stand to be tickled. I'll have it out of you in five seconds." He poked her under the ribs and laughed when she lurched away.

Danny's eyes widened before he started laughing with his dad. "Get her, Dad."

"Cut that out," she demanded as Andy's fingers fluttered against her side again, "or I'll kill you."

Danny's mouth dropped open, and Andy gave her a hard look.

"What Miss Lucy meant to say—"

"Was that your dad was mean to tickle me," she interrupted, realizing she couldn't talk like that in front of Danny. "But I shouldn't have said that last part. I was only teasing."

The little boy's nod was punctuated by his wide-eyed gaze. "There's good teasing, and there's bad teasing. Right, Dad?"

"Right," Andy said, sending him a proud, paternal smile.

Apparently Lucy needed to work on her conversation around little people. The kids she spoke with usually were grown-ups in little bodies, wizened by everything they'd experienced in war. "I'm sorry."

Andy bumped her with his hip. "Forgiven."

"It's okay, Miss Lucy," Danny said, gazing at her with those big puppy eyes now. "You didn't know you were being bad."

Indeed. It took some effort not to laugh at his sincerity.

Andy cleared his throat. "How about we grab a table?"

"Good idea." She held her arms out to Danny. "I had Dad reserve one in the corner for us."

"Thinking ahead like always," Andy said as Danny jumped into her arms without fear.

Andy grabbed their drinks, and together, they meandered to the open table. She smiled at the dancing leprechauns, arching rainbows, and pots of gold on the wall.

"What are you smiling at, Miss Lucy?" Danny asked, leaning his elbows on the table and staring at her.

"This place," she said, feeling warmth for her dad's bar roll through her heart. "Some things never change."

"No, some things don't," Andy said with a soft smile as he settled onto the bench across from her like he had hundreds of times growing up.

As she gazed at her best friend in her dad's bar, Lucy was grateful their friendship had never changed either. Despite the sparks of attraction she'd occasionally felt for him, nothing was worth risking their connection.

# Chapter 7

Danny was so engrossed with talking to Lucy, Andy had to remind him to eat his hamburger and fries at least ten times. Everyone else was equally enthralled. Even Moira, Matt, and Natalie, who'd known Lucy growing up. Jane and Blake were new to the Lucy show, and they shoveled in their Cobb salads without looking at them as his best friend answered Danny's rapid-fire questions.

Had she ever seen an animal eaten by a lion? He squealed when she told him she'd seen *a whole pride of lions* eat an antelope, going into grisly detail only a five-year-old boy would want to hear. In response to Danny's question about whether she'd ridden a camel, she told him she'd lumbered through the pyramids in Egypt at sunset on one of the hairy, spitting beasts. And when his son asked her if she'd ever found buried treasure, her response was to tell him about the incredible tombs in the Valley of the Kings, where dead people were transformed into mummies and entombed with all their worldly possessions.

"Do you mean like a Wii or football?" Danny asked, seeking clarification on this entombing stuff.

"Take a breath—and then a bite of your hamburger, Danny," Andy repeated again, hoping Lucy's stories weren't going to give his kid nightmares. "And don't talk with your mouth full."

"Exactly like an Wii or football," Lucy said, her eyes sparkling. "But not just small things like that. We're talking about beds, chests of gold, and statues of their family members. The ancient Egyptians believed they needed all their things around them so they could make a home in the afterlife—the place they went to after they died."

"I like this idea of being buried with my football," Blake said, putting his arm around Natalie. "Babe, let's keep that in mind. And I'll want a statue of you, of course."

His wife socked Blake in the arm and gave him a look. "Not funny."

Danny propped his chin up with his hand on the table. "I thought people went to heaven when they died. Dad, does Mom have her things with her? I can't remember."

Andy's chest constricted, and for a moment, he couldn't breathe. Everyone at the table stared at him, and Lucy went from sparkly to stricken in the space of a second.

"The ancient Egyptians didn't know about heaven," he said cautiously, trying to formulate a response that wouldn't scar his kid. "Your mother has everything she needs. Trust me on this."

"Maybe we should visit her tomorrow and check to make sure," Danny said, his brow furrowed now. "I don't want Mom to be without her favorite things. If I were in heaven, I'd want to take my Wii and the football Blake gave me. And my bike. Oh, and my stuffed hippo."

His son thought about death way more than any child should. Andy knew it was only natural. He'd read basically all the psychology books ever written about children and grief, and they all agreed on that point. He'd heard the same things from the child psychologists he'd spoken to in preparation for ushering his son through their shared loss.

Heaven wasn't a tangible concept to a five-year-old, he'd realized early on, but even young kids understood angels. He'd told Danny that his mother was an angel in this beautiful place called heaven, which was kind of like a magical garden where everyone you loved who'd died came to live with you. Danny had liked the thought of his mom being with her grandma, who'd taught her how to quilt. Andy hadn't seen the harm in telling his son those stories. They were a comfort, a balm.

But this... How was he supposed to keep Danny from wanting to leave an assortment of Kim's favorite things at her gravesite? He rolled his shoulders to relieve the tightness and felt Moira put her hand on his back in support.

"Danny," Lucy said, clearing her throat, causing everyone to look at her. "Your dad is right. The ancient Egyptians had a different way of saying goodbye to the people they loved. Why, almost every place I go has a special way."

Andy had to bite his tongue to keep from telling Lucy to stop talking. Judging from the puzzled look on his son's face, she was only making things worse.

"But do you know what, Danny?" she continued, staring earnestly at his son. "The one your dad chose for your mom is absolutely the best. Because he's the best and smartest dad ever. Right?"

And then Lucy smiled—that smile that transformed everything around her.

Danny grinned back. "Right. He *is* the best and smartest dad ever!"

To punctuate the sentiment, his son turned in his seat and gave him a smile big enough to fill the world with sweetness. Andy felt his stomach settle back into his gut as Moira patted him on the back.

All of the adults around him released slow breaths.

Lucy met his gaze briefly before returning her laser-like focus to Danny. "Did I tell you about the time I took a horse and rode through the ancient ruins of Petra like Indiana Jones? Please tell me you've seen the Indiana Jones movies. They're like your dad's favorites."

"Of course I've seen them!" Danny said. "But Dad has me close my eyes for the scary parts."

"Like the scene where all the bugs crawl over them?" Lucy asked, gagging. "I hate that part!"

"We're not supposed to say 'hate,' Miss Lucy," Danny said quietly. "Right, Dad?"

"Right," he answered, leaning over and kissing Danny on the top of his head because he needed to. Frankly, all he wanted to do was down Lucy's Jameson, take his kid home, and tuck him into bed.

"Oopsy daisy," Lucy said with a shrug, doing her best to lessen the tension at the table. "Guess I'm still learning what's okay to say. You keep reminding me. Okay, Danny?"

"Okay," Danny said, bouncing in his seat. "Have you ever seen—"

"How about you and me find the foosball table?" Matt interrupted, standing up. "I'm in the mood for a little competition."

Andy knew his brother was trying to give him a moment to recover his balance, and he appreciated it. Danny's questions were becoming more inquisitive as his mind developed. Sometimes Andy wondered how many times he'd have to deflect a particularly tough question about death and how it related to Kim.

The hardest part was that he knew it wasn't going to end any time soon—as a little person grew, so did his questions. Right now, Andy was looking at somewhere around ten more years of this line of questioning. It stretched before him like an open-plank bridge over a gorge.

The rest of their party stood too. Lucy sought his eyes, and in them, Andy could see her regret for her earlier comments. He smiled at her to assure her it wasn't her fault.

Blake picked Danny up and threw him in the air, causing him to squeal. "I'm going to beat your pants off tonight, munchkin."

Danny giggled. "No, I'm going to beat *your* pants off, and then you'll have to walk to your car in your underwear."

"That would be a sight," Natalie said, laughing out loud.

"Might make a few women faint," Jane added, joining in.

"Undoubtedly," Moira agreed, giving him a playful wink.

"I'll catch them as they fall, man," Matt told their brother-in-law, his shoulders shaking.

Blake shook his head. "You all wish you could have this body."

Matt clapped him on the back, and the group of them left the table and headed for Hairy's game room, leaving Andy and Lucy alone with Moira. He gave his sister a look, which she returned.

She fussed with her hands. "Lucy, I'm sure you heard, but I up and left my old job after a few too many run-ins with my boss. I'm planning to take a break in Dare Valley before looking for a new one, and I was hoping...we might get together sometime. What with you being back and all. Plus, I'd love to talk to you more about photography. You're one of the best out there, and it's a special hobby of mine."

His sister was as close to babbling as he'd ever seen her. Good Lord, was she having another fan moment?

Lucy was watching her with a neutral expression, but he could feel her gathering herself. Talking about photography was probably the last thing Lucy wanted to do outside of the classroom. Not that Moira had any way of knowing that.

"Let's give Lucy some time to settle in," he said, deciding to intervene.

Moira's mouth parted slightly, a sure sign she was surprised by his response. "Of course. Any time you'd like, Lucy. I'll just join the others and let you two catch up."

A smile flickered on Lucy's face. "Andy's right. I have a lot of things to see to right now, but I'm sure we can chat at some point. Good luck finding a new job, by the way."

His sister sought his gaze once more before nodding and darting off in the direction of his family.

"You need a Jameson after that?" Lucy asked him point-blank. "I guess your sister didn't realize how upset we both were. Me because of the situation with my eye, and you because of my mistake with your son."

"It wasn't that bad," he told her, trying to be nice. "And I don't use liquor to handle my stress."

She tapped her finger on the table. "Well, *I* sometimes have a drink when I've had a moment. I'm sorry I caused Danny to ask those questions. I would never do anything—"

"I know," he said, interrupting her. "He's smart, and he's curious. It's not the first time he's asked something like that after hearing what should have been a simple story. Kids who lose parents young often have a fascination with death."

Whereas all he wanted to do was run as far as he could in the opposite direction. He wanted to believe Kim was in a place called heaven, but when it came down to it, he just didn't know.

"I walked right into it with all that talk about mummies and the afterlife," she said, picking up a cold French fry and throwing it across her plate. "So, if you won't have a drink with me, what can I do to make up for it? Let's see. How about we dart over to the ice cream parlor and grab a cone? We can snarf it down before we return so no one will know."

Leave it to Lucy to suggest ice cream. A cone share had always been her go-to comforting suggestion when they were at school together.

"Mocha almond fudge and butter pecan, here we come," he said.

"Let's blow this joint," she said.

She rubbed his back, giving him a full-wattage Lucy smile. He shrugged his shoulders to relieve the tension as her fingers worked some magic. Her hands were strong, something he'd never realized. But they were also gentle as they traced the knotted line of muscles running across his shoulders.

He was about to comment on her strength and skills—and tease her about picking up the latter in a Turkish bath internship overseas.

And then he noticed her eyes.

Suddenly he couldn't speak.

The color was greener than he remembered. He stared into them, noticing the gold rings around her pupils. She continued to smile at him, kneading his trapezius. There was a light in her eyes, he realized. Even though her right eye had been injured, it hadn't been dimmed.

How had he forgotten how beautiful they were? They contrasted with her fair skin and the spattering of freckles she'd always hated on her nose. *Good God.*

*Lucy's beautiful.*

He hadn't felt this intense punch of attraction since high school. Sure, he'd felt a spark for her at her homecoming party, but this was different. This ka-pow was the kind that made everything around him seem to slow down. The fingers massaging his shoulders felt hot all of the sudden. *Oh, no. Not again.*

He stumbled back, feeling light-headed.

She grabbed his arm and eyed him with concern. "Are you okay?"

His nod was crisp. "Yep." Not freaking out here. Not at all.

Of course, Lucy O'Brien had always been bright and beautiful. It was a constant—like the oxygen levels in his blood.

But she hadn't been beautiful to him for nearly twenty years, and he didn't want to be reminded of all that. Not when he'd already decided that their friendship needed to stay that way.

"Are you sure you're okay?" she asked, tilting her head from side to side, looking into his face. "Why don't you sit down for a sec?"

"No," he said, shaking it off. "Let's grab that ice cream. Then you can tell me what our mothers are plotting."

He waited for Lucy to precede him to the door. People were watching them again. They had been all night. While he wasn't surprised, he was annoyed. Isn't that why he'd brought Danny with him even though he had multiple willing babysitters? He was single again, and Lucy was back. The town gossips would wag their mouths anyway, but he didn't plan to fuel their fire.

Except a very old flint and steel had sparked a fire *inside* him. For her.

His freak-out was in danger of reaching epic proportions if he didn't rein it in. Outside, the night was warm, and he took some deep breaths to clear his head. After they ordered their ice cream cones, he started to ask for the check, but she cut him off and paid for both of them. Suddenly he felt awkward and unsure of himself. If he had paid, it might have meant something. Like they were going out.

He tried to tell himself he was overthinking things. This was only an ice cream with Lucy, his childhood best friend. He'd only left his son with his family so she could tell him about their mothers' latest crazy stunt.

But as she led the way to one of the corner tables away from the rest of the crowd, he couldn't suppress the growing awareness inside him. She really was beautiful. This was a hell of a time to realize it again, but he'd managed to push aside those thoughts in high school for the betterment of their friendship. He could do it again.

Andy wrapped his cone with a napkin like he was wrapping up his feelings and tucking them away. "You might have realized Danny never stops talking."

She was studying him in that serious way of hers, like she was trying to figure out why he'd gotten all flustered back there. He scanned the room casually, trying to act cool, something he definitely didn't feel.

"He's different from you that way," she said, licking her scoop with delight. "You were always a quiet kid."

It was hard not to notice how sexy she looked eating her ice cream. "He got that from Kim."

An awkward silence descended—as uncomfortable and unwelcome as snow after Easter.

"I really am sorry about earlier," she said, fiddling with her napkin. "I talk to kids who've lost their parents all the time. You'd think... Well...those kids are used to people dying. They don't..."

When she trailed off, he fought the lump in his throat. Suddenly he couldn't hold back his own sadness—the grief he felt every time he had to tell his sweet little boy about things like angels and heaven when all he wanted to do was see Kim standing right in front of their son, loving him and doing normal things like taking him to school and teaching him how to ride his bike.

"They don't what?" he asked, hearing the rasp in his own voice.

She took a deep breath, lowering the cone. "They

don't ask a lot of questions about where their parents have gone after they've died. At least not to me. They...it's not right or wrong. It's just the way it is. They're so concerned with surviving, getting their next meal, maybe getting into a school so they can be educated. I...hate seeing anyone so young lose a parent. I don't like that part of this world."

Her grief was palpable, and the earlier brightness in her eyes faded to something darker. This was the Lucy he sometimes knew online—the one whose inner light was sometimes dimmed by the things she saw, the things she chronicled with her camera. Seeing this Lucy in person tore at his heart.

How many times had he raved at the injustice of losing Kim before realizing he needed to accept that bad things happened to good people? It sucked, and he didn't understand it, but Lucy was right—it was just the way things were. Kim had gotten cancer and died. He was alone now, and his job was to raise their son in as loving and happy of an environment as possible. And he wasn't doing a bad job, if you asked him, dammit.

"On that we agree," he simply answered, not wanting to debate the big questions of life and death in this ice cream shop.

He was a doctor, and it was something he dealt with on an ongoing basis. He tried not to let it bleed into his off-time more than it naturally did.

"How about you spill this secret now that we've gotten all deep and everything?" he added, making himself take another taste of his ice cream.

She stared at her cone. "I hesitate to mention this after our conversation earlier."

"*Lucy,*" he said, gesturing with his hand.

"My mother bamboozled me into telling you this because April didn't feel like she could. Your mom doesn't want to stir up unhappy memories. And after tonight, I can kinda see why."

His stomach twisted into a knot. "Just spit it out."

"Our mothers have decided to raise money to support breast cancer," she told him.

He narrowed his eyes. "Why would that bother me? I think that's a great idea. If you ask me, we need more money for research and mammograms and the like."

"I'm happy you feel that way," she said, tracing circles on the counter with the tip of her cone. "It's how they plan to do it that might give you pause."

"What are they going to do? Knowing our mothers—"

"Exactly," she said, taking a bite of her ice cream. "Ever watch the movie *Calendar Girls*?"

"Uh...yes," he answered with a sinking feeling. Surely they didn't...

"They asked me to take photos of them and ten other people who have lost someone to cancer." She swiped a rivulet of ice cream cresting down her sugar cone. "Here's the kicker. They're going to be the humorous, risqué kind. They suggested using cantaloupes to cover their..." She gestured to her own chest, making him super uncomfortable after his earlier awareness of her.

"Cantaloupes." And then it hit him. "Oh, no. *No.*"

"Oh, yes," she said, biting her lip. "And they've recruited some men too, apparently. Dr. Jeff is one of them."

He sat back in the booth. "You're kidding! What are they planning to do? Buy out all the cantaloupes and hot dogs in Dare Valley?"

She thrust out her cone. "That's what *I* thought at first. And then I saw Jeff's face when he told me his mom died of breast cancer."

He swallowed thickly at the compassion threading her voice now. He knew that face. She could break his heart with that face.

"Everyone is dedicating their month to the person

they lost," she continued. "Your mom is dedicating her page to Kim."

Now it all made sense. "I understand why she was afraid to tell me. We haven't talked about her recent scare with the lump in her breast. I...couldn't."

She reached for his free hand. "She knows. This is her way of doing something about it all, I think. I've come around to the idea."

He could see why. It was a beautiful gesture, but also the kind of kooky thing their moms normally got up to together.

"Andy," Lucy said softly, bringing him back. "Your mom's calling it The Calendar of New Beginnings."

"Oh, crap," he said, setting his cone down so he could pinch the one place guaranteed to prevent his tears from leaking: the bridge of his nose.

He'd learned about that spot while working at the hospital in the weeks after Kim's death, when anything and everything seemed to trigger an episode. A young woman dying of cancer like Kim. Another who lay still and emaciated in her hospital bed, her family unsure if she'd ever awaken after a car accident. And then there were the ones who'd passed on. Hearing their families weep with abandon had crushed him. But a doctor couldn't cry in front of his patients, particularly not the ones who were already hopeless and grieving, so he'd learned to pinch that pressure point and keep the tears inside until he could be alone. Later he would release all the pain he'd gathered that day, like rain in water buckets after an afternoon thunderstorm.

Lucy held his hand while he gathered himself together.

"It's okay to cry, Andy," she said, tightening her grip. "I won't think any less of you."

No, she wouldn't, although many women might.

"I can take it," she added softly.

He looked up and saw the soft light shining again in

her beautiful green eyes. "I know you can, Lucy. I'm glad you're doing the calendar."

"Me too," she said softly. "Here. It's time to swap cones like we always used to."

They ate each other's ice cream as she held his hand, and just like that, the sorrow in his chest didn't feel quite so heavy.

# Chapter 8

It was a day of new beginnings, and a Monday to boot. In the morning, Lucy was moving into the small rental home she'd dubbed Merry Cottage, and at three o'clock in the afternoon, she would teach her first class at Emmits Merriam's School of Journalism. She'd accomplished a lot after only a week in Dare Valley.

Since Lucy didn't have more than a couple of suitcases with her, she was able to pull off the move without much fuss. Her mother's cleaning crew had vacuumed and dusted every available space, making the worn furnishings gleam. The air smelled of lemon, and Lucy sneezed as she wandered through the small home. The carpets and the upholstery on the Victorian couch and armchair all showed vacuum tracks. The windows sparkled in the sunlight, showing a rare streak from the cleaner. It was a gesture she'd happily accepted.

After living in anything from hotels to barracks, huts to compounds, this little cottage made her feel cozy. Even though none of the furnishings were hers, this place was her safe haven for the moment.

She let herself out the French doors into the backyard. The view was one of the things that had drawn her to this cottage. Mountain peaks rose up all around her, dotted with pines and other conifers. A small pond drew her across the lawn—freshly cut, courtesy of her father. She looked into the water and studied her reflection.

She *did* need a haircut, but the world wouldn't end if she waited a few days. Her face still hadn't filled in, and the gauntness of her cheeks made them look sunken. Dark circles lay under her somber eyes.

This was the Lucy O'Brien her students would see, but was this really her?

Where was her sparkle, her vitality? Seeing Andy's pain the other night had made the walls surrounding all of her bottled-up emotions start to crumble. She'd experienced loss too.

And it sucked.

Her hand unconsciously reached up to touch her right eye. She'd always taken her twenty-twenty vision for granted, and without it, she was floundering. Who would she be if she wasn't able to take photos, to travel around the world and be an award-winning photojournalist again?

No one understood the magic, the courage, the technique it took to capture the perfect picture. Sure, Andy was right—if her vision didn't improve, there were ways she could adjust to her new reality. She could take photos using her left eye, but that would be like asking Michelangelo to paint with his right hand. Would he have been able to paint the Sistine Chapel if his left hand had become useless? She didn't think so. She could try and switch to taking only black-and-white photos, but again, if Michelangelo had painted the Sistine Chapel in only black and white, would it have been considered a masterpiece?

When she'd agreed to take photos for The Calendar of New Beginnings, she'd told herself the quality wouldn't have to be up to her usual levels. She could use it as an opportunity to learn how to take photos with her left eye. But that wouldn't do justice to the project, not considering the depth of loss Andy, Jeff, April, her mother, and all the rest had been through. She felt the pressure to produce perfect photos for the calendar, and something told her these couldn't simply be playful, risqué photos. Anyone could do hot dogs and cantaloupes.

Her new idea was to capture the truth of loss and the courage it took to keep living after experiencing grief. Maybe each subject could hold a photo of the person they'd lost or a memento from their life.

Today was as good a day as any to see if she could take photos—any photos—since she'd be teaching young minds about photography later in the afternoon. God, her first class. The thought of teaching something she feared she could no longer do made her sick to her stomach. It actually made it worse that her students were so excited to work with her. According to the administrator she'd spoken with at the school, there was a sizable wait list to get into her class.

She pulled her phone from her jeans pocket with a trembling hand and brought up the camera function. Maybe it would be best to start out by taking pictures on the simplest mechanism out there.

But even holding the phone made her miss her babies: an old manual Leica for when she didn't have access to electrical power and the new digital Leica M9 model—the smallest, quietest full-frame camera on the market. She'd scrimped and saved to buy that camera. Her bag of Leica lenses gave her the versatility she needed for any shoot, anywhere in the world.

Lucy had bought Leica because her hero, Henri Cartier-Bresson, had talked about the camera brand becoming an extension of his eye in his biography, which Lucy had read hundreds of times. The famous French photojournalist had mastered the art of candid photography, and Lucy had pored over his body of work and everything written about his life to search for the secrets of his success. She loved Ansel Adams' black-and-white landscapes of the American West, but her very soul was touched by Henri's photos of world events like Gandhi's funeral and the last days of the Chinese Civil War.

Henri had claimed his photography style was grounded in the concept of the decisive moment, which was the title of his first book. It was a notion she intrinsically understood. To capture such a moment of pure, uncensored truth, you had to always be present and ready.

The camera phone didn't feel right in her hands, but she wasn't ready to take her Leicas out. Since the accident, she hadn't touched them except to pack. Hadn't been able to. She'd captured some excellent photos of the attack on the Congolese village before the explosion that had knocked her out, but she couldn't bear to look at them yet. At least the soldiers hadn't stolen or destroyed her equipment in the melee.

She raised the camera and sized up the shot. Since it was a flat-screen viewer, she could use both eyes to frame it. Her depth perception wasn't an issue here, thank heavens, since it only affected her when she tried to pick up the objects closest to her.

Sinking to her haunches, she angled the phone until it captured the exposed rock a few feet away in the water. She lowered the camera to look at the scene with her naked eyes, and when she closed her left eye, as she was apt to do out of habit, her vision immediately went blurry. And darn it all to hell, she could hear in her head her doctor telling her not to do that.

She almost lowered her phone in defeat. Taking photos shouldn't make her feel helpless and weird.

But she was made of sterner stuff than that. Adjusting the camera again, she took a few photos of the sunlight illuminating the water around the rock. Her new inclination to close her right eye like she was some pirate photographer with an eye patch wasn't a longterm answer. It certainly wasn't comfortable.

It didn't surprise her that the photos were all wrong. She wasn't used to the technology and her timing was off. But how was she going to make this calendar happen when she couldn't even capture a decent photo with a camera phone? Could she back out? But no, despite her initial reluctance, she was determined to see it through. She'd just have to go back to the basics.

She was going to have to relearn her craft until she was surer of the fate of her right eye. God, she was going to have to investigate buying a new camera model; one with an electronic view finder. It sucked, but Lucy knew better than to rail at fate. That wasn't who she was. And she wasn't a quitter either. She was an award-winning photojournalist, and she was going to continue to be one. Somehow. And dammit, she was going to be a freaking awesome teacher too.

As she deleted the photos of the pond, her phone chimed. It was from Andy.

*Good luck with your first class today. You're going to knock them on their butts.*

Nice of him to send her a text when he was working. Sharing their ice creams had cemented their bond in a whole new way. There'd been some unexpected intimacy, but Lucy knew that was from Andy's vulnerability. Still, the way he'd looked at her a few times...

But they were just getting used to looking at each other again, right? That was normal.

She texted him back. *I'm a little nervous, but I have decided to be the best photography teacher they could ever find in Dare Valley.*

*I don't have any doubts,* he responded. *We'll have to huddle again later so you can tell me all about it.*

Huddle. Friend talk. Her mind flashed back to the awkward look that had crossed his face after she strong-armed the bill for their ice creams.

*You'll have to see my new digs. It's like Strawberry Shortcake meets Jane Austen.*

Her phone immediately buzzed. *No kidding. I'm almost afraid to cross the threshold. Gotta run. A nurse just buzzed me. Good luck!*

Good luck indeed. She went inside to prepare for her first class. Again. She might not be able to take the kind of photos she wanted to right now, but by God, she could teach others how to take their own.

By the time Lucy drove to the university later that afternoon, she felt calmer and more decisive. The faculty parking lot was easy to find, and she'd snuck into enough journalism classes as a teenager to remember the path to her new department. If only Arthur Hale had still been teaching at the time—back in the eighties, he used to teach one coveted class every year.

The administrative assistant to the dean showed her to her new office, leaving her with a warm welcome and a shiny brass key to the lock on the door. The office had one lone window, and Lucy was happy for the light.

"I was hoping I might catch you before class," she heard a man say from behind her.

Turning, she smiled. "Hi, Tanner."

"Hi, Lucy," he responded, leaning against the doorframe. "I remember my first day as a teacher, so I thought I'd pass along the best advice anyone has ever given me. It comes from my sister-in-law Jill."

It was impossible to keep her mouth from twitching. Jill Hale had been making waves since childhood, and Lucy had always enjoyed running into her on her trips home. "Knowing Jill, I'm sure it's a doozy."

"She told me not to be boring," he said with a slow grin. "And Meredith reminded me most kids here want to be like us, so we'll have a cult following, like it or not."

She sat on the edge of the desk. "Do they follow you around and hang on your every word?"

He shrugged. "Most of the time. Unless I've given them a bad grade on an assignment. Then they try and work their way back into my good graces."

She laughed. "Well, that's going to be weird. I might ask for some tips on handling that kind of adulation. I'm not used to it."

His brow knit then, and she stilled. He was easing into something, and Lucy feared she knew what it might be.

"How much do you know about why I'm back?" she asked boldly. "Because I'm happy to hear your pointers about how to deal with a cult following, but that's not the only reason you're here."

He ran his tongue across his front teeth. "My wife might be a little younger than you, but she's always looked up to you. And then there's Arthur... They're worried, and since we all have black ink in our veins, as the Hales say, I made some calls."

Lucy tapped her foot on the carpet. "I knew it was possible Arthur might look into things, but I underestimated your connections. I...didn't think." She'd been too busy worrying about everything from healing to the future of her career to returning to Dare Valley.

"I didn't come here to get into your business, and you can tell me to buzz off." He pushed off the doorway and walked toward her. "I might have come to Dare Valley for different reasons initially, but I was burned out too. I didn't know anyone when I arrived—unlike you—but I lucked my way into the best family around. The Hales and O'Briens are close. And you and me...we've been in some of the same places, same situations."

She nodded, feeling her chest grow tight.

"I'm here as a friend if you want to talk about what happened with someone who knows what it's like to work in war zones." He ran his hand through his hair. "Being here taught me not to do everything alone. And that's what I came here to say."

He was more than sweet to extend that offer. She knew it couldn't have been easy for him. The journalists who covered wars tended toward a lone-wolf mentality—she needed to look no further than herself to see evidence of that. But sharing her story with Andy had soothed her. Perhaps sharing it with Tanner would do the same.

"They're not sure I'll regain full sight in my right eye," she began, clenching her hands together. "I don't have to tell you what that might mean for my career."

He didn't move. Didn't say anything. Just waited for her to continue. And so everything she'd been through simply flowed out. At one point during her telling, he helped her into her black chair and grabbed the empty one in front of her desk for himself, positioning it closer to her. How he'd sensed that her legs were trembling, she would never know. When she finished, she felt messy and vulnerable and hollow. But she also felt *heard*.

Since she'd listened to hundreds of people talk about the tragedies they'd suffered, she knew it wasn't easy. Not everyone was capable of listening to the hardships of others. Tanner was most certainly one of the prize few, which had no doubt helped him become the successful international correspondent he had been.

"Is there anything I can do to help?" he asked. "I know you're taking care of everything, but is there anything you need? A drive to the eye doctor in Denver? You tell me, and it's done. Mere might be close to having our baby, but we're here for you, Lucy. Arthur is too. You know how he is. He likes to poke and prod as much as any salty journalist, but that man would give you the shirt off his back if you needed it."

She wiped a few tears away from her eyes. "I'm sorry I'm so emotional. I was just thinking about him as I walked here today. I've always regretted I was too young to attend the classes he used to teach here."

The corner of Tanner's mouth lifted. "Arthur said you used to sneak into journalism classes when you were in high school."

"He knew about that?" she asked.

"Sure did. Who do you think told the teachers to look the other way? You were interning for him, after all. Plus, he founded the journalism school. He kept them from busting you."

She sat back in her chair. "He never said a word."

"No, but he was bursting with pride as he told me about it yesterday." Tanner looked over his shoulder at the plain white wall clock. "Your class starts in twenty minutes. I should let you get ready. We can talk again."

"I'd like that," she said as he rose.

"Arthur would also appreciate hearing your story," Tanner said at the door. "He'll tell you the truth helps lower his blood pressure, but really, all it will do is ease his worry."

She rubbed her brow. "I'm not sure hearing my story is going to make him worry less."

Tanner knocked on the door, confusing her.

"He's tougher than wood," he explained. "Don't treat him like an old man. He's more tenacious than men half his age. He only knows you were injured in that village. It's for you to decide if you want to share the rest, not me."

"You're right. I'll go see him."

"Good luck with your class," Tanner said. "I might sit in sometime if that's okay."

She smiled. "I promise to look the other way."

After he headed out, she went over her notes one last time. Her syllabus was unorthodox, but then again, so was she. If they wanted to learn how to capture decisive moments in photos, they would have to be prepared.

Her classroom was packed, just like she'd been told it would be, when she arrived at three o'clock. Thirty-three students gave her their full attention when she stood at the front of the room.

"As you know, I'm Lucy O'Brien," she began. "Since you're here, I don't need to tell you who I am or what I've done. All you need to know is that I'm really good at what I do. I assume you're here because you want to be really good at taking photographs."

A few of the students nodded, and God help her, some of them looked like they should be in high school. Most of them were green as grass—like she'd been. A few had obvious attitude. And Tanner was right. She noticed a sizable number of them were hanging on her every word.

"I'm going to teach you some camera techniques," she said, handing out a stack of syllabuses to the person on the end of the front row to pass along. "But I'm also going to simulate extreme moments of tension and noise during which you will be required to take a photo that will be graded. If you're scared of what happens in conflict zones, you might want to drop out right now and give one of the twenty-two other people on the wait list your spot."

She paused for a moment and scanned the class. People were shifting in their seats. Many of them weren't making eye contact now.

"Just so you have a sense of what you're getting into, for one exercise, I'm going to play a particularly grisly scene from a recent battle in Afghanistan, captured by an award-winning cameraman, and ask you to take a picture as it's being played. The dean has graciously given me permission to use the planetarium for this purpose. You're going to see people getting shot, dying, moaning, screaming. Hear machine guns being fired. Your hand is going to shake. Your adrenaline is going to rush."

A kid in the front row gulped, and she stared at him before continuing to scan the crowd. These were her students now, and she felt a new sense of responsibility. It was up to her to teach these kids what she knew so they could survive in war and be successful if they followed a career path similar to her own.

"I can't simulate people trying to kill you as you take a picture," she said, walking to the other side of the room. "But I can help you gain some understanding of what that's like. And how freaking hard it is when you're trying to take the perfect photo to capture what's unfolding around you. To create an image that will reach out and grab the throats of people sitting a world away in London or Hong Kong or Dare Valley."

Someone held up extra copies of the syllabus, so she walked to the last row and took them from him. She kept her pace slow and deliberate as she made her way back to the front of the room, taking time to settle into her new skin.

"We're also going to take photos of starving animals at the local pound and dead animal carcasses on the road. I can't find a starving child or someone dying of a machete wound here in Dare Valley, but we can start initiating you into the world of an international photojournalist."

She pulled out her camera phone and waggled it in the air. Her students' eyes latched onto the object.

"Who plans on using this camera for class?" she asked. "You'll notice I didn't specify a professional camera as a class requirement because they can be incredibly expensive."

All but a few outliers raised their hands.

"This used to be your best friend," she said before setting it on the table in front of the dry-erase board.

"It's a good camera for a college student. You're in journalism school because you're still learning and deciding how you're going to specialize. I'm going to show you different camera models a professional would consider. Personally, I'm a Leica fanatic, and if you don't know Leica, you'd better Google it once class finishes. As far as I'm concerned, if you don't even know about the most famous camera models out there, you're going to be in trouble in my class."

Several people were furiously writing in notebooks while others tapped on their tablets and laptops. It was weird to see that kind of technology in the classroom. She'd gone to college when the most advanced item a student could bring to class was a graphing calculator.

"You're also going to become intimately familiar with Henri Cartier-Bresson, who's considered the father of photojournalism. You're going to read a few of his books during our time together. Don't worry about writing this down. It's in the syllabus."

The students gave her their attention again. She had them on edge now, she could tell. This class was more than they'd bargained for. Jill would be proud—no one would be be able to accuse her of being boring.

"Papa Henri—as I like to call him—said a lot of things about this magical art called photography. You'll read about them in his books, and if you miss a particularly important insight, I'll point it out here in class. He's going to be teaching you too, so don't think it's only going to be me up here."

She put her hands behind her back as she strolled to the dry-erase boards. Choosing a purple one—at least it looked purple—she uncorked the lid. "My favorite quote from Papa Henri is this: 'It is an illusion that photos are made with the camera...they are made with the eye, heart, and head.' When you take a photo for my class, make sure you're using all three."

The words touched her anew. What if she had lost

one of the three critical elements needed to capture a moment of reality in a photograph? She shook off the fear. This wasn't the time.

Turning, she folded her hands and regarded her students. "Now. I want to hear your names, and why you're here."

# Chapter 9

After a quick run through the park after work, Andy showered and headed over to his mother's house. He hadn't called to tell her he was dropping by, but he knew she'd be there alone. Moira had agreed to help arrange it.

His sister was free and clear of her old job, having cleared out her office on Friday. They'd celebrated with drinks afterward. His sister hadn't asked him about his protectiveness toward Lucy at Hairy's the other night, thank heavens. Then again, she knew him well enough to deduce he had his reasons.

When his mom opened the door and saw him, she immediately tightened up. It wasn't like him to stop by without warning, let alone at five thirty on a Monday.

"What's the matter?" she asked, looking over his shoulder. "Is something wrong with Danny?"

His heart sank, and he knew he had been right to come here. It was past time for him—for them—to face their demons. "No, he's with Jane and Moira. Jane agreed to give Danny and Rufus some dog training after I begged. And Mo's soaking up all the auntie time she can get during her break from the day job."

"Moira told me she was heading to Jane's, but she didn't mention seeing Danny." Her shoulders sagged with relief, and a slow smile flickered across her round face. "You were a good daddy to let Danny have a dog. I know Rufus isn't easy, but he makes him so happy."

"I tell myself that daily," Andy said with a laugh, pulling her into a hug.

"Lucy told you about our calendar," his mom said against his chest.

He nodded. "Yeah. How about we sit and have a drink?"

She fussed with the hem of her cream blouse before turning and striding off to the kitchen. He followed her, aware of the tension locking her shoulders in place once again.

"Mom," he said as he entered her bright apple-green kitchen, "I'm not upset about the calendar. I was just...bothered you were afraid to tell me about it."

After handing him his favorite beer, she busied herself with pouring a glass of Cabernet. Giving her a moment to stew, he retrieved the shamrock bottle opener, popped the top off his beer, and took a deep draw. The IPA wet his whistle, but it didn't soothe his dry throat.

"Mom, we need to talk about it," he said, and she turned around so quickly, the wine sloshed a little in her glass.

He took it from her and led the way to the kitchen table. She kept an array of bright tablecloths on it now, but when they were growing up, the bare surface had played host to a record number of ketchup stains and spilled milk. He and his siblings used to finish their homework at this table after their afternoon snack. Once complete, they'd packed up their individual book bags and gone outside to play. Usually, Lucy was waiting for him in the yard because she always finished her homework faster than anyone alive.

"Lucy said you were afraid you'd stir me up with this calendar," he said after they both sat down. Reaching for the clenched hand in her lap, he said, "Mom, it's not the calendar. We...never talked about how I reacted when you told me about the lump in your breast."

She looked down, not meeting his gaze.

"Hearing you had a lump—even a benign one..." For a man who said and read the word *benign* more than the average citizen, it stuck in his throat like a wishbone.

"It scared the shit out of me, Mom."

She didn't rebuke him for his language. She only gripped his hand tighter.

"I can't imagine how scared you must have been too. And I know why you kept it from me at first. From all of us. I'm so glad Natalie found out like she did, because I'm not sure you would have told us otherwise."

Her lips formed a tight line before she said, "No, I wouldn't have."

He scooted his chair closer until their knees met. "That's why I'm here. Mom, what happened to Kim was horrible. There are no words to describe what her loss meant to me and what it still means to me. But you're *my mom*..."

Crap. He swiped at the tears gathering in his eyes with his free hand. She sniffed, but didn't let her tears fall.

"You're my mom," he continued, trying to breathe. "We're supposed to support each other. And I'm a *freaking* doctor. If I can't help my own mom when she gets a call from her doctor saying they found a lump in her breast, what good am I?"

She cupped his cheek like he was a little boy again, and his heart broke clean in half.

"What good are you?" she asked with a soft smile. "You're the most amazing man I could ever imagine, and the bonus is you're my son. You were dealt a blow that would turn most people bitter, and yet you continue to be a bright, shining light. Not just for this family, but for your beautiful son and everyone else in this town, including your patients."

"Ah...Mom," he said hoarsely, totally at sea with his emotions.

"Andy Michael Hale, from the time Dr. Getties put you in my arms, you have been a miracle to me and everyone around you. But my health is my health. I dismissed telling you all about the lump initially since I had Ellen to lean on. A mother doesn't want to worry her children needlessly."

Needlessly? "But Mom—"

"Andy, I know you are still grieving over Kim. That you're doing the best you can. I admire the hell out of you for it. But if you think I would add one more worry or hurt to all the ones you already carry..." This time her voice broke. "I'm not sure I would have told any of you about the scare even if Kim *hadn't* passed away."

He narrowed his eyes at her. "That's just crap."

"I mean it, mister," she said, narrowing hers back in return. "You're a parent. There are things you don't share with Danny."

"He's a kid," he protested, reaching for his beer and taking a fortifying drink.

"And you're *my* kid," she said, her face filled with love. "That never changes. No matter how old you get."

He sat back, drinking his beer. She didn't let go of his hand, but took a sip of her wine as well.

"I hear you," he finally said. "But I don't want you to ever think you can't come to us for support. You're our mom, and we love you more than anything. Promise me you won't keep something this serious from us again."

He didn't want to say so out loud, but she'd done the same thing about her marital problems with their father. One day, after nearly forty years of marriage, she'd up and walked out, saying their father wasn't interested in being married anymore. Unfortunately, she'd been right.

"I won't make a promise like that, Andy," she said quietly.

Her eyes entreated him to understand. But he'd also learned a thing or two at her feet. "Mom, I *need* to be there for you."

"You *are*, honey," she said, setting her wine glass aside and cupping his cheek again. "But I'm not your responsibility. You only feel that way because of all the pressure your father and I put on you as the eldest child in the family. I don't want to repeat past mistakes. You're a man with his own family. I can take care of myself."

"No one doubts your ability to take care of yourself, Mom. That's not what this is about."

"Then?" she asked, searching his face. "You're afraid to fail me like you feel you failed Kim."

He hung his head. "You sound like Lucy."

A soft chuckle reached his ears. "She's always been a smart one. You might be a doctor, Andy, but you're not God."

"More's the pity," he mumbled. And because he was sure she was going to sock him for being irreverent, he added, "Think of all the people I could help on a daily basis if I were."

"Oh, honey," she said in that aggrieved tone he recognized from his childhood. "What do you think you do every day at the hospital?"

He didn't have a response to that. Since Kim's death, he'd questioned everything, including his purpose as a doctor. His mother and Lucy were right about him. In one very dark moment in the middle of a long, sleepless night, he'd asked himself: What kind of doctor couldn't save his own wife from dying of cancer?

Fortunately, between his hours at the hospital and his responsibilities as a single father, he'd had little time to sit with that question. But this business with his mom's health scare and Lucy's eye... He was being faced with his own helplessness all over again.

"I'm glad you're doing the calendar, Mom," he said, reaching for his beer. "I'm all for anything that's going to help raise money and awareness for breast cancer."

"Would you be willing to be featured as one of the twelve?" she asked.

He gasped in horror. "Good God, no."

"I was only teasing." She laughed with gusto. "We needed to lighten up. I'm looking forward to being Miss April, by the way."

"Not April," he said, groaning. "Even I know you were called Miss April in high school."

"College too, dear," she added. "I was quite a beauty in my day."

"You still are," he said, leaning over and kissing her cheek. "Don't let Dad spoil that."

"I won't. That I *can* promise you."

They both reached for their drinks again and sipped in silence. Through the curtains in the kitchen, Andy took in the orange and pink hues of sunset. Fall was creeping into Dare Valley. Soon the snow would come, but for now, the leaves were starting to turn, resembling the sunset outside.

"I'm glad we both moved back to Dare Valley," he said.

"Me too." She let go of his hand, and he realized his chest wasn't as tight.

"I love you, Mom."

"I love you too, honey," she answered, draining her wine. "Since we're on the subject of things I'm willing to share, would you kindly let your siblings know that I plan to start dating again? I feel a sufficient amount of time has passed since the divorce was finalized, and I've sorted out who I am and who I want to be."

His mother was planning on dating again? He supposed he should have expected it. She was still young and beautiful and had a lot to give.

"Maybe I'll see you out there," she added, jostling his shoulder.

It took him a moment to realize what she meant. "Mom. Really. I'm still easing my way into it. I don't—"

"I know you don't," she finished for him. "But Kim would want you to."

That meant his mom didn't know about the letter Kim had sent him. He'd assumed Natalie wouldn't share the information with anyone but Blake, but he'd never had the guts to ask her outright.

"I know Kim would, but I have to be the one who wants to date again. Despite the agreement I made with Natalie."

"That was smart of you," she said with a slow shake of her head. "Those two belong together." A pause hung between them, and then his mother said, "Speaking of the calendar, Lucy's mother and I are worried about her. Has she told you the real reason why she's back? She told her dad a few vague things about healing from an attack on a village, but that's all we know."

So Lucy had opted for a highly censored version of the real story. He considered his options for a couple moments. "You know I would never keep anything from you, but out of respect for Lucy, anything she might have said to me will remain between us. She's my best friend, Mom."

"But she's Ellen's daughter and as hard-headed as her father," his mom said, her mouth suddenly grim.

Personally, Andy didn't think Lucy had inherited her hard head from Harry, but he wasn't going to say that to his mother. "I'm not getting into the middle of things."

"Andy, it's for her own—"

"Good," he finished. "I know. But trust me. Lucy feels like you do about your life and your health." Funny how he hadn't realized how similar their stances were until now. "You independent women."

She shook her fist playfully. "Don't say that again, buster, or I'll box your ears. If you ever have a daughter, you'll be happy if she's independent. Like me and your sisters."

But they took it too far sometimes, he personally thought, though he would only admit it under duress or bone-deep worry. "You're all rock stars," he said to be agreeable.

"And you're full of hog manure sometimes," she said, standing up and taking his empty beer bottle over to the blue recycling container. "Since you asked me for a promise earlier..."

"Which you didn't grant," he pointed out.

"I bet you're the only one who knows the real story about why Lucy's back in Dare Valley, so promise me you'll look out for her," she continued, bold as the blue jay squawking in her backyard.

"*Mom.*"

"*Andy.*"

They faced each other down in the kitchen. "I'll look out for her."

"Good," she said simply, giving him a warm smile.

But when he left a half hour later, he realized he hadn't made that promise just because his mother had asked it of him.

Andy was used to doing things for other people—so much so that he sometimes forgot to ask himself what he wanted. *This* was something he wanted. He wanted to look out for Lucy for himself.

# Chapter 10

Lucy's first class had rejuvenated her faith in the next generation. The celebratory beverage she had with her father at Hairy's afterward made her spirits soar even higher. He shouted a toast across the bar, making all happy-hour-goers turn to look at them. "To my amazing kid, Lucy," he said, hoisting his Guinness in the air. "And to all the young minds she's going to mold."

She wasn't so sure about the mold part. It sounded too much like the green, stinky fungus. She preferred the image of being a lighthouse for young minds. But her dad was sweet, so she drank her pint with him and then had some heavenly fish and chips for the second time in a week. Her mother had wanted to bring her a meal to commemorate her first day of class, but Lucy had decided to draw some boundaries. While she loved her mother, she didn't want her to start popping over all the time—even if her cottage was located in the boonies, as her mom kept saying. Like Dare Valley had boonies. It *was* the boonies.

Dr. Jeff kept her company at the bar again, and while she enjoyed talking to him, she didn't want to give him any encouragement. Dating wasn't high on her list of plans for her time in Dare Valley.

As she was leaving the bar, a car honked. She looked over and saw Andy rolling his window down and slowing his car to match her pace.

"Hey!" he called. "I was just swinging by to see if you were at your dad's after your big day."

"I decided to head out," she said and then gestured for him to pull into the space at the end of the block. "Enjoy my new digs."

He leaned toward the passenger seat window as she walked over. "How was your first day of class?"

"Epic," she said with a grin. "Where's the munchkin?"

"With Jane and Matt and Moira. I begged Jane to work with Rufus."

"Good idea," she said, resting her hands on the open window. "I could go back in if you want a drink."

"Or you could show me your place?" he asked with a mischievous smile. "I'm intrigued by your description. What was it again? Strawberry Shortcake meets Jane Austen. Not something you hear every day."

"I'm parked around the corner. You can follow me home." Then a thought struck her. "Wait! Have you eaten? I don't have much in my refrigerator yet. Dad gave me a mammoth serving of fish and chips."

"Some things never change," Andy said, shaking his head. "Mom fed me after our talk today."

She gazed at him over her nose. "Talk, huh? That sounds ominous. You okay?"

"Yeah," he said, his voice even and sure. "Now hustle it over to your car, O'Brien."

"As you wish, Andy Cakes," she said, giving a playful hip wiggle.

She didn't hustle since she was healing. At her pace, a snail could have beaten her. Or a turtle. Totally embarrassing.

But Andy didn't pressure her or act impatient. He

pulled up behind her when she rounded the corner, then followed her on the meandering route to her house. When they arrived, she cut the engine and took a moment to soak in the view. Merry Cottage.

The yellow house with the lavender shutters and front door warmed her insides. As someone who'd intentionally chosen to live like a nomad, it was weird to feel this attached to a place. Over the course of her adult life, she'd made sure not to get attached to anything but her cameras. Otherwise it would have been too difficult to move on. Besides, early in her career, she'd reminded herself she could always return to any places that felt particularly special and meaningful. Unfortunately, war sometimes destroyed those places, which had taught her to enjoy the moment.

When she exited the car, Andy gave a shrill whistle. "You weren't kidding about the cottage. It's out of a cartoon. I don't know if I can walk in there and retain my Man Card."

"My dad said the same thing when he came over to mow the grass, but his manhood is still intact. I think you'll be okay."

He scanned the yard. "If you end up getting a poodle to go along with this house, I might have to schedule an intervention."

Like she'd ever own an animal. It didn't suit her lifestyle. "No worries there. Come on in."

She dug into her purse for her key. Her dad had given her a key chain with the Hairy's logo on it. The leprechaun's charming smirk put a smile on her own face. Of course, most people didn't lock their doors around here, but she would sleep better at night knowing the deadbolt was securely fastened. Opening the door, she gestured grandly for Andy to precede her.

"Ladies first," he said, so she stepped inside ahead of him.

"Make yourself at home," she said, looking for

somewhere to drop her purse. Everything was still so new she hadn't settled on the right spot yet.

"I have to say, Luce," Andy exclaimed. "You sure know how to pick them."

"It's charming and homey!" she shot back, setting her purse down on the window seat in the parlor.

"It is if you like lace, tea, and crumpets," he said, rocking back on his heels. "Seriously, Luce. I can see why this place hasn't been rented, but at least it doesn't smell like an old basement."

Old basement indeed. "Would you like a beer? Dad made sure I was stocked for visitors."

"I had one earlier, but I wouldn't say no to another." He followed her into the kitchen, chuckling under his breath. "What did your mother bring you?"

"Besides eggs, milk, and butter?" she asked, gesturing to the selection of beer arranged on the shelf in the refrigerator door. "Cosmopolitan fixings."

"Figures," he said, grabbing one of her favorite microbrews from Portland.

She took one for herself and handed him the bottle opener—another piece of Hairy's swag—after popping her own. "To good friends."

He clicked his bottle against hers when she extended it. "The best."

They took a drink to seal the toast. "Come sit at my green 1950s aluminum table with matching vinyl chairs. Mom couldn't believe it. Isn't the set incredible?"

"Green? It looks...ah..."

"What?"

"Blue to me," he said, clearing his throat.

She wasn't exactly surprised, but her spirits sank all the same. "Really?"

He rubbed her arm. "One of those blue-green colors. Like aquamarine."

She started tracing the scuffed-up metal edge of the table as she tried to shake off her tension.

"I'd forgotten how much you like vintage," he said, watching her carefully. "You were always wearing something old in high school. Antique."

She narrowed her eyes at him and let herself fall into their usual easy banter. "It was fashionable. Besides, I like things that have a story."

"This table sure has a story," he mused, shaking his head. "I shudder to think what your bed looks like. Princess and the pea meets...Marie Antoinette or something."

Snorting on a laugh, she said, "It's one of those old-school brass beds."

He started laughing. "You'll have to show it to me." Then a shadow passed his face. "If that's not too weird."

"Weird? Why would that be weird?"

When he shrugged and looked away from her, she asked, "Are you acting all awkward because you asked to see my princess bed?"

He swung his gaze to meet hers, and she noted a flush on his ears.

*"Seriously?* It's only a bed, Andy Cakes." But her heart started hammering. Had she been right the other night? Had he been thinking about her in a weird way?

If so, she wasn't sure she wanted to know. They'd been friends forever. He was not going to mess it up by turning all guy on her. Not Andy. She set her beer aside and grabbed his hand, pulling him out of the chair.

"What are you doing?" he cried as she led him out of the kitchen, back through the parlor, and down the short hallway on the right side of the house.

"Getting this whole bed thing out of the way," she said, ever rational.

"Come on, Lucy," he responded, tugging on her hand. "I don't need to see it. You're embarrassing me here."

"You're making too big a deal of it," she said as she hauled him into her room. Haul was a strong word. She was too weak to haul anyone.

"Now *you're* being weird," he said, forcing her to a halt in the doorway.

Yeah, she was, but she wasn't going to allow any weirdness between them. "Ta-da!" she exclaimed, sweeping her free hand across the room. "One antique brass princess bed."

"Great!" he said, his cheeks flushed now. "I've seen the bed. Can we go back to the kitchen, please, and drink our beers?"

Teasing him was too fun to pass up. She let go of his hand and ran across the short expanse of the bedroom, kicking off her shoes as she went. She jumped on the bed, careful of her mending back, and gave it a gentle bounce, making it squeak.

Andy looked like she'd doused cold water on his face.

"Mom discovered how noisy the bed was, of course, when she helped me put on the linens."

"You're going out of your way to embarrass me," he told her, pinching his nose. "I'd forgotten how much you love to do that. What are the scarves for?" He pointed to the row of scarves she'd arranged over the brass footboard.

He was trying to change the subject. "To monitor any change in my color vision. Dr. Davidson suggested I buy different shades of the color spectrum so I could monitor my progress at home. They have a retailer they recommend to patients around the corner from their office. The store person helped me select the right ones after my appointment."

"That's a great idea," he said, zeroing in on the scarves, all professional now. "What color is this?" he asked, pointing to a red one.

That did it. "Don't go all doctor on me. It's weird!" she ordered, bouncing again to draw his attention away from the scarves, sending another squeak through the air. "We're friends. There's *nothing* weird about seeing my bed. Heck, in high school, you used to sit on it with me and do your homework. Or have you forgotten?"

Now his whole face was flushing. "That was a long time ago."

And they hadn't been two consenting adults then, some distant part of her mind insisted.

She narrowed her eyes at the thought. Who was getting weird now? "Did you ever think of me as a girl back when we were listening to the radio on my bed or sharing the answers to Mr. Tarleton's horrible math homework?" Like a boil, this whole weirdness needed to be lanced. The direct approach was the best approach.

He put his hands on his hips and kicked at the worn blue wool rug covering the oak floor. The silence stretched between them, making her nervous. *Oh, no,* she thought. He really *had* thought of her that way when they were hanging out in her childhood room. More often that she'd imagined.

"I was a guy," he finally said, lifting his shoulder. "Correction. I *am* a guy. We have strange thoughts when it comes to girls and beds. What can I say?"

For the life of her, she didn't know.

"Why are we having this conversation?" he asked in an aggrieved tone.

"Because you got all weird on me," she said, regretting she'd taken it this far. "It scared me. You're my best friend, Andy. My oldest friend. Don't get weird about my princess bed."

The corners of his mouth tipped up. "I won't get weird. I promise. You're my oldest friend too, and I...I'm glad... Crap. I need to say it. You're the only one who doesn't treat me with kid gloves anymore."

She inched to the edge of the bed and wrapped her hands around the brass footboard. There was something in his voice. "Kid gloves?"

"I like that you're not afraid to call out the weird, the

awkward, the tough things in life," he said, rubbing his brow. "You never shy away from anything, Lucy. And since Kim died, you're the only person who really listens to me and puts the tough crap on the table."

She didn't know any other way. "You said you were at your mother's earlier. I'm guessing you talked about the calendar?"

"Yeah. I decided I needed to confront her." He kicked at the rug again. "I hate how much my family worries about me. Did you know that Blake wouldn't tell me the real reason Natalie left him because I was too mired down in my own grief?"

"What was the real reason?"

"It doesn't matter," he said, throwing his arms out. "The point is that everyone in the family knew but me. If I'd known, I would have talked to Natalie. I would have told her she was making a mistake, and maybe they wouldn't have lost so much time together."

There was too much missing from that story for her to parse it right now, and she wanted to get to the core of what was bothering him. "What's really the matter here, Andy? Because I'm not following you all the way."

He blew out an aggrieved breath. "I don't know. I'm just...tired of people not talking to me about what really matters. I suppose I'm saying you're the only one who does, and I...I appreciate that. Even if you didn't initially tell me about what happened to you."

She ran her finger along the edge of the bedframe. "I don't think that's what you're saying."

His gaze met hers.

"I think," she continued, "you're angry at yourself for not saying how you feel about things or asking...uncomfortable questions. Like why Natalie really left Blake. Or how you felt about your mom's health scare. You're mad at yourself for letting them protect you."

He closed his eyes briefly, his pain obvious.

"Or why she couldn't tell you she had a lump in the first place," she finished, knowing she needed to say it. "I didn't tell you about my accident mostly because I didn't want *anyone* to worry. It's important for you to know that."

Since he looked like he'd lost a patient at the hospital, she pointed to a place on the bed beside her.

"Come over here," she ordered, "and don't get all weird on me."

He kicked his shoes off like the responsible guy he was and sank onto the bed next to her. "This mattress is terrible."

"It's better than most of the ones I had overseas," she said, scooting closer. "And don't change the subject. You're worried you've closed yourself off to the people you love and their problems."

"Crap," he said, leaning back on an elbow. "I really am. I keep letting them down."

"Be nice to yourself," she said, playfully socking his arm. "You were dealing with your own stuff. Losing Kim was horrible. I can't even imagine how horrible. They were trying to protect you. All you did was let them."

He gazed at her with hope in his sad eyes, which looked more dark brown than hazel to her now.

"It doesn't mean you stopped loving them, Andy. So lighten up."

She gave him a gentle nudge in the shoulder for good measure, which made him smile.

"All right, I'm lightening up," he said, nudging her back. "Just so we're clear, I'm expecting you to let me know how things are going because I care about you."

"I know you do. And I care about you." Care was a tame word, but after the earlier bed weirdness, she wasn't about to say she loved him. Even so, she couldn't deny that part of her had no trouble seeing him as an attractive man resting on her bed. It had been a long time since she'd had anyone in her bed, and okay, she could admit it...here be weirdness.

"You have this look on your face," he said, touching the tip of her nose. "Now who's getting weird?"

"Fine," she shot out. "I was just thinking I haven't had an attractive man in my bed in some time. How's that for weird?"

He pursed his lips for a moment. "I was just thinking that I haven't sat on another woman's bed since before I started dating Kim."

She made her mouth drop open in horror. "My God, that's like over a decade ago."

The snort he gave made it easier for her to shake off this...this whatever was going on with her. He made no move to stand up, so she simply crossed her legs lotus-style on the bed.

"Are you over being angry with yourself?" she asked.

He nodded.

"Do you want to cuddle now?" She bit the inside of her cheek to keep from laughing.

"Shut up," he said without heat.

Scooting closer, she settled her head against his shoulder. "You're too hard on yourself."

"Me? Maybe, but you're too tough," he said, putting his arm around her.

"Probably," she said, liking the comfort of his arm around her. "I wish you'd been closer after my accident. I might have called you. At night when I couldn't sleep, all I wanted was someone to wrap me up and tell me everything was going to be all right."

"I felt the same way when Kim was sick—and after she died."

She had only been able to come home for the funeral, something she still felt guilty about. "No one can ever guarantee it's going to be all right, can they? Look at me."

He pulled her in even closer. "You're right, but I would have come halfway around the world and more to be there for you."

Tears gathered in her eyes as he kissed the top of her head, ever so sweetly.

"How was your first class, by the way? I got distracted. I was planning on buying you a celebratory drink."

Since a change in conversation was more than appreciated, she ran him through the high points. He kept his arm around her as she regaled him with a description of her unconventional syllabus and the looks of horror it had painted on some of the kids' faces. When he went still all of a sudden, she edged back to look at his face.

"What *are* you thinking?" she asked.

"I always wondered how you learned to take photos of...starving kids and people who'd died or were dying," he said softly.

She lifted her shoulder. "I wasn't trained to do it. I was thrown into the fire on my first couple of assignments. I bawled after visiting a hospital filled with kids dying from famine and puked my guts out after photographing my first massacre. The camera might capture the moment, but it can't capture the sounds or the smells. I'll never forget the buzz of flies on the bodies. And the stench." She gave a full-body shudder. "Do you ever have a physical reaction to a patient's illness?"

"Not much anymore. There were moments in my first year in medical school. I especially remember a young man who was brought in with a head wound. Half his head was caved in. He'd been riding his motorcycle without a helmet. I'd never seen brain matter mixed with shards of bone before. I puked my lunch out once I left the ER."

"What happened to the man?"

"You would ask," he mused. "He didn't make it. Too much brain trauma. He coded on the table."

Somehow she hadn't realized they were linked like this through their professions. He tried to heal hurt people while she took photos of them to raise awareness and support. And both of them dealt with a reality few people faced on a daily basis: that death was a part of life.

"It's hard," she said, "watching people die and not being able to do anything about it." She tucked her knees up and wrapped her arms around them. "I suppose you do something, but deep down, I don't believe it's only up to us. Don't get me wrong, I always try to help whenever I can. I've raged at military officials for not letting humanitarian supplies through. I've hauled gallons of water to people in old gasoline barrels. But half the time it's too late."

"The body can live without food for a time, but not water," Andy said in a serious tone, rubbing the bridge of his nose. "You're right, though. Sometimes we're helpless to save the people we'd like to help."

She laid a hand on his arm. "It wasn't your fault Kim died. I know we've talked about it a little in our chats, but not in person. You were too raw for me to say it before."

His shoulders rose to his ears from tension, and while the last thing she wanted to do was hurt him, she made herself continue.

"And it wouldn't have been your fault if your mom had been diagnosed with cancer. And I know I've said this to you before, but if my right eye doesn't recover, that won't be your fault either. You're just another actor in this big stage of life, Andy Hale."

"You've gotten way more philosophical in your old age," he mused, his dark eyes weary.

"I used to struggle against all the injustices I saw. I got pretty worked up. Like ulcer-in-my-stomach worked up. But I met a relief worker in Congo who helped me see things in a new way. His name was Davy, a quirky little British guy, and he'd been in some of the worst hotspots imaginable. Like Rwanda in April of 1994. He was one of the few doctors who didn't evacuate the country when the genocide broke. He chose to stay and help anyone who managed to live through the attacks. You know there were hardly any guns used, right? One million people were killed with machetes and knives. Right up front and personal."

This time he was the one who shuddered. "God. I didn't know that."

"Anyway, Davy said we all have a part to play, and since there are often forces bigger than us at work, our only choice is how we play our part. He told me to play mine well. I've never forgotten him."

"You met a lot of people like Davy, haven't you?" Andy asked, leaning back on his elbow.

"Yes," she said fondly. "They made everything worthwhile. I never knew when the next miracle would occur." Or the next nightmare. But she had learned they were as inextricably linked as a Janus coin.

"You know, I always wondered if we'd grow apart," Andy confessed. "The farther away you went, the more I worried. But it never happened. Not even when I married Kim."

She'd wondered the same thing, especially with the very different paths they'd chosen. "No, it never happened. I hope it never will."

A smile lifted his face for a moment. "Me too."

Her mind sized up the subject before her like she was taking a photo. Andy was sitting on her over-the-top bed and gazing at her with a familiarity she'd rarely experienced in her travels. This...this was a moment she wanted to capture. "I'd like to try and take a picture of you. Right as you are now. Is that okay?"

Her palms broke out in a sweat when he studied her for a long moment before nodding. Pushing off the bed, she retrieved her smart phone from her purse in the parlor. When she returned, he was sitting up as stiff as an over-starched puppet.

"You've tensed up," she chided, trying to calm her own nerves. "Lean back on your elbow like you were before."

He let out a tortured sigh. "I'm no good at this, Luce."

Her hands were shaking as she brought up the camera function and positioned the frame on him. *"Please.* I need to try to take pictures when I have the urge. Even though I'm scared I can't capture what I see anymore."

Leaning back on his elbow again, he watched her with compassion. She took a few steps to the right and the left, judging the angle and the light, closing her right eye. Her weird vision pissed her off, and the phone still felt unfamiliar in her hands. She missed the feel of her Leica.

"I want you to think about me," she told him, determined to proceed. "How you and I have weathered a lot of years and a lot of miles together to stay friends."

Even though he was still embarrassed, a reluctant smile crossed his face. "That we have."

"And I want you to think about how you play your part every day by being the best dad in the world to Danny, a son to your mom, and a brother to your siblings." She started taking photos, missing the feel of her finger pressing the shutter. With the Leica, she had all the precision of a sniper taking a shot. The touch screen wasn't the same.

"Andy," she said softly. "Think about Kim and how you were the best husband she could ever have imagined."

His face contorted, but he didn't shift out of his pose. His eyes flickered down, but she knew she'd captured the depth of his love. The depth of his loss. She lowered her phone to her side.

"Thank you," she whispered, her diaphragm tight.

His chest rose on a tortured breath. "You don't pull any punches as a photographer."

"A great picture doesn't just capture a moment in time, it captures emotion. You have a lot of emotion inside you, Andy Hale."

Although he rolled his eyes, he made no move to get off the bed. "Well... Are you going to show them to me or what?"

"Huh?" she asked.

"The pictures you took? I want to see them."

Her hand curled around the phone. "They're not... It's only a camera phone. I don't... Shit. I don't want to show them to you." Truth be told, she wasn't sure she wanted to see the flaws in her work.

He patted the bed beside him this time. "Come over here, Lucy Lu. We'll struggle through them together."

He was right. Where was her courage? She prided herself on doing things no one else would. Besides, how was she going to improve if she wasn't willing to study the flaws in her work? She hopped up beside him on the bed and opened the photo album in the phone's directory.

She clicked on the first photo of him. He made an agonized sound in his throat.

"Delete," he begged.

A reluctant laugh emerged. "You look cross-eyed. Must be thinking about our friendship. Besides, the composition is all wrong. And the light...terrible."

"The composition?" he asked dryly. "My name is Andy."

"No, silly," she said, pointing to the next photo. "The composition is—"

"Lucy, I know what composition means," he informed her, nudging her in the shoulder. "I was trying to get you to lighten up. You're all tense."

"I'm allowed."

They clicked through the rest of the photos, and her insides shriveled at the poor quality. Sure, she'd managed to capture some heartfelt emotion, but the photos didn't have the clarity or crispness she was used to with her Leica.

"These are really great, Lucy," he said softly when they reached the end. "Do I really look like that when people mention Kim to me?"

"Yes," she said, handing him the phone so he could take a better look. "You loved her, and now she's gone. How did you expect you'd look?"

He gave her back the phone like he couldn't bear a further viewing. "I don't know. I guess I hoped I'd look peaceful. I don't... God, I don't want Danny to see me like that. He's only a kid."

"But he lost his mother too," she said, putting her arm around him this time. "He probably doesn't have many memories of her. Am I right?"

He was silent for a long time. "No, and it breaks my heart. I tell him stories and keep her picture around..."

"I expect he's more aware that he doesn't have a mom like the other kids since he's in school. Do moms still bring in cakes and cookies for class?"

"Yeah." He cracked his neck. "It's the bane of my existence. And PTA meetings are pure torture. It's usually just me and the mommies, although some of the other dads show up. Weird doesn't begin to describe it."

She hadn't thought about those ongoing aspects of being a single parent. "Is your courage flagging, Hale?"

Just like she'd hoped, it was enough to add some steel to his posture. "Never. He's my kid."

"A bunch of mommies aren't going to intimidate you," she added, dropping the phone onto the bed and putting her hands on her hips, mimicking a tough guy.

"Usually," he said with a sardonic twist to the mouth. "But I maintain the right to be terrified by the mommies who want to set me up with their single or divorced friends or the divorced mommies who have a kid in Danny's class."

He'd told her about the agreement he'd made with Natalie, but he obviously wasn't ready to date yet. "There's nothing wrong with wanting to be on your own after what happened," she said. "If you ask me, the world would be a lot happier if love found people instead of people chasing it down by trolling bars or the Internet."

He bit the inside of his cheek. "You've never mentioned anyone special in all these years. I've wondered..."

"What?" she asked, feeling her familiar defensiveness rise. "If I'm a lesbian?"

"No!" he answered, clearly horrified. "Not that it would be a problem, but..."

"How about that I have commitment issues?" she continued, her mouth flattening. "I've heard them all. I've dated a string of men over the course of my time overseas. Most of the relationships were short given the nature of our work. There were a few who had longterm potential, but we all had our individual careers. Once we left the country, things fizzled."

She'd tried to meet up with a few of the guys she'd liked in places like Rome or London between assignments, but that hadn't worked out well either. The honest truth was she hadn't cared enough about any of her past flings to change her schedule for them.

"There was another guy—an agricultural specialist I met in northern Uganda. He wanted me to give up my work and settle down with him on a ranch in Idaho."

"And you'd never settle down," Andy said, his tone deeper than usual.

They shared a look. She went for the truth after all these years. "It's why I never let things get romantic with you in high school. I didn't want to stay here, and we both knew it."

"So you had thought about us back then," he said, softly. "I always wondered."

Her throat thickened. "I guess we both did. You know, it's not that I don't want to have someone in my life. If I met a man who understood how much traveling is a part of me, I would consider marriage."

He looked away. "Marriage might work with your job, but kids wouldn't."

"You're wrong," she told him flatly, feeling defensive again. "If I wanted to have kids, which I do if the right situation presents itself, I would adjust my travel schedule to accommodate my family. Why do we have all these rules about what it means to be a wife and mother? Men travel for business all the time. Why do you think I left Dare Valley? There was no room for what I wanted here."

She'd gotten so impassioned, her heart was racing. She took some deep breaths to relieve the pressure in her chest, not sure if it was from defending her position or from hearing them both admit to the way they'd felt back then.

"I knew you felt trapped here," Andy said, sliding off the bed and reaching for his shoes, "but until right now, I never knew how much."

She watched him put his shoes on, his back taut with tension. "Are you mad at me because I didn't want what you wanted? I told you I wanted to see the world and take pictures. It's who I am."

"I know," he said, but his voice was sad this time. "I only wish you would have realized you could let someone love *you* and still be what you wanted."

He might as well have struck her. "Are we talking about you?" How had they gotten to this?

"No, we're not talking about me. You made it clear in high school that you were going on to bigger and better things. And I knew what I wanted. To be a doctor, have a wife and kids, and live in Colorado close to my family."

He was making it sound like she thought she was better than him. "I was going on to *different* things, Andy. Ones that mattered to me." She slid off the bed and stood. "Why are you this upset?"

His scowl was as wide as the Serengeti. "I don't know."

"Yes, you do," she said, getting in his face. "What is it?"

"You're going to leave again," he said, his eyes flashing with an unusual fire. "And dammit, I don't want to start caring about you all over again and looking forward to hanging out with you at Merry Cottage. And I damn well don't want to start liking you like a girl again."

She froze in place. She didn't answer right away, giving the smell of gunpowder in the air time to disappear. He kicked at the floor again.

"If your eye gets better, you're going to head back to those dangerous places." He paused. "You're so damn tough you might do it even if your eye *doesn't* recover. Lucy, you could get hurt again. Or worse."

*"Andy,"* she said softly.

He looked up, breathing hard. She could tell he was thinking about Kim and losing the people he loved. He was scared to lose her too, but she didn't have the words to soothe him. The only thing she knew that would help was a hug. So, that's what she did. She wrapped him in her arms and squeezed him tight.

The rigid muscles and locked frame of his body eventually relaxed. "I'm sorry," he whispered. "It's not you. It is, but—"

"I know," she said, rubbing his back.

He edged away to look at her. "It's only... Lucy, you really mean a lot to me, and I've missed you. I don't want to see you hurt again. Not even for something you love."

Their eyes met as he reached up to push the hair behind her ear. The hands holding her suddenly felt warm. Awareness rolled through her again, unwelcome and alluring all at once.

A man's hands were holding her in a way she enjoyed. More shocking was the realization that they were Andy's hands. *No, no, no*, she thought. This could not be. It could never be. He was still in love with his wife, and she still planned to leave Dare Valley again.

"It's getting late. You need to pick up Danny, right?" She stepped out of his arms and crossed the room to put on her own shoes. It didn't matter that she didn't plan to leave the house. It occupied her hands and kept him from seeing her face.

"Why do I have the feeling things got weird again?" he asked, his feet planted firmly in the doorway.

She stood and shook her head, striving for as normal an expression as possible. "We're fine."

He glanced at the watch on his wrist. "I have another half hour before I need to pick up Danny."

As a dare, it was a good one. He was essentially saying: if it's not weird between us, then you won't mind me staying.

But she did. She couldn't seem to have control over herself right now. Her eyes were seeing his body in a new light—or an achingly familiar one. He'd always been in top shape as a runner, but for some reason, his muscles looked more manly, more lust-inspiring than ever before. His broad chest filled out his shirt, and his shoulders looked like they'd been carved from granite. Her brain wanted her to assess more, but she wouldn't let it.

She could control herself. She'd always been able to control herself. This awareness was only something she needed to block out. He was right—she was planning to leave Dare Valley. It would hurt them both if they did something stupid and gave into these odd moments of attraction. It would ruin their friendship forever.

She told herself not to make too big a deal of these sparks between them. He was handsome. He always had been. It was a simple fact. Like one plus one equaling two.

Once she was used to being around him again, his muscles and all that handsomeness would become as normal as the awe-inspiring mountains surrounding Dare Valley.

"Okay, let's finish our beers," she said, pasting a smile on her face.

His gaze dropped to her lips. Was she imagining it? Clearly she had lost her mind, so she hustled past him to the kitchen, trying to control the panic rising inside her.

She was not going to become attracted to her best friend again.

# Chapter 11

Moira cruised to her cousin Jill's house for happy hour in what she was now calling her old car. Once she landed her big new job, she was going to splurge on a Range Rover. It was easy on the eyes *and* good on the road. Another thing to look forward to now that she'd decided to make a change.

Cleaning out her office on Friday had sucked. A few of her colleagues had teared up, both because she'd be missed and because no one wanted to lose their buffer from Taylor. Everyone had wished her the best, though, and more than one person had whispered she was brave to leave. A few had asked where she was going, but she'd only given them a mischievous wink and said she'd be happy to share the news as soon as she was able. There was no way she wanted anyone outside of the family to know she was still looking.

She needed to focus on her job hunt more. She had the final version of her resume ready to go. She'd talked to a headhunter. Everything was gelling. And it felt nice to have a little break—some time to reflect on what she wanted next. For the first time in years, she was waking up without an alarm. Plus, she was having a good time staying with her mom and hanging out more with her family—especially her cute-as-a-button nephew. Her mother hadn't stopped hinting that she should look for a job locally, and Moira had to admit it would be nice. But she wasn't holding her breath.

One thing she would have liked to do was spend more time with Lucy, but Andy's message had come through loud and clear. She wasn't going to push things. Andy knew better than anyone what Lucy needed right now, and if it was time to settle, Moira was going to give it to her. There would be plenty of opportunities for them to get to know each other better.

Besides, Moira was plenty busy too. There was a lot of groundwork to do for her job search, and she was hanging out more with her cousins. She couldn't remember the last time she'd spent an afternoon with just Jill, so when Jill had asked her to swing by her house to have a drink—just the two of them and the twins—she'd been excited. At family gatherings, everyone took turns playing with Jill's adorable girls, but today they'd be all hers.

When Jill answered the door with a gurgling Mia in her arms, Moira couldn't help but laugh. They were both wearing matching purple tutus.

"I love the look," she said, patting the puffy tulle around Mia's chubby baby waist. "Did you have them made?"

Jill gave her a smacking kiss on the cheek. "Yep. A woman in town sewed them for us. Brian is praying for a boy next time. I told him he has a whole lifetime of girly stuff ahead of him, so he'd better get used to tutus and glitter and ribbons."

"Brian's a good egg," Moira said, following Jill inside.

Violet, cute as a button in her own matching tutu, screeched when they entered the kitchen. Moira smiled at the woman holding the toddler and then shifted her gaze to the famous billionaire beside her. Well, surprise, surprise. They had company.

"Hey, Margie," Moira said casually. "I'm going to come by the bakery tomorrow morning for another one of your fabulous cinnamon rolls. They're an integral part of my mental health program while I'm looking for a new job."

Jill's former barista at Don't Soy With Me, now the owner of Hot Cross Buns Bakery, gave her a brilliant smile. "We appreciate your patronage. Moira, have you met my fiancé?" she asked, setting the toddler down on the floor. "Wow, I still can't believe I'm calling you that."

The man in question ran his hand down her short black hair and gazed at her adoringly. "It's currently my favorite word in the English language." He crossed the room and extended his hand to Moira. "Evan Michaels."

"Nice to meet you," she said, trying to keep it cool. She couldn't very well say, *So, you're the billionaire everyone is talking about.* "The endowment you gave Emmits Merriam for the new inventor's center is very impressive."

"It's going to be so much fun," he said, looking young and playful. It was obvious he meant it.

Moira suddenly remembered she and Evan were the same age. And didn't that make her feel like a bit of a loser. Here she was cruising for her first six-figure job while this guy had made billions with his top-secret inventions for the military.

"What can I get you to drink?" Jill asked in an odd tone. She was crouching on the floor, pretending to play with the twin's blocks as she covertly watched the rest of them.

Moira's radar went on. Jill had lied to her about it being just the two of them this afternoon. Something was up.

"Jill, you have the L upside down," she said dryly, gesturing to the letters her cousin had placed together to spell Love.

Her cousin corrected it immediately. "Oops. Brian and I are trying to teach the twins special words."

Moira narrowed her eyes and walked over to her. Kneeling down, she pulled over the blocks she required. "T-R-U-T-H. Truth."

Mia clapped her baby hands while Violet grabbed the H and started gumming the corner, drooling everywhere.

"Am I that obvious?" Jill asked.

Moira gave the red curls falling over her cousin's shoulder a good-natured yank. "As your hair."

"She did it for me," Evan said, crouching down beside them. "Jill thought you might be able to help me."

"Help you?" Moira asked, so surprised Mia managed to unbalance her by climbing onto her leg.

He gave a lopsided grin. "Yeah. You know about my Artemis Institute of Innovation. That saves a lot of explanation."

She stayed where she was, sitting on Jill's kitchen floor as Mia snuggled in her lap. "Hard not to. It's the talk of the town."

"Right!" He grabbed one of the blocks. "I've been thinking about who I need to hire to make it work, and Jill explained how Mac Maven specifically recruited her for his new hotel because of her local knowledge and connections."

Moira suddenly knew where this was going.

"Jill told me you're a successful human resources director at a top Denver engineering firm who's looking for a new job, and she got to thinking—"

"I'll bet," Moira said, and the poor guy froze for a moment. "Please continue."

"I need someone to manage the center. I'm not talking about the finances or anything. This person will act as the director—they'll be in charge of hiring and managing staff, meeting with clients and press. The scope will be beyond human resources, but Jill says you're a jack of all trades and good with people. And I want the person to be young. There will be a lot of students involved. I'm hoping to include more budding inventors over time. It's important to me to foster a creative, hip environment for inventing."

Moira had to blink a few times before she answered. "You think I might be that person?" Her mind reeled. This job would be in Dare Valley, like her mom had been hoping. Had she and Jill dreamed this one up together?

"I'd like to talk to you more about it, and I'll need to see your resume and have my CFO, Chase Parker, interview you, but yes, I'd like to see if it would suit both of our interests."

Margie was standing behind him from his position on the floor, nodding and giving her an encouraging smile. "You'll like Chase, Moira. He runs Evan's company."

"So I can focus on my inventions," he added.

"I've read about Chase in *Fortune,*" she said. The man had radiated power in the photo on the cover of the magazine. "He's well regarded for taking your company into the billionaire club. Not that your inventions wouldn't have done that on their own."

Evan laughed. "Oh, I like you already. Jill said you were balls-to-the-walls honest. Chase will like that too. Oops. Can I say that in front of the kids?"

Jill shrugged. "They know the word ball. Just not in the way you meant."

Evan cleared his throat. "That's...good. Sorry about that, Jill. So, Moira, are you interested?"

It would be crazy not to consider it. She'd been hoping for more management responsibility, and this position would launch her into a whole new realm. "Of course, I'd need to hear more about the position, salary, and benefits. Do you have a job description?"

"Nope," Evan answered unabashedly. "That's why we need you. Just kidding! I'll talk to Chase and have our people hammer out something to send you. What's your contact info?"

He dug out his smart phone, and she dictated her information.

"Do you have anything in your past that would preclude you from receiving a security clearance? Jill didn't think so, but I wanted to be sure."

Her cousin plucked Mia up and made a silly face at her. "Does toilet-papering Grandpa Hale's house with Meredith and Matt count? I still remember how much he hollered about that."

Aunt Harriet had thought it amusing, but not her uncle. She couldn't remember why in the world they'd ever thought it a good idea. "Other than that incident, I'm a safe bet."

That only made Jill laugh harder.

"I've never toilet-papered anything," Evan said, rubbing his chin. "I feel a little left out."

"Yeah, you geniuses had it rough," Margie said, patting him on the back. "All right, let's get going so Moira can chew Jill out for setting her up."

They said their goodbyes, and Margie pulled Jill into a hug. "Thanks for looking out for my man."

"My pleasure," Jill said, giving Moira a conspiratorial wink. "I'll do anything to get all my Hale cousins back in town."

"Moira, it was great to meet you," Evan said, shaking her hand warmly. "I'll be in touch. I want to move fast on this. We're setting up a makeshift facility at the university right now until we break ground on the actual center. Maybe I can give you a tour."

"Sounds good," she said, trying to visualize what an invention center would even look like. Probably sleek and modern with lots of high-tech toys.

After they left the house, Jill headed to the refrigerator. "I never did get you a drink. What would you like? I have wine, beer, and cocktail fixings for anything from cosmos to Manhattans."

"Red wine would be great," she said, smiling down at Violet when the little girl whacked her with a cloth-bound book with a red dog on the front. "You're not out of the woods yet, you know. Please don't tell me you plotted this with my mother."

"Nope! The machinations were all on my own." Jill pointed the wine bottle at her own head. "I'm a genius too. Now I just need to make billions like Evan. He's great, right? And this new center? It sounds all sci-fi meets *American Idol.*"

Moira wasn't going to waste brain cells pondering that comparison. "To be honest, I never thought I'd find a job opportunity here with the kind of responsibility and compensation I'm looking for."

"Evan's company is huge, and it's got the bucks you're looking for," Jill said. "It could be the stepping stone to bigger things. The headquarters are outside Washington D.C., and they have offices all over the world."

Her cousin should have been in sales. "You're terrible, but I love you."

Jill brought over her glass of wine and plucked her pumpkin beer off the counter. "Here's to considering new possibilities."

Moira lifted her glass. "Here's to."

## Chapter 12

Lucy's mother had orchestrated her introduction to The Calendar of New Beginnings' volunteers with as much mystery as would surround a spy ring. She'd even purposely invited Lucy late so everyone could enjoy appetizers and cocktails beforehand to loosen up.

The plan was for the volunteers to introduce themselves in order, starting with January. Apparently, a few volunteers had expressed preferences for certain months, like April Hale, while the order of the rest had been chosen by drawing the remainder of the names out of her dad's ball cap. The kicker for Lucy was her mother's insistence that each person come into the room one at a time to maintain the element of surprise.

As soon as Lucy arrived, she'd been led to the empty family room, which now featured a makeshift bar stocked with enough alcohol to intoxicate all the citizens of Dare Valley.

Ellen's infamous cosmopolitans shone bright-pink in her crystal punch bowl. Lucy's grandmother's sterling silver ladle was sticking out—a reminder of why her mother had helped orchestrate this calendar. An array of beers lay nestled in a bed of ice in a red barrel. And there was an assortment of wine, whiskey, and bourbon, which made Lucy wonder if the female volunteers were hardcore grain alcohol drinkers or if there were more males in the group than she'd expected.

It was an uncomfortable situation, made more so by the element of surprise. Had her mother somehow corralled one of her grade school teachers into posing? How mortifying. She forced her features to take on a blank slate as the first woman sashayed into the family room.

"I'm Miss January," Deidre Gadlons said, posing like a woman who had always hoped to be in *Playboy*. "I'm hoping we can rig up special sparklers around these beauties."

A cheer erupted from the kitchen, where her mother had parked the waiting volunteers. When Deidre gestured to the breasts underneath a fake-fur vest shot with silver thread, Lucy's good eye twitched.

"I might be nearing fifty, but men around town have been hoping to see me naked for decades," she continued. "Fortunately my Eddie decided he wouldn't get bent out of shape because this is for such a good cause. He's usually the jealous type."

The poor woman. "Good to see you again, Mrs. Gadlons. You're looking as great as ever."

"I know. It's been years since I've seen you, Lucy, but please call me Deidre."

Her mother popped out from behind the kitchen doorway, scaring the bejesus out of Lucy. "Might be best if you call everyone by their first names. After all, you'll be on an intimate basis with all of us."

She held her tongue about her new idea for The Calendar of New Beginnings, wanting to listen to the volunteers' thoughts first. So far, the sparkler comment wasn't exactly encouraging.

"Next," her mother called, and in strolled the only male volunteer Lucy knew about.

"I'm Mr. February," Dr. Jeff said, flipping open the

gray suit jacket he'd worn over designer jeans. "Like Deidre, I have a feeling all of the women in Dare Valley have wanted to see me naked."

The women hooted from the kitchen, and Dr. Jeff executed the splits like John Travolta on *Saturday Night Fever*.

Oh, God. Did every volunteer have some secret fantasy posing for this calendar would help them fulfill? "Are you hoping for a hot dog as a prop?"

More people guffawed, and Dr. Jeff looked down at his crotch. "Depends on the kind. It would need to be a kielbasa or a frankfurter. I'll leave that to you." The hoots continued as he headed to the bar.

The next woman entered. "I'm Miss March. You know me better as Linda Feathers, from your mother's bridge club."

And her cosmo-drinking comrade in all the pictures her mother sent her overseas. "Hello, Linda."

She tucked her head like she was suddenly shy. "I was thinking... Well..."

"Spit it out, honey!" her mother shouted. "We're all in this together. There's no shame."

"Well, my idea is to cover my lovelies with white feathers...since that's my last name. I found some beautiful feather fans at an online vintage shop. I think they'd be captivating as well as concealing. My husband, Harold, doesn't want anything really good to show."

The husband factor wasn't something Lucy had considered, probably because her dad wasn't concerned about her mother posing in her unmentionables. She'd pretty much showed it all during her breastfeeding fair and afternoon hot tub sessions.

"Thank you for sharing, Linda," she said, annoyed to hear the primness in her voice. "Next!"

April Hale stepped forward and gave her a wide smile. "Miss April, obviously. Lucy, we've discussed the cantaloupes."

"They're out of season," someone shouted from the other room, causing a ripple of hilarity to start again.

"That's what I said," her mother interjected from the doorway. "We might need to use bowling balls for April's tits."

"Mother!" Lucy cried.

Snickering could be heard amidst the laughter.

"Oh, lighten up, Lucy Lu," her mother said, rolling her eyes. "What are you planning to do? Pretend we don't have parts?"

*Nice one, Mother.* "Thank you, April. Next."

A sweet old lady stepped forward, wearing a yellow knit dress and sensible flats. She seemed vaguely familiar, but Lucy couldn't remember her name.

"Miss May or Joanie Perkins. People around town call me and a couple of my friends the Easter Brigade since we wear pastels. Since April has her month namesake, we decided to move me to May."

The forethought of the group astounded her. It wasn't going to be easy to convince them all to go along with her new idea. "I'm sure you'll make a lovely Miss May, Joanie."

"I was thinking I could frolic around a May pole. Maybe some colorful ribbons could cover me up."

"Won't cover much," an older woman shouted, a voice Lucy recognized as Ester Banks, her mother's cousin.

Ester made her mother look like a Puritan. Lucy was doomed.

"How does your boyfriend feel about this, Joanie?" Ester shouted. "Let's hope you don't give Arthur Hale a heart attack when the calendar comes out. Would be a shame to have him go that way after all he's done for our town."

Lucy's mouth dropped. "Mr. Hale?" she asked blankly.

Joanie gave her a saucy wink. "He's my boyfriend,

dear. I know he thinks the world of you."

Lucy flushed from the compliment as much as the surprise. Arthur Hale had a lady friend? How had her mother not mentioned this? He was nearly eighty. They both were. Not that age should matter. But Arthur had loved Harriet like crazy... Lucy reminded herself life moved on. She was happy for Arthur. Joanie seemed like a nice lady—pole and ribbons and all.

"Thank you, Joanie," she said. "Next."

Joanie hustled off to the makeshift bar and poured one of her mother's famous cosmos. Lucy was going to need a few after the introductions wrapped up.

"Mr. June," the next man said as he entered, grabbing her full attention.

She might have lived overseas, but even she knew about the famous super-chef, Terrance Waters.

"I was thinking a meat cleaver," he said, his face deadpan.

"I'd be happy to hold it for you, Chef T," Ester barked out from the other room.

Lucy blinked as the women all dissolved into giggles, but she had to admit he was drool-worthy in a white T-shirt and faded jeans.

"Are you sure they make a meat cleaver big enough, Chef?" her mother asked from the doorway.

The mega-watt glare Lucy sent in her direction didn't even dim her mischievous smile. Landing Chef T for the calendar was a big coup. Interestingly, her mother hadn't told her. Then she realized why. This calendar was going to sell buckets if Chef T was baring all, covered only by a meat cleaver. Which meant people outside of Dare Valley would hear about this project and Lucy's involvement in it. Her glare deepened. Not that it had any effect on Ellen O'Brien, who gave her a saucy, checkmate wink.

"Good to meet you, Lucy," Chef T said, reaching out to shake her hand. "Jane says you're the tops, and that's important in my book. Look forward to working with you."

They shook hands, and he stepped aside as an even taller man walked in at her mother's signal—one who was actually more masculine than Chef T, to Lucy's mind. He had a devil-may-care smile, guaranteeing the kind of fun that could get a person in trouble.

"Mr. July," the man drawled.

This had to be the famous poker player and Jane's former boss. "Rhett Butler Blaylock, I presume."

He raised a hand to his forehead like he was tipping his hat to her. As an old-school gesture, it was charming. "We haven't met, Lucy, but everyone I care about cares about you. As far as I'm concerned that makes us friends."

His sincerity made her smile, even though she had to crane her neck to meet his eyes. Good Lord, he was as tall as a sycamore.

"My wife is expecting," Rhett informed her, "so being a daddy and all, I'd like to keep my photo a bit...I can't believe I am saying this...in good taste."

A chorus of boos sounded from the women in the kitchen and those gathered around the bar. Someone emitted a hiccup as well, clearly intoxicated by her mother's strong cosmos.

Rhett turned to face the women standing in the family room, putting his hands out like he was reining in a mob. "Ladies, please. Try and be understanding. God knows, I've done plenty of things in bad taste, but my wild days are behind me. When Ellen asked me to participate, I couldn't rightly say no, what with it being for such a good cause and all. My great-uncle Jackson Lee died of lung cancer when I was a sprout. He was the first person to teach me poker, and I miss that old man like crazy." Rhett turned back to Lucy. "But my wife...she's a bit modest, if you understand me. Plus, I have a teenage stepson and one on the way. I need to be a role model."

"That's very admirable," she said, liking him already. "I'm sure we can come up with something that'll please you both."

The next woman emerged—the one Lucy feared more than anyone. Ester Banks might be eighty, but she was no one's version of a good grandma. The older woman and her mother had been friends since meeting in a stained glass class when Lucy was a girl. She had a blue streak running through her silver hair, a low-neck top showcasing her double D's, and a fake candy cigarette in her mouth. Ester also had a potty mouth that could beat out Betty White.

"Hello, Lucy," she said in a throaty voice, pretending to smoke her candy cigarette. "I'd prefer to include my current boyfriend—he's at the retirement home—but your mama's being a real bitch about doubles. How do you feel about it?"

With the fake cigarette pointed in her direction, Lucy struggled not to laugh. "Honestly, I have to agree with the bitch," she said, making everyone laugh, including Ester, like she'd hoped. You couldn't show fear to that woman. She ran over people like tanks rolled over protesters. "I don't do couples, Ester."

"Then you're a bitch too," she said in a throaty voice, laughing. "Well, I had to try. If it's only going to be me, I'd like to lie naked in the back of my red '67 Pontiac Firebird. I had a lot of fun in that car with my husband, Howard, before he died of prostate cancer fifteen years ago. Seemed like the thing to capture."

Lucy suspected Ester had never planned to include her current boyfriend. She was only going for shock value like she usually did.

"I appreciate the compromise," she said as Ester blew fake cigarette smoke in her direction and walked to the cosmo punch bowl.

When Hairy's' main bartender, Mike Dougal, walked

in next, Lucy was knocked off balance.

"Hiya, Luce," he said, giving her one of his lady-killing grins. "Mr. September at your service."

"Does my dad know about this?" she asked him before swinging her head to stare down her mother.

Her mom crossed her arms over her chest. "Your father doesn't want to know any of the details about this calendar. We made an agreement."

Likely to preserve his sanity as much as to prevent her mother from embarrassing him with tall tales of the photo shoot. Her dad was one smart cookie. "Fine. Mike, what do you have in mind? To be honest, I'm almost afraid to know." The bartender's reputation as a ladies' man was well known, but he'd never so much as looked at her wrong. Her dad would have killed him, and he knew it.

"I was thinking you could rig something of me building a Guinness at Hairy's," he said, gesturing to his front. "Beer has a head, after all, and—"

"Stop! I get the picture. Thank you, Mike. Next!"

Jill sauntered in. "Personal introductions aren't needed," she said saucily, hiking up her hip like an old movie bombshell. "Miss October in the flesh."

Lucy expected her cousin to suggest adding milk foam to cover her sizable rack or something since she owned the town's coffee shop. A headache spread across the base of her neck to her temples.

"I should have guessed you'd volunteer," Lucy said, cocking her brow.

Jill was going to be worse than Ester, and she proved it by sticking her tongue out at Lucy.

"As I told my cousin recently, I'm a genius. So, Lucy, I've been racking my brain for the best pose, and I think I want to go all Latin."

Chef T spewed out his bourbon and started coughing like it had gone down the wrong pipe. Poor guy. Her mother had regaled Lucy with the hilarious stories of

Jill teaching Chef T Latin dance moves so he could win a date with his now-fiancée, Elizabeth.

Jill looked over her shoulder at him. "Sure you don't want to pose with me, Chef T?"

More hooting erupted as the chef narrowed his eyes. "Not a chance in hell," Chef T ground out.

"Your loss," her cousin said, executing a flawless salsa move.

"I see you have hidden skills," Lucy said, crossing her arms.

"They aren't so hidden anymore," Jill informed her. "You'll have to come to our Latin dance class, Luce. It's so much fun and a great workout. Now back to my pose. I was thinking feathers too—the kind women dancers wore in old movies—but if Mrs. Feathers wants to use them, I could use a hat covered in fruit to cover these beauties." She extended her hand to her boobs like Vanna White introducing the next letter on *Wheel of Fortune*.

Chef T groaned and covered his eyes. Like that would do any good. The image was already seared into Lucy's brain. "Very Carmen Miranda of you. Thanks for sharing."

"I have more ideas!" she declared.

Lucy turned her around and pushed her toward the bar. "I think that's enough for the moment. Next." She was starting to feel more in charge as each new subject emerged, and it felt good. This was going to be her photo shoot, and her mother needed to understand that.

She blinked rapidly when Old Man Jenkins shuffled forward in a plaid shirt tucked into brown pants. Lucy didn't know when everyone had started calling him Old Man Jenkins, but she'd never heard him called anything else. He used to be one of the biggest volunteers in Dare Valley, always leading one church or town improvement committee after another.

"Mr. November," he said in a gruff voice through a

lopsided grin. "I'm the oldest of this motley crew. I'm ninety-one."

He was adorable. Lucy gave him a soft smile. "We're lucky to have you."

His scoff made everyone chuckle. "I might not have a young body anymore, but I've fought in two wars and devoted a lot of my time and energy to this town. I run Bingo night now when I'm not spending time with my friends at the senior citizens' home. I'm representing all the old folks who've lost someone to cancer. While some people suggested I incorporate a Bingo theme—which I nixed because the balls are too small—I was hoping you could drape a flag over me since I'm dedicating my month to my brother. He died in Korea fighting beside me."

Any laughter generated by his Bingo ball comment faded. Everyone seemed moved by his earnestness, and in that moment, Lucy knew she was going to treasure hearing his stories while she photographed him—her way—capturing the hard angles of his cheeks and mouth, chiseled from age and experience.

"Thank you so much for sharing, Mr. Jenkins," she said. He nodded crisply and shuffled over to the bar to shake hands with Rhett, who led him over to the table and poured him a bourbon.

It did Lucy's heart proud to see a younger man giving proper respect and care to the older man. So many of the cultures Lucy had experienced around the world respected the elderly in a way she wished people in the West would.

Lucy turned and saw her mother standing in the doorway, waiting for her full attention. *"Mother.* Somehow I am not surprised to see you're rounding out the year as Miss December."

Her mother gave an impish grin and sauntered forward. "I thought it fitting since I've won the Best Decorated House for Christmas award in Dare Valley five times—a town record."

Lucy refrained from pointing out that her dad was the one who climbed his ever-faithful ladder in the snow each year to hang her mother's extensive assortment of decorations and lights. Growing up, Lucy had hated decorating for Christmas. All the work had turned into a chore, so whenever she couldn't come home for Christmas, she comforted herself with the thought that at least she wouldn't have to help create the O'Brien Winter Wonderland.

"And your idea?" she asked because she would give her mother the respect she'd given everyone else. "Still thinking of mangoes?"

A few of the women snickered while Jill hooted out loud. "Mangoes," Jill cried. "You can do better than mangoes, honey."

"You're the one who wants to cover your boobies with a hat made of fruit," her mother shot back.

"Ladies!" Lucy cried, noting how the men had clustered together in solidarity, not that she blamed them.

"Mom, please share your idea with us," she said, giving Jill a hard look.

"I, too, have been thinking about what I'd like to convey to our readership," her mom said in a dramatic voice. "I was wondering if dressing up like Cleopatra might be intriguing enough. There are tales of how she hid in a rolled-up rug, wearing nothing but a headdress, to get to Julius Caesar."

"Very Katy Perry of you," Jill said, tapping her mouth. "I love it!"

Lucy didn't. It was exactly the kind of cheap theatrics she rebelled against. "Thank you for sharing, Mom," she said kindly, facing the twelve volunteers before her. "And thanks to all of you again for being a part of this. I'm really happy to be involved as well since it's for such a great cause, and it honors the people we loved who died of cancer."

She made sure to pause, hoping to shift the mood in her favor by reminding them all why they were here.

"I have to confess that this calendar isn't the kind of photo shoot I normally do." Her hands broke out in a sweat at the thought of taking photos of any kind, but they couldn't know that. "I'm willing to keep an open mind about the kinds of poses you'd like to do. This might make some of you feel vulnerable. For others, it will be a walk in the park."

She gave a pointed glance to Jill and Ester, who both started laughing.

"As you probably know, I've taken photographs for some of the biggest global organizations' calendars out there, raising money for anything from human rights to women's empowerment. I know what works, and while I really like this idea of taking fun, risqué photos, I wanted to suggest another approach for you to consider."

Her mother jammed her hands across her chest and stared at Lucy with fire in her eyes.

"Since you're all making a dedication to someone you lost in the calendar," she continued, "why not pose with the person's photo or a special memento. Like the flag Old Man Jenkins mentioned. It personalizes the story in a beautiful way. Or we can even shoot you in the person's favorite place—like the convertible Ester mentioned, or somewhere special you used to spend time together."

A few people were nodding now, and she smiled at them in solidarity.

"I got laid plenty in that car, God bless my Howard," Ester said, finally eating her candy cigarette.

Her mother walked toward her. "Lucy, we discussed this. I don't want this to be one of your sad calendars."

The bubble of solidarity she'd been creating burst, and her mother's insinuation gripped its claws around her. "I'm not saying you have to make it sad, Mother. Only meaningful. Authentic. If you're telling the story of your loss, why not have a photo that captures it?"

Everyone looked at her mother, sensing a showdown.

"Lucy, this calendar shows that life moves on," her mother said in a hard tone. "That people still laugh and have fun. That's why it's called The Calendar of New Beginnings."

"There's no reason the photos I'm suggesting wouldn't fit that theme," she said diplomatically. "Surely you understand that considering Chef T's participation, not to mention a few of the others in your group, this calendar could be sold nationally, perhaps even internationally. I just want a product that is going to be equal to that level of exposure." Even if she wasn't sure how she was going to pull off her part of the bargain.

"You mean *your* level," her mother said sternly.

"Ellen," April said, laying a hand on her mom's shoulder. "Lucy makes a good point. Maybe we should discuss this more with her once everyone leaves."

"We *did* discuss it with her," her mother said, making the others look away in discomfort. "If you didn't want to do it, you should have just told us. I could have asked Farley Higgins. He has a pretty good photography studio here in town. But I was hoping you might be willing to use your God-given talents to help us out since you're back in town. Clearly, this isn't your thing."

Her mother could throw guilt around like ninja stars. "Mom, I'm not saying I don't want to be involved. I was only sharing a concept that came to me as I was thinking about this calendar. I hoped you would listen to my idea since I was respectful enough to listen to yours. It's not like we couldn't take more than one photo." She considered the possibility. "We could have one that's about the loss and another funny one about the joys of moving on."

A few people were scratching their chins. Even Lucy wasn't sure how that would work.

"Sounds like you two have some personal problems to work through," Old Man Jenkins said, calling a spade a spade. "I'm old, and I'm tired. I'm going to head on home. When you two figure things out, give me a call."

A few people nodded, and Ester shrugged. "I gave Old Man Jenkins a ride here, so I have to go. But he's right. Work it out. Ellie, I'll see you tomorrow at Latin dancing."

Pretty much everyone else followed them out the door, fleeing like a herd of water buffalos that scented lions. Too bad she and her mother were the lions. Lucy didn't want to battle it out, but she knew it was inevitable.

Jill gave her an encouraging hug before she left. April whispered something in her mother's ear as they hugged goodbye.

When they were alone, her mother turned to her, fire and brimstone flashing in her eyes. "We need to get something straight."

Cue the showdown.

# Chapter 13

Ellen O'Brien had been a lot of fun growing up, but she could be as tough as a rebel leader. Lucy was about to receive one of her mother's firm butt-kickings. Since she'd been through them before, she went to the bar and ladled out a hefty cosmopolitan.

"Lucy Marigold O'Brien," her mother began, making Lucy's mouth turn sour despite the sweet cocktail she'd just sipped.

She'd always hated her middle name, not only because it made her sound like some misplaced flower child, but because marigolds smelled like ass, if you asked her. Taking another fortifying drink of her cosmo, she turned around. Her mother was breathing hard enough to make her mangoes heave.

"I'm sorry you didn't like my idea, Mom," she said, striving for peace. "I was only trying to add something to the calendar from my experience."

Her mother charged over to her. "The calendar was fine without your idea! This stunt you pulled was an embarrassment to me and yourself. These people signed up for The Calendar of New Beginnings, not The Calendar of Death."

So much for peace. "Mom, I'm not suggesting—"

"Yes, you are," her mother interrupted, slicing her hand through the air. "If you think you're too good for us and this calendar, I can ask Farley to take the photos. I meant what I said, Lucy. We don't need you to lower your standards for our sake. We might not be as well traveled as you are, but we're good people, and the calendar is fine just as we planned it."

Her mom's voice, just below a shout, was making her head hurt. "You're not listen—"

"Why didn't you come to me with this idea beforehand? You blindsided me in front of all our volunteers."

Since her mother wasn't calming down any, Lucy set her cosmo aside. "I thought I'd see what the whole group thought of the idea, Mom. It came to me after I talked to you and April."

"Bull! Let's lay it all out, shall we? You didn't think I'd consider your idea, and you were right. Lucy, sometimes I just don't understand you."

There it was again. The unsolvable issue between them. They *didn't* understand each other. It was like trying to talk to someone speaking a different language. Why couldn't her mother accept her for who she was?

"I'm going to head out," she said, unable to continue the dead-end conversation. "We can both think about what's best for us and talk tomorrow. I love you, Mom." The words were hard to utter.

Her mom was stiff as she kissed her cheek. Lucy hustled out of the room, stopping to pick up her purse in the entryway. When she exited the house, she pressed her hand to her aching head. Her vision suddenly seemed worse. Hadn't her mother's mums in the terracotta pot looked crisper and clearer earlier? Hadn't they looked red? Now they were almost rust-colored.

Lucy took a moment to scan her surroundings, blinking her right eye slowly, hoping to correct her vision. But it didn't change. Everything looked worse than it had before.

She felt the claws of a panic attack sink into her skin.

*No, no, no,* she told herself. *We're not going to freak out.*

Her vision hadn't altered like this since her hospital stay, and then it had only changed for the better. This wasn't supposed to happen. Her vision was supposed to improve, not worsen. Could it be the stress from the fight? She had no idea, which made it that much scarier.

She glanced at her car. Right now she didn't trust herself to drive. Her spirits sank. She couldn't even take care of herself. Powerlessness overwhelmed her. She needed help, and if there was one thing that grated on Lucy's nerves more than anything, it was having to depend on anyone.

She set off down the sidewalk to Andy's house, hoping he'd be home. There was no way she was asking her mom for a ride after their altercation, even if her mother had known the truth. Her dad would drop everything at Hairy's and run her home. But then there would be questions.

After passing Washington Elementary, she finally reached Andy's A-frame house, which seemed gray to her. There were a few white thingies in the yard alongside a T-ball set. Baseballs, she realized. She had to close her right eye to count them. Four in total. The grass was a little long, showing Andy hadn't had the time to mow it in a while.

When he opened the door, he immediately said, "What's wrong?"

"How did you know?" she asked, noting the Labrador next to his legs. "I was going to ease into it."

He wrapped his arms around her before she could say anything. "It was your face. You look...scared. Is it your eye? I don't see your car."

All she wanted to do was burrow against him. "Yeah, it's my eye. I had a fight with my mom over the calendar. My vision went all funny as soon as I stepped outside—funnier than usual. I don't understand how that could have happened—"

"I'm glad you came," he said, keeping his arms around her. "It's going to be okay."

Crap. Now he was going to make her cry. "I know. Maybe it's just stress from the fight."

"Doubtful. From my research, traumatic optic neuropathy doesn't usually see visual acuity worsen. Even from stress. This is...puzzling. How's your color vision?"

"Worse. You looked it up?" she asked, even though she wasn't surprised.

"Of course I did. I might not be an ophthalmologist, but I'm a doctor. I wanted to be informed in case I could help."

"No one can help," she said, embarrassed by her woe-is-me tone.

"You must have had some fight with your mother," he said, sweeping his hand up and down her back in the most wonderful way.

She was sure she wasn't supposed to notice how good it felt. She also wasn't supposed to notice he smelled like pine and earth. At least her sense of smell hadn't changed.

"Hey!" he said, tightening his arms around her. "You're scaring me here. I think this is the single longest hug we've ever had. How bad is it?"

She pressed her head into his chest, noticing how hard the muscles were underneath his dark T-shirt. "It's bad enough that I decided not to drive home."

He was silent for a moment, stroking her hair, something she realized was more than comforting. No one had ever stroked her hair with that much tenderness before.

"Will you call your doctor, please, if you haven't already?" he asked softly. "I know I said I wouldn't push, but it seems like the smart course of action."

Rubbing her head against his chest, she nodded. "I

think I probably should. He said to call if there was any change."

"I can take tomorrow off and drive you to Denver for the appointment," he said, tucking her closer, all protective-like. "We'll figure it out, Lucy."

It moved her something fierce that he would cancel his work at the hospital to help her. "I can make it to Denver. Tanner offered—"

"I'm taking you! Don't even try and argue with me. You'll just piss me off."

She hung her head against his chest, wanting to weep suddenly. "I'm not used to people helping me. Usually I'm the one helping."

He hugged her tightly. "Well, get used to it, Lucy Lu. I'm here for you, and damn it, you'd better let me help."

"Thanks, Andy. I don't know what else to say." Her voice was hoarse, she realized.

"You should tell your mom and dad, you know." He shushed her when she went rigid in his arms. "Your mom wouldn't have picked a fight if she knew what was really going on."

"I'm not so sure about that," she said, her spirits sinking further. Her mom's precious project had been threatened. She might have chosen a different way of putting Lucy in her place, but she would have done the same thing regardless.

"All right. I won't try and convince you." He finally let go of her, but his hands were still on her waist and he was staring into her eyes.

It took Lucy a moment to realize he was trying to assess her condition...like the doctor he was.

She gave him a gentle shove in his middle, making him grunt. "Stop. I don't need you going all doctor on me. You can't see anything wrong with the naked eye anyway. Can you take me home? I wasn't sure if Danny was around or not."

Andy continued to study her—zoom in on her was

more like it. "He's at Latin dance with Natalie and Jane. They took him once as a lark because I was working late, and he got hooked. The oldest male is close to eighty, and Danny is the youngest. He goes once a week. It's good cardio, better than soccer even."

Laughter was the best balm in the world, especially in life's dark moments. "That's gotta be the best story I've heard in weeks," she said, chuckling despite herself. "And to hear you calling it good cardio..."

His gaze was soft as he pushed her hair behind her ear. "Wait until he wiggles his hips to the merengue. You'll be a goner."

Her eyes might be playing tricks on her, but she'd be a goner if he continued to look at her like that. Suddenly her chest was tight. It was happening again. This weird, strange, otherworldly attraction for him.

"I can't wait," she said, hearing the breathless quality of her voice.

His nostrils flared like he'd heard it too, and everything inside her stilled. His hands tightened on her waist before falling away. He stepped back, and she could have sworn he shook himself.

"How about a beer?" he asked, putting his hand on the edge of the open door.

"Sounds good," she responded, aware he was looking over her shoulder.

Somehow they'd both forgotten they were standing in the doorway for all his neighbors to see. Oh, how the Dare Valley gossip mill would turn if someone squealed that the now-eligible Andy Hale had kept his arms around Lucy O'Brien for a couple of minutes.

"Anyone see us?" she decided to boldly ask.

"I think we're safe," he said with a wry twist to the mouth. "Come on in. This is Rufus. He's a good dog, but he's a handful. I'm going to put him in Danny's room so he won't bother you and then grab us a beer."

The minute Andy closed the door, he took her hand

and led her down the hallway to what was clearly the family room.

"I'll be right back," he said, sitting her down on the tan couch and leaving the room with the dog.

Trucks, trains, and books lay in a makeshift circle on the floor in front of a dark bean bag chair, clearly Danny's perch. Next to it sat an adult-size one as well—green, she thought. Lucy liked the image of Andy sitting beside the boy as he played. The fireplace was bare, but to the right sat a basket piled with fresh-cut wood ready for the cooler fall nights approaching.

She glanced at the clock. Just after seven o'clock. All she wanted to do was go home and crawl into bed. Right now, she felt like giving up. It wasn't her usual, but she decided she was entitled to a pity party. Cold glass touched her shoulder, and she turned to see Andy handing her a bottle of Guinness.

"I know it's not as good in the bottle," he said, coming around to sit with her. "But it'll hit the spot."

Her two sips of her cosmopolitan didn't count as mixing, so she took the beer and drank while he sampled his IPA.

"Feeling pretty sad, aren't you?" he asked, putting his arm around her after setting his beer aside.

She turned her head. "How can you tell?"

"Please. When you're sad, your shoulders sag." He kneaded them. "Plus, it's written all over your face. Who can blame you? You had a fight with your mom, and your visual acuity and color vision has worsened with no clear explanation. That's what I'd call a pretty bad day."

"I hate feeling sorry for myself," she admitted, kicking her legs out and crossing them at the ankle. "But I'm feeling a truckload of self-pity right now. I just want my eye to get better. I want to take pictures again. I want—"

"Everything to be like it used to be," he finished for her, kissing her temple. "I know. I have my days too."

"What do you do when it happens?" she asked, glad she'd made the decision to come to him. She didn't just need a ride, it turned out—she needed a friend.

He blew out a breath. "Well, you saw how I got the other night, which I'm still a little embarrassed about."

She set her beer on the coffee table, and this time she was the one who leaned closer to him. "Don't be. I'm glad you can share how you feel with me. We never held back in our chats online."

"Seems a little different in person," he said, pressing her head to his chest. "Right now, I'm happy to be the one comforting you. Don't laugh."

He'd always been sensitive about people laughing at him. Why, she could remember how upset he'd been in third grade when the class clown made fun of him for wearing brown cords to school in May. Lucy had shoved the boy later on the playground and told him she'd beat him up if he ever made fun of her friend again.

"I won't laugh. I know it's hard to be the one bleeding out." If only the human body had a shutoff switch to flip when it was hurting.

"I look at stupid stuff online like lawnmowers or power washers instead of going to bed," he said. "I sometimes can't face going to bed alone. I miss..."

"What?" she asked when he trailed off.

His inhale sounded like an airplane engine firing up. "I miss hearing someone breathe next to me in the dark. I'm better now, but I have nights. After Kim died, I couldn't sleep in our bed. I slept on the couch when I wasn't sleeping by Danny's bedside. After Kim died, he'd wake up crying for her."

"You never told me that," she said, trying to imagine the kind of toll that must have taken on him. On both of them.

"I'd lie in bed for hours, and even though I was exhausted, I couldn't fall sleep. When I did my residency, I didn't sleep much, but this was different. It was like I was numb or something." He kicked out his legs, crossing them at the ankles. "Shit. This is pretty depressing. I should be trying to cheer you up."

"You don't have to cheer me up. Do you have a quilt? It's stupid, but I'm suddenly cold."

"It's the emotion," he said, rising and grabbing a blue and yellow quilt. He wrapped it around her and kept his arms around her too, rubbing her skin to generate warmth. "I know the things you saw in the field made you sad sometimes. What would you do to feel better?"

"Well...I usually wrote you," she said, and when he shifted to look at her, she turned to face him as well. "You were always a link for me when I was pretty low, especially when it was too dangerous for me to go outside. I'd pull up my computer and write to you. It always helped. I don't know if I've ever fully said it, Andy, but our chats have meant more to me..."

She cleared her throat, unable to go on. He'd been her lifeline in so many ways.

"They meant a lot to me too," he said softly, tucking her hair behind her ears again.

The moment lengthened. She stayed where she was, looking back at him, feeling like she was seeing him in a different way than she ever had.

"Lucy—"

"Dad!" Danny yelled out, making them jump apart like two high school kids caught sitting too close together on the couch. "Rufus! Where are you?"

"Guess they're back," Andy said, rising and walking to the front door. "Hey, big man! How was Latin dance tonight?"

"The best!" the little boy said, appearing in Lucy's line of sight. "Hey, Miss Lucy. Are you having dinner with my dad? Aunt Natalie, Aunt Moira, and Aunt Jane took me to Brian's restaurant so I've already eaten."

"Hey, Danny," she said, giving a little wave. "No,

we're not having dinner. Just a beer." That seemed like the understatement of the day.

The women appeared, all dressed in workout gear. They kissed Andy on the cheek. There was no mistaking their interest in her presence.

"Dad, where's Rufus?"

"I put him in your room since Miss Lucy is here," he answered.

"You look like you've had a tough day," Moira said, coming over and sitting beside her on the couch.

"It wasn't easy street," she responded with her usual flair. "How's the job hunt going?"

"It's taken an interesting turn," she said, frowning, and Lucy could all but feel the questions turning in her mind.

Natalie came over, pointing to the quilt around her. "Are you sick?" she asked.

"Nah," she said, shaking her head. "Just got cold. Weird, right?"

As Jane walked over to greet her, Moira and Natalie exchanged a look and then glanced over at Andy, a silent question on their eyes. He gave them a blank look back—oh, that silent sibling communication—and took Danny's hand, positioning the little boy in front of Lucy.

"Why don't you show us what you learned tonight, Danny?" Andy asked, taking his seat beside her again.

"Are you sure Miss Lucy's okay, Dad?" Danny asked. "She looks kinda sick to me too."

Lucy forced a smile. "I'm used to tropical jungles and hot savannahs, remember?" she said, ad-libbing on the spot. "Dare Valley feels cold to me. Now how about you show me how you break it down. Your dad has been chatting up your merengue."

The little boy wiggled his hips. "Aunt Jane, can you put on our playlist? It's better with music, Miss Lucy."

"You have a playlist?" Andy asked.

"Yep," Jane said. "Danny picked his favorites, and

Elizabeth shared her music with us."

"You'll have to share it with my dad, Aunt Jane," the little boy said, "since I'm too young for a cell phone yet."

Andy was already shaking his head. "Man, I think my head just exploded. My five-year-old kid is talking about having a cell phone."

His son put his hands on hips. "Dad! All the older kids have them."

Even Lucy felt her mouth twitch. Then Jane's phone started playing a fast, Latin beat, and Danny launched into his moves. His little legs executed a fast but effortless salsa. Lucy looked over at Andy in shocked delight.

"He's really good," she whispered. Andy's smile glowed with parental pride, and she couldn't help but smile back.

Danny did a spin, which had Lucy clapping. Then the Hale sisters jumped up and joined him. Jane followed suit, and all four executed the moves in tandem. When Danny slapped himself on the butt during a spin, Lucy had to bite her lip to keep from laughing.

But she couldn't contain it when he ran his hands down his sides like a diva and wiggled his little body for all he was worth. Andy started laughing with her, and he put two fingers to his lips and gave a shrill whistle.

When the song finished, Danny ran over to his dad and jumped on his lap. "Dad! You've just got to come to class with me sometime. It's so much fun."

Andy ran his hand over the boy's mussed hair. "You know I prefer to run, but I'm glad you've found something that makes you happy."

"It's so much more fun than baseball," Danny said as Jane shut the music off. "Even if I'm the only kid. Miss Lucy, you should come too."

"Even though I was one of the worst dancers at Dare Valley High School, I do love to dance. Especially to songs with a fast rhythm. Maybe after I settle into town a little more." Although it might prove problematic to follow along in class considering the peripheral vision in her right eye was shot.

"Okay, you let me know," Danny said, bouncing on his dad's lap. "We need more backup dancers. Right, Aunt Natalie?"

"Always," she said, laughing.

Andy made a show of sniffing his son. "Someone needs a bath. Why don't you say goodbye to your aunts and Miss Lucy and head upstairs? I'll be up in a jiffy. You know how to start the water."

"All right, Dad," the boy said, giving them hugs. Then he turned and gave her one too before racing up the stairs. "Rufus! I'm coming."

"Are you sure you're going to be able to take me home?" she asked Andy.

Then she realized all the women were staring at her with open curiosity.

"I don't have a ride, so I walked here," she explained with a shrug. "Long story."

Natalie narrowed her eyes. "Wasn't today the meet-the-volunteers party?"

"Wait!" Andy called out. "How do *you* know about the calendar?"

"I might have mentioned it," Jane said with a grimace. "Elizabeth told me about Terrance's involvement. She couldn't keep that to herself."

"Terrance volunteered?" Andy asked, his mouth agape. "You're kidding."

"She's really not," Moira said, fanning herself. "This calendar is going to sell like Chef T's hotcakes with his famous salted maple syrup."

"She's right," Lucy said, remembering his meat cleaver suggestion.

"You didn't hear it from Mom?" Andy asked his sisters.

"No way," Natalie said, making a face that matched Moira's. "Personally, I'm glad they didn't ask me. Blake's football friends would never let me live it down if I posed for a calendar like that. They'd probably put my photo in their locker rooms just to rile Blake."

*Now that would be funny*, Lucy thought. And it would make the calendar's popularity spread even further.

"Care to share who else volunteered?" Natalie asked, turning to face Lucy. "Jill can't keep a secret worth spit, so she spilled her involvement weeks ago."

"Terrance is terrified of her," Jane said, sputtering.

Moira wiggled her hips. "She's never going to stop torturing him. C'mon, Lucy, who else has volunteered besides our mothers and those two?"

She didn't even consider playing coy. She ticked off the list, delighting in their facial reactions. When Old Man Jenkins' name came up, Andy actually slapped his forehead.

"Him! And Rhett too? You're right, Moira. They are going to sell like hotcakes. Personally, though, I'm not sure I want to see Mom in all her glory as Miss April."

"Me either," Moira said, crossing her eyes. "It's a good thing Lucy is doing the calendar. There's no one in Dare Valley who could match her ability as a photographer."

Andy's laughter faded. It was obvious he was thinking about her eye—just like she was—so Lucy gave him an encouraging smile.

"Could one of you stay a little longer with Danny?" he asked. "I need to take Lucy home after I get him bathed and in his PJs."

"I can get the munchkin bathed and into bed," Moira said. "You don't have to wait to take Lucy home. You guys feel free to head out. You too," she said, turning to face Jane and Natalie.

Jane grinned. "Matt told me he's opening up one of

my favorite wines. But I can stay if you need me to."

"Me too," Natalie said.

Moira shook her head. "You get to be with Danny all the time. It'll be fun for me to have some alone time with him."

They both nodded, and there was a round of kissing and hugging as everyone said goodbye.

"I'm going to say goodnight to Danny," Andy said to Lucy. "Cover up until I get back. You're still cold."

He was right. She felt like she'd swallowed icicles.

As soon as he disappeared up the stairs, Moira sat down beside Lucy and narrowed her eyes. "I'm not stupid. You *are* sick, aren't you? That's why you came home. I told Andy something was up."

She didn't like hearing they'd discussed her condition behind her back. "I'm not sick," she said, gripping the quilt. "Please don't ask me any more questions, Moira."

After hearing how quickly the news of the calendar had made the rounds, the last thing she wanted to do was tell one more person about her condition. Even if she thought Moira would respect her privacy.

"My brother is worried about you," Moira said, "and so are your parents. I won't ask any more questions, but I'm glad you're relying on Andy. It's always made me happy how you two have stayed close friends all these years. It's pretty rare, especially when someone gets married."

"Kim knew I wasn't a threat, thankfully."

"That isn't the only reason she was glad you and Andy were friends," Moira said matter-of-factly. "Andy pours so much energy into taking care of other people, and because of that, he doesn't always tell us how he really feels about things. But he could share those things with one other person besides Kim. You."

But their agreement was changing, Lucy realized. Even though she was doing her best not to let Mr.

Responsibility take care of her, here she was, relying on him for a ride because she couldn't drive. And now he would be driving her to the doctor too. She was entangling him in her problems, and though she didn't want that, she wasn't sure how to stop.

"He's the best friend anyone could ever have," she said in all seriousness. "It's been hard to make longterm friends given how much I travel. Andy has been a constant in my life forever."

"And you've been one in his," Moira said, giving her a smile. "You might be a bit older and my brother's best friend, but I've always liked you. Considering the way I blabber every time I talk to you, I'm sure you know I admire you and all you've accomplished."

"Thank you," she said, not sure how to respond except directly. "Are you saying you'd like to be my friend too?"

Moira laughed. "Yes. Hope that doesn't make you uncomfortable."

Andy walked back in. "Ready?"

Nodding, she rose. "Thanks, Moira for—"

"You don't have to say it," she said. "It's what *friends* do. Don't rush back on my account, Andy. The munchkin and I are going to have some fun."

"Thanks, Mo," he said, crossing the room to Lucy and extending his hand to help her up like she was too weak or blind to walk alone. When he grabbed the quilt to bring with them, she wanted to bristle.

"I'm not that cold," she hissed.

He gave her a look. "Humor me. See you in a bit, Mo."

After leading the way to the garage, he opened the passenger door and stood beside it until she was buckled in.

When he tucked the quilt around her, she blurted out, "I'm not an invalid."

"I know you're not," he said softly before closing the

passenger door.

But as he drove her all the way out of town and to her house, all she could think about was that she *was* an invalid. She couldn't even drive herself home. Those seven miles between her house and his felt like the longest she'd ever traveled. They drove in silence, and she was glad he didn't try and engage her in conversation. When they arrived, she threw the quilt in the backseat, undid her seatbelt, and exited the vehicle. Sure, she still felt cold, but she would get over it.

It was her vision that troubled her. It hadn't improved yet, and she feared she'd slipped backwards. Was this it? What if it never got better? What then?

He was waiting for her at the hood of the car, and while he didn't touch her, she could feel his support as they walked to her front door. She inserted the key into the lock with a heavy heart.

"Your mind is spinning all sorts of horror-story scenarios, isn't it?" he finally asked when she opened the door.

She had to press her chest to her tight diaphragm to breathe. "Hard not to. I'm trying not to freak out."

He pulled her into his arms. "It's okay to freak out. My mind is spinning with all sorts of things too. How about we have something to drink?"

She had one bottle of champagne she'd bought just because. Lucy thought everyone should have a bottle of champagne in the refrigerator.

"I'm going to pop some champagne. Because fuck it. Why not? I'm still here, and I'm going to find a way to be happy—regardless of what happens with my eye. I won't let this destroy my life."

Even if it felt like it would. She didn't know who she was or what she'd do if she couldn't take photos and travel. Lucy O'Brien was a globetrotter with the world as her address. She wasn't some college professor living back in her hometown of Dare Valley.

He rubbed her back. "So we'll have champagne. You should call your doctor's service first. It's late, and the office will be closed, but there will be a way to get him an urgent message."

He let her go and walked in the direction of the kitchen, turning on the lights as he went.

"Yeah, Dr. Davidson gave me a special number to call." She'd hoped she would never have to use the handwritten number on the business card he'd given her. But she bucked up and called it, leaving a voicemail in a shaky voice she hated.

Andy pulled the champagne from the refrigerator. "Let's sit on the couch while we wait for him to call you back."

Her throat closed. "You really don't have to wait with me."

"You're crazy if you think I'm leaving you alone. Do you have champagne glasses?"

She shrugged, unable to speak, so he started rummaging through the cabinets. Sure enough, Mrs. Weidman had some old-school crystal champagne glasses that could have graced Joan Crawford's hand in an old movie. He poured the champagne and led the way to the couch.

"To good friends," he said as they sat. They clinked glasses for the toast.

"The best," she said and took a drink.

The bubbles exploded in her mouth, and she made herself imagine they were like a hundred fireworks exploding inside her, shining color into the blackness she feared might become her reality.

Andy removed her cell phone from her clenched hand and placed it on the coffee table in front of them.

"I'd like to hold your hand while we wait for the doctor to call," he said in a calm tone, but his gaze told her a different story.

He reached for her hand, and she curled her fingers

around his, and they waited in the quiet room, staring at the phone, sipping champagne.

# Chapter 14

Even though Andy wasn't waiting in an oncologist's office for Lucy, he found himself tapping his foot on the floor, unable to read the health magazine in his hands. While staring at the ceiling in his dark bedroom last night, he'd reminded himself that her vision wasn't an issue of life and death. Not like Kim's illness. But that fact did nothing to ease the knots in his belly.

He'd picked Lucy up at eight o'clock, over three hours ago, after dropping Danny off at school. One look at her pale face had told him she'd slept no better than he had. She mumbled that she was lucky not to have class in the afternoon, then stayed silent for most of the drive to Denver. So did he. About an hour into it, she finally broke the silence to say her mom had texted to ask why her car was still on the street in front of their house. The lie she'd responded with was at least encased in truth. She'd told Ellen that Andy had taken her home after a few drinks at his house.

Andy assured her that he and Matt would drive her car back to Merry Cottage after the appointment. The bigger question was what she'd do if she couldn't drive, but neither of them put voice to that. Instead, he reached out and held her hand, and didn't let it go until they arrived.

Now he was gritting his teeth in the waiting room. Andy hadn't asked to accompany her inside Dr. Davidson's office, and when she hadn't offered, he'd steeled himself to wait.

After what seemed like an eternity, Lucy returned from the back of the building. She looked in his direction, and he watched as her chest rose and fell on a deep exhale. Then she squared her shoulders and walked over to him. There were other people in the waiting room, but he didn't care. He pulled her into his arms. She folded against him like sails dropped when the wind went out of them.

The news wasn't good.

When they finally released each other, he led her out of the doctor's office to the parking garage. He remained silent until he steered the car above-ground.

"It's almost lunchtime," he said, turning away from the office building.

"I'm not hungry," she said, leaning her head against the back of the seat like all her energy had been zapped.

"I know you don't want to eat, but you need to keep up your strength," he said as gently as he could. "Did you eat breakfast?"

She shook her head. "Oh, you're probably hungry. Feel free to stop and get something. Unless we need to get back right away to pick Danny up from school."

The tension inside him was rising. "Jane is going to pick him up."

He'd known better than to ask his mother. She would have asked all sorts of questions about this impromptu trip to Denver, which would make their way back to Ellen. As far as he knew, Lucy still planned to keep her condition from her parents. In fact, he was starting to wonder if she was going to tell *him* the whole story. So far she hadn't said a word about the appointment.

"I'm going to stop at a café I like and grab a sandwich," he said, heading in that direction. "Maybe something there will sound appealing to you."

"I won't starve if I miss a few meals," she replied in the most forlorn voice she'd ever used with him. "Trust me. I know what it takes for that to happen."

Jesus. She was spiraling into serious depression right in front of him. "All right. I don't know what to say to you now, but why don't we start with you telling me what Dr. Davidson said?"

"He said he couldn't see any clinical reason for this sudden fluctuation in my vision," she said with an edge in her voice. "Apparently, sometimes it's a patient's *perspective* that causes them to see fluctuations."

The ire in her voice could have punctured a tire. "What else?"

She threw out her hands. "He made me feel like I was imagining things. I'm not crazy! I see what I see. And my vision got worse after my fight with my mom. Of course, he gave me this BS song and dance about how important timing is for diagnosis. He might have seen something yesterday, but it wasn't there today."

Andy kept his face neutral. He understood what Dr. Davidson was saying. It wasn't possible to confirm heart palpitations after the fact using an EKG.

"Dr. Davidson did confirm their 'presumptive' diagnosis that my optical nerve had been damaged. Yay, right? Today the nerve finally looked white, which shows after the initial injury."

A healthy nerve looked golden, Andy knew. "Well, that's something."

"Is it?" she railed. "My color vision still sucks. We did those stupid color panels again. Those kimchi hara things."

"Ishihara?" he asked.

"Whatever. They're stupid, and I failed. I couldn't

distinguish a red number or letter in a sea of orange dots or a blue one in a bunch of green dots."

Personally Andy thought the color test was ingenious—the inventors had found a way to keep the brain from making guesses on the colors. "Your color vision can still improve, Lucy."

"But it hasn't since the first couple of weeks after my injury! I mean, sure, I can close my right eye and look with my left, but I'm not supposed to. And right now, my brain isn't accurately computing what it sees when I'm looking with both eyes like a normal person. Maybe it will never adjust. Dammit!" She kicked the glove compartment.

His stomach flipped at her violence. "What else did he say?" he asked as calmly as possible.

"Dr. Davidson said I can still drive. The vision in my left eye is twenty-twenty like it used to be. My right eye is the same twenty-fifty it was when I had my last appointment."

He knew better than to try and point out that the doctor's news could have been much worse. It would be like pointing out to someone who'd lost a kidney that they still had one functioning. He didn't want to be the "you should be grateful" asshole.

"Dr. Davidson said it's still all a waiting game," she continued, tracing the window's edge. "Things could continue to improve. We need more time to see."

How many times had he told a patient the same thing?

"Don't take this personally, but sometimes you doctors suck. I don't know why we even drove all this way. He had nothing useful to say, beyond implying I was a crazy psychosomatic woman. You took a day off for nothing, and I'm sorry."

"I know it seems like this didn't produce anything useful," he said, reaching across the console for her hand, "but you confirmed a diagnosis. That's huge! And it was smart to check things out."

She scoffed.

"Lucy, I would take off a week if it were necessary. You're not alone here. As for doctors sucking, I pretty much thought the same thing about all of Kim's doctors in the end. Not to mention myself. There are limits to what we can do, and I freaking hate that."

She curled her fingers around his hand and gripped it suddenly. "I'm sorry. I'm stirring things up for you, and I don't mean to. And I don't mean to be angry and pathetic either. I keep trying to tell myself I'm going to be fine, but all I can think about is not being able to take photos like I used to. See the world like I used to. I know I should try to teach myself a new way, but it's going to take a while. Mostly, I just want to curl into a ball and cry. It's not fair."

"So you stay in Dare Valley as long as you need and figure it out," he said, stopping at a red light. "There are worse places to be. You have me and your family."

There was a decided sniff in the car. "I don't feel like I have much of anything right now, but you're right. I guess I'm going to have to find a new way to think about my mom. I'd be an idiot to fight with one of the few people in my camp."

"I still think she'll be easier to deal with if you tell her the truth," he said, pulling into the parking lot of the café.

"No, she won't," Lucy said in a hard tone. "She'll treat me like I'm a child and insist on doing everything from driving me around to making my meals. All the while she'll tell me this is for the best because it was never safe for me to be overseas in the first place. I can't do that."

He schooled his features as he left the car, only to realize she wasn't getting out with him. Going over to the passenger side, he lowered his head until he could see her through the window.

"Are you going to come inside?" he asked through the glass.

She shook her head, burrowing in the seat.

His patience was wearing thin, so he didn't open the door and cajole her. Kim would have dragged herself out of the car, as much for him as for their son, who had been so young at the time of her diagnosis.

When he opened the door to the café, he reminded himself Lucy wasn't Kim. He needed to tailor his support to fit *her*. After finding a table, he ordered a Reuben and ate it by himself, mulling over the issue. He was tempted to order Lucy something, but he didn't want to force food on her. She was already bristling over her version of how Ellen would treat her. No, force wasn't the way.

He kept an eye on her in his SUV, but she hadn't moved in the seat. Was she asleep? He doubted it. The sandwich had about as much flavor as gravel since his taste buds weren't firing this morning, a common effect of stress in the body. He finished off the meal because it was fuel, asked for two to-go cups of water, and then walked back to the car. Barely fifteen minutes had passed.

When he handed her a water, she took it, but she didn't drink it. He put his in the cup holder and buckled up. "I'm sorry if I'm being too pushy, Luce. I…don't always know what to do in these situations, and I can't read your mind. You're going to have to help me. What do you want me to do?"

"Can you just take me home?" she asked, clutching the plastic cup. "I need to do some thinking. Be by myself."

He didn't like the sound of that. If he left her alone, she might fall into a deeper depression. "Please do one thing for me, okay?"

She finally looked at him. "What?"

"Remember I'm your friend." He had to swallow the

lump in his throat.

"I know you are," she whispered. "I'm just...I need space."

Nodding, he turned on the ignition and headed to the highway that would take them back to Dare Valley. The ride back seemed as long as the one to Denver. They didn't speak at all, and she didn't drink the water. She only sat there, huddled in the seat with the cup clutched in her hand.

When they arrived at Merry Cottage, she crawled out of the car and headed for the front door.

"I'll text Matt so we can pick up your car," he told her as he followed her.

"Oh!" she said, stumbling suddenly as she turned around. "I can go with you, since Dr. Davidson said I could drive. Don't bother him."

His ire was growing. He hated seeing her this way. And he hated not being able to fix it.

"It's already organized," he told her flatly.

"Okay, thanks," she said, shoulders slouched. "I'm sorry I'm Debbie Downer right now. I'll snap out of it."

That did it. He grabbed her shoulders. "You don't have to apologize to me for feeling how you feel."

Then, without pausing to consider the ramifications, without planning it like he planned almost everything, Andy Hale kissed her smack on the mouth and released her.

"Now, go inside and rest."

He headed back to the car, taking deep breaths. Lucy just stood there in the shade of the front door, and he could see her press a hand to her mouth as he pulled out of the driveway. It was then he fully realized he'd kissed Lucy O'Brien for the first time.

"Oh, shit."

# Chapter 15

If being accused of being psychosomatic wasn't bad enough, Andy Hale had just kissed her for the first time. In all the years they'd been friends, he'd never *once* kissed her on the mouth. Friends didn't do that in the U.S. of A. Sure, they did it in other countries, but Lucy could rattle those off by name. It sure as hell wasn't ordinary here in Dare Valley.

It had been a fast kiss, driven by reflex or subconscious instinct. She hadn't seen it coming, and it had been over before she'd processed what was happening.

But even though it had felt a little weird, it had felt a little right too. Her lips were still warm and tingly from the unexpected contact.

She watched Andy drive away, wondering if she should call him and ask him what the hell had just happened. But she was too tired and vulnerable right now. Maybe she'd feel more prepared to face him after she took a nap.

And so when she heard the crunch of tires in her driveway a little while later, she stayed where she was, lying on the brass princess bed that had caused all that weirdness with Andy in the first place.

She supposed something had changed between

them that night.

She could finally admit to herself she was attracted to the man he'd become, the man who would swap ice cream cones with her. Who would make her laugh and bare his soul to her. Who smelled of pine and earth. Whose embrace made her want to lean into him forever. She'd loved him for as long as she could remember, but it was strange to feel a new kind of love for him. That feeling, so unexpected and disarming, made her want to open the door when he knocked softly. But she ignored it, and moments later, she heard a car drive away.

Everything was changing. Everything was falling apart. She'd come to Dare Valley in the hopes that it would give her clarity, but while she knew these streets and these faces, the path ahead was still shrouded in fog. And coming home after so much time away had only shown her how very different everything was...

Andy, for one. He'd kissed her, and now they were going to have to talk about it. If that kiss meant he wanted to be more than friends, she'd have to seriously consider it. She *wanted* to consider it. But she needed to emphasize yet again that she still intended to leave Dare Valley and resume her career.

She heard a car come up the drive again and groaned. Had Andy stewed and decided to come back and face her? If there was one truth in the universe, it was that Andy Hale wasn't a coward. She wasn't either. It was one of the reasons why they respected each other.

So when a knock sounded distantly from the front door, she dragged herself off the bed and steeled herself for the more-than-friends chat.

Opening the door, she gaped. "Mother."

"You and me need to have a talk, missy," she said, steamrolling past Lucy into the cottage. "I just saw Matthew Hale drive off in your car. Andy was following him. What's wrong with you?"

"Nothing," she lied again. "They were just doing me

a favor."

"I know when something doesn't sound right. Did you leave your car outside the house to make me worry?"

Lucy was shaking, unable to handle her mother's drama but unwilling to tell her the truth. If the car incident upset her this much, how would she react if she knew about Lucy's injury?

All she needed to do was find some way to make peace with her mother. She was staying in Dare Valley for the foreseeable future. Her life would be easier if they weren't at odds.

"No, Mother, I did not leave my car there to make you worry. I walked over to Andy's house and had some drinks with the Hales. Moira stayed with Danny, and Andy drove me home. No big deal."

"You do look hung over," her mother said, narrowing her eyes as she studied her. "I noticed it the minute you opened the door. Goodness me, Lucy, you must have tied one on over there."

All she could do was nod. It stung a little that her mother thought she was hung over rather than sick, but then again, Lucy was encouraging the lie. Guilt coiled around her like a poisonous vine. She just couldn't take this on right now.

"I'm sorry I worried you, Mom," she said. "Why don't you come inside?" She decided sitting down on the couch was a good idea. Her legs were a little shaky. "I'm sorry we fought. You were right. I did blindside you."

Her mother sat beside her, clutching her purse in her lap. "I'm glad you could admit that."

Through the haziness of the future, one thing became clear. If she and her mother were going to keep the peace between them, she'd have to relent.

"We'll do the calendar your way," she said, trying not to look on it as a defeat. She could do mangoes and feathers and meat cleavers. It was the universe's greatest joke on her that she'd have to relearn the way she took photos using cliché props, but she had to start somewhere.

Her mother only blinked at her.

"You're right," Lucy continued, feeling numb now. "My idea *is* sad. No one wants to dwell on death and loss. There's plenty enough of that in the world."

A part of Lucy really meant it. She didn't want to entangle herself in all that sadness right now. It might depress her even more. Maybe this way would be fun. God knew she could use a laugh. But a part of her—the part that wanted to capture truth and meaning—was dying inside her.

She let it die.

"This is a pretty big turnaround," her mother said, peering at her closely. "Even for you."

"I might choke on the words, Mom, but even I can be wrong."

Her mom's mouth twisted. "Dammit. I was all fired up, and you had to go and apologize."

Lucy cleared her throat. "It doesn't happen often, so enjoy it."

That prompted a laugh from her mother. "We have that in common, I suppose, although I can count the number of times your father has apologized to me. Three."

Lucy really didn't want to hear about them right now. She just wanted her mother to leave so she could curl back up on her princess bed and pretend she was somewhere else, someone else.

"Please tell the volunteers we'll start soon. I need to find a place for us to shoot."

"Oh, I didn't have a chance to tell you yesterday," her mother said, her face brightening. "Chef T offered the media room in The Grand Mountain Hotel. He uses it for his TV shows and promos. It's fully equipped with all the lighting and sound stuff—not that we'll need sound. But it would be funny to make a video about the making of this calendar, don't you think?"

Right now all Lucy could focus on was the challenge of taking good enough photographs. "Let's stick to the photos, Mother. I'm sure some people will get all weird when they have their clothes off. A videographer would only make them tense up."

"You make a good point there," her mother said, flicking her blond hair over her shoulder. "Not everyone is as comfortable with their bodies as I am. Except Chef T, perhaps. He's posed for some pretty big magazines, showcasing those hot tattoos of his."

Lucy had to be depressed—even the thought of seeing Chef T's rippling muscles and hot tattoos didn't ping anything inside her.

"I'll check out the media room," she said.

"Before he offered, it occurred to me that the university might have something available for you to use," her mother said, "but it didn't seem appropriate. You might think I don't care about your reputation, but you're wrong."

That somehow soothed her. "Yeah, imagine what the Dean of the Hale School of Journalism would say if he heard that his newest adjunct professor was using university property to take pictures of town citizens wearing nothing but fruit and frankfurters."

Her mother fell back against the Victorian couch, laughing. "Fruit and frankfurters! That's a good one. But you're not laughing, which means you have a pretty bad head. Heavens knows I've nursed your father enough. How about the O'Brien Hangover Remedy?"

Lucy gulped. "Does it still involve raw eggs and tomato juice?"

Her mother nodded.

"I'll pass." She made a show of putting her hand to her head, trying not to feel guilty for perpetuating the lie. "I just need to rest."

"Good thing you don't have class today," her mother said, rising. "How about I make you some tea before I go?"

"That would be nice," she said, recognizing it for the peace offering it was. She rose too, forcing steel into her spine. Right now, she felt like the weakest person on the planet.

"Get into bed," her mom said, patting her on the fanny. "I'll bring your tea."

Lucy headed back to her sanctuary, climbed back under the sheets, and assumed a fetal position, staring at the wall. Since her vision was unfamiliar and unwanted, she closed her eyes.

Part of her wanted to keep her eyes closed forever, but sooner or later she would have to face reality. Even ostriches had to take their heads out of the sand. Just not right now.

When her mom hustled into her room a few minutes later, she kept her eyes closed, pretending to be asleep. The rattle of china echoed in her ears. Then a warm hand touched her forehead, a throwback to her childhood when her mom used to tuck her in.

"Love you," her mother whispered.

Lucy let the tears roll out from under her eyelids as soon as she was alone.

# Chapter 16

Andy knew he was in trouble when Natalie and Moira showed up at the park to join him and Matt for a run that afternoon. They were waiting in the lot when he pulled up in his car.

He got out and put his hands on his hips. "Is this an intervention?" After spontaneously kissing Lucy on the mouth earlier, he probably needed it.

What in the hell had he been thinking? Truth was, nothing. He'd looked into her gorgeous green eyes and acted on instinct. She was beautiful and vulnerable and pretty much one of the most precious people in the entire world to him. Jung had called such impulses the subconscious mind. But it was really no excuse.

He'd messed things up, that much was clear. Lucy hadn't even come to the door after he and Matt dropped off her car.

Even so, he wouldn't lie to himself or her any longer. To say he'd missed her cheek and hit her mouth would insult them both. He could no longer hide his attraction to her, a feeling that had only increased in intensity since the night of her party.

But he'd kissed her on one of the worst mornings of her life—without her permission. He was an ass.

Certainly not the best friend he claimed to be.

"Let's run," Matt said, staring down their two sisters.

Andy was glad for the reprieve, however temporary. His siblings would probably pounce after the run. They knew he'd be more amenable if given the chance to expend his pent-up energy. They were all like that.

He didn't keep pace with any of them, going for a fast, hot burn. The path flashed before him as he ran full out.

Matt finally matched his speed at the one-mile marker. "You're running like the hounds of hell are after you," his brother said.

"Yeah," he ground out, glad his brother didn't press him for more conversation.

At mile two, Andy had lost track of how far ahead he was. Honestly, he didn't care. All he could think about was how the most important friendship in his life hung in the balance because of a spontaneous kiss on the mouth.

It hadn't even been a *good* kiss, but a hard, fast kiss fueled by pent-up longing. He increased his speed again.

At mile four, he finally looked over his shoulder. Matt was still behind him, but he was pretty far back now. The girls were nowhere in sight. Even though he didn't want to talk to his brother, he slowed his pace until Matt caught up to him again.

"Don't spill your guts yet," his brother said, shaking his head. "If you do, you'll only have to repeat it when we get back to the park."

His mouth twisted. Crap. He hated talking about himself, and Lucy sure as hell wouldn't want him talking about her. "There's nothing to say."

"Bull," Matt said in a hard tone. "Brace yourself for Sibling Sharing Time."

Leave it to Matty Ice to call it that. Andy increased his pace again, leaving his brother behind in the dust.

When he returned to their starting point, his sisters were talking by the edge of the park, a good ways from the path. Obviously, they had turned around at some point. They turned when he slowed, twin frowns twisting their features.

The realization that they'd all taken time from work save Moira to talk to him—before he picked Danny up—made his gut quiver. Matt stopped beside him, breathing hard.

"You kicked my ass today," he panted. "I think you were running an eight-minute mile."

"Too bad I wasn't competing in the New York marathon," he said wryly.

"You should consider it when you're pissed," Matt said, bending over at the waist. "I haven't seen you run like that since…"

His brother trailed off, unable to say it. They never could call it out.

Andy's heart wrenched. "Since Kim got sick and died."

Back then, he'd run until his body couldn't continue in the hopes it would drive away the fear and the pain. Or make him tired enough to sleep. But it never had. All it had done was release all the pent-up emotion inside him, and, trying to be scientific about it, he'd let himself cry out the grief, knowing it was as much of a natural body function as urinating.

His brother put a hand on his shoulder. "Come on. It's time to tell us what the hell is going on."

When they joined Natalie and Moira, he blew out a breath. "You must be pretty worried to have joined us for a run."

"We are," Natalie said, not mincing words. "Why couldn't Lucy drive herself home last night, Andy? We know something's going on."

"I can't tell you that," he said. "Lucy made me promise, okay?"

Moira put her hand on his arm. "Is she sick? I know she said she wasn't, but..."

He shook his head. "No, she's not. Thank God. But what's going on is tough, and that's all I can say."

Matt started stretching his calves. "I don't like this. You're bottled up tighter than I've seen you in forever."

His brother still couldn't say Kim's name. "You can say it. *Since Kim.* And you're right. I haven't been this upset since Kim got sick and passed away."

He hated the way Natalie's lip quivered, and Moira's eyes went blank. They'd all dealt with their pain in their own way.

"I know you're worried," he told them. "And I appreciate your concern. But it doesn't change anything. Lucy needs a friend, and that's me." Something he might have blown to smithereens with that kiss, but he wasn't about to tell them *that*.

"Fine," Natalie said, all matter-of-fact, a clear sign she was frustrated. "We won't ask you to break a promise to her. All we want you to know is that we're here for you. We can help out with Danny if you need to be with her more."

"Where were you and Lucy this morning?" Moira asked, putting her hands on her hips. "It's not like you to take off work."

He stared her down. "You're one to talk."

She frowned. "You can be such an ass sometimes."

"Then stop poking at me," he said.

"You all but told me to leave her alone that night at Hairy's," Moira said, "which I respected because you're her best friend and know more about what's going on with her."

"She doesn't need everyone asking things of her," he said. "She has a lot on her plate."

"That isn't an answer," Matt said, sounding like the lawyer he was. "All we know is Lucy suddenly returns, looking sickly. She wasn't able to drive her car last night for some reason, which prompted you to take a day off work today."

Leave it to Matt to lay it all out. "Dammit, don't box me into a corner here. I gave her my word."

"Her parents don't even know what's going on," Moira said, letting her hand fall away from his arm. "Neither does Mom. Although Mom said Lucy and Ellen had a huge fight yesterday about the calendar."

"Look," he said, holding up his hands. "She just got back to town, and while she remembers you guys, you're not...her friends."

"Everyone needs support," Moira said. "I told her I'd like to be her friend last night."

"Like any of us are good at letting people in," Andy said, rolling his eyes, not wishing to outright tell Moira to dial back the fangirl thing she had going on with Lucy. "We Hales are as tough as they come."

"We're getting better," Natalie said, putting a hand on her hip. "I'm back with my ex-husband, after all. And Matt is getting married."

"What about me?" Moira asked. "Don't leave me out because I'm still single."

"You left behind a dead-end job for something better," Matt said, raising his hand for a high five. "Back in the day you might have sucked it up and stayed just to spite your boss."

Moira's hand smacked Matt's so hard his brother winced. "I told Natalie when we were driving over here, but Jill encouraged Evan Michaels to consider me for the director position of the Artemis Institute here in Dare Valley. Being connected to a man like Evan and a company like Quid-Atch would open up big doors for me."

Andy put his hands on his hips. "Jill strikes again. Be good to have you back home. Danny would be over the moon to have another aunt in Dare Valley."

"I know," she said, a smile crossing her face. "I

decided the pros outweigh the cons. I could finally get a nice house with a view of the mountains, and whenever I miss city life, I can just drive back to Denver and stay with Caroline. Of course, I haven't met with Evan's CFO yet, but I'm going to knock him dead."

"If you do knock him dead," Matt said, rubbing the red spot she'd left on his hand, "call Andy Cakes here so he can resuscitate him."

They all chuckled a little. Matt even bumped into Andy playfully.

"We're here for you, Andy," Moira declared. *"All* of us are here for one another. That's why I pulled a calf muscle trying to keep up with you."

Andy crouched down to look at her calf, but she shoved him away.

"You *said* you'd pulled a muscle," he said, giving her an exasperated look.

"It's fine," she said, making a show of shuddering. "I'm not going to let my brother check out my muscles. Even if he is a doctor."

Andy ran his hand through his hair, realizing he was sweaty. He probably stank too. "Fine. Put some ice on it when you get home and take an ibuprofen."

"Thank you, Doctor," she said in a nasally voice.

"I need to get going," he said, checking his watch. "Danny needs to be picked up soon."

"I can grab him and take him back to the house with me," Natalie offered. "Blake would love the company. Besides, Touchdown and Rufus could have a doggie play date."

Andy never understood why dogs had to have play dates. He appreciated the need to socialize animals, but the word just weirded him out.

"I don't know," he said, thinking about Lucy. He'd have to face her sometime about the kiss he'd stolen. Part of him wanted to delay the inevitable conversation, but that would only make things fester.

He'd learned in his marriage that conflict was like an infection. With early prevention, the effects subsided with little harm to the patient. Delay treatment, and things turned ugly.

He didn't want to have to use the paddles to resuscitate his friendship with Lucy.

They were all watching his struggle as intently as if it were must-see TV, so he shot them a look. "Fine. I appreciate the offer."

"If she needs anything, we're here to help too," Moira said. "You're right, she doesn't know us well anymore, but we grew up with her. Plus, she's your friend, which means we'd do anything for her."

"Unless she and Ellen are at odds," Matt said, making a scary face. "That woman wouldn't hesitate to knock you in the nuts if you got in her way."

"She wants to knock our dad in the nuts," Moira said, "let me tell you. The things I hear from Mom's kitchen when they think I'm still sleeping... It would curl your toes."

Matt put his hands over his ears. "Please don't tell me. I have a delicate constitution."

They were all laughing as they walked back to the parking lot. He kissed his sisters on their cheeks and hugged his brother. "Thanks, guys."

"We've got your back," Natalie said.

The look she gave him spoke volumes. They had both loved Kim fiercely, and now they were both trying to rebuild their lives. It felt good to do it together.

Then he heard Matt yell, "Natalie! Dammit. You slapped that bumper sticker on my ride when I was running with Andy."

His sister gave him a saucy wink as she opened her car door. "You better believe it."

"I helped!" Moira volunteered, grinning.

Andy detoured to the back of Matt's SUV. Sure enough, there was a new pink bumper sticker on his brother's ride—the latest battle in Matt and Natalie's ongoing war.

"'I Love Mr. Darcy'?" Matt exclaimed, pointing to the offending sticker, which featured a red heart next to the phrase. "Seriously?"

"Jane loved it," Natalie said as she and Moira got into Natalie's car. And with that parting phrase, they drove off.

"My future wife had a hand in this?" his brother said, all Matty Ice now. "Oh, she's so going to get it when I get home."

Since he knew his brother was only joking, Andy slapped him on the back. "Go show her who the big dog is."

His brother cut him a glance and then smiled. "I'm pretty lucky to have her, aren't I?"

"Yeah, you are," Andy said, heading to his car.

At one time in his life, he'd thought he was the luckiest man alive. He'd had everything: the most beautiful, loving wife in the world; the happiest kid on the planet; and the best job out there.

Then it had all come crashing down.

But that didn't mean he had to stay down forever. He still had the happiest kid on the planet and a really great job here in his hometown.

And now his best friend was back.

He wondered how lucky he was going to feel after he and Lucy talked about their kiss tonight.

# Chapter 17

When Lucy's father showed up around suppertime with fish and chips, one of his classic hangover cures, Lucy tried to smile and choke down a few bites. Her vision was still scaring the bejesus out of her, despite what Dr. Davidson had said. Lucy was trying to look at everything with her good eye, and it took a lot of concentration since it wasn't her dominant one.

"It's not like you to tie one on," her dad said, drinking a Guinness at her kitchen table. "Even if you and your mom went twelve rounds."

"I'd hardly call it twelve rounds, Dad," she said, pushing around her coleslaw.

"That's not how she tells it," he said, leaning his meaty forearms on the surface. "I'm still trying to figure out what happened with your car. That doesn't wash."

What? Was she in tenth grade again? "Dad, I'm way too old for this kind of interrogation. Unless you're planning on trying to ground me—which I can tell you is impossible with your nearly forty-year-old daughter—I suggest you finish your beer and head back to the bar."

He stared her down. "You're only thirty-six, and if I want to worry about you, I will. You asked me to respect your wishes and not ask more questions, but that's not working for me right now."

It wasn't working for her either, truth be told, but she wasn't ready to tell him everything yet. No, if he knew, her mother would know. And she couldn't handle being smothered just now. She and her mom were having enough scrapes as it was.

"Everything is fine, Dad," she told him, something she'd been repeating to herself often enough.

"That Hale boy knows what's going on," he ground out. "I have half a mind to go talk to him."

Great. Maybe Andy would blurt out that he'd finally gotten up the nerve to kiss her. They should call the newspaper, have Arthur run an article. "Leave him be. He has enough on his plate without you poking at him."

"I'll poke at him if I want, Lucy Lu," her dad said. "You can keep your cards close to the vest for only so long, kid."

That would only be true if she couldn't drive, but Dr. Davidson had assured her she could. After all, people who only had vision in one eye did it all the time. She'd just have to find a way to be comfortable behind the wheel given her new reality. Maybe driving twenty miles an hour everywhere was the answer.

"I'm an adult, Dad," she said, shoving her uneaten food away. "I need you to respect that."

He was frowning as he stood up. "If I hadn't said those same words to my father when I told him I wanted to bartend instead of going to college, I'd keep at you. But you're tired, and I'm tired, so I'll just go back to my sanctuary and hope you'll trust me when you're ready."

Her heart broke, hearing him admit he was tired. "Oh, Daddy."

He pulled her out of the chair gently and wrapped his arms around her. "I know part of what's holding your tongue is worry about your mother. I wish I could promise you that I wouldn't tell her the whole truth. I've watched you two knock heads all your life. She means well. She just has the courage of her convictions—rather like someone else I know."

If she hadn't been so tired, she might have stuck her tongue out at him. "Then we're both stuck between a rock and a hard place."

"I'm glad you have Andy to help you," he said, letting her go and putting his hands on her shoulders. "But I swear to the Almighty that if you don't let me help you if you need it, I'm going to…"

"I'm too old for you to paddle my butt," she quipped.

"I never liked doing that," he said with a heavy sigh. "All right. I'm going. You get some rest and text me tomorrow to let me know how you are. Your mother might fool herself, but I know this isn't a hangover."

She watched as he walked out of the kitchen. The front door opened and closed. Sitting back at the kitchen table, she reached for her Guinness. Part of her wished getting drunk would help her mood, but that would be stupid. She'd felt this same temptation before, after a massacre in Sudan. There had been so much misery and death and darkness around her, she'd wanted nothing more than to keep drinking gin and tonics with her peacekeeper friends until she passed out. But the tension in the country had been too taut for her to take the risk.

Closing her eyes again, she let herself fall into the blackness. As a child, she'd never been afraid of the dark. She'd learned to fear it overseas—sometimes there were scary things in the dark, especially if the power went out because of an explosion. But not here. Not in this kitchen. It was just her, and the darkness felt comforting somehow.

She stayed that way for so long her left leg fell asleep, so she rose to shake it awake. A knock landed on the front door. She was reluctant to leave the blackness, but the person was persistent, which made her guess it was either Andy or her mother.

At the moment, it was a toss-up who she'd rather

see.

When she opened the door, he seemed to fill up the space, rather like he was filling up the entire frame of a photo. He had on a suede coat over a dark T-shirt and jeans, and since he rarely dressed casually, she knew he'd selected the outfit intentionally. Was he hoping it would lighten the mood? Regardless of the reason, he looked good, and she felt her body responding to him.

His eyes scanned her face as if gauging her reaction to him post-kiss. Perhaps it was the fusion created by that kiss, but her brain sent a signal to her eyes—she knew about such things now—and she found herself looking at the sexy, soft lips that had covered her own earlier in the day.

His body suddenly seemed too big, too warm, and she realized her chest was tight with tension. But her belly was also soft and liquid—a sure sign she was aware of him as a man.

"You know I had to come," he said after a long silence. "We both care about each other too much not to talk about what I did earlier. Can I come inside?"

That he would take full responsibility for the kiss didn't surprise her. "I didn't think you'd pretend it hadn't happened or say you'd missed my cheek. Come on in."

She detoured back to the kitchen because it seemed like the smart place to have a tough conversation, and this one was going to be tough.

When he shrugged out of his jacket, she took in all the hard muscles of his arms and shoulders. Her mouth went bone dry with the desire to reach out and touch him.

"You look like I'm about to give you a root canal," he commented, hanging his jacket all neat and tidy over the chair. "I'm sorry. I know it's been a rough twenty-four hours."

They were counting time now? "No, it's best we get

it out in the open. I...ah...knew you wanted to talk about it earlier...when you brought my car back with Matt. But I just couldn't then."

He turned the chair and straddled it—like it was a shield between them. "I know. It's probably for the best. I had a nice, hard run this afternoon, and it helped me see things more clearly."

Her stomach flipped over. *Oh, no, here it is.*

"I didn't plan to kiss you like that," he said, gripping the rungs of the chair like a man behind bars. "If I'd planned it, I would have done a better job. I mean, as a kiss, it pretty much sucked, and for that, I'm sorry too."

Cripes, he was even apologizing for his technique. "Andy—"

"No," he said, holding up his hand. "Let me finish here. If you interrupt, I won't be able...to...hell...get this out."

Her hands suddenly felt odd and unsure against her body, so she clutched them together, which didn't feel any less weird. Everything was weird, and she'd never felt more adrift from him or their usual easygoing rapport.

"I'm scared to hear it," she admitted.

He heaved out a breath. "And I'm scared to say it. Trust me, you don't know how much. Would you...please sit down? You look like you're going to run out of the room the moment I say something wrong."

She felt a little rabbity, she realized, but if he was brave enough to say his piece, she could muster the courage to listen. Sinking into a chair, she faced him.

"Thanks," he said, rocking his chair in place. "Lucy...even though I've tried like hell to ignore it, there have been moments where I've...oh crap, I can't believe I'm about to say this... I find you attractive. You were right to pick up on my moments of weirdness, and I know this is the last thing we both wanted, but I can't deny the way I feel. My subconscious finally overrode my conscious will—"

"You're going to go all Freud on me?" she asked, her mouth dropping open.

"I was thinking more Carl Jung," he said, his ears changing color now.

"Like that makes it so much better," she said, shocked to realize she was hurt. "I thought..."

He scooted his chair closer, and she felt caged in. "You thought what?"

"That you decided to kiss me because you wanted to—even if it was a snatch and grab—and you left right after."

His head lowered. "I don't know what to say. I'm so happy you're back, but I'm scared to ruin our friendship. I'm afraid I already have, and just when you need a friend. I'm not proud of myself and my timing, okay? I feel like I threw a grenade into an already burning building today."

"Only an idiot does that," she said in a no-nonsense tone. "Not a trained soldier for sure."

"So my analogy sucks," he said, rocking the chair again as he looked at her. "What do you want me to do? I did want to kiss you, and I'm sorry for the timing and even sorrier that I didn't ask you. Lucy...*please* tell me we're still friends."

The hoarseness of his voice put tears in her eyes. She laid her hands over his on top of the chair. "We're *always* friends—even if you did kiss me because of some subconscious mumbo jumbo. Now would you please turn your chair around and sit in it like a normal person? I feel like I'm hearing the confession of someone on death row."

He let go of her hands, stood, and turned the chair around. "I *feel* like someone facing death row. I thought this might end our friendship."

"I wouldn't let it," she said, shaking her head, feeling her throat tighten. "Andy Hale, you are the best friend

I've ever had, and I'm not going to let something like a quick kiss ruin that."

He pursed his lips, considering. "What if it hadn't been a fast kiss?" He paused. "Lucy, that subconscious impulse forced me to realize the truth."

The hair on the back of her neck stood up. "What's that?"

He shoved out of his chair and paced. "I came over here, hoping we could talk ourselves past this, but it grabbed me again when I saw you standing there in the doorway. You're beautiful and so...freaking dear to me."

Her heart was slowly coming out from its hiding place.

"Lucy, I still want to kiss you."

*Whoa.* There it was. When he said it like that, the secret place between her thighs clenched. "If we're being honest...oh sweet mother." She was going to do it. She was going to tell him.

"What?" he pressed, his frantic energy tangible.

"I might want to kiss you too," she whispered. "I've never...shit...I don't want you to think I've been pining for you all these years. Yes, there were some moments in high school, but I never once felt anything romantic for you when you were married to Kim. I need you to know that, Andy."

"I never thought you did." He swallowed thickly, sitting back down and taking her hands in his. "I didn't either."

A heavy silence hung in the room. With every word they uttered, they were changing the fabric of their friendship, and she was scared what the tapestry would look like when she took a step back to see the full display.

"I also don't want you to think I only kissed you because you were vulnerable," he told her, tracing her skin with his thumbs.

"I never thought that," she said with a reluctant

laugh. "If you kissed everyone who looked vulnerable, you'd be known around town as that kissing doctor."

"Leave it to you to make a joke," he said, snorting softly.

"It's what we do. Andy, we need to be logical here."

"I knew you were going to say that," he said, shaking his head. "I've through all the pros and cons a hundred times, but I keep circling back to one undeniable truth."

"What's that?"

He heaved out another anguished breath. "That I haven't wanted to kiss anyone since Kim. Lucy, I can't deny that."

"You haven't?" she asked in a soft voice. Somehow that had never dawned on her.

"No, I haven't," he said, looking oddly embarrassed. "And if losing Kim taught me one thing, it's that life is precious. That every moment is precious, and you have to make the most of them."

She felt the same way.

"You're here now," he continued. "I don't know for how long, and yeah, I'm afraid of you leaving, but I don't want to miss one single minute of the time you're here. I want to eat ice cream with you and go hiking in the mountains like we used to. And yes, I want to kiss you—even though I'm scared of that most of all."

She made herself ask, "Why?" and the question lingered in the air between them.

"I'm scared because I don't know what will happen between us if we do," he admitted, rocking in his chair again. "But mostly I'm scared...ah shit...there's no way easy way to say this...I didn't expect to want to kiss anyone else after I met Kim, and when she died..."

There was agony in his voice now.

"I still didn't because there wasn't anyone who tempted me. But I do now, and..."

It took all her willpower to stay still and let him gather himself together.

"I'm afraid I'm going to like kissing you," he whispered harshly, "and that it's going to break my heart all over again because it will mean Kim is gone for good."

Lucy gripped his hand, wishing she knew what to say to that.

"I don't say that to hurt you."

"I know," she whispered, leaning forward on the edge of her chair until the sides of their heads touched.

They sat like that, cheek to cheek, knees touching, in the silence. Her heart twisted for him and the choice before him. If he kissed her for real this time, he would be choosing to move on.

When he finally pressed back and looked into her eyes, she had her answer. He tucked her hair behind her ear.

"Lucy, I want to kiss you," he said, his body clenched with tension. "Will you let me?"

# Chapter 18

Andy stared into her beloved face, feeling the soft texture of Lucy's auburn hair between his fingers. His heartbeat was pounding in his chest. *Please don't say no. Not when I've put everything out there.*

Her thumb slid over his hand in an unmistakable caress. "Let's try this again," she said, and this time, she leaned forward and tentatively touched her lips to his.

It was still a shock feeling her mouth on his, but somehow it helped that she was as tense as he was. He ran his hand down her arm, hoping it would help them both relax. Her lips brushed his once, twice, filled with heat, and when that sweet connection ended, he pressed forward again, fitting their mouths together more completely. Her breath rushed out, and the urgent warmth of it inflamed his senses. She was sweet and lush and tentative, but she was here.

This was a kiss he wanted them both to remember.

He tilted his head to the side, experimenting with the angle, flirting with the fit of their mouths. Her bottom lip was too lush to ignore so he kissed it. Then her upper lip had to receive its fair share as well. And soon they were kissing as if they'd been kissing forever.

The gasp she made was unfamiliar but welcome

when he ran his tongue along the seam of her lips. And when she ran her tongue sensuously over his, he was surprised to hear himself groan. He needed to be closer to her. He tugged her off her chair and onto his lap.

Sliding his hands into her hair, he continued to kiss her in slow, sensual passes. She traced his collarbone and then cupped the back of his neck. That one simple touch made him feel edgy, out of control. He kissed her one last time, drawing things out, then forced himself to inch back, mostly because he didn't want to stop.

She was breathing as hard as he was. The light shining in her eyes touched the soft spot he'd carried in his heart for her all these years. But the flush on her cheeks and the redness of her lips tantalized him.

"You're so beautiful," he said, sliding his finger along her cheek. "I've never told you before."

Her brow furrowed, and then she cuddled closer.

"What's the matter?" he asked, wrapping his arms around her.

"The earth just shook," she said matter-of-factly. "Didn't you feel it?"

"It *was* a great kiss," he said, happy to feel a smile cross his face after so much turmoil. "But the earth shaking? You flatter me."

She sat up straighter on his lap. "That's not what I meant. It shook because it was a big decision—for both of us. Andy, I already love you, and this just strengthens everything. It scares me. I don't want..."

His heart clutched, as much from her profession of love—he knew how she felt, but after kissing her, it struck a different chord in him—as from the regret lacing her voice. "What?"

"I don't want to need you," she whispered, "and feeling like this when I already care about you so much and respect you and enjoy spending time with you..."

Being with Kim had taught Andy that needing someone didn't have to be a bad thing. "You're looking at it differently than I do. It's not needing. It's only enjoying someone more than you enjoy other people."

She took a moment. "I like that. Andy, so much in my life has changed recently, and here we are in my new kitchen in Dare Valley. We've known each other our whole lives, but I'm sitting on your lap, and we just kissed for the first time. I feel like everything I thought I knew is falling away."

"Our bond might be changing," he said, his voice deep, "but it isn't falling away."

"I know it was only our first kiss—I'm not counting the earlier one, by the way—but it was a big moment for both of us."

He was glad she understood. "The biggest. I need you to read something." He carefully pulled a letter out of his pocket and handed it to her, his gut gripping with tension. "Natalie is the only other person who's read this. I showed it to her to encourage her to be with Blake. But after what just happened between us, I...want you...to read it."

"Okay," she said quietly, opening the letter slowly. "Oh...my. It's from Kim." Her gaze shot to him, searching his face.

He swallowed thickly. "Yeah...it's from Kim."

She bit her lip, and he knew why. Kim's words did that to him every time he had the courage to read them. Of course, he knew them all by heart now.

*Dear Andy,*
*I asked you to open this letter today because it's now been a year since my death. I can't imagine what you've been through. After I learned I was sick, I would lie in our bed at night listening to you breathe and try and imagine how I would feel if you were the one who had cancer and died, leaving me alone with Danny. Even though imagining it created the most incredible agony inside me, the reality is probably much worse.*

*I knew it would hurt you too much if I tried to talk to you about finding someone else to love after losing me, so that's why I wrote this letter. A part of you probably still feels bound by the vows we made even though I'm not there anymore. While you may not want to hear it, and honestly I don't want to say it, I want you to find someone else to love.*

*You won't rush. That much I know. Heck, you didn't even rush when we first started dating and were so hot for each other. You always take your time. That's why you were meant to be a doctor. With every relationship, it's like you are always monitoring the vitals, the progress, looking for a change in the status.*

*I won't tell you to choose a good mother for Danny because I know you will. I won't even tell you to choose someone who makes you laugh because you'll find the right person for you. And why do I believe that? Because I believe in angels, and when I get to heaven and it's the right time, I'm going to ask God to let me come back and help you find the next woman of your heart.*

*I only ask that you let me.*

*This is hard to write, and I'm crying, partly because I know you're probably crying as you read this. But you'll know when you're ready to start being open again, putting yourself out there. As someone who had the privilege of being loved by you, no one knows better how much love you have to give.*

*Give it, my love, when the time comes.*

*I'll be there, rooting you on, wishing you every happiness always.*

*I love you,*
*Kim*

"Do you go to pieces every time you read this?" Lucy asked, handing him the letter and wiping at the tears swimming down his face.

He slipped the letter back into his jacket, feeling the love in it against his rapidly beating heart. "Yeah, but I needed you to know...oh God...that you helped me open my heart again. And that Kim is rooting for you and me. Things will only get easier from here."

"Will they?" she asked, searching his face. "I just read one of the most heartbreaking and brave letters imaginable after hearing you say you *love* me."

He had to grip his knees to control the trembling of his hands.

"Andy, what I feel for you is stronger than anything I've ever felt for another person. It's just... I love you so much, and you've already been through so much with Kim. I..."

When she paused, he couldn't draw in a solid breath.

"I don't want you to get hurt again. I...want to be with you, but there's so much we don't know. What happens when I leave? I mean, I don't know if I'll ever be able to take photos up to my standards again, but I *want* to keep working. To keep traveling. I don't know—"

He pressed his finger to her mouth. "I know it's hard to live with all those questions. All I can promise is that I'm here and that I love you. Don't worry about hurting me. That's the wrong perspective. Focus on loving me—for as long as you want to."

Her hands cupped his face. "Even though we just kissed for the first time, I can't imagine ever wanting to stop loving you."

As far as he was concerned, that was the only thing that mattered. "So when the questions come up—for both of us—let me hold you and kiss you and tell you that. We'll face things together."

She looked down and fiddled with the edge of his T-shirt. "And what about sex? At some point, we'll want to do that too, right? Of course we will. We love each other. Doesn't that scare you?"

This time he gulped. "It does a little. It would be another big enough step for both of us. When we end up making love, we'll talk things through. There's no need to rush anything."

The healthy adult male inside him knew what he wanted. Hot sex. Meaningful sex. It had been a long time, and yes, it would mean severing yet another connection with Kim, but it would also be a happy step forward if it was where he and Lucy decided to go. And after kissing her just now, he wanted to go there.

But he was also older and wiser. A lot was changing—in her life and between them. He wanted them both to feel comfortable and to take care with each other.

"So are we dating now?" she blurted out. "I mean, showing me Kim's letter seems to imply that and more. I mean, neither one of us is the booty-call type unless you have some really dark secrets I can't imagine, and I think I just said 'I mean' twice. I'm babbling."

"You did repeat that." He couldn't help the slow smile he gave her. "I like 'booty' as much as any guy, but that's not my thing. And please don't ever sext me while I'm at work. When Kim and I were first married, she did it as a joke, and I just happened to have my phone lying on my desk. The nurse I was talking to saw the message when my screen lit up, and she dropped a patient's file."

Holy crap. Why had he told her that?

"I'm sorry. I shouldn't be telling you stories like that."

"Like what?" she asked, tilting her head to the side. "It seems silly for you to say that after showing me her letter. Andy, you were *married*. You have stories. It's all right if you talk about Kim. You always did before."

Yeah, he had, but somehow everything had changed. "I don't...oh hell...I don't want you to ever think I'm comparing you to her. I mean—heck, now I'm saying it—I didn't want her letter to imply you're..."

"The consolation prize?" she asked in that bold-as-brass Lucy way of hers. "If you feel weird, tell me. I'm glad you showed me the letter, Andy. You never mentioned it to me before."

He hadn't been able to—not even in an email. He'd been too raw, and the words were the final ones he had from his wife. For a long time, he hadn't been ready to share them. Someday he'd show it to Danny when he was older, but not for years.

"I never want you to stop remembering Kim or your life with her," Lucy went on. "It's not just important to you, but to Danny. I only want..."

"What do you want?" he asked, so bowled over by her, by *this*, that he couldn't see straight.

She lifted her shoulder. "I only want us to be honest with each other. Like you did when you showed me the letter. This *is* weird. We've been best friends forever, and now I suddenly want to jump your bones."

He couldn't help it. He started laughing. "You want to jump my bones? Did you have to say it that way?" But then he realized why she had. Lucy O'Brien was tough, and when she was scared, she got tougher. This was uncharted territory. "How about we try calling it making love?"

And that was all it took to make tough-as-nails Lucy O'Brien squirm before his eyes.

"I mean it," he said, wanting to squirm a little himself. "We *love* each other—even if this other kind of love is new. We know almost everything there is to know about each other. And now we want to be together. When we decide to have sex, it won't just be sex. Honestly, I wouldn't want it to be. We both care too much about each other for something that simple."

"What if this whole I-want-to-kiss-your-face-off thing fades?" she asked, her eyes vulnerable. "Maybe we won't make it to sex."

"I would never have showed you that letter if I believed that," he said, and he realized it was the God's honest truth.

Because he needed the confidence building as much as she seemed to, he leaned in and kissed her again. She made a show of trying to keep reserved, but soon she was fisting her hands in his hair and opening her mouth, giving him a whole other impression of heaven on earth. This time he couldn't stop himself from running his hands down the sides of her body, and when she inched back on his lap to make space, he set those same hands to her breasts.

She moaned into his mouth, and the kiss turned wild. His tongue thrust into her mouth, and she met him stroke for stroke. She shifted in his arms until she was straddling him, and he almost lost control when he felt her core press against him.

"Okay," he said, breathing hard. "Now we'd really better slow down."

She gave him some space, thank God, but stayed close enough for him to stroke her back. "I guess we might be heading toward sex, after all," she said, gasping for air.

"Seems so," he said, smiling softly against her hair. "Would you go to dinner with me sometime soon? After all this kissing, the least I can do is take you out and show you a good time."

"So we *are* dating," she said, making a face. "This is so weird! We've hung out a million times, but this feels different."

"You didn't answer my question. Will you go?"

"If we go out together, people are going to know. Are you ready for that to happen? Maybe we should wait a while? Until we're more sure."

He shook his head. "People are already talking because that's what this town does. I would like to take you out and have some fun. What do you say?"

"Okay," she said softly. "Sounds like a plan. But you don't need to fuss and bring me flowers. I'm low-maintenance."

He was going to go the extra mile because she didn't expect it. Because he deserved it. They both did.

"What are we going to do about our families?" she asked, her mouth twisting. "They're going to know something is up."

"I'll tell them we're starting to date, but it's early so they need to leave us alone." Yeah, that would work. His mind flashed back to his earlier Sibling Sharing Time, as Matt had called it.

"Our mothers are going to be thrilled," she said, laying her head against his shoulder. "What are you going to tell Danny?"

He took a moment to gather his thoughts. "I'll tell him you're really special to me and that I like having you around a lot. And that his mom really liked you too."

Her eyes gleamed with unshed tears.

"You mentioned it before. Kinda. But you like kids, right?"

"I love them." She leaned back, smiling. "And I would never do anything to hurt him."

"That's not what I was asking," he said, his voice gruff.

"Yes, it was." Her voice was whisper-soft as she traced his brow. "It's okay. Kim will always be his mother, but I'd like to be his friend."

Okay, so it hadn't gotten easier after the kiss and showing her the letter. His ribcage felt like it was inside a trash compactor. He didn't think Danny would fully understand what it meant for him to *like* a woman other than his mother. But it still worried him.

"It will be fine," he told her, making himself smile.

"We have a lot of things to talk about," she said,

crossing her arms behind his neck.

"Good thing we've had all that practice talking," he replied, sliding his hands down her back to her hips. "There are a few areas where we still need some practice."

"Like I haven't heard that before."

"I don't mean it to be a cliché." He tugged her closer against his body again. "I'm glad you kissed me back this time, Lucy."

"Thank God for the subconscious mind," she said, laughing under her breath.

"Shut up," he replied and kissed her senseless.

# Chapter 19

Moira was nervous about her meeting with Chase Parker. Evan had shown her around the center's temporary location at Emmits Merriam University a couple days ago. The tour had made her more excited about the opportunity, but there hadn't been a single butterfly in her stomach from start to finish. Of course, she'd been on cloud nine from the happy news that her brother and Lucy were dating—the whole family was elated. Plus, Evan was funny and approachable and kind of geeky, it had turned out, once you got over the whole billionaire genius inventor thing.

Then there was Chase. Totally different ball of wax.

He was coming to town for meetings, and he'd asked to meet her at High Stakes, Chef T's fancy restaurant in the Grand Mountain Hotel, on Friday afternoon.

Moira arrived in a navy business suit, one she'd made a special trip to her apartment in Denver to pick up. The hostess immediately ushered her into a private dining room and closed the door behind her.

The man she'd researched thoroughly rose from the end of the long table where he'd been checking his phone. He was tall and ruggedly handsome—the kind of man who still wore his Wyoming rancher heritage in his broad shoulders but who'd found a way to wear the sophistication of an Italian suit with total ease.

Power radiated from him, and Moira fought with the raw awareness he generated in her. Most women found Chase Parker handsome, and she was unhappy to discover she was one of them.

"Hello, Moira," he said in a baritone voice. "I'm Chase Parker. It's nice to finally meet you. Evan has been telling me good things about you."

He didn't span the distance between them to shake her hand. Unlike Evan, who was eager and somewhat jittery, Chase was the kind of man who expected people to come to him. Moira had rather expected that.

"Mr. Parker," she responded. As she walked down the long length of the private table, her eyes fell on the copy of her resume laid out carefully by Chase's phone.

"Chase," he corrected, taking the hand she extended to him in a firm clasp.

"Thank you for flying out to meet me," she said. "I told Evan I would have been happy to visit you at headquarters. I know you're a busy man."

He gestured to the chair to his right. "Please sit. This project is important to Evan, and given the press the Artemis Institute is receiving, I want to make sure it receives the proper attention from the ground up. We're here today to see if you might be the anchor. Evan seems to think so."

She took a seat and crossed her legs. "I'm glad Evan has expressed such faith in me. Not that I'm surprised. My cousin, Jill Hale, has been working on him. Plus, we're the same age, and Evan wants the institute's director to be young and local. I fit the bill. But we both know there's more to running a center like Artemis. I hope I'll be able to persuade you that I'm up to the task."

She'd thoroughly researched Quid-Atch and concluded she wanted to be a part of a company like that, one with a global reach and vision. That she could do so in Dare Valley was a bonus. The more time she spent here, surrounded by her family, the less she liked the thought of leaving.

His mouth turned up as he settled back in his chair. "Evan said you would call a spade a spade. I'm surprised you'd bring up Jill's campaign to see you land this position."

"As a human resources director, no one is more sensitive to issues of nepotism than I am." Her bland stare did nothing to change the steady regard he gave her. "I want to be hired because I'm the best candidate for the job."

"I'm glad we can dispense with the small talk then," Chase said, tapping his finger to her resume. "You have less experience than I'd personally like to see for this position. Evan and I have a slightly different idea of the kind of director needed to successfully run the center. Most of your work has involved only human resources. I'm more convinced we need someone with more management experience."

She'd expected him to raise this concern. "With my recent employer, Peterson Engineering, I significantly widened the scope of my work. While Peterson doesn't deal with inventions per se, it does highly technical work. I had to be fluent in the jargon to be successful. I managed a staff of seven people directly and had indirect supervision over another thirty. Beyond approving staff hires, I was personally involved in the decision-making process for every senior management position."

"Including your former boss?" he asked, crossing his arms over his massive chest. "I take it she's the reason you resigned your position before you had a new offer in hand."

Since Jill had told Evan all about her bitchy boss, she'd had no choice but to paint the full picture. Evan had been sympathetic. Chase wasn't going to be that easy.

"I did everything possible to work with Taylor, but she wasn't interested in cooperating. I concluded she saw me as a threat to her position. The situation wasn't going to improve, so I decided it was in my best interest and the company's for me to call it."

"Did you recommend the company hire her when you interviewed her?" he asked, and darn it all if she wasn't impressed with his line of questioning. She would have asked the same question.

"No," she said, "I told them I was concerned she wasn't a team player. I was overruled." Their decision to hire Taylor had been a slap in the face.

"If your opinion was so valued by management, why didn't they listen to you?" he asked, turning his phone over when the screen lit up with a text.

She appreciated him giving her his full attention, although right now she felt like the circus lion being nudged about by a lion tamer.

"They didn't see what I saw," she said, going for full honesty. "Taylor acted different with me when we were alone, which didn't give me a good feeling. She didn't even agree to give me two weeks to transition my work to another staff member before I left, which is customary."

There was a knock on the door, and Chase called out, "Enter."

A server brought forward a tray with a bottle of sparkling water, two glasses filled with ice, and a bowl of lime wedges. "As you requested, Mr. Parker," the man said, setting the tray down beside them.

"Thank you," Chase said, and Moira was happy to hear him say it. Many of the senior executives she'd known felt so entitled, they'd forgotten the meaning of politeness.

"I thought we could start with some water," Chase explained as the server poured. "Of course, please order anything else to drink you'd like."

If they were going to work together, he needed to loosen up a bit. She couldn't work with such a starched shirt. "Even champagne?" she joked.

His eyes narrowed for a moment before he smiled. "As you wish. I have plenty of martini lunches in D.C. with the Defense Department. Government types never shy away from drinking when a contractor is footing the bill."

The server was patiently waiting. "I'm good with water to start, but if you could bring me an espresso, I'd be most appreciative."

After he left, she leaned forward conspiratorially. "Chef T makes really great espresso."

"Personally?" Chase asked, looking more relaxed now. "I'm surprised he's not off shooting one of his TV shows."

"He's here now, and he knows we're meeting. Chef T is connected to our larger family."

"The Hales. Your great-uncle is the legendary Arthur Hale, and everyone expects your brother, Matt, to be voted in as the new mayor this November."

"We try and tolerate their presence," she said blandly. "They're both crusaders for justice in their own ways."

He studied her. "And are you? Someone in human resources often has to right wrongs done to employees in a company. Have you ever had to fire anyone?"

"Of course," she said, sipping her water after adding a lime wedge. "If they deserve it, I keep it short and sweet. If they're being laid off, I keep a box of tissues on my desk, but I still keep it short and sweet."

"I see a pattern." His mouth quirked up, and it was hard not to notice the rugged planes of his jaw. *Fortune* hadn't airbrushed anything. "I wasn't sure what to expect after what Evan told me about you. He said you were really nice and funny."

This time she rolled her eyes. "Showing off my intelligence to an inventor wasn't really on the table. What was I supposed to do? Talk about the best way to structure a job description or create a human resources manual?"

Chase laughed, and it was one of those loud, gusty ones, which she found herself immediately liking. "Evan's eyes would have glazed over the minute you said job description. I was the one who insisted I write one for my position. If it were up to Evan, he would have just hired me and let me do whatever I wanted."

This time she was the one who laughed. "I have a feeling you probably still do whatever you want—even with a job description."

"You're right," he said, chuckling darkly. "But Evan is the boss, and I try to remember that mostly. He and I—"

"Are perfect examples of complementary leadership," she interjected. "Sorry, I got excited. I sometimes interrupt."

He took a drink of his water. "No, I'm glad you aren't one of those stiff, inflexible human resources types."

"Oh, don't mistake my good humor. If we agree on a job description, I'll follow it to the letter unless we agree on expanding the scope. And if we have a manual in place for how to run the institute—"

"You'll make sure every I is dotted and every T crossed," he said, interrupting her this time.

She traced the rim of her glass, feeling the mist from the water's bubbles on her finger. "I understand the importance of compliance, especially in a high-security facility housing people's inventions. I wouldn't be laissez-faire about that. Dare Valley might be a small town, but intellectual property theft is still possible. We don't want someone walking in off the streets to steal some head-in-the-clouds inventor's prize project."

Chase lifted his glass and saluted her. "I'm glad you understand that. One thing Evan and I have always agreed on is the need to protect his inventions."

"It's important to protect everything from the ideas and the prototypes to the final inventions," she said. "Evan explained the invention process to me in great detail. I assume you'll have visitor and press protocols in place as well."

He nodded. "Yes. Evan and I are still discussing the security protocols. He wants the institute to have an open and creative energy, but he recognizes most inventors are pretty tight-lipped about their projects. We've agreed to have low-profile guards and special access-only rooms beyond the high-tech security system I've finalized with our current provider."

"But there's also the danger that students might try and steal each other's ideas *within* the institute," she said, shaking her head. "Not everyone is ethical. We could create an ethical protocol and provide mandatory training for everyone in the institute."

"I'm trying to persuade Evan to go a step further and make them sign a legally binding agreement about the use of their work and collaboration within the center."

Moira had a hard time imagining Evan going for that idea, which would essentially give the institute an opportunity for legal action in the event of a breach of contract. "It's a tough spot to be in, isn't it? The institute's inventors won't technically be employees, but they'll be doing important work that needs to be protected. You also don't want anyone to use the institute's resources to invent some new form of a chemical weapon."

Chase set his glass down. "No, we don't. Not all inventions are for the good of the world. Evan doesn't like to sit in judgment over people's ideas, but as an institute, we have a responsibility to ensure no harm is done."

Moira uncrossed her legs and leaned forward. "It's going to be an exciting give and take, especially in the beginning. Selecting people worthy of using the institute is going to be—"

"A pain in the ass," Chase said, scowling now. "Evan doesn't agree on the need for background checks in applicants."

"Well, that's just crazy! Of course you need to do background checks. You can't let any Tom, Dick, or Harry into a place like this and give them access to the resources and support the institute plans to provide."

He took a drink of his water, studying her over the rim of the glass. "I'm glad we agree on that."

She could only imagine the power struggle that would erupt between Chase and anyone who stood in his way. Surely this was a man who was used to getting his way. "While we're talking about agreements, I would need it to be clearer who I report to directly. Evan clearly will have a role as the creative genius behind the institute, and it sounds like he plans to work with inventors on their projects from time to time."

Chase sighed, running his hand through his dark hair. "I'm dreading that part. I told Evan his first priority has to be to inventing for Quid-Atch, but he gets distracted by good ideas. It's what makes him brilliant. Plus, he always geeks out with other inventors. So far, I've only witnessed this with Rajan Singh, the head of our R&D, and our team, but with this extra influx of people..."

"He's going to be in inventing heaven," she finished for him, smiling wryly. "He might have mentioned it."

"You're smart to ask who you'd report to," Chase said, casting a glance at her resume. "But it won't be so clear-cut. Evan will be the creative mastermind, as you said. Plus, he lives here now. He'll want to do things we technically aren't supposed to do. That's why I'm going to be involved. Evan and I have been engaged in the battle between invention and management since we first met."

She'd suspected that tension going into the interview. "I don't want to be caught in the middle. I'm not eager for a lose-lose situation here, especially since it involves me relocating back to Dare Valley."

Chase added another lime to his water. "I can't promise easy waters every time, but Evan and I always figure out an agreement in the end. I don't expect you to be a party to that."

"If I were offered the job," she said, looking him squarely in the eye, "I'd want there to be an agreement upfront about that."

"There are always scenarios we can't foresee," Chase said, waving his hand. "Look at me. I'm sitting in Dare Valley, talking with you about a job at a new invention institute. Trust me, even though Evan's like a brother to me, I didn't see this coming. But we adapt. Evan *is* a genius and a visionary, don't get me wrong. But he sometimes needs people to help him think through his plans in terms of practicality and budget."

"Visionaries aren't always the best managers," she said, thinking back to one of her first bosses, who could rally a board of directors but lacked the strategic ability to lead the company into a new market.

"I also won't be here 24/7," Chase said. "I need someone who has a good head on her shoulders who can handle such issues on an ongoing basis."

"You need someone who will keep the ship running, keep you informed, and keep the institute's burgeoning reputation intact."

"Exactly," he said as another knock sounded on the door. "Your espresso, I presume. Enter."

The server came in carrying her coffee. Chef T had certainly had a hand in making it—he knew her preferences, and there was a small jar of honey with a silver spoon on the saucer instead of brown sugar.

"You take your espresso with honey?" Chase asked. "That's very Italian of you."

She raised her brows. "What can I say? When it comes to some things, the Italians know best." She refrained from mentioning the fine cut of his suit, but the unbidden thought prompted another issue they hadn't discussed. "Beyond the ethics protocol and training, I hope you plan on including sexual harassment protocols and training. I'm not sure how many female inventors will be selected, but it's important to make sure inventors with less than ideal people skills understand the law."

She added her honey to her espresso and took a sip. Heaven.

"That's serious human resource talk," Chase said, "but I like it. Evan didn't have good people skills in the beginning either, but he's grown up. I expect we'll be dealing with some inventors who have them and others who don't. Inventors run a wide swath, I've discovered. And as for female applicants, I can say from our experience with Quid-Atch that there's not near enough of them involved. Our R&D team is composed of mostly men since they still dominate the math, science, and engineering fields."

"Unlike human resources, which boasts nearly all female employees," she said, making a face. "Hopefully more balance will be achieved over time."

"Agreed," Chase said. "Let's order some lunch. I have some questions to ask you about your background."

As Moira looked into the shrewd eyes of Quid-Atch's chief financial officer, she knew she had a ways to go before she convinced him she was the best candidate for the job.

But she had no doubt she would.

# Chapter 20

Lucy's first photo shoot happily landed on the day when she'd awoken to discover the vision in her right eye marginally improved. It had only taken a couple weeks, thank God. When she closed her left one, she was able to make out the painter's signature in the corner of the fake Monet hanging on the wall in her bedroom in Merry Cottage. Her doctor's words about psychosomatic changes echoed in her ears, but she decided not to look a gift horse in the mouth.

She'd immediately grabbed her phone from her bedside. Her mom had already sent her a text. Shocker.

*Are you sure I can't come for the photo shoot? I promise I won't be in the way.*

Lucy thought about screaming her frustration into a pillow, but decided not to waste the energy.

*Mom, we talked about this. I'm working with the volunteers individually. People do better with less distractions. Talk to you later. Love you.*

She hoped that would satisfy her for the moment. That woman was like a dog with a bone when it came to the calendar. And her hounding hadn't stopped just because Lucy had agreed to do things her way.

Well, she wasn't going to let her mom dim her

happiness over the improvement in her vision, so she texted the one person she knew would be thrilled. Well, he was the only one who knew, besides Tanner, who was basically a vault, but...

*Hey, Andy Cakes! My vision suddenly seems marginally better. I can make out some finer details. Stay tuned. Oh, and thanks for a wonderful time last night. Dinner out with you and Danny was wonderful. Have a great morning.*

Clutching her phone to her chest, she focused on the scarves on the brass footboard. She still couldn't make out the differences between the two red ones, she discovered, when she closed her good eye, or the deeper mustard yellow from the sunshine scarf next to it.

She'd focus on the progress. That's what she wanted, after all.

Certainly there had been progress in her relationship with Andy. They'd fallen into the dating thing pretty easily over the past couple of weeks, thrilling their families. They'd had years of experience talking, hanging out, and laughing together, so that aspect of their relationship felt as natural as breathing.

Then there was the new joy of watching each other while thinking of getting the other person naked—or so Lucy liked to joke to herself. And the touching and kissing? The man had skills there, and if it ever got awkward, like it did the first time he took her bra off last week, they knew how to defuse the weirdness with laughter. Both of them had busted up laughing at her joke about him finally making it to second base. But then they'd quickly discovered second base wasn't going to satisfy them.

Her phone buzzed. *That's great. Let me know if Dr. Davidson wants to see you, and I can take off. I had a good night too. Gotta run. Rufus just barfed, and Danny won't put his pants on. If you don't hear from me in a few hours, I've run away to Bali.*

An irrepressible smile spread across her face. He always made her smile. Laughter was the best medicine, he'd say, and he wasn't kidding. Her spirits were better. Classes were going well. She was grading her first photos of road kill, discovering she had no trouble whatsoever judging their technique or composition.

But she hadn't taken any more pictures herself. Not until today. She'd been hoping her vision would miraculously correct itself, so she wouldn't have to learn a new way. At least her vision was back to the condition it had been in before her fight with her mother. Would it improve a little more with time? God, she hoped so, but she couldn't wait any longer to take the photos for the calendar. Her mother had made that clear.

Another text came in. *Good luck capturing Jill's maracas. Please don't feel like you need to share the details. I've been scarred enough today between my dog and kid. Call me if you need me.*

The last part of his message made her heart clench. They didn't focus on the problems with her vision, but they didn't dance around them either. A couple of nights ago, while they were sitting on the couch after Danny had gone to sleep, he'd asked her to describe what her vision looked like now. In halting terms, she'd tried to explain it, and afterwards, he'd held her quietly until she finally made herself drive home.

As she dressed, she decided to call Dr. Davidson to tell him the news. Though she dreaded that he might tell her she was imagining it, making the call was the right thing to do. The phone call was brief because the doctor was in the car on the way to the hospital, but he agreed that her news was encouraging. Afterwards, she drove over to The Grand Mountain Hotel to face her demons.

She'd already checked out the media room Chef T had volunteered for today's shoot. It was equipped with the kind of state-of-the-art equipment Lucy never had in the field, taking photos for humanitarian organizations' calendars and the like. Yet her work hadn't suffered for it.

Once again, the volunteers had agreed to draw names to establish the shooting order, and it was Lucy's luck to begin with Jill. She was grateful her mother's name had been drawn last, although that meant her mother had more time to shop for a headdress worthy of Cleopatra.

When Lucy entered the hotel's fancy lobby, Jill met her in a surprisingly conservative white blouse and navy shirt, in keeping with the hotel's elegant ambiance.

"Are you ready, Lucy?" the quirky redhead asked, practically bouncing in her pink ballet slippers, the only nod to her away-from-work style. "Just to get Chef T's goat, I threatened to show up in his kitchen with only my fruit hat on. He took the day off out of fear. Coward. Since he deprived me of my fun, I asked Moira and Natalie to come and drink mimosas with us. I hope that's okay. Your mother really wanted to watch, but I told her I'd like to keep it to us girls."

So her mom had gone around her, looking for Jill's permission to be there since she didn't have Lucy's. Lovely. But even though Jill had denied her request, thank God, Lucy wasn't off scot-free. Moira was going to be a problem. She was probably going to ask her a bunch of photography questions and notice if she made any mistakes. Great. Like she wasn't already nervous enough.

Lucy had never taken photos while drinking a mimosa in her life, but heck, it sounded pretty good about now.

"No mothers," Lucy said as Jill put an arm around her tense shoulders and led her up the hotel's wide staircase to the office area where the media room was located. "I figured you probably needed some space for your first photo shoot."

"You too, Lucy," Jill said. "We all know this isn't

your normal. I hope it at least can be fun for you."

Was Jill being all sweet and sensitive now? Lucy almost didn't know how to take that. Had Andy said something to her? No, he wouldn't have. "Am I that obvious?" It wouldn't hurt for the volunteers to think she was nervous because this wasn't her usual subject matter.

"Yep," Jill said, shaking her playfully. "But we'll get through this together. Brian says my *maracas* are pretty inspiring."

*Oh, good Lord, here we go.* "I'm not sure I'll be able to handle that much inspiration, Jill."

Snickering, she replied, "That's what he says."

"You're so bad," Lucy said as they made their way down the hallway.

When they entered the media room, Natalie and Moira lifted their glasses in salute.

"Welcome to the Fun House," Natalie said, pointing to Jill's hat in the center of the small coffee table.

To say it was a mere sombrero covered in fake fruit would have been an insult to every cross-dressing *caballero*. Jill hadn't selected only tasteful fruits like cherries and apples. No, she'd stuck four bananas, partially raised, in the shape of... Well, any idiot could tell.

"I don't think I've ever seen anything like it." Truthfully, she hoped she never would again.

"I made it myself!" Jill said, linking their arms together and leading her over to the cushioned benches in front of the coffee table. "I didn't like the ones online, and Brian joked that since I was bitching about the selection so much, I should just make one."

"He now regrets that decision, I bet," Moira said, chuckling with Natalie.

"How many mimosas have you two already had?" Lucy asked, shaking her head. This photo shoot covered a lot of firsts for her—it was starting to look like it would be her first tipsy shoot too.

"Moira's only had one," Natalie said, biting her lip. "She can't hold her liquor."

"I really can't," Moira said, putting her finger to her nose like Doris Day in *Pillow Talk*. "You're not much better with your Natalie shows."

"That takes a lot—"

"Let's get started, shall we?" Lucy said, interrupting Natalie. "Jill, I thought we should start off by talking about who you're dedicating your month to. You didn't say at the volunteer party. Is it your grandma?"

"Yep," her cousin said, shucking off her pants without so much as a what-for. "If Grandma Harriet were alive, she'd think this calendar a hoot. She would have loved my hat."

Lucy blinked as Jill threw her pants in the corner. Natalie hooted. Moira hiccupped, which might turn out to be a blessing in disguise. Lucy had thought she would have to make Jill comfortable. She should have known better. When her top flew off, Lucy covered her eyes.

"Do you mind?" she asked. "I haven't had a mimosa yet."

They must have thought she was joking because they all guffawed. But before she could blink, Natalie pressed a glass into her hand. She looked at it and thought, what the hell, and downed half the contents.

"This is going to be so much fun," Moira said. "Part of me wants to see you shoot photos of Mom too, but the other part..."

"We might be scarred for life," Natalie said, "although I have half a mind to send the photos to Dad anonymously at the hospital."

"That would be the day," Moira breathed out. "Our dad's turned into a real prick, in case Andy didn't tell you."

She cleared her throat. "He's mentioned it."

Setting her mimosa down on the table, Lucy

unpacked the soft yellow drape she'd chosen for the shoot. She'd thought a uniform color would work best for the calendar, despite what she'd originally told the volunteers about using different settings. Andy had assured her the background she'd chosen was lovely.

While her mother hadn't initially been on board with a uniform setting, she'd relented after Lucy had explained it in technical terms that had made Ellen's eyes glaze over in a minute. Besides, she'd agreed that they wanted to keep the focus on the subjects, not what was behind them.

Lucy hung the drape on the center background wall and checked the lighting she'd set up the day before. The dressing bench she'd selected from her mother's bedroom was already situated in front of the drape. Some people were going to sit, she expected, while others would stand. Lucy would have to see what worked best.

This wasn't anything like her usual process for shooting a calendar. Normally she created a story with her photos, building on the theme of the project, strengthening the emotion in each of the images. This time, her subjects had already chosen their months and their themes. All she could do was try and make it look as visually appealing as possible.

"Do you need some help?" Moira asked as she was turning on the strobes. "I know I only dabble, but I love photography."

*Oh brother, here we go.*

"It's more than dabbling, Lucy," Natalie said. "Moira is pretty darn good. She took one of the best pictures of Blake and me at our first wedding."

"I know it won't surprise you, but I wanted to be here today to watch you work." She gave a slight shrug. "I know Andy said to give you time to settle, but I still...really want to see how you do what you do. I promise to contain my enthusiasm. I hope that doesn't make you uncomfortable."

Actually, her interest made Lucy's stomach roll even more. "I'm not uncomfortable," she lied. "Are you going to have another mimosa?"

"I'd better stop, or I won't be able to watch you work your magic." Moira gave her an encouraging smile.

*That's why I suggested it.* "Jill, do you have a robe or something?" Turning, she realized Jill was drinking her mimosa in her birthday suit. "Seriously, Jill. You could have at least kept your panties on. I'm not taking any pictures south of the border."

Jill gave her a smoky glance and walked toward her. "All right, Mr. DeMille, I'm ready for my close-up," she purred like Gloria Swanson herself.

"Oh, good Lord," Natalie said, reaching down and throwing Jill's shirt at her. "Put something on, for the love of Pete."

"We're all girls here," Jill said, picking up her red-and-green-striped maracas and shaking them madly.

Moira snorted out a laugh.

"Don't encourage her," Lucy said in exasperation.

Nothing felt like it was under her control. Here she was taking photos of entirely naked people—so not her thing—being watched by her own peanut gallery. *These* were the conditions in which she was supposed to relearn her art. To top it all off, she would never hear the end of it when her colleagues got wind of her involvement in this calendar. She wouldn't be surprised if a few of them suggested that she follow it up with a study of monkeys wearing top hats.

"You've turned green," Moira said. "Is it the nudity or the harsh realization that you're not doing your normal calendar?"

Now that made her laugh. "Both. All right, let's get this done."

Jill fitted her garish hat on her head and picked up the maracas. Equipped with her props, she arranged herself on the bench, stretching out, of course.

Lucy unzipped the case of her new camera, her fingers trembling as she picked up the Leica SL, the company's first 35 mm format digital camera with an electronic view finder. She'd bought it last week after concluding she had to learn to use an EVF in case her vision didn't improve enough for her to return to her old way of taking photos.

All she had to do was look at the small view finder and click the button. It couldn't be that hard, right?

She'd stayed in the Leica family both because their cameras were the best on the market and because she knew their lenses in and out. Until this new model emerged, none of the electronic view finders on the market had been equipped to handle the kind of high-subject contrast she needed in the field. Even so, she hoped the viewing contrast issue wouldn't drive her nuts. This model's view finder supposedly refreshed fast enough for her to shoot on the fly and see the images she was taking with minimal blur.

"I'm surprised you use an EVF," Moira said.

Lucy's belly quivered. Moira had already noticed something was off, and she'd barely started.

"I have a lot of cameras. I thought an indoor shoot might be easier with an EVF." God, she hoped so. Sizing up a shot using a view finder was going to feel weird at first. She would have to pray she had enough courage and skill to adapt.

"Can I hold it a sec?" Moira asked, stepping closer. "I've never seen one of these babies in person. I have a Nikon. I'm sorry. I know I said I was only going to watch."

"Hey!" Jill called. "I'm getting cold over here."

"Maybe later," Lucy said, walking over to her subject, thankful for the reprieve. "Jill, you're not Rose in *Titanic*. For heaven's sake, would you sit up a minute? And can we lose the maracas please?"

She handed them to Moira with a scowl. "I ordered these special from Mexico."

"*Lo siento,*" Lucy replied automatically in Spanish. "Sorry. They're not right for what I have in mind. Take the hat off and put them over your…natural maracas. The fruit is casting weird shadows on your face."

"Man, you're bossy," Jill said, slapping the hat to her chest. "I'm only following your orders because you know what you're doing."

Her red hair shifted over her shoulder as she flung it back, and suddenly Lucy saw it. The perfect pose.

"Wait! Stay there." She grabbed the hat Jill was holding and arranged it so it covered the rim of her nipples, showing off Jill's ample cleavage. "Tuck your legs up a little on the bench. Like you're spooning."

The hat's curves blended into Jill's curves, creating a pleasing feminine line.

"Nice," Moira said, earning her a glare from Jill.

"What's nice?" her subject asked. "I don't understand."

"Let Lucy do her thing, Jill," Moira said, giving her space. "Girlfriend is in the zone."

Andy's sister's keen interest made her palms sweat, but the compliment did raise her spirits some. She still had it: the ability to size up the perfect shot. Despite the ease with which she'd graded her students' shots, she'd wondered.

"Put your head on your hand. Elbow here. Now turn and face me."

"I've never seen you this intense," Jill mumbled.

Because Lucy was falling back into herself, becoming once more the artist who could capture a special moment of time for eternity. She felt complete again, like she had her purpose back. She wanted to jump around and shout "Hallelujah."

Shifting the camera in her hands, she rubbed her palms on her thighs. All she had to do was capture the image. Trying not to notice how bulky and unfamiliar the Leica felt in her hands, she pointed the camera at Jill. The view finder was alien. She knew it was against the rules, but she closed her right eye first to see the finder more clearly. Well, Dr. Davidson could write an X on her chart. Seeing her subject in that tiny window felt downright unnatural.

When Lucy put her right eye to her old Leicas, she felt like she was part of the scene. Now she felt an unnatural fissure between her and the scene she wanted to capture. She pressed the camera to her chest for a moment, trying to connect it to herself. Make it a part of her.

"Are you okay?" Moira asked, peering at her curiously.

"Yep," she replied crisply. "Just a little ritual I do." What a lie. Like she'd ever had the time in her normal job to take a moment and pray.

"Interesting," Moira replied, and Lucy had to bite her tongue to keep from telling her she was in the way.

Because right now, Lucy felt like she was in Moira's internal view finder and the woman was seeing all sorts of things Lucy would rather not have exposed to the light. Andy had been right to keep his sister at bay. She'd have to thank him later.

*Just start taking the pictures*, she told herself, struggling with the new process. She focused on the view finder, moving around Jill, pressing the shutter again and again. The little window made it harder for her to see if she was capturing what she wanted. So she just kept on shooting. Surely there would be a winner in the lot. She had to trust herself.

Her gaze volleyed between her subject and that tiny view finder like a tennis ball being bandied across the net. But her brain was having a hard time zooming in and out on the scene.

"Tell me something I don't know about your

grandma," she told Jill. "Something special."

A shadow crossed her face before she smiled, one of those glowing smiles only a rare love could generate. Lucy pressed the shutter.

"One time I broke one of her champagne glasses in two," Jill said, shifting a little more on the bench than Lucy would have liked. "I'd taken it out of her china cabinet to use for my tea party. I wanted to have champagne and not tea because I saw the adults drink it after Grandpa won another Pulitzer. It looked more fun."

The story was as magical as her expression, and Lucy sank to her knees to capture her face. Jill's eyes widened at her unexpected closeness.

"So you broke the glass," Lucy said, looking back and forth between her subject and the view finder.

"Right," Jill said, falling back into the memory. "Grandma caught me trying to bury it in her backyard. I knew someone would find it if I put it in the trash. All she did was take her gardening trowel from my hands and wink at me, saying she'd never liked those champagne glasses much anyway. She picked up the pieces and led me inside. After throwing them in the garbage, she washed my hands and poured orange juice for us in two champagne glasses. We drank them at my small table with my dolls."

"Oh, that's so freaking sweet," Natalie cooed. "No wonder you like mimosas."

"I hadn't really put that together," Jill said, tears filling her eyes.

Lucy captured the shock on the woman's face, thinking yet again about the power of the subconscious mind. Andy would love this story when she saw him later.

"It seems fitting that you drank one before taking these photos to honor Aunt Harriet," Moira said, still a little too close for Lucy's peace of mind.

"I miss her sometimes," Jill said, her tears falling now. "She never got to see Violet or Mia."

Lucy continued to take the photos, each image telling the story of the woman's love for a grandmother now gone.

"She would have loved them," Natalie said, and she sounded closer, making Lucy wonder if she was standing next to her sister now.

"Yeah, she would have," Jill said, brushing away the tears on her face. "I'm so sorry, Lucy. I'm a mess. Please don't take my picture like this."

She lowered her camera and smiled at Jill. "You've never been more beautiful or real, and there's nothing wrong with showing it."

Jill gave her a watery smile, and Lucy resumed. After taking what seemed like a hundred shots, she finally called it.

"I think we have a winner somewhere in here," she said, setting the Leica on a table. "You can sit up now, Jill, but please, for the love of Pete, keep the hat where it is."

That made everyone laugh, diffusing the lingering emotion in the room.

Jill set her hat aside, more somber now, and slipped on her underwear and her shirt. Crossing to Lucy, she pulled her into a hug.

"Whoa," Lucy said, returning the embrace.

"Thanks, Lucy. I didn't expect it, but I felt Grandma here."

Goosebumps broke out all over Lucy's body. "When Violet and Mia start having tea parties, you'll have to dig out those champagne glasses one day and fill them with orange juice."

"Aunt Harriet would love that," Natalie said. Jill released Lucy and bounded over to hug her cousins.

"Once I check out the photos," Lucy said, "I'll send you the one I think is the best."

Right now, there was a peace inside her fostered by the certainty that among the trove of photos she'd taken, there would be a photograph worthy of her pride. Besides, she could run it by Andy. He didn't have a professional's eye, but he would tell her what he saw.

"I can't wait to see what you choose," Jill said, her face glowing.

"Me too," Moira said enthusiastically. "There were a few moments there where I knew you had the perfect shot. You know, the kind you feel in your gut."

Yeah, Lucy knew that feeling. She thrived on it. "Thank you for saying that." And she meant it.

"It was great to see you in action," Moira said, "although this is probably pretty tame compared to what you're used to."

"It's fine," she said, not feeling as sad as she might have before. Taking photos again—even like the ones today—had restored a part of her soul to her.

"This really is the best idea ever," Jill said, prancing about, swinging her pants in the air. "And now it's official. I'm a calendar girl. Oh, Brian is going to be a happy man tonight."

Natalie laughed, and Moira slapped her hands over her ears, singing, "La-la-la-la," like that would stop Jill.

Lucy simply stood there, feeling more grounded, more settled inside herself. Things might not be perfect, but they were looking up.

And that was something to be grateful for.

# Chapter 21

When Lucy opened the door of Merry Cottage and flung herself into his arms, Andy clutched her to him. Her enthusiasm had all the force of a runaway train.

"I got through it," she said, laughing. "I took photos again! And it felt terrific."

The sound of her laughter made his heart feel funny. Being with Lucy pretty much made it feel that way all the time. He cuddled her closer, happy she was happy. And then his mind had to intrude.

*She's going to leave you.*

He told that thought to go to hell and focused on her, how her body was pressed against him, how her arms were squeezing him. She was here now, and he didn't want to start missing her before she was gone. "That's great, babe. I'm so happy for you!"

"Babe?" she said, pushing away from him. "Do I have a new nickname now?"

His ears started to burn. "Maybe. Is it too soon?" Shit. Now he was being a moron. "Do you like it?" He couldn't stop talking. "Lucy, I—"

She pressed her mouth to his, silencing him, thank God. Her hands slid up his back in the most arousing caress, and he reminded himself how lucky he was to have her. Even if it was only for a while. She was everything good in the world, and each day they spent together, the sun seemed to shine a little brighter.

Her tongue traced his lips, and he was lost. He groaned as he tightened his hold on her, not caring that they were standing in the doorway of her cottage. It wasn't like anyone could see them all the way up here. The cool fall air felt delicious against his fast-heating skin, and it was a pleasure to be with her out here with millions of stars over their heads.

She hummed as they kissed, inflaming his blood. God, he wanted her. Was greedy for her.

Her phone buzzed in her pocket, and he edged back. "Do you need to take that?"

"No," she said, breathing hard. "It's probably my mother again. She's been nagging me to see the photos I took of Jill today."

"How about I distract you?" he asked, seeing the shadows reappear in her eyes.

Their mouths met again, and a flash of heat rocked through him when he felt her tongue tease his bottom lip. He picked up her slim body, stepped inside, and slammed the door behind them. Suddenly, he couldn't control himself. She wrapped her legs around him, making him groan like a caveman as he walked through her house. He knew where he was going. When he reached her bedroom, he laid her down on that girly princess bed and lowered himself beside her.

All he wanted was to touch her skin, and so he tugged her blue shirt over her head and then freed himself of his own. He brought her against his chest, loving the feel of her lacy turquoise bra rubbing against his skin, teasing him with the soft, enticing flesh they encased.

She pulled back, panting. "Are we really doing this?"

Her bold question doused some of his fire. "I got a little carried away. I want you like crazy." Feeling it felt great. Saying it made him a little uncomfortable. "But it's a big step. I don't want our first time to be an unplanned tumble."

With each happy moment with Lucy, he felt like his memories with Kim receded further into his subconscious—that same subconscious that had caused him to kiss Lucy in the first place. It was all so confusing.

"You're thinking again," Lucy said, letting him go and sitting cross-legged on the bed. She pulled her shirt on and handed him his.

He looked at it and shook his head, struggling to swallow his messy emotions.

After he put on the shirt, she took his hand. "It's okay. We both got carried away. When you brought me back here, I thought…"

"I wasn't thinking," he said, pressing a hand to his forehead. "And I should have. You deserve better than that. I'm sorry."

"Stop!" she said, rising on her knees and facing him. "There's nothing to be sorry about. We want each other. Bodies are always ahead of brains."

He snorted. "That just about sums it up, but we're not ruled by our bodies. Lucy, do you want to make love with me? After today, you might be…" He broke off, unable to finish the thought. They were getting into dangerous territory here.

"Oh," she said, sitting back on her heels. "You think I'm going to pack my bags and head off because I had one good day of shooting photos? Pfft."

"*Pfft?*" he repeated. "What kind of answer is that?"

She scooted closer, making the bed squeak. "Andy, I'm happy because my first photo shoot wasn't a complete disaster, and even though I still think they're weird, I managed to use a camera with an EVF with your sister watching my every move. I might not have selected the best image yet, but that's pretty much a miracle. But if you think I'm comfortable using it, you're crazy. Besides, it's not like I could use it overseas. Well, I could, but it's louder than my babies, and I can't imagine trying to use it in a battle or a street protest. For a controlled studio setting, it's fine, but... You look lost."

"I am," he said honestly. "You lost me with EVF."

She explained that and a whole lot more, and he nodded because he understood most of it. Then she launched into a description of various camera models, making his eyes cross.

"Are you still listening, or have you zoned out?" she abruptly asked.

He tugged on his ear. "I hear words, but it's like you're speaking camera Klingon."

"Funny," she said, crossing her arms tight over her chest. "So, back to the whole sex thing. I want to do it finally. I think. Wait a minute. Yep, I'm pretty sure."

He found himself smiling despite himself. "Well, that's a ringing endorsement if I've ever heard one."

She moved like quicksilver, pushing him onto his back and crawling on top of him. "Is this better? *I want you. Only you. All of you.*"

While her throaty voice suggested she was putting him on, he found it terribly arousing. "Are we back to joking about this? Lucy, we need to be serious. Consider the implications. Heck, we haven't talked about sex histories and birth control yet." He'd waited to bring it up, wanting to allow things to deepen between them.

She blinked, and he knew he had her attention.

"I can get a blood test if you need it," he said, "but I can assure you I'm clean."

"I can show you my last TB test," she said, shoving his shoulder playfully. "Andy, you're taking all the fun out of this."

"And you're trying to make it too simple," he said, cupping her chin. "I still don't know how you figured it out when I lost my virginity freshman year of college, but I think you know...oh, shit...I've never been a player."

"I know," she said, all serious now. "I'm not making fun of you. I'm only trying to get us through this awkward conversation."

He studied her. There was extra color on her cheeks, he realized. "You're embarrassed? Funny, I didn't expect that."

She shoved him. Harder this time. "Why not? It's not like I'm promiscuous. Did you think I was?"

He ran his tongue over his cheek. "No. Other than our talk a couple of weeks ago, you've never really discussed guys with me."

"It's not like you wanted to talk about girls with me either. I only figured out you'd lost your virginity because I know you so well."

"And you poked at me pretty bad that day," he said, remembering how angsty he'd felt after ending their phone conversation. "Part of me had hoped you might be a little jealous. It's hard for me to say that."

She was silent for a long moment. "I was. It's hard for me to admit that."

There was a tug in his heart. "There's a part of me that feels rather vindicated right now."

"Good," she said dryly. "So let's finish up the stroll down sex lane. I lost mine not long after you lost yours, to an English major who loved photography. His name was Hugh, and he was okay, I suppose. He wrote me a poem, which was kinda sweet."

Hearing her talk about her past was making his diaphragm tight. "Was it a good poem?" he asked, pitching his tone to give it a double meaning.

"It was terrible," she said, shaking her head. "There were a few other guys in college. Interesting ones. I like interesting. And then I went overseas and there were a few more—like the agriculturalist I told you about—but I had to be more careful. The communities I worked in didn't respect women who slept with men who weren't their husbands. I...wanted to maintain my reputation and honor their feelings. But there were certain ways to engage in a romantic relationship without major consequences."

As he listened, he realized there was so much about her time overseas that he didn't know about.

"Some of my female colleagues recommended going on the Pill in case I got raped," she continued, distant now as she remembered. "Some also suggested I wear a wedding ring and pretend I was married so I would get hassled less, but I couldn't do that either."

"Good Lord, Lucy," he said, sitting back in shock. "I had no idea you had to deal with things like that. No woman should."

"It was part of the life I'd chosen," she said matter-of-factly. "I never had unprotected sex with anyone. Even if they said they were clean. There are too many expats who have sex with locals. It's not like I suspected my boyfriends would cheat on me, but I didn't want to risk getting AIDS either."

Right. AIDS. The disease that especially plagued some of the African countries where she'd worked. "Can you come here?"

Her eyes came back to him. "What?"

"I need to hold you for a minute," he said, his chest feeling tight with the realization of all the danger she'd been in.

She rested her head on his shoulder when he wrapped his arms around her. "It's fine. But I didn't love them. I cared...in my own way, and there was always kindness and respect."

But they would have more than that. "You know I love you, right? That being with me isn't going to be that simple." Not after Kim, who had shown him how beautiful sex could be.

"You never were one to settle for half measures," she

said softly, tracing his chest.

"Neither are you," he answered, sweeping his hand up and down her back in a soothing motion.

"I can't promise what the future will hold, Andy. I'm just not sure yet. If that bothers you, maybe we shouldn't have sex. I...dammit, I don't want to hurt you."

She didn't include herself, but he knew she could be hurt too, and that it worried her. "I want to make love with you, and...I'd rather do it without any barriers between us. Would you be willing to go on the Pill? That is, if you're not already."

Silence hung heavy in the air.

"I'm not right now," she said, trying to inject a trace of humor in her voice, but it fell flat. "I have heard it's nicer that way. But it will take a month to become fully effective, as you know."

"We can use condoms until then," he said, setting her back from him so he could look into her eyes. "And it is better without them. But it's going to be magical either way, Lucy. That I can promise you."

She cocked her eyebrow. "How can you tell? Do you have some magic sex crystal ball?"

Refusing to be baited, he brought her hand to his heart. If he had to be the one to put it out there, he would. "I love you. I want you. Making love with you couldn't be anything but magical."

This time an anguished breath crested out, telling him she couldn't hold back the emotion rising inside her. "I love you too. I'm just...a little scared. Don't laugh."

His heart rolled over. "I know. Lucy, trust me. It's going to be okay. And it's not going to keep you from making your own decisions about the future or taking the photos you love." He loved her too much not to say it, especially after seeing the joy she'd felt after today's photo shoot.

"I don't mean to hurt you," she said, wrapping her arms around him. "My career is who I am."

He wasn't sure of that anymore. She'd always been Lucy to him, not some famous photographer. But she wasn't ready to hear that yet.

"I want you to be who you are," he said, kissing her softly on the lips. "You're the one I love. You're the one I want. Even if I am afraid of what will happen between us if you leave."

She startled against his mouth, and he could hear her wondering whether he was talking about the long-term again, and perhaps he was. They were so good together, and she got along so well with Danny. And while he wasn't sure where things were going, he was close to being sure about where he wanted them to go. Real close.

"Blake has a cabin in Vail," Andy said, forging ahead as she sat back. "I thought it might be nice for us to get away for the weekend. I want our first time to be special, and this way, I can wake up with you and give you my full attention all weekend. I've never spent two nights apart from Danny since Kim died, and I think it's time."

While she was trying to disguise the exaggerated cadence of her breath, it was unmistakable. "Are you sure you're okay with leaving him like that? I know it's a big step for you."

It was a big step, but he'd realized it was the healthy thing to do. "It's not like he won't have a blast with his aunts and uncles or my mother. Since Kim died, I might have gotten overly...ah...attentive to him. It was a lot of pressure at first, worrying about being a father and mother to him. But he's fine, and I need to have my own life outside of being a father and a doctor. I'm more than that."

She looked down suddenly.

"I wasn't talking about you," he said, but he felt like he might have been. A little.

"All right," she said with a no-nonsense nod. "I'll make a doctor's appointment this week and get tested and...go on the Pill. Will you...ah...buy the condoms?"

He nodded. His relief was tremendous. If she was taking this step, she was still committed to exploring this blossoming thing between them. "If you know you have a clean bill of health, you don't have to worry about the tests."

"It's important to you," she said evenly, "and it's easy enough to do when I go in."

Silence hovered between them.

"So...we're really doing this finally," she said. "Lucy O'Brien is going to get it on with Andy Hale."

Her teasing was starting to annoy him, but he told himself to be patient. She was still scared of what was happening between them, and if he were being honest, so was he.

He made his mouth curve. "Seems so," he said.

# Chapter 22

Blake's cabin in Vail, which showcased stunning vistas of the mountains and the changing leaves of fall, was the warmest, most welcoming cocoon of a place Lucy had ever been in. Western blankets decorated with buffalos and Native American designs were slung over the arms of comfy leather couches. Everywhere there was shining honey-colored wood. Lucy plopped down on the couch cushions as Andy hauled in the luggage, something he'd insisted on doing without her help. It wasn't like she had much more than a duffle, so she'd let him make the gesture. As a world traveler, she'd always packed light.

The high ceilings caught her eye, and she stared up at the light pouring in from the windows. In the past week, she'd had two doctor appointments. One with Dr. Davidson, who said the increased clarity of her vision in her right eye was encouraging. Of course, her color vision had not improved, which still worried her, but there was nothing either of them could do about that.

The second appointment had addressed the change she and Andy were about to make to their relationship. She hadn't been with many men, but most of her interactions had been spontaneous. Some had been fun while others had generated from loneliness or despair.

She might joke about them doing the horizontal mambo, but it was mostly a show of bravado. Deep down she was afraid having sex with Andy would only strengthen their bond. Worse, she feared it would tie her to him and Dare Valley, preventing her from making a logical decision about leaving if and when the time came.

"Do you want to help me unpack the groceries?" he asked. "I'm starving."

So he wasn't going to haul her off to the bedroom right away. She hadn't thought he would, but her mind had generated a few scenarios. Her phone buzzed, and she pushed off the couch to pick it up. Her mom was asking when she could talk to her about the upcoming photo shoots with Rhett and Old Man Jenkins next week. Great. Her mom wasn't even going to leave her alone while she was away with Andy.

"I can help with that," she said, turning off her phone, "or if you'd rather, I can make us some sandwiches."

"Sandwiches would be good. I'd like pastrami and mustard. With an apple."

"On top of the pastrami?" she asked smartly, earning her an amused look.

She followed him into the kitchen and brought out the ingredients. "Are you going to judge me if I eat the potato chips I brought? I seem to recall this is a vacation of sorts, which involves eating junk food."

He kissed her on the cheek and started putting groceries away. He was always doing sweet things like that, and she liked it. She liked it a lot.

"Other than an occasional ice cream, I don't really eat junk food." He drew out the three bottles of wine from a brown bag.

"Ice cream isn't junk food. It's an essential food group, and one I missed terribly when I was overseas."

His hand caressed the back of her head quickly. "Then we shall find ice cream around here and have it as often as you like."

That wasn't all they'd be having as often as they liked. He might want to be a gentleman, but frankly she was too fidgety to put up with it.

"Were you planning to wait until after dinner to make your move?" she asked, biting her lip to keep from smiling.

He dropped the milk jug on the counter. "Are we on some kind of timetable?"

She cleared her throat to stop the nervous laughter catching in her throat. "No, but I realized it was silly to wait for the guy to make a move. Dinner is about eight hours off. Why wait? Besides, I rather like having sex in the sunlight."

His hazel eyes, which looked more brown to her brain now, heated and the look he gave her made her all molten inside. "Come here then."

She almost asked why he couldn't come to her, but that would be silly. Bounding across the room, she wrapped her arms around him. A slow smile broke out across his face as he caressed her cheek.

"It's still a little weird, thinking about getting naked with you," she admitted.

He arched a brow. "I'm sure we'll get through it fine. We've managed to get through everything else together."

It was true. His keen understanding of her, of them, had helped dissolve every boundary.

When he slid his hands around her waist, he looked her straight in the eye. "I love you. Come make love with me."

Her heart started racing, and an aching vulnerability washed over her. She wasn't going to be able to tease or joke about this simply being fun. This was Andy, and he'd always known her soul.

"I love you too," she said, reaching for his hand and leading him out of the kitchen. "Are you sure you can wait for your sandwich?" she teased because she couldn't seem to help herself.

His fingers were already edging up her shirt, caressing the bare skin of her waist. "Oh, yeah."

They journeyed up the stairs to the master suite. A set of deer antlers jutted out above a stone fireplace. Lucy wanted to pop out some joke about them, but she couldn't get the words out. It was like her funny bone had been decommissioned, replaced by something raw.

Scanning the massive room, she noticed their luggage nestled together in the corner. It was weird to see their things together. Growing up, Andy had had his house and she'd had hers, and even though they'd spent hours hanging out, they'd never had sleepovers. Boys and girls in their town just didn't do that when they were only friends, so until now, there'd always been his space and hers.

"We've never spent the night together," she said, "even after all of our years of friendship."

"Are you nervous?" he asked, holding her close.

"Probably. I don't know. Sure." She made a face. "What about you? Are you thinking about Kim?"

His head darted back. "We agreed to be honest with each other, so yeah, I am. A little. I know she's happy I'm with you. She always liked you, you know."

Lucy swallowed the lump in her throat. "I liked her too. I was so grateful she never got jealous, you know? When you first married her, I was a little worried. But she wasn't like that."

"No," he said with a sad smile. "She was glad I had you. In fact, she used to say she decided I was a keeper when she learned I was still best friends with a girl I'd met in kindergarten."

"Really?" Somehow that sweet, insightful comment made her miss Kim. So she sent her a quick thanks for...well, everything.

"Kim thought our longstanding friendship meant I was a nice guy, and since she'd dated a few assholes in college, she was looking for something else."

Andy Hale was a nice guy, and Lucy realized she'd never been with one of those. Those other men had been interesting and smart and courageous, but none of them had been nice in the way Andy was. "Do you feel guilty? About what we're about to do?"

He took his time answering. "I've had my moments since I first started wanting you like this, but I've let it go. Lucy, you make me *so* happy. Having you back here, first as my friend and now like this... Well, it's pretty damn perfect."

"You really do love me," she said, studying his face. "All the way."

"Is that finally sinking into your thick skull?" he asked, fighting a smile and losing.

Her heart twisted in her chest. "Seems so."

He leaned in until he was inches away from her mouth. "Let me show you how much."

Their lips met with a newness she could only marvel at. Her arms wrapped around him as he pressed lush kisses to her upper and lower lip.

She cupped the back of his neck and stood on her tiptoes to press her mouth more firmly against his. He opened his, and so did she, and she fell into the lushness of the slow slide of their tongues against each other. He was rarely in a rush, she'd discovered, always content to let the heat and friction work their magic.

Her breathing turned heavy, like the feeling in her belly, and she felt the beautiful tension of male arousal against her center. She pressed closer to him, rocking her hips, making him groan.

"Let's get some of these clothes off you," he said harshly, edging back.

They helped each other get bare to the waist. And of

course, he had to check the healing wounds on her back, kissing each of them in benediction. His hands cupped her breasts, making her head fall back in pleasure. Her knees were turning weak, she realized, and she walked until she sat on the edge of the bed. He sank to his knees in front of her, opening her jean-clad legs and sliding between them. Oh man, that was really hot.

He pressed his mouth to one of her breasts as she ran her hands over the hard muscles of his shoulders. His chest was strong and built, and she couldn't get enough of him. He seemed to feel the same because he started to tug on her nipple in the most urgent of ways, making things below clench and tighten. She made a soft sound when he switched to the other breast and plunged her fingers into his dark hair.

When he finally released her and looked up at her from his position between her knees, her mouth went dry. A tidal wave of lust crashed over her. She pushed him onto his heels and climbed into his lap, pressing her mouth to his in a hot, wet kiss. Locking her knees around his waist, she gripped him as he rocked against her. He groaned, clenching his hands on her bare skin, and then slid his hands down the back of her jeans.

She jolted against his mouth at the caress, pressing away and standing. Her hands unzipped her jeans and pushed them down her legs. He took one of her feet into his hands to slowly slide her pant leg and sock off, all the while kissing the exposed skin of her thigh.

Lucy thought she was going to die. "You're driving me crazy."

"Good," he muttered, kissing the inside of her knee, a place she'd heard was an erogenous zone.

"I had no idea someone kissing your knee could feel so sexy," she told him.

He might have snorted, but since her ears were ringing, she couldn't be sure. "How about here?" he asked.

Her eyes crossed. "Yep. Bull's-eye."

"You're a talker," he said, pulling her last sock off. "I don't know why I'm surprised."

Standing before him in nothing but her underwear, she put her bare foot on his bare stomach, getting his attention. "Is that a complaint?"

A slow sexy smile crossed his face as he slid his hand up her foot and then all the way to her core. She might have squeaked when he arrived at his final destination.

"Not for a second," he said, sliding a finger inside her panties. "Talk to me."

He caressed her slowly, gently at first, but when he increased the pressure of his touches, she decided she'd had enough.

"Take them off," she said, shoving her panties down her hips.

"A talker and an impatient one at that," he said, all honeyed-voice man now.

"I'll show you impatient," she said, toppling him over until he lay on the rug.

"There is a perfectly good bed behind you," he said, chuckling softly. "In case you somehow missed it."

"Shut up," she said, kneeling beside him and reaching for the zipper on his jeans. "If you're going to drive me nuts, I'm going to drive you nuts."

"I think I'm going to like that," he said as she undid his jeans and slid her hand into his briefs.

He closed his eyes, his face a mask of tension. "Yeah, I like that. God, Lucy. More."

She managed to get his jeans and briefs down to his thighs, and he helped her the rest of the way. Like he'd done with her, she took his socks off while kissing his muscular legs. Then she sat back as the full view of him came into focus. Her mind sized up the subject before her. Andy Hale was lying naked and aroused on the bedroom floor, and he couldn't have been more freaking sexy.

"You're so gorgeous," she said, putting a hand on his muscular thigh.

He sat up and cupped her face. "And you're beautiful. Now, come here."

She shifted onto his lap, and the jolt of lust she experienced from the naked contact of their bodies had every nerve ending tingling. This was a level of lust she'd never felt before, and she could feel the last vestiges of humor and control vanishing.

She wanted him. All of him. Now.

Pressing her mouth to his, she kissed him again, and this time every wild impulse in her broke loose. She ran her mouth over the hard planes of his shoulders, savoring the taste of him. Her breasts tingled against his chest, and she gasped when he shifted, rising off the floor with her wrapped around him.

"I want you in bed," he said against her mouth before laying her in the center.

They kissed, but soon it wasn't enough. He made his way down her body, discovering all the places that made her cry out. The crook of her elbow. The sides of her breasts. And her core. That most of all.

He lingered over her, teasing her heated flesh, urging her on with his mouth. She was too mindless to protest the intimacy of it all. And when he flicked his tongue over the center of her, she came in a rush, crying out.

She felt him shift on the bed. As she watched, he reached for a foil packet on the nightstand and rolled on the condom. It was oddly sexy and intimate in a way it had never been before.

Spreading her legs even wider to accommodate his body, he stretched out over her. All that bare, taut skin just inches away from her pretty much made her mouth water. She noticed the pillow in his hands before he grabbed her hips with one hand and tucked it under her. *Whoa.* This was new. And a whole lot of vulnerable. It was impossible not to gulp as he rose over her, all naked, aroused man.

"Hey," he said softly, caressing her face. "Stay with me."

Like there was anywhere else she could go.

He edged forward, and she felt the press of him as he slid inside her. She dug her head into the mattress at the pressure of him, the heat of him.

"All right?" he rasped out.

She nodded, feeling suddenly overwhelmed. Her heart was changing in her chest, and then she realized why. This *was* making love. How could she think otherwise as she looked into his face? The light in his eyes seemed to reach all the way into her soul, and for the first time, she knew what it meant to feel complete with someone inside her. Totally complete.

"Andy," she whispered.

He swallowed thickly and held his hands out to her, which she gripped tightly. "Right here, Luce."

Then he slid deeper and retreated. The slow slide of him inside her made her reach for him, and soon he found a gentle rhythm that pleased them both. Her knees gripped his body when she needed more, and he seemed to feel it because he increased the pace of his thrusts.

And she was lost.

She rocked against him, mindless from the passion rising within her again, but this time with a hard edge that could not be softened or controlled. Urgent cries sounded from her mouth as he pounded into her, never releasing her hands.

"Lucy," he called out, and she sought his face.

Tension radiated from him as their gazes met. He gripped her hands even harder.

"Let go," he said, rocking into her.

She tilted her head back as he pressed deeper and felt everything gather and then flash inside her. Her body contracted around him, and she cried out, thrashing against him. He thrust wildly and then froze above her, calling out her name.

The very sound of his voice like that broke something free around her heart. She felt the pieces shatter, and when he folded over her, this time the wave she felt was of the greatest, fiercest love she'd ever known for another human being. Her body seemed to be falling, almost like she was plummeting from a tall cliff. But instead of hitting the ground, she floated, because there was no body after all.

Surrendering to that weightlessness, she felt this new heart of hers expand until she was sure its energy was cocooning him as well. And when he nestled close and pressed his sweaty head to her neck, she breathed him in. The love she had for him continued to expand, and so she surrendered to a place where words and thoughts were no longer needed.

# Chapter 23

Andy knew he was probably crushing Lucy, but he couldn't seem to muster the energy to push away. His breath was still coming out in heaving gasps, his heart was pounding, and sweat was coating his skin. Holy freaking Christ. What had just happened?

He hadn't been with a lot of women, but he'd had a lot of sex. Good sex. Great sex. The kind of regular married sex that used to put a smile on his face throughout the day. It had gotten better with Kim the more they'd done it, the longer they'd been together.

He'd thought that was how things worked.

Lucy had just blown that theory to hell. Sex with her was like jumping to light speed, and he was flailing to wrap his shorted-out mind around it.

Things had pretty much gone as expected at first. There had been humor between them, and she'd gotten pushy. He'd known she would play an active part.

But something had changed the moment he'd entered her. She'd gripped his hands and opened everything she was to him, and he'd felt like the deepest parts of each of them were merging together. And then she'd come, harder and hotter than he could have ever imagined. The passion between them had been crazy and urgent, and the last threads of his control had splintered. The force of his climax had been absolute and unwavering. His body felt hollow now, but there was this odd expansion in his chest, one that felt all warm and comforting.

He nuzzled her neck, wanting to touch her, to be close to her, to never be apart from her. There was love here. So much love he felt small in the face of it.

She was quiet, her breathing smoother than his, and so soft and pliant beneath him. He forced himself onto his elbows and realized their hands were still wrapped around each other. Her auburn hair was mussed, a lock of it laying against her soft, white cheek. The rusty line of her eyelashes curled in the most appealing way. He'd never realized how long her eyelashes were before. He saw every freckle, every pore on her face. It was like every atom that made Lucy O'Brien was suddenly visible to him.

She was beautiful, breathtakingly so.

Her lashes flickered, and her eyes opened. There was wonder there and so much love his heart seemed to fill with it like a water bucket from a well.

"Hey," he said softly.

The only response he received was a smile, and it was enough.

He gathered his strength to shift off her, but she tightened her legs around him.

"No," she whispered. "Stay."

"I don't want to crush you."

"You're not," she said, all soft and warm under him.

"Let me take care of this," he said and dispensed with the condom.

Coming back to rest on top of her, they stayed that way until he got a crick in his neck from being on his elbows too long. When he shifted onto his back, she cuddled against him.

Hours seemed to pass. They didn't speak, and it

might have been the longest they'd ever gone without saying a word. Her hand rested on his chest like she was counting his heartbeats while he ran his hand along the side of her back, marveling at the smooth line of her vertebrae.

Finally, his stomach grumbled, and he sighed.

"You're hungry," she said, still quieter, still more peaceful than usual.

"I can wait a little longer," he said, not wanting to interrupt their reverie.

She made no move to rise, only rested her face on his chest. When his stomach made more noises, she finally pressed up. Her hair looked a bit tangled, which pleased him somehow, and her eyes were like luminous jewels.

"Come on," she said. "You need to eat."

He tugged her back, drinking in her soft gaze. "I don't want to leave this."

A half smile touched her face. "We won't."

But she kept her back to him as she rose and pulled on a robe from her bag, and he could feel that they were once again on unfamiliar ground. At least there were puffy clouds beneath their feet.

She was making sandwiches when he joined her in the kitchen. He wrapped his arms around her middle. The sweep of her mustard-covered knife slowed on the bread.

"*Well,*" he said in a deep voice. He hadn't heard himself sound this way for some time, husky and satisfied, replete from lovemaking.

"*Well,*" she replied, resuming her task.

"Can you stop making the sandwiches for just a minute, please?"

She set the knife down on the counter and turned around. There wasn't a smile on her face, but her eyes were serious.

"Are we going to talk about what we're feeling here?"

he asked, suddenly awkward again. "I...it was cataclysmic for me. You?"

"Same," she said, leaning back against the counter. "I was trying to credit it to the pillow."

A smile tugged at his lips. "Seriously?"

Her shoulder lifted. "I've never..."

"Ah...it's an anatomy thing," he said, putting his hand next to hers on the counter. "I studied anatomy, remember?"

"You always were an A student," she responded, giving away nothing.

"It wasn't the pillow. It was us. This."

She heaved out a slow breath. "I know. I thought it would be good, but I didn't see this coming, frankly."

It was hard not to grin. "Neither did I, but as my mother always says, 'Don't look a gift horse in the mouth.'"

She punched him in the chest, righting the easy balance between them. "Thanks for making me think about your mother after I just had wild sex with her son."

Since she was starting to seem more like herself, he pressed a little closer. All he wanted to do was put her on the countertop and gobble her up. "It was more than wild sex."

"Yes, it sure was. As I was making the sandwiches, I finally realized why."

He couldn't keep from sliding his arms around her waist. "Enlighten me."

She pressed her lips together like she was trying to find the words. "When I was out on a particularly tough assignment, I would come back to wherever I was staying feeling numb. It was like everything inside me was frozen after what I'd seen. If I had Internet, I'd pull up my computer and write to you—even if you weren't awake."

How many nights had he done the same with her?

Especially after Kim had died. She'd been his salvation in a way, the one person with whom he could share his deepest and darkest hurts and fears.

"When I finished writing you, I could feel my heart again."

He was stunned for a moment when the words sunk in. "Oh, Lucy."

She took his hand and placed it over the spot that reverberated in steady, easy beats.

"I felt like that again after we made love," she said, and he knew it was the first time she'd used that term instead of sex. "Andy, you help me get in touch with my heart. You always have. And today...today you put me into a deeper connection with my heart than I've ever experienced." She looked at him, and he was alarmed to see tears gathered in the corners of her eyes. "I didn't expect that."

His own heart thundered in his chest.

"You've always helped me feel my heart too," he said quietly, "even when I didn't think I had one left."

She cupped his chin. "I love you."

"I love you too," he said, lowering his head until his mouth was inches from hers. "Thanks for helping me find it again."

And then he kissed her softly on the lips, feeling their hearts dance around each other all over again.

# Chapter 24

After the photo shoots with two of the male volunteers, Lucy found herself grading her own photos with nothing better than a C for the final product, like the average students in her class. At least her instincts on capturing the perfect moment still deserved an A+.

The lighting on Jill's face in Lucy's favorite photo was too harsh, to her mind. The sad-yet-hopeful expression on Old Man Jenkins' face was a winner, but the flag he was holding looked blurred on the corners. And Rhett Butler Blaylock's whimsical smile as he kicked back wearing an open leather vest...well, the focus was off ever so slightly on the best photo of the lot. They would need a lot of touching up, and while she knew the images were great, she couldn't help but feel frustrated.

Andy loved them and kept telling her that she was her own worst critic. But she was three photo shoots into the project, and she was floundering. Doubt seeped into her like unwanted water in a leaky basement. Her mother's frequent calls and texts didn't help. Today's had been short but sweet.

*Lucy, I want to see the photos you've taken so far. Stop ignoring me. I know your tactics, missy. I have a right to see them.*

Perhaps she did have a right, but Lucy didn't have enough confidence to show them to anyone but Andy. She was tight every time she picked up the new camera, and her nightmares had changed from twisted memories of the village bombing to garish versions of the calendar photos resembling fun-house mirrors. Everything she captured seemed distorted right now.

The only part of her life that felt in focus was her relationship with Andy. She'd never been more in love with anyone. Never imagined it could be possible to want to be with someone every day and night and still want more. Of course, they couldn't be together every night because of Danny. They'd agreed not to spend the night together in Andy's house. It didn't feel right. That meant they met at her house during his lunch hour or spent time together while a family member took care of Danny.

Tonight they were going to have dinner together at Andy's house and play Wii afterwards, something he and Danny did a couple times a week. Lucy had attended a few of the boy's T-ball games and hung out with the Hale clan at Sunday dinner.

They were weaving more than their hearts together. They were beginning to weave their lives together. She was trying not to freak out about what that meant for her and her career.

Her vision hadn't improved past the day of Jill's photo shoot, but Dr. Davidson assured her it still could. Her color vision wasn't better, though, and that bothered her.

She was sitting in her home office, grading photos of starving cats and dogs at the local pound, when her phone rang. She picked up her phone because there was no evading the caller any longer. "Hello, Mother."

"Hello, Lucy. I thought April and I could come over and see the photos you've taken so far since you don't have class today."

Lucy pushed her sandwich aside. There was no way she could eat any more rye and Swiss. "Mom, how many times do I have to tell you? I prefer to assemble the calendar in draft and show it to all of you at the same time. Most of the people I work with prefer it that way. They can see the complete—"

"I'm not most people," her mother said crisply. "I'm your mother. Stop putting me off. When I asked you to do this, I thought we could have fun together. I've respected your wish not to have me present at every photo shoot, but I want to see what you have so far."

"Old Man Jenkins would have been uncomfortable with you in the room, Mother," she said, trying and failing to keep the aggravation out of her voice. "And Rhett probably wouldn't have been as relaxed if there had been any bystanders besides his wife."

"You're underestimating Rhett," her mother replied in a hard tone.

Lucy didn't think so. Under that tough, devil-may-care attitude was a vulnerable man full of emotion. He'd gotten all teary-eyed while telling her stories about his uncle. And so had his lovely wife, Abbie. More than one tissue had been passed around. Of course, Rhett blamed it on his impending fatherhood. Lucy knew better.

"Edith said she wouldn't mind if I come to her photo shoot this weekend," her mom said, using her words like a railroad worker pounding nails for Union Pacific.

Lucy decided to stop arguing with her. "Mom, I'm really serious here. Can't you trust me?"

"This isn't about trust," her mother said, her tone growing sterner. "It's about the calendar, and since April and I came up with the idea, we want to be more involved. That means seeing the photos you've taken so far."

This was going to be a disaster, but she knew her mother. Reason and compromise weren't in her lexicon.

She was done taking no for an answer. Lucy could show them the photos she'd taken and explain the reasoning behind her selections, all the while making it clear they weren't completely touched up to her liking. Heavens knew that was the case.

"Fine," she said rather petulantly. "Come on by in the next hour or so. After that, I'm going on a hike and then over Andy's."

"We'll be there in a jiffy," her mom said and hung up.

Lucy pressed her fingers between her brows. Her mother wasn't going to see things the way she did. She never had. Rising from the table, Lucy threw out the rest of her sandwich and decided to make her bed to keep her hands occupied until they arrived.

She was tugging on the pillowcases when she heard a knock on the door. As she walked to open it, she told herself she was a grown woman with an award-winning career in photojournalism. People admired her work. When she saw her mother's sour expression, she had to admit the harsh truth.

Her mother wasn't one of them.

Part of her still didn't fully understand why her mother had asked her to do the calendar in the first place.

April gave her a hug first, which was telling, and her mother's greeting was perfunctory.

"Can I get you anything to drink?" she asked, hoping to soften the rolling tension coming from her mother.

"That would be nice, dear," April said, giving her an encouraging smile. "How about hot tea? You can feel fall in the air. It's going to be a cold winter, I think."

"Yeah," she said, falling into the weather talk—the last vestige of civility between people who were at odds with each other. "I had to bring out my down jacket for the first time last night."

"Andy said you two went on a moonlight walk last

night after Danny went to sleep," April said, taking her arm and leading her into the kitchen.

She cast a last look at her mother before she walked through the doorway. She was stiff and sour-faced and radiating anger. Tea wasn't going to soothe her. She wasn't willing to be soothed.

"Yes, it was nice of Matt and Jane to come over and stay with Danny," Lucy continued, grateful to have April there as a buffer.

"Everyone is all too eager to help you and Andy spend more time together," April said, standing beside her at the counter as Lucy set the old flowery teapot on the stove. "Don't be shy if you need a night here and there. It can't be easy sometimes, wanting to be alone with a little boy in the house."

Lucy fumbled with the tea box, and it shot out of her hands, bouncing along the counter. Oh good Lord, was April really going to bring that topic out into the open?

Andy took his role as a father seriously, and so far, they'd only had one sleepover, courtesy of Natalie and Blake, who had watched Danny for the night. Not wishing to add more talk to the gossip mill, he had come to stay at Merry Cottage, teasing her that he was rather coming to like her princess bed.

"That's very kind of you," she told April, taking the box of tea from her when she handed it back with a knowing smile. "We're all managing the newness of everything."

April gave her a wink. "Good. Every time I see my son, I can't believe the change in him. It's like he's come alive again."

Lucy's heart clutched. She was coming alive too, in a way she hadn't expected. "He's a good man. Always has been. We're lucky to have each other."

The future was as out of focus as many of her photos, but she could say that much without pause.

April put her arm around her and gave her a loving

squeeze. "We're so happy you're back, Lucy. All of us."

She looked over her shoulder, and when she didn't see her mother, said, "Except her, it seems."

April also checked to make sure they were alone. "She is, Lucy, truly. You two just butt heads a lot. Being away made that easier. Your mom wouldn't have asked you to shoot the calendar if she hadn't wanted to spend quality time with you. But you've kept her on the sidelines and that hurt her feelings—something she'd never admit in a million years."

Crap. April had to go all Oprah on her. "You're right. We have always butted heads. I was hoping this time we wouldn't because this calendar…"

She broke off, realizing she had almost admitted how pivotal and important it was to her as well.

"This calendar?" April encouraged, her round face gazing at Lucy with openness and love—rather like her son did when she was feeling vulnerable.

"Well, it means a lot to me too, especially because of Andy." As a save, it wasn't bad.

"Then let your mom in a little," April encouraged, turning the burner off when the teakettle gave a piercing whistle.

"A little?" she asked with a laugh, rubbing the hard ball in her sternum. "Are we talking about the same woman here?"

April laughed too. "If you're going to stay in Dare Valley—which I very much hope you do—you're going to have to find a way to meet each other in the middle. Otherwise you're going to implode and kill each other."

She wasn't wrong, and since Lucy wasn't thinking long-term at the moment, she decided to stick her head in the sand a little longer and just get through today.

"Are you two finished lollygagging around?" her mother asked, walking into the kitchen.

Lucy's eye twitched. "We were just making tea, Mother."

"Sounds like you were making a lot more than tea to me," she said, her mouth carved in a stern line.

"Oh, Ellie," April chided. "Sit down at that table over there, and let us finish off the tea. We're going to be civilized here."

Her mother sat while Lucy poured water carefully into the mugs. It wouldn't do to miss the cups because of her depth perception issues. Fortunately, she'd learned the trick of putting her finger on the rim of the cup to guide her.

After dunking the tea bags a few times, Lucy brought out the honey and lemon. She set everything on the table, and they all sat down and reached for their mugs. Lucy gulped her orange pekoe and immediately started coughing on the too-hot liquid.

"Boiling hot water will do that to you," her mother said like Lucy was an imbecile.

April shot her a look.

"Why don't you show us the photos while we're having tea?" her mother suggested.

Lucy stood up immediately. There was no point in delaying. She headed into her office and grabbed the photos off the antique desk. Since she had access to high-resolution printers at the university, she'd printed off her favorite photo of each subject with the intention of using a magnifying glass to manually catch the defects. Of course, she'd found plenty and hoped to touch them up.

When she returned to the kitchen, Lucy set the photos down on the table next to her mom. Resuming her seat, she picked up her tea. Jill's photo was on top.

"Oh, she looks so lovely," April said, a warm smile on her face. "I don't think I've ever noticed how soft or beautiful Jill is. I mean I knew she was pretty, but...goodness, Lucy."

"She has *tears* in her eyes," her mother said indignantly, grabbing the photo and shaking it in the air. "I told you we weren't doing one of your sad calendars, Lucy!"

April's eyes widened. "Let's look at the other two, Ellie."

Her mother slapped Jill's photo down with enough force the cups shook, making the tea rock back and forth like the weather in the room had turned stormy.

"Old Man Jenkins looks sad too!" she exclaimed, glaring at Lucy. "Dammit, what did you do to them?"

Her tone was a harsh slap across the face. "I didn't do anything to them, Mother. I only asked them to tell me a story about the person they were honoring."

Her mother shoved out of her chair. "Why would you do that? The past is dead, Lucy. All you're doing is dredging it up by asking questions like that."

She gripped the bottom of chair to keep from facing off with her mother. "Their memories aren't dead, Mother. They matter. It's the whole reason they're doing this calendar."

Her mother emitted a sputter as April set a hand on her arm. "Ellie, she's right. These pictures are really great. I mean, Old Man Jenkins is still sitting there with an American flag on his lap and he looks...so sweet."

"It's supposed to be funny, not sweet," her mother said in a shrill tone. "April, he's ninety-one years old and wearing nothing but a flag. And yet my daughter somehow managed to suck all the humor out of the scene."

Lucy shot out of her chair. "Fine! I'm a humor sucker, Mother. The photos need considerable touching up, but I happen to think they're wonderful."

Her mother grabbed the last photo—the one of Rhett. She thrust it into April's face. "My daughter even managed to suck all the charm from Rhett Butler Blaylock. God help us."

Her mother's friend lowered her head, as if she didn't quite know what to say. Lucy couldn't blame her.

"He's more than his charm, Mother," she said, fisting her hands at her sides. "He has a heart, and he misses his uncle. Do you know that when Rhett was a little boy, his uncle used to let him sit on his lap during his poker games? His wife, a staunch Southern Baptist, told him he'd go to hell for gambling. And do you know what he'd tell Rhett? That a real man has to make his own fate in this life and not let anyone else tell him what's right and wrong."

Her mother's brows drew together like two wasps colliding in midair. "Are you saying I'm trying to tell you what's right and wrong? You're darn right I am. I gave birth to you. That's my job."

Lucy's stomach was burning now, like her ulcers had grown back. "But your job is done, Mother, and you refuse to see it. You refuse to see me. You won't let me be me. I do calendars all the time—perhaps not like this—but I know what works, and you won't *listen* to me. You never do."

Her mother's hands cut through the air like a knife. "I'm a terrible mother, I know! I don't know how you can even stand to be around me."

"Ellie!" April called out.

Ignoring her, Lucy's mother strode to the kitchen doorway. "You're wrong this time, Lucy. Life *is* filled with humor and fun. Even after you lose someone or something. That's what gets people through things. You're only dragging everyone back into the thick of their grief. Rhett can never play poker with his uncle again. That's a fact. You're cruel to make him remember something that can never be."

Lucy's breath sucked in at the attack. "That's it! If you feel that way about me, you don't know me at all. I'm a good person, Mother. I listen to the stories of people who have nothing left but the memories of the people they loved. It doesn't matter if it's Rhett or a ten-year-old kid in Congo who lost both parents to AIDS. I honor the person they've lost and their memories of them. And I show them how beautiful they are while they're being human. You have no bandwidth for the full range of human emotion, and I'm sorry for you."

She was heaving out her breath now. April shook her head, she noticed, as if immeasurably sad.

"If that's how you feel, then not only should you not do our calendar, but you shouldn't ever talk to me again. Because I can hear the judgment in your voice, Lucy, and I'll be damned if I'll let you imply I'm a bad person."

Her mother turned around and stomped out of view.

"Oh, Lucy," April said, rising and hugging her with heavy arms. "I know you're not my daughter, but I hope you can take a minute to hear what you just said to her."

She pressed away from the woman she'd always respected. "Didn't you hear what she said to me?"

"Yes, but I heard what you said back. Neither of you is right."

April walked out of the kitchen, and Lucy heard the front door close moments later.

She studied the three photos on the kitchen table. Her mother was mistaken. She had to be.

If she were right, everything Lucy believed in was wrong.

# Chapter 25

Andy was preparing Danny's current favorite for dinner: macaroni and cheese. Some idiot who ran the lunch program had served this nutrition-free meal three days ago, and Danny had refused to eat any of his old favorites over the last few nights. Only macaroni and cheese would do. Andy had finally caved after a two-night-long protest.

Lucy had texted him to say she was running late and not to hold dinner for her. He'd told her that was for the best since their menu sucked. She'd seemed off in her text, but he'd been too distracted to press her. He could figure out what was going on with her when she arrived. Right now he was stuck in food hell.

He'd found a recipe online, which he'd thought would be more nutritious than using a box. It had horrified him to see how much butter and cheese was involved in a homemade recipe.

He told himself he wasn't a bad father as he fumbled with the white sauce. Crap. Even meals with no nutritional value were beyond his cooking competence. He almost admitted defeat and dragged Danny to the store to buy a box, but he bucked up. He could do this. It was only a white sauce. But his looked pretty lumpy...

Danny hated lumpy food—he wouldn't even eat mashed potatoes and gravy if there was the tiniest lump in either.

His son was never going to eat this.

Danny ate it. All of it. And after he'd snarfed down the broccoli Andy had insisted on including, his son threw his arms around his neck and given him a smacker on the cheek.

"That was the best meal ever, Dad! Thanks."

Then he hopped off his lap, leaving Andy to stare stupidly at Rufus. "Sometimes I don't understand anything."

The dog whined in solidarity. The doorbell rang, and Danny gave a "Whoop."

Andy smiled for the first time since he'd caved in to his little food monster. Seeing Lucy always brightened his mood. She was becoming one of the greatest joys in his life—a life that felt more balanced with her in it.

Right now, he was surrounded with the people and things he loved: Danny, Lucy, his family, his work, and Dare Valley itself. He hadn't been this happy since he'd realized Kim was the one. Even though he was trying not to get ahead of himself, he knew Lucy was the one too. She was just way too skittish to hear that yet. And he was way too uncertain of what would happen if she was able to resume her career.

"Grandma!" Danny shouted, catching Andy off guard. He headed out of the kitchen to see what had brought his mother over tonight.

Danny was telling her all about the macaroni and cheese, and while she was listening, she had one eye on the kitchen doorway as he came through it.

He knew that look. It meant trouble.

"Hi, honey," she said, giving him an encouraging smile. "I thought I'd stop by and see if I could play with Danny tonight and put him to bed. It's my favorite thing in the world." She ruffled his son's hair. "He's *my* macaroni and cheese."

"I'm not pasta, Grandma," Danny said with as much exasperation as a five-year-old could muster. "I'm a boy!"

"Are you?" she said, crouching down and smelling him. "You smell kind of cheesy to me."

He scrunched up his nose. "I don't smell cheesy, Grandma. That would be silly."

"Yes, it would be, wouldn't it?" she asked as he wrapped her up in a hug. "My mistake. How about you go pick out some books for bedtime while I talk to your dad?"

"Great! I'm going to pick a lot of them, Grandma." He raced out of the room and pounded up the stairs, Rufus barking behind him.

Andy crossed his arms. "All right. This is unexpected. Anything you need to tell me?"

The smile her grandson had put on her face faded. "Lucy and her mom had a big fight today."

Shaking his head, he said, "I'd hoped it wouldn't come to that."

"Well, it has, I'm sad to say. I thought perhaps you two might want to be alone for a while. Natalie said Lucy was coming over for dinner tonight, but it didn't sound like anyone was babysitting later, if you know what I mean."

Even though he was a full-grown adult and a doctor, a flush broke out over his ears. "Jeez, Mom."

"Please," she said, waving her hand. "It's been a while, but I know what adults who love each other do. Plus, I thought you might be able to reason with Lucy a bit if you were alone together. I'm doing my best with Ellie, but she's too angry and hurt right now to listen to me. You'll have your hands full with Lucy."

It explained why her text had sounded strange earlier. "Thanks for coming over, Mom."

"I have a bag outside," she said, giving him a saucy

wink. "I'll just go get it. You might call in tomorrow late if you can."

The flush spread from his ears to his cheeks. "Could you stop, please?"

She laughed as she went to retrieve her bag. "No way. This is way too much fun."

He was glad someone was enjoying it. Detouring to the stairs, he took them two at a time. His son was sitting on the floor, pulling books out of his bookcase right and left. What had been a reasonably clean room before had become a minefield of children's books. Man, they had a lot of books, and while he was glad his son had a healthy appreciation for reading, it was a freaking mess. One he felt a little guilty about leaving for his mother.

"Hey, buddy," he said, sitting on the floor as his son threw an unwanted book toward the corner near a teddy bear. "Whoa! Watch out for civilians."

Danny laughed. "You're funny." The next book on the bookshelf made its way into the teetering pile between his little legs. "Where's Grandma?"

"She went to get her bag," he said, choosing his words carefully. "She realized she couldn't live without you, so she's spending the night."

"Cool!" he exclaimed as the pile of books fell like a row of dominoes.

"And since she wants to do the whole Grandma thing, I'm going to spend the night with my best friend."

His head shot up. "Lucy? I thought she was coming over. I was going to show her how to play Backyard Football. Blake taught me some new plays, and I'm rocking it. She was so going down tonight."

There was nothing wrong with a little healthy competition. "Maybe you can play with Grandma."

He shook his head. "I tried one time. She's horrible, Dad. She couldn't even figure out what buttons to push."

"That's awful," he said, trying not to laugh. "I don't know how you can handle her being your grandma. Okay, give me a kiss. I'll pick you up after school tomorrow, okay?"

Danny climbed onto his lap for a hug, squeezing him with all his might. "Have fun with Miss Lucy."

He held his son's little body against him, inhaling the sweet scent of little boy and enthusiasm. "Will do. Love you. Have fun with Grandma."

He had risen to his feet and was halfway to the door when his son asked, "Dad, are you going to marry Miss Lucy?"

That question pretty much made his head explode. He stilled and turned. His son was holding *Where The Wild Things Are* to his chest, looking decades older than his age.

"Why would you think that?" he asked, his chest growing tight.

His son clutched the book and shrugged. "My friend, Bobby, said he heard his mom and her friends talking about how much time you've been spending with Lucy. I told Bobby that Lucy's your best friend ever, and she's really funny and nice. She even took that picture of the camel with the funny face for me," he said, pointing.

The reminder warmed his heart. Even before their connection had bloomed into romance, she'd supported him and his son in a way few others had.

"She's a really special lady. Like I told you a few weeks ago, I want to spend lots of time with her now that she's back home and have her spend time with you because you're pretty special too."

Walking back over, he sank down on the floor beside his son.

"I'm your son," Danny said matter-of-factly. "Of course I'm special."

Andy smiled. "No one is more special."

"Even Miss Lucy?" he asked, peering up at him.

Andy pulled him onto his lap. "Do you think you're any less special to me because I like to go running with Uncle Matt or hang out with your aunts?"

Danny shook his head. "They're our family."

"That's right," he said, remembering how many times he'd told his son that. "Lucy is my family too. She and I have been friends since I was your age. She's been away from home for a long time, which is why I want her to come over here and hang out with us. I'd like for you two to get to know each other better."

"But you kiss her sometimes, and Bobby says that means she's your girlfriend," Danny said, blowing his mind yet again.

What in the hell was he supposed to say to that? Sometimes he felt totally unprepared for conversations with his kid. "Yeah, she's my girlfriend." Man, that sounded weird. He was thirty-six. Too old for that term.

"I love Lucy," he told Danny, deciding to be honest. "She makes me happy. Like you do."

"Like Mom did?" his son asked. "I heard Aunt Moira tell Aunt Natalie she hasn't seen you this happy since Mommy died."

His throat thickened. "I loved your mom. So much. And I wish she was here instead of being an angel, but God needed her more."

Danny nodded like that made sense to him. He breathed a sigh of relief.

"When Lucy came back to Dare Valley after being gone *forever*," he said, using Danny's favorite concept of time, "I just couldn't help it. I fell in love with her. And yes, I kiss her sometimes." He should have been more careful. Danny must have snuck out of bed and seen them on the couch or something.

"She's kinda pretty," Danny said, putting his finger to his cheek. "And she's so funny. She put those straws up her nose when we had sodas at Hairy's."

Yeah, that had been pretty funny.

"I'm glad you like her, Dad. I think she likes me too. Otherwise, she wouldn't give me photos or play Wii with me."

Simple gestures of love were the truest ones—a lesson he was proud to have taught his son. "She likes you a lot," he said.

He just wasn't sure if she loved Danny enough to join herself to their family. Lucy had said she'd adjust her schedule to have a family, but he didn't yet know if that was something she wanted with him.

"So, are you going to get married, Dad?" Danny asked again. "Bobby said when adults have sleepovers they get married."

Andy wanted to curse Bobby and his older siblings. Surely that's where Danny's friend had gotten his ideas. "I haven't asked Miss Lucy."

He realized he was scared to. If she said no, he didn't know where they'd go from there. Besides, she was dealing with enough pressure from her injury. And now her mother. He hadn't wanted to add to it. But he realized his son was asking the kind of questions that would make an impact on his young mind. Andy needed to remember his responsibility as a parent. Being Lucy's boyfriend couldn't trump that.

"What would you say if I asked Miss Lucy to marry me and come live with us?" he asked, deciding to go all out. His son was already thinking about it.

"She's fun," Danny said, the highest compliment his son could pay anyone. "And she makes you laugh. Mom likes seeing you laugh."

Suddenly he couldn't breathe. "Mom?"

His son nodded. "She visits me sometimes," he said, smiling brightly. "She wants us to laugh more. That's why I tickle you so much. She tells me to."

His heartbeat pounded in his ears. "Danny. Listen to me. When did you talk to your mom?"

"After you tuck me in sometimes. She sits by my bed

and talks to me until I go to sleep. She told me she's always liked Lucy, and she's glad she's back in Dare Valley."

Could his son have actually talked to Kim? It seemed crazy, but Andy had been a doctor long enough to wonder. "What did your mom look like?"

Danny snorted. "She looked like Mom, but she glowed like the blonde lady in *Pinocchio*."

The fairy godmother in luminous blue? It could be a figment of his son's imagination. And yet the hairs on the back of his neck were standing on end. "What did your mother say?"

His son's face seemed to be lit from within, and Andy clutched his heart. "She said she's happy to see you so happy, and that you know what to do. Mom said to always follow your heart."

Tears gathered in his eyes. His logical mind was hesitant to believe in things like spirits, but his heart did. "She's right," he said in a hoarse voice. "You should always follow your heart."

Pulling Danny onto his lap, he held his little body to him, filled with that huge, crazy love he had for his son.

"It's going to be okay," Danny told him. "Go have fun with Miss Lucy. Tell her hi for me."

Andy pulled himself together and kissed his son's soft brown hair. "I will." Rising from the floor, he shifted a few steps, off balance. "Have fun with Grandma."

Danny was restacking his books. "Okay."

As he walked to the door, Andy tried to calm the wild cadence of his heart.

"Wait, Dr. Serious!" Danny shouted.

Andy jolted and gave a full-body shiver. No one but Kim had *ever* called him that. The nickname had been a private joke between them. Danny couldn't have remembered it. He turned around, chills covering his body.

"What, Danny?"

"I forgot to tell you," Danny said with a grin. "Mom has the coolest angel wings ever. They're bright blue and *really* big."

His lips trembled as he tried to smile at his son. "You tell her I love her when she visits you next time."

"Ah, Dad," Danny said, shaking his head at him. "She knows that. Duh!"

Andy turned back around and headed to the door, unable to keep the tears from streaking down his face.

# Chapter 26

Lucy was shaking off her bad mood when she heard a knock at the door. God, please don't let it be her mother. Or her father for that matter. He'd called her to say he'd heard about the fight. Of course he wanted them to work things out, but things had gone too far this time, and Lucy wasn't sure their relationship could recover. It was impossible to think about anything else, and Lucy had vacillated between lying on her bed in a sad funk and pacing the small cottage in anger.

She peered through the window to identify the car and was puzzled to see it was Andy's. She detoured to the front door. "What are you doing here? I'm sorry I needed more time. I was in a mood, but I was just about to head out."

He stepped closer to her and framed her face with his hands. "Do you have any idea how much I love you?"

The intensity with which he said it, combined with the heat of his touch, seemed to turn some wheel inside her. Well...this was unexpected. "Yes. I think so. Sure."

"Let me show you," he said in a deep voice before covering her mouth with his.

He danced her inside the house and closed the door behind them, making her wonder what in the world was going on. Then he swept her into his arms and carried her to the bedroom all Prince Charming-like. It was a little weird and surprising, but his mouth was so hot and insistent on hers she let all the questions flee her mind for the moment.

She fell back into that place of pure heart, pure sensation with him—a place she'd never known *until* him. After depositing her on the bed, he kissed his way down her body, dispensing with her clothes as he went. His fingers glided over her skin in reverence. His kisses were a benediction to flesh and bone.

Something really was different. But it felt so wonderful, she was content to meet whatever mood he was in.

His mouth gave worship to her breasts and the sensitive core between her thighs, causing her to cry out in pleasure. When she came apart, he continued to love her, causing her to come again.

He was on fire for her, and she was on fire for him. Panting, she rolled onto her side and put her hand on his heart. Arousal had tightened his muscles, but the love shining in his eyes made her heart expand beyond its previous limits. *So this is love, big love*, she thought, and leaned forward to kiss him again and share her piece of it.

She kissed her way down his skin, just as he had done for her, and as she removed his clothing until they were completely bared to each other, the only wish she had was to love him—all of him—and to help him feel the wild beauty he'd unleashed in her heart.

The tips of her fingers tingled as she ran them across the hard planes of his body. Her love was so great, so large she could have hugged the whole universe. She honored the differences between their bodies in a whole new way, and when he finally slid into her, holding her gaze, it felt that they were floating up in the stars.

When she resurfaced, she realized he was sprawled

across her, his elbows preventing him from crushing her. He was always so careful about that. Their hands were still linked, which made her smile. His warm, rapid breathing tickled her ear, making her giggle.

He shifted until he could see her face. "Wow," he said in a stupefied voice.

Her body felt like a small container for all she was in that moment. "Yeah. Wow."

Rolling onto his back, he drew her onto his chest, not that she needed urging. Her favorite place in the world was to be cuddled against him, listening to his heart beat, feeling the rise of his ribs as he breathed.

"I'd like to analyze what happened," he said with a snort, "but after this evening, I'm pretty much open to anything."

She inched higher so she could meet his gaze. "Sounds like you have an interesting story." She had no desire to share hers in this special moment.

His smile was soft. "I do," he said and proceeded to tell her about Danny's visits from his mom, who had blue angel wings.

By the end, they were both brushing away tears.

"As I was driving over here," Andy said, "I couldn't stop thinking about it. Kim wanted me to know she was still watching over our son like she promised she would before she died. She told me she'd find a way—even if it took petitioning God multiple times."

Ah, that sweet woman. Lucy wiped at more tears running down her face.

"But Kim also wanted me to know how happy she was that I'd found love again. With you. I didn't need her blessing—she gave it to me in the letter you read—but it still feels...pretty darn great to have it."

Lucy could tell the last pinches of guilt he had felt about moving forward with his life had dissolved on the way to her house. It was no wonder their lovemaking tonight had taken them to a whole new level of love and connection.

"I'm so happy for you," she said, tracing his chest. "And for Danny. I'm glad he still has his mom in some form."

"You really believe it?" he asked.

"I really do. The things I've seen overseas... I believe in spirits. I've even felt a few of them help me in moments of danger. Call them angels or whatever you'd like, but there was something there. I don't think I'd still be here otherwise. Plus, they say kids are so much more open to the otherworldly than adults."

He was nodding. "I'm going to tell my rational mind to take a hike and simply say thank you. I know what I want to believe."

She kissed his cheek. "Good plan."

"Now," he said, turning on his side so they were facing each other, "why don't you tell me about what happened between you and your mom?"

Her mouth parted. "Who told you? You mother?"

"She's the one spending the night at my house to give us some extra time together," he said, giving her a knowing look.

*"Oh."* She'd assumed someone was babysitting, and it made sense April would have interceded after their earlier discussion in the kitchen.

"Yeah. *Oh.*"

"It wasn't pretty," she began. "I was trying to get rid of all my negative energy before I came over. It was...taking a while."

Talking about the fight pretty much erased her earlier sensation of floating in the clouds. Plunging to earth again sucked, and her nerves were stretched tight again by the time she finished.

"Are you going to tell me it wasn't one of my better moments?" she asked.

"Would I do that?" he asked, a smile tugging at his lips.

"Yes."

"But gently, I'd like to think." He rubbed her arm. "So you both said some pretty tough things to each other. What do you plan to do about it?"

She'd thought about that all afternoon. Of course, she'd been mad enough to want to throw things and cheer as they shattered. But that didn't exactly make her feel proud or mature, and really, it was her heart that was shattering. That was nothing to cheer about.

"My mom doesn't like me," she whispered, feeling the pain spread to her bones. "And I don't like her. I know that's a terrible thing to say, but it's true. I'm not even sure we love each other anymore. Otherwise, how could we have said those things to each other?"

His sigh was heartfelt. "I'm not saying it's the same situation, but sometimes I think that way about my dad too."

"You mean the asshole who didn't treat your mother right?" she asked in an impassioned voice.

He gave her a bland look, but his eyes wrinkled with humor.

"So I might still have a lot of anger inside me," she explained, not that she needed to.

"Good to see you're not repressing it," he said with a wry smile. "I don't know what to tell you, Luce. I do believe your mother loves you. She just doesn't love you like you want her to."

How was that love? "She doesn't *see* me. Not for who I really am." She punched the pillow in defeat. "And that means she's loving some version of me that I'm not. That's why she gets so mad when I don't live up to her expectations. I've thought about little else since she stormed out. She thought I came home because I finally decided my career was too dangerous—something she's been saying for years."

She waited for him to comment, but he didn't.

"And in coming home, she hoped I'd go back to

being some silly girl who only wants to experience the fun side of life."

"You were never a silly girl," Andy told her, cupping her face. "You organized a student protest to raise awareness about female genital mutilation when we were juniors in high school."

Yes, she had. "I forgot about that. I read about that happening in Sudan in *U.S. News & World Report*. At first, I didn't even know that was anatomically possible. Then I couldn't believe it was happening. I mean, who would hurt women and girls like that?"

"Bastards," he said, gazing at her seriously. "I could name other protests you organized. What about that film from France—?"

"On human trafficking in Russia," she said, nodding. Goodness, she'd forgotten about these moments.

"Lucy, you were always trying to change the world for the better, even when you were living here in Dare Valley."

"My mother didn't like it then," she said, putting the final pieces of the memories together. Arthur had always encouraged her to pursue her interests, especially after her fights with her mom.

"And yet, your mother organized a breastfeeding fair because she was angry that women needed to hide a natural function in public."

She gave him a look. "Are you trying to say the apple doesn't fall far from the tree?"

He returned the look.

"You're pissing me off," she said without heat. "I want to be right here. Dammit! I want my mother to be wrong. Oh God, I'm a terrible person."

"No, you're not," he said, tapping her on the nose. "You're human. I want my dad to be wrong. I want to say he's the biggest jerk out there for not loving my mother enough and for not fighting for her when she asked for more. I want to punch him and tell him he's not a man for letting her walk out without a word."

"Now who's angry?" she asked, blinking at the force in his voice.

He blew out a breath. "I don't want to believe my mother did anything wrong. She's one of the most amazing women alive."

"But it takes two to tango, as Arthur Hale always says."

"Yeah." Now he sounded as down in the dumps as she did.

She curled up against his chest again. "I don't know what to do. My mom won't listen to me. I've never seen her this mad before. And it doesn't change the fact that she hates the three photos I've selected for the calendar so far."

"I happen to like the ones you've taken so far," he said. "In fact, I'd like you to send me the photo you took of me when I was thinking of Kim. It's...I want Danny to see it when he's older. I was scared to have him see it before, but now...I think it's the kind of thing he'd love to see."

"I'll send it. Andy, when it comes down to it, I think my mom's right. Someone else should take the photos instead, someone who understands their importance. What about your sister?"

"Moira?"

"Yeah," she said, mulling over the idea. "Her questions might have freaked me out at Jill's photo shoot, but she does know her stuff. Plus, she's here right now, waiting to hear about the job at the Artemis Institute. Maybe I can help her touch up the photos behind the scenes or something."

"It's a reasonable idea, but it won't solve the overall problem between you and your mother," Andy said quietly.

"I've tried to talk to her before," Lucy said, feeling defensive. "Why do you think I finally blew my top today? All the pressure of not being listened to reached its max. I felt like I'd turned into a volcano."

"I could make a joke about being familiar with your molten heat, but I'll refrain."

She punched him, making him grunt. "You know what I mean."

"I do," he said, kissing her on the check. "Let it settle a bit more. Maybe my mom will help Ellen see some reason."

"Somebody needs to," she said, "because not even my father has been able to all these years. He called me this afternoon, and he sounded more worried about us than ever before. Not that I can blame him. But my dad accepts and loves my mom as she is, flaws and all. What am I missing here? Am I letting my hurt feelings color everything?"

"Big questions. Ones for you to sit with." He made a face. "But if it makes you feel any better, I love you and I see you."

Crap. How had she gotten so lucky? "I know you do. You always have, and I'm grateful for that. Andy..." Her heart was growing again, and she took a big breath to grow with it. "I love you to pieces, but somehow, the words never seem big enough for what I feel."

Oh, the smile that spread across his face: a touch of heat mixed with an extra measure of love. She was a goner.

"How about we leave this for now, and you let me love you to pieces again?"

She climbed on top of him and smiled down. "How about you let me love you to pieces back?"

As she did, she became one giant heartbeat.

# Chapter 27

Andy finally gave into his gut urging to go see Ellen during his lunch hour the next day. Sometimes when his siblings were at odds, he'd been able to broker a peace. He didn't see why Lucy and her mom would be any different.

Besides, he kept coming back to the photo Lucy had taken of him after she'd asked him to think about Kim. She'd sent it to him on his way to work. Seeing how he looked when he thought about the wife he'd lost had changed him. Perhaps explaining that to Ellen would help her see Lucy's side of things. Deep down, he knew she needed to take the photos for the calendar—not just for herself, but for the future of her relationship with her mother.

Last night, Lucy had begrudgingly admitted Ellen might not be completely wrong, or her completely right. Common ground had been forged on lesser things.

When Andy knocked on the front door, Harry opened it.

"Oh, hi," he said awkwardly.

"Lunch break?" Harry asked, clapping Andy on the forearm in solidarity when he nodded. "Ellie's in the backyard. Good luck. I've gotten nowhere with her."

His gut urging turned into an upset stomach. "That sounds ominous."

Harry made a fist in the air. "That woman. I love her, but I swear sometimes... How's my girl?"

Andy hadn't expected that question. Heck, he hadn't expected Harry to be home. "She's upset too. Wishes things were different."

"When Lucy was growing up, I was the sole peacekeeper in the house," Harry said, making a face. "It's nice to have help."

Yeah, that was him. Peacekeeper Andy. Part of him wished he'd worn a suit of armor or something. Ellen was going to blast into him. And knowing Lucy, she wouldn't be all that happy to hear he'd come here.

"I'll see what I can do," Andy said, coming inside when Harry stepped out of the way.

"I'm heading to my bar. If you need a drink afterwards, there will be one waiting for you."

"That's kind of you, but I have to get back to the hospital."

Lucy's father grabbed a jacket from the hall closet. "After, then."

"I'm going to spend some time with Danny." He'd texted his mother a picture of himself making a funny face, wanting to make Danny laugh before he left for school. "My mom babysat last night so I could talk to Lucy." There was no way he was mentioning he'd spent the night with her.

"April was here this morning after dropping Danny off at school, so I know the score," Harry said, picking up his wallet and keys from the wooden bowl in the hall table. "Ellie didn't listen to your mom either."

Terrific. Harry and his mom were batting zero with Ellen. How was he supposed to do better? "It's about more than the calendar."

Harry's mouth twisted. "Always has been. Well, your next drink in my bar is on me, and if you get my girls to reconcile, you have a free pass on anything I serve for a year." With that, Lucy's dad left.

Andy felt a little weird walking through the house on his own, but when he opened the patio doors, that weird feeling morphed into red-hot embarrassment. "Sorry, Mrs. O'Brien!" he cried out the moment he saw Ellen—all of Ellen—in the bubbling hot tub. He was so shocked he'd reverted to calling her Mrs. O'Brien like he was twelve. "Harry didn't mention you were...ah...." *Sweet Jesus, put me down right now.*

"Good heavens, Andy Hale!" Lucy's mom called back. "You'd think you've never seen a naked woman in a hot tub before. Besides it's not like you can see anything anyway."

If that's what she thought, she'd never seen her cleavage. He was going to have to wash his eyes out with soap or something.

"I'll just wait inside for you," he said, bumping into the patio doors.

"No need," she called out. "You can talk to me here. If it bothers you so much, don't look."

Right. That was a good suggestion. "I'm just going to turn around now." And stare at the wall.

"You'd think you wouldn't be so embarrassed. One, you're a doctor. Two, you're sleeping with my daughter. *This* is what you have to look forward to."

Not in a million years was he going to go down that track. "Could we please talk about why I'm here?" he asked. Okay, pleaded.

"Dammit, I look good for my age!" Ellen railed on, confirming that she was more than riled up.

"I'm sure you do," Andy said to placate her. "I'm here about Lucy. I wanted to show you a picture she took of me after she arrived."

"Well," she barked out. "Come over here and show me."

His insides shriveled. He'd have to get closer to the

hot tub. "Ah...could you please meet me inside to talk about this? I...don't want to drop my phone in the water." There. Genius.

"I'll bend over the edge and put my hands out," she responded. "Don't be bashful, Hale. It's nothing you haven't seen before."

Why did people always say that? He had a license to practice medicine—not ogle naked people.

"Mrs. O'Brien, I'm really going to have to insist you put on a towel or robe." He was going to hold his ground.

There was a grand huff behind him. "You really are a prudish man, aren't you? I hope Lucy knows about this. Given how strong she is in her opinions, it might concern her that you're uncomfortable looking at naked people."

There was a small boulder in the garden to his right, and he had the sudden urge to bash his head against it. Was this what Lucy had to deal with? No wonder she'd lost her cool. Maybe he should just go.

"All right," she called out. "I'm decent."

He turned around, eyes half mast in case she was lying. She was wearing a short red kimono that skimmed her knees. He'd call it progress.

"Well! Are you coming over here or not? I'm growing cold here. I'm wet in some places."

"Coming." Anything to escape from this lamebrain conversation. Matt was going to laugh himself silly when he told him about it.

"I know you and Lucy have your opinions about things," he said, "and I'm not here to get into that." He'd grown up with three sisters, so he knew better. "But I wanted to show you this picture and tell you what it did for me."

She grabbed her purple reading glasses from the picnic table. "Better not be one of those boudoir photos." Then she barked out a laugh. "Not that I could imagine you posing for one after all your fussing about seeing me in the hot tub."

He was so not going to mention the mind-blowing sex he'd had with her daughter last night. Three times. But he was tempted. God, she brought out the devil in him. "No, it's this one."

After drawing out his phone, he punched in his code and brought the photo up on screen. She peered closer before taking it from him.

"You look sad!" Ellen declared, thrusting it back at him. "And no wonder. I swear, I don't think my kid can take anything but sad photos of people. In fact, I've concluded after talking to her yesterday that she's flat-out lost her funny bone. And I'm sad for her. Laughter is what makes life worth living."

Andy wanted to shove his phone in his pocket and storm out. But he loved Lucy enough to stay and defend her. "Your daughter is one of the funniest women I know. She can laugh in the face of life's conflict and suffering in a way you rarely see in people, and I cherish her because of it."

Her brows rose all the way to her hairline. "You're really in love with her, aren't you?"

"You're darn right I am," he said, his voice rising. "Lucy hasn't lost her funny bone, and I'm sorry you two can't set aside your differences enough to see each other. This photo she took captured my face when I was thinking about Kim."

"That's twisted," Ellen said, frowning. "You're dating!"

"It's not twisted," Andy said, his breath coming out hard now. "Your daughter has no problem letting me talk about Kim or how much I've missed her or how much I loved her. She never stops me from feeling what I feel."

Ellen's eyes narrowed to dangerous slits. "Are you saying I don't?"

He pulled himself back from that argument. "I'm saying that when I saw this picture of myself, I understood what my son must see when I talk about his mother. It made me sad to see it at first."

"That's my point!" Ellen said, thrusting her hand into the air in frustration. "No one needs those reminders. The past is the past, and dredging it up is a mistake."

"It's not a mistake. This picture helped change my mind about that. Sure, it captured my loss, but it also captured the love I had for Kim."

She looked about ready to smack him upside the head. "Of course it did, you numbskull. Kim was your wife."

He was bungling it. "You're not hearing me. This picture captured the love I still have for her—even though she's gone—and that's...well, that's a beautiful thing to remember. For me and my son." So much emotion was coursing through him, he had to take some deep breaths to steady himself.

"I still don't understand you. Did you need reminding that you still love Kim? Were you feeling guilty about being with Lucy?"

"This was before I started dating Lucy, but that's not the point," he said, pushing the phone under her nose. "This photo showed me I'm living with the love *and* the loss. This is what Lucy has captured for Jill and Rhett and Old Man Jenkins. She is capturing that life goes on, yes, but we still love them and miss them and wear silly costumes to commemorate them."

Ellen stared at him and then slid her glasses down her nose. "You know. I think you're as half-cocked as she is."

That did it. "Then you don't know your daughter for who she really is. If you could see her the way I do, you'd know she is one of the most amazing, powerful, loving women on the planet. I thought medicine was tough, but Lucy makes that look like baking a cake. And if you knew how hard this calendar is for her and everything she's gone through to make it happen..."

He broke off, horrified. Ellen grabbed him by the forearm, and for an older lady, she had the grip of wrestling champion.

"What in the world do you mean by that?" she barked out.

He was dead meat. "Nothing. Trying to compromise her vision to work with you has been hard on her."

"Bullshit!" Ellen cried, tightening her grip. "You know the whole story about why she's back, don't you? Of course you do! You were always thick as thieves and now you're doing the horizontal mambo."

So that was where Lucy had gotten the term. "I do love your daughter. Maybe she's right about you two not being able to see eye to eye. I'm going to go. I did what I came to do. What you decide to do is up to you. All I know is that you have a wonderful daughter who's back in Dare Valley. It would be sad if you miss your chance to get to know the woman she's become."

She started to sputter, and so he left.

Then he heard the footsteps running behind him. Dear God, was Mrs. O'Brien chasing him through her house in a kimono? He increased his pace.

When he reached the sidewalk, he didn't slow down.

"You're wrong, Andy Hale!" she shouted behind him. "I *love* my daughter."

As he locked himself in his car, he shook his head. Funny. He'd never mentioned her not loving Lucy.

Only not knowing her.

# Chapter 28

Lucy was still a little shaken when she finished class. Today, she and her students had ventured to the planetarium to take photos under pressure. Each had taken a turn, but she'd stood in the theater the whole time, her arms crossed over her chest to help quell the inner anxiety she felt from the blaring sounds of battle from the film footage. This was another wound she'd suffered in that village—another hurt that didn't show.

A couple students had dropped their phones. A few more promising students had stayed calm in the face of all the noise and gore, pointing and shooting with efficiency. Lucy had been impressed with their composure. She couldn't wait to grade this next round of photos once they touched them up.

When she pulled into her driveway, she frowned. Her mother was sitting on a worn bench in what used to be a garden before Mrs. Weidman got too old to tend to it.

She'd expected there to be another face-off, but she hadn't expected one this soon. Frankly, she wasn't up for it.

Exiting the car as her mother stood and started walking toward her, Lucy said, "I just got home from class. Can we chat another time?"

"No," her mother said in a harsh tone. "We cannot. Not when I have Andy Hale taking me to task for not knowing or loving my daughter. Not when he knows the real reason you're home, and I don't."

Her breathing shattered. Andy had visited her mother?

Crap. Of course he had. He was a fixer. Fiery rage flashed through her. He *knew* she didn't want him to interfere in her life. Well, she would deal with him later. Right now she had to figure out a way to appease her mother.

"Look. I didn't know he was going to see you. If I'd known, I would have talked him out of it."

Her mother's face was pinched tight with tension. "Do you have any idea how hard I try to understand you?"

That stopped her in her tracks. "How hard you try?"

"Don't belittle me," her mother scolded. "Since you were little, you were different than any other kid I knew. Do you have any idea how hard it was to be a mother to a child like that?"

Her words were a hard slap to the face. "So it's my fault for being different?"

"That's not what I'm saying," her mother said, clutching her hands together. "I'm trying to tell you that I didn't know how to be a mother to a girl like you. You never liked the same things I did. When you were in high school, all you wanted to do was go to school, hang out with Arthur Hale, or rail about human rights issues in places I didn't know anything about. Not once did you ever want to go shopping or get your nails done. Not like other girls."

Lucy set her leather briefcase purse on the ground. This was going to take a while, and she didn't want to have this confrontation while confined in her small house. "You're right, Mother. I'm not like other girls. I didn't want the things most girls want. But you make me feel like I'm bad. For being me."

Her mother's eyes narrowed. "Well, you make me feel like a bad mother. You think I'm shallow for wanting to do a funny and risqué calendar to honor people who've died of cancer. And then you shame me in front of my friends."

"I never shamed you!" she said, shaking her head.

"Sure you did!" her mother shot back. "You did it with April and the other volunteers. This morning your father looked at me with more judgment than I've ever seen. Then Andy Hale came by to deliver the final punch. I'm not a bad person!"

But she clearly felt like one, or she wouldn't be talking this way. "No, you're not, Mother. I'm not either. We just...don't speak the same language. I hoped that could change. Even though I'm thirty-six years old, I hoped..." Oh, crap, she wasn't going to say it.

"What?" her mother pressed.

"Nothing." Lucy shook her head. "We aren't going to resolve this, Mom."

"We certainly aren't if you don't finish what you were about to say. Tell me."

She looked down at her feet, wishing the ground could swallow her. "I just wish that you could be proud of me for one teensy, weensy second. And that's stupid because I'm the only one who should care about my accomplishments. I hate that I still want your approval."

"Join the club," her mother said dryly.

Lucy blinked. "You want my approval?"

"What do you think I've been trying to say?" her mother asked. "Ever since you could walk, your father has been everything to you. I never measured up, and since we didn't have any more children after you despite all our hoping and trying, I didn't have anyone else to..."

*Have a second chance with*, Lucy thought. As a kid, she used to ask her parents why she couldn't have a brother or a sister like Andy did, and they'd always told her it was in God's hands. She'd stopped asking when she was ten, sensing it upset them.

Her mother seemed to shake off the old memories. "Then you left here and did all this...stuff I didn't understand. I felt like you judged me for staying here and living an average life. When you came back, I hoped the calendar would bring us together. Not tear us apart."

So she hadn't been too far off last night. Neither one of them was completely wrong—or right. "That's what I wanted too," she said sadly.

"Then Andy Hale shoved his camera in my face today after I got out of the hot tub."

The hot tub? Served him right for interfering. "Seriously?"

"He's a real prude, Lucy. I'm a little worried for you, but that's not the point. He showed me the photo you took of him while he was thinking about Kim."

The one she'd sent him earlier in the morning. "He didn't like it at first."

Her mother nodded. "That's what he said. But then he realized you were capturing the love he still had for Kim despite everything. That he was moving forward and living with it. He said that was what your photos of Jill and Rhett and Old Man Jenkins showed too."

If Lucy had had a chair behind her, she would have sat down. He got it. He got *her*. She'd thought so last night, but this confirmed it one hundred percent.

"I got to thinking about what he said," her mother continued, twisting her wedding ring. "I'm not saying you're completely wrong about the photos, but I'm not saying I'm completely right either."

For her mother, it was a giant admission. "I'd come to the same conclusion. Even though I wanted you to be wrong." She gave her mother a wry smile.

"Your father said we're alike that way," she said, smiling in return. "That's why we always butt heads. He also gave me the first ultimatum he's ever given me in our forty-plus years together. He told me to say I'm sorry. That you're our daughter, and we won't lose you because of this. And I don't want to lose you, Lucy."

Lucy's heart finally broke open, and the hurt rolled through. "I don't want to lose you either, Mom."

Her mother sniffed. "So, I'll say I'm sorry and really mean it. And I'll try a little harder to understand you, and I'll hope you'll do the same for me."

In her whole life, her mother had never apologized to her. "Thank you for saying that. I know it wasn't easy. I'm sorry too, Mom."

"And I want you to do the calendar," she said, "but I'd really like you to share the process more with me if it wouldn't be too much trouble. It's hard to admit I really don't know you and why you chose those photos. But I'd like to."

Well, that put a lump in her throat. "I'd like that too."

"Oh, come here," her mother said, grabbing her in a hug. "We might fight like cats and dogs, but I still love you."

Lucy couldn't help but laugh. "That's what some people call tough love."

Her mother pushed her back and stared into her eyes. "It's about to get tougher. Why *are* you home, Lucy? Because it's damn well past time you told me the whole story and not that vague crap you told your father. I know you've gotten cozy with Andy Hale, but it chaps my hide that he knows why you're back and I don't."

Lucy sighed. "Why don't you come inside? I'll make some tea and tell you. Just promise me you won't turn all crazy on me and become Caretaker Mom."

"Like I'd agree to something like that in advance," her mother said, grabbing her forearm and leading her toward the house. "Do I look stupid?"

"Never," Lucy answered. "But I'd still like you to agree to try and be reasonable when you hear why I'm back." Hopefully, it wouldn't change her mind about Lucy's suitability for doing the calendar.

Her mother stopped her as she opened the front door. "It's that bad?"

"It's not great."

Her mother pushed her inside. "Then I'll try, and whatever it is, we'll face it together."

Lucy could live with that. She headed to the kitchen to make tea.

# Chapter 29

Moira finished up her call for a potential job in Denver and tried to whoop and holler about the offer they'd laid out. She'd crushed the interview last week. Blown them out of the water. Now they were offering her a fabulous position with greater responsibility and a better title. Plus, the offer was in her salary range and came with great benefits. She'd told them she would think about it.

But it wasn't the job she wanted. It was, at best, a good Plan B. What in the world was taking Chase Parker so long to get back to her? She'd run into Evan at Margie's bakery the other day, but he'd held up his hands and said the ball was in Chase's court. She'd gritted her teeth to keep from asking more questions.

The man was thorough. Industry standards suggested good human resource practice was to ask for three references. Chase had asked for five and checked them all personally, which showed his seriousness. A man of his position didn't usually check references. She was so fed up with the waiting. Being without work gave her way too much time to think about things. She needed to take a second Latin dance class or something to release all this frustration.

The doorbell rang, and Moira went to answer it, grateful for a distraction.

She was surprised to see Lucy on the other side of the door. "Hi, Moira," she said, sounding a little nervous.

Of course, Moira knew why she would be nervous. Her mother was deeply upset about the fight between Lucy and her mother. "Hi, Lucy. If you've come to see Mom, she's out at the store."

She shifted on her feet. "I'm here to see you, actually."

Moira tilted her head, puzzled. Something told her this wasn't a social call. "Okay. Come in. We can talk in the kitchen."

Once Lucy was settled at the table, Moira asked if she wanted anything to drink. Lucy's request for water confirmed she wasn't here for a drink and a laugh.

Moira set the glass of water in front of her and sat down beside her. "What's on your mind, Lucy?"

Her exhalation was more an explosion of pent-up energy. "I just spoke with my mother about the calendar, and it's going forward as I'd envisioned. I assume your mom mentioned the fight."

"In epic terms," she said, making a face. "I'm sorry."

"Don't be," Lucy said, running her finger over the blue flowers on the white tablecloth. "Things are better. For the moment. We still have a long way to go."

"Rome wasn't built in a day," Moira said, wishing she had more than clichés to offer.

"So...about the calendar," Lucy continued, taking a quick sip of her water. "You might have wondered what was going on at Jill's photo shoot."

Moira blanked. "You'll have to help me out here."

Lucy laughed self-consciously. "So, you didn't realize I was having trouble taking photos that day?"

"You seemed pretty nervous, and I remember you having some issues with your new camera, but I don't remember thinking anything was wrong."

*"Whew!"* Lucy put her hands on her head and laughed a little harder. "I told your brother I was sure you were on to me, but he said you hadn't said a word to him."

On to her? "Lucy, now I'm really confused. Help me out here."

Lucy lowered her hands to the table and gripped the edge. Moira's gaze flew to her face, and suddenly she knew the other woman was about to confess something big.

"Let me tell you why I returned to Dare Valley. And why I need your help with the calendar."

And so she began. Halfway through her story, Moira extended her hand to Lucy. When Lucy's voice broke at this small gesture of compassion, Moira knew she had been right to give it. Usually when someone was telling her a difficult life story at her work, she tried to keep a step back from them. But this was her brother's girlfriend. One of her idols.

Moira felt tears gather in her eyes as Lucy described her fears about taking photos again. She found her heart breaking a little for this brave woman she admired so much. Moira enjoyed photography, but it was Lucy's life and blood.

"I'm going to do the calendar," Lucy continued after drinking more water, "but I talked to my mother about having you help me. You...understand what it's about. Because of Kim."

She really had to blink back the tears this time. Kim had been a shining light in all of their lives and when she'd died, it had felt like the sun had been stolen from their family.

"I'd be happy to help," Moira told her, clutching her hand. "Lucy, I know I'm not as good as you are. I never could be. But I'll do my best."

"We'll figure it out together," she said, returning the

grip. "I don't want these photos to suffer because of my current limitations, and I know you can help offset those. I'm still adjusting to the electronic finder, but the biggest issues are that it's hard for me to see whether the lighting is right and if the picture is blurry as I shoot. There could be a problem—"

"But you can't distinguish it as easily on the fly," Moira finished. "I can't imagine how horrible this must be for you."

Truthfully, she was amazed Lucy had even agreed to do the calendar in the first place. Now she understood why Andy had told her to give Lucy some space.

"The only people who know about my...situation are your brother, Tanner—because he's been in the same hot spots and gets it—and my mother," she said, "although I expect my dad will know soon enough. I need to tell him the whole story myself, but it's...been a day."

Moira nodded. "No doubt. I'll help you any way I can. I don't want you to worry. I have your back."

Lucy gave her a weak smile. "You Hales."

The way she said it made Moira smile back. "What are you going to do long-term? About your career."

"That's the million-dollar question," Lucy answered, suddenly pushing out of her chair like she couldn't be contained any longer.

Moira let go of her hand and stood. "You should head on home, drink some wine, and take a bath. We can talk about the calendar in more detail when you're ready."

Lucy reached for her oversized bag hanging on the back of her chair. "I wanted to show you my choices for the three volunteers so far. I...showed Andy, but he doesn't have a photographer's eye. And your mother liked them... We won't talk about what my mother said yesterday. We came to a new understanding today. They need to be touched up a lot more than usual, but I hope what they've captured is as good as I think."

Lucy's hand was trembling as she drew the photos out and arranged them in a row on the kitchen table. Moira immediately zeroed in on the photo of Jill.

"Wow! You captured Jill perfectly. I've never seen her softer or more timeless."

"Whew, that's a relief," Lucy said, a smile dancing on her lips like she couldn't quite sustain it.

Moira peered closer, studying the remaining two. "The one of Old Man Jenkins almost breaks your heart, doesn't it? It should be funny, right? A ninety-year-old guy is sitting with nothing but an American flag in his lap. But there's wisdom and power here. You want to sit at his feet as he tells you how to navigate this thing called life."

"Exactly!" Lucy said, and Moira heard excitement in her voice.

She turned back to the third photo. "I don't know Rhett as well as Jane, but I've gotten to know him some. I have to say you captured a vulnerability I expect few have ever seen in him. He's such a force of nature, you know?"

"But here he is, holding the poker cards given to him by the uncle who taught him the game."

"It's wistful and haunting and ridiculously sweet," Moira said.

"But technically," Lucy pressed. "I still think there are a few places to improve."

Moira leaned over them, starting at the outer edges of the photo and then going to the center. "There's the smallest shadow on Jill's left cheek. And I would sharpen the color of the fruit in her hat a little more to add punch."

When she straightened and looked up, she realized Lucy was brushing tears away.

"Hey!" Moira said, putting her hand on her arm. "I can't tell you it's going to be all right, but I'm here to help."

Lucy bit her lip and nodded bravely. "Can I leave these with you? I have other copies. I'd like you to take your time with them. I can send you the electronic files when I get home."

"That would be great," Moira said, giving her an encouraging smile.

"Well, I'd better run. You're right. It has been a long day. And I haven't even talked to your brother yet."

"What did he do?"

"Besides visit my mother as an emissary of peace while she was in the hot tub?" Lucy asked, rolling her eyes.

Moira couldn't help it. She burst out laughing. "I hope he burned his eyes out. I mean, I love my brother, but sometimes he gets these ideas in his thick skull about fixing things."

"I know!" Lucy said, and they shared a smile of understanding. "But he's pretty great, and it did end up helping. I'm trying to decide how angry I am."

"We've all struggled with that conundrum at one point or another," Moira said. "You've known him forever, so you know he means well. I'm sure you'll find a way to draw the line with him."

"One would hope," Lucy said, pulling her into a hug. "Thanks, Moira. I was so scared to tell anyone what was going on with me, which is why I kinda...kept you at arm's length. I'm sorry about that. I hope we can be friends."

"That would be great, Lucy," Moira said, wishing she could high-five herself. "I'm honored you trusted me enough to ask for my help with the calendar."

"Well," Lucy said, shrugging, "you Hales are a pretty special lot. Tell your mom I said hi."

"Will do," Moira said and saw her to the door.

As she walked back to the kitchen, she was smiling. Lucy O'Brien had just agreed to be her friend and let her help with the calendar photos. Talk about awesome.

She scanned the photos again. It felt good to be involved in something that mattered. If she got the job at the Artemis Center, her whole career would be devoted to making a difference in the world. She'd had a long time to self-reflect over the past several weeks, and no question, that was what she wanted.

*Dammit, Chase Parker! Call me back and offer me the job,* she thought. *You know you want to.*

Then she realized she wasn't going to give him another day to call her. She had an offer in hand. Why not call and tell him about it?

When he came on the line, she went for honesty. "I have a pretty competitive offer from another company in Denver. You checked five of my references personally. How much longer are you going to take to offer me this position?"

Because her gut told her the job should be hers.

"Hello to you too, Moira," he said in that even-Steven baritone voice of his. "Evan said you were pestering him for a progress report at the bakery."

She made a face. Good thing he couldn't see it over the phone. "I don't pester. I ask reasonable questions."

*"Oh,"* he said, sounding amused. "Is that how you'd qualify the question you just asked me?"

"Truth or dare," she said, putting it all out there. "When was the last time you personally checked five references on someone?"

"You mean other than the defense minister of the former Yugoslavia?" he asked blandly.

She knew better than to ask if he was joking. "Exactly."

"Our HR director sent the offer to our lawyers for final review yesterday," Chase said. "I'll give them a call and make sure they know I want the final copy ASAP. Would that be agreeable to you, Ms. Hale?"

*More than.* She executed a salsa step, grinning like a

loon. "You can call me Moira," she told him primly to get his goat, "and yes, it would be."

"I'm going to like working with you," he said, chuckling softly over the line.

"You'd better have put together a better offer than the other one I have on the table," she told him. Okay, she wasn't planning on taking it regardless, but still... He needed to understand what others were willing to offer.

"Don't try and bluff me. You don't want that other job, but you'll be happy to know Quid-Atch has a reputation for offering its people top dollar. It encourages company loyalty and productivity."

God, he was attractive when he talked all corporate like that. "Don't forget about employee retention."

"Exactly." His soft chuckle made her smile. "Did I mention top executives receive signing bonuses?"

She jumped in place. Forget the salsa. "No, you forgot to mention that," she replied, trying to keep the excitement out of her voice.

"Care to ask what that might be?" he said, the glee apparent in his tone now. "I have a mind to break through that exterior reserve you put on so well."

It couldn't be that much, could it? Normal signing bonuses ran anywhere from two to ten thousand in her line of work. But this company wasn't exactly normal. "Okay, shoot."

"Are you sitting down?"

There was no mistaking it. He was laughing at her. "I'm fine standing."

He named the number. Moira's knees gave out, and she struggled her way into a chair. For a moment, the only thing she heard was the buzzing in her own ears. *Holy freaking baloney.*

"Are you still there? I assume that's acceptable since you don't have a witty comeback for me."

He had her number all right. "Does it come with a

company car?" she asked, just to be punchy.

He sputtered, and this time she laughed silently.

"In Dare Valley? Please. You'll have to drive like two miles at best."

"But I'll be working in a high-tech facility," she pressed, loving the process of negotiation, particularly with him. "Evan has a Maserati."

"This week," Chase said with a sigh. "And Moira? The whole car ploy is a no-go, but please do keep those kinds of tactics in mind when you're meeting with potential donors to the Artemis Center. I like people who push for more."

Oh yeah, this was going to be fun. "I'll look forward to seeing the offer."

*"Really?"* he drawled. "Please don't sign it in purple ink. I understand from Evan that your cousin Jill has a fondness for purple tutus. I wasn't sure whether an affection for that particular color runs in the family. I'll only have to send back the contract, you see."

"I don't have a purple pen—or purple tutu, for that matter—so you're safe," she said dryly, tucking away the reminder that Evan apparently shared a great deal more than business impressions with Chase.

"Thank God. We'll talk again once everything is official. You can jump up and down and cheer now."

He hung up. And she did jump up and down, shouting the numbers of the signing bonus out loud.

She was going to be able to do something meaningful in the world, and that was important.

But she was also going to be able to pay for her new car in cash.

Like the calendar she was helping Lucy with, she had the makings of her own new beginning in Dare Valley.

# Chapter 30

Andy had this niggling feeling in the back of his mind that he really shouldn't have talked to Lucy's mom. Perhaps he should have left the moment he saw Ellen soaking in that hot tub. Matt sure as heck had laughed himself silly when he'd told him about the ordeal. He'd agreed Andy could never unsee that horror. Oh, and wouldn't it be funny if Ellen ended up being Andy's mother-in-law? his brother had teased. According to Matt, that was going to be a story for the kids he had with Lucy.

Was it any wonder Andy was stirred up inside?

Thinking about having kids with Lucy—*seriously* thinking about it—had made him a little queasy. After all, he'd married Kim thinking it would last forever. That they would have babies and grow old together.

But Andy couldn't deny that the thought of marrying Lucy made him happy. After waking up next to her this morning, he'd pretty much decided he wanted to wake up with her every morning. She was a snuggler, and he liked that. Plus, she laughed at normal things like bed head and bodily functions—not something every woman could do, he'd learned as a doctor. He liked the thought of them still swapping ice cream cones and wisecracks when they were eighty.

He loved her, but he'd been dancing around a future with her, letting her take the lead. It was time for him to admit he was in this for the long haul. To craft a possible vision of their future together for her to mull over. Funny how making that decision had erased his fear of losing her.

Lucy had been silent all afternoon despite a couple of texts he'd sent her to check in. That didn't bode well. Her silence indicated the news of his unceremonious meeting with her mother might have reached her. He could be in deep shit for all he knew.

Well, as Uncle Arthur liked to say, he needed to pick up his Man Shovel and dig his way out. He was going to apologize to her for talking to her mother behind her back, whether she already knew about the hot tub chat or not.

Since Matt had continued to text him hot tub jokes after their brief call, he asked his brother to come over and watch Danny for a little while. Danny was already asleep by the time Matt and Jane arrived, so they were sitting on the couch browsing on Netflix when he left.

Only after he pulled into Lucy's driveway did it occur to him that he should have brought a peace offering like roses or ice cream. Why the hell hadn't he thought of that before? Because he was an idiot. He'd blame it on the shock of seeing her mom in the hot tub. Clearly it had shorted his brain.

But he couldn't very well reverse out of her driveway. Not when she was already peering out her window to identify her caller.

She already had the door open as he walked down the path to her front steps. "I'm still a little mad at you," she said, crossing her arms over her chest.

So, the cat was out of the bag. "I don't blame you. I meant well. Somehow I failed to comprehend how bullheaded your mother can be when she feels cornered.

I should have made my retreat the moment your dad opened the door and told me he hadn't gotten anywhere."

She continued to stare at him blandly.

Hitting his head with his palm, he said, "What was I thinking?"

"You were meddling," she said sternly, "which I thought we'd discussed. Besides, you must have said something about me having a special reason for returning to Dare Valley. She blasted me for telling you the whole story and not her. She was pretty worked up."

"Did she tell you I found her naked in the hot tub?" he asked, trying to make her smile. "I'm going to have to pay your dad back for that one. You don't do that to a brother."

She rolled her eyes. "From where I'm sitting, you deserved to catch her in the hot tub after what you pulled. I hope the image is burned into your corneas so you never do this again."

Ouch. "I'm sorry, Lucy. I really am. Are you going to let me come in and grovel?"

"No groveling is needed. Why don't you just come inside and tell me what you were thinking? I have some ideas. I talked to your sister, who told me you've done lamebrain things like this for all of the Hales. I might have remembered a few examples after I got to thinking."

"Which sister?" he asked.

"Moira, but I'll tell you about that after we talk about you."

He followed her inside to the kitchen, finally cataloguing she had on pink and brown plaid pajamas. It was no wonder she was exhausted if she'd had another confrontation with her mother.

"Do you want anything to drink?" she asked, opening up the fridge and pulling out a bottle of fizzy water.

"I wouldn't mind some of that water you're so fond of," he responded, feeling awkward standing in her kitchen. "I don't want things to be weird."

She poured two glasses of water and crossed to him. "I don't either, so let's sit down and talk."

Right. Their relationship had become so much deeper and stronger, but they were still friends. They knew how to talk to each other.

"To be fair," he began, watching the bubbles dance and fizz, "I would have talked to your mom even if we weren't involved."

Sitting back, she crossed her arms again. "Really? You never did that sort of thing when we were growing up."

"I used to be terrified of your mom, something I thought adulthood had changed. My mistake." He gulped the water to wet his throat. "I wanted to show Ellen that photo you took of me when I was thinking about Kim. I thought I could help her see what you helped me see."

"So she said. Keep going."

His chair squeaked when he rocked back on its legs. "I wanted so badly for you two to understand each other. Lucy, it broke my heart to think about you and your mom fighting like that. Especially when you need all your friends and family in your camp right now."

She gave him a bland stare. "I know you meant well, and if we're being honest, you did help my mom see things in a different light."

"I'd like to say 'then what's the problem?' but I already know."

"I know your M.O.," she said, giving him a stern look. "But you know how much I hate having other people interfere. Have you forgotten how many times I've told you to let me deal with my own problems?"

Game. Set. Match. "Yes, but—"

"You're lucky I talked my mother out of believing I'd

put you up to it, or it would have been World War III. Trust me. Then you really would have been in trouble."

He winced. "Listen, I know I...overstepped. I'll say it again. I'm sorry."

"I know," she said, lifting her glass and toasting him. "That's why you're inside Merry Cottage drinking my fizzy water. Now, let's talk about how you put my mother on the scent about why I came home."

Shit. "How bad did she dog you?"

She crossed her eyes in a move he hadn't seen since third grade.

"After a surprising come-to-Jesus talk with her, I ended up telling her the whole story. We even agreed I'm going to do the calendar my own way with Moira's help. That's why I went to talk to your sister."

His mouth must have dropped open because she shook her finger at him.

"But you listen to me. I'm going to remind you of the same thing I just told my mom. I don't want anyone meddling with my life because of this whole eye thing. Or talking to me about the dangers of working overseas. Or about why it's so much smarter for me to settle down in Dare Valley forever."

That seemed like a reasonable segue to his earlier thoughts, so he said, "About settling in Dare Valley forever..."

She set her water glass down with a clunk. "I beg your pardon?"

He settled back into the peace he'd felt earlier. "I had other reasons for going to talk to your mother today. Okay, this is going to sound a little crazy, but it's partly because I was thinking about you and me as a unit."

Her face was losing its red ire—not a good sign—so he rushed to continue.

"If you were at odds with your mom, I was too, and I didn't want that. Then things would be weird with my mom because she's your mom's best friend. Is this making sense?"

"You sound like some mutant version of the telephone game right now." Her eyes were narrowed in deep concentration.

"Okay, so let me try and muddle this out." He took a moment to think through the best way to convey his feelings. "When I realized how stubborn your mom was being in refusing to see you for who you are—something I never fully got until today—I grew incensed. I went a little crazy on her."

"She told me," Lucy said, a smile touching the corners of her mouth.

"The reason I went a little crazy is because I'm completely crazy about you. I went from trying to reason with your mother to defending you. Something I hadn't expected. And taking things to a whole other level of crazy...I told Matt about talking to your mom in the hot tub."

"He must have wet himself laughing," she said, fighting a bigger smile now.

"Pretty much," he admitted, shuddering. "Some things can't be unseen, Lucy."

"You deserve it," she said, echoing her earlier sentiment.

"Fine, it's my penance for interfering. But then Matt told me it would be a great story to tell our kids."

She blanched, going several shades paler.

"I know! My brain pretty much exploded, but then I got to thinking... Well, I thought about what it would be like swapping ice cream cones with you when we were both old and gray and laughing together and all that jazz."

Her face wasn't very encouraging, so set his glass down with a clunk too.

"Lucy, I'm not proposing right now because I'm not prepared with a ring or anything, which you deserve."

"Holy shit! You're—"

"Let me get this out. I never thought I'd want to marry again. But then I thought about how wonderful things could be if we stay together in the years ahead... I realized I want to put a possible future out there for you to consider."

Her mouth gaped, and she stared at him.

"Lucy, I'm not afraid anymore." And after all the fear he'd lived with for the past couple of years, he knew this marked a turning point for him.

She didn't move a muscle—not one.

"You say you can't know what your future will look like because of your vision," he continued, "but I don't think that has to be true."

He was tempted to get down on one knee, but he realized from her agitated breathing that it wouldn't be the best move. Instead, he inched his chair closer to her so their knees touched.

"Lucy, I love you. I want you in my life forever. Not just as a friend, although that connection has always been so special between us. I want to wake up with you and laugh with you. I want to share my days with you—and tell you everything, from the random to the profound. You appreciate both, and I love that about you. I want to share Danny with you, and I want to create more beautiful little people with our genes that we can raise together."

She shoved him back with a hand to his chest. "And you say you're not proposing? You need to stop this right now."

When she pushed out of her chair, he grabbed her shaking hands. "I'm not proposing right this second. I'm sharing my vision of the future. Our future. Our paths were connected when we were young. Then you went away, and they forked, but now you're back. We're walking the same path again."

She put her hand to her temple like he was giving

her a headache. "Andy, you don't get it. No one ever walks the same path. That's what my mother finally understood today. Her, you, me—we all walk different paths. We're all our own people. Don't ask me to stay here and become something I'm not."

He pushed out of his chair. "I am not asking that. Lucy, you're not hearing me."

"I may have trouble seeing you like I used to, but I can hear you just fine." Stalking over to the counter, she put ten feet between them. "Why are you doing this? We've only just started this other thing between us."

He stayed where he was, watching her small frame tremble across the room from him. "Lucy, you know I usually take my time about making big decisions, but with some things, I just know. I feel that way about this, about you and me. And you're not being honest with yourself when you say this just started. You and I have always connected on a deeper level than most people do. Normal rules don't apply to us."

She edged back even further from him—bumping into the counter. "You don't think I'll get my full vision back, do you? Oh, my God, is this your way of trying to save me?" The fire in her eyes was scorching. "I know you love me, but you can't save me from an uncertain future, Andy Cakes."

The derision in her voice crushed his heart. "Every fear you have is rising up and casting a shadow over us. I don't want you to give up who you are. I'm saying I want to be with you. Forever. However that looks. Whether you get your vision back or not. Whether you work overseas again or stay here."

Her head was already shaking in denial. "You originally said I couldn't have children and do what I do. Andy, I know you like I know myself. You could *never* be happy with a wife who traveled the world for work. And I couldn't give that up. Not for you. Not for our kids. I wouldn't want to. I would want to show our children *anything* is possible—even a marriage that isn't conventional."

He took three steps toward her, but the look she gave him—like a wild animal caged—halted him. "I do love you. What I'm telling you is that I want to find a way to have a shared future. And yes, that includes a family."

She threw out her hands. "You're way too conventional to have a wife who has to leave for a month here and there to visit a war zone. I wouldn't want to worry you. You could never take hearing what my life was really like."

In all the years they'd known each other, she'd never gone below the belt. "You're pissing me off, Lucy. You were the one who decided I couldn't take it. Why don't you trust me more?"

"You had trouble with Kim getting sick and dying," she spat out. "There are plenty of things I knew better than to tell you, and that was before we were together. Like the time I managed to evade five child soldiers who bribed the hotel manager for the key to my room so they could gang rape me. Or when I hid behind a burned-out garbage can while soldiers shot a bunch of street children because I knew I'd be killed if I tried to stop them. How would you feel about getting that kind of phone call from your wife?"

God. Is that what she'd gone through? His face tightened as emotion jolted through him. "It's cruel of you to say I couldn't handle things with Kim. I did my fucking best, okay, like any other person after finding out their beloved young wife is going to die. No one knows how they're going to react when they're faced with impossible situations. You're projecting because you're scared I could actually love you as you are. Lucy, I'm not your mother, dammit!"

Her harsh breathing filled the kitchen. He took a moment to compose himself.

"How did we end up yelling at each other?" he asked in a softer tone. "We never do that."

She smiled sadly. "It appears we are, and I'm sorry."

"Me too."

"Please don't do this," she said more softly now. "Let's see how things go between us, and whether my vision changes. We can talk about the future when it comes."

Now he strode across the kitchen and gently put his hands on her shoulders, looking into her scared green eyes. "I don't want our decision about whether to have a future together to hinge on whether your vision improves. That's not fair to either of us. I love you. I would want you even if you were blind. It's you I want, Lucy. However you are."

The muscles in her shoulders were stretched taut under his fingers. "Well, it matters to me. I need to know who I am and where I'm going. I can't just agree to throw all that aside and stay in Dare Valley."

Suddenly he felt as helpless talking with her as he had while talking with her mother. "You're still not hearing me."

"We're not hearing each other, and that breaks my heart. We've always been able to understand each other." She hung her head. "Perhaps this was inevitable. We've both wanted different things our whole lives."

He shook her gently, sensing he was losing her. "No, we haven't. We've always wanted to be in each other's lives. We love each other now more than ever, and people who love each other find a way to forge a future together. That's what I want with you. That's what I've been trying to drill into your thick head."

Her eyes flashed, but she didn't respond.

"You need to think about what I said," he told her, releasing her. "And I'll think about what you said. Lucy, I mean it, the situation with your vision doesn't matter to me. All I want is to be with you, share Danny with you, and make a family with you. I'd like to stay here, but I'm willing to talk about that."

From the shuttered look on her face, he knew she didn't believe him.

"I know you're scared I'm asking you to give up on yourself, but I'm not. The truth is that I plan to bring my lawn chair to your game of life and cheer you on like I cheer for Danny at T-ball. I want you to remember that."

He made himself kiss her on the forehead and walk out of the kitchen.

# Chapter 31

After a sleepless night, Lucy decided to pay a visit to the man who would understand her the best: Arthur Hale. So, after drinking her morning coffee, she drove to the office of the newspaper that had helped steer her course.

Main Street was bustling with pedestrians enjoying the warm fall day as she walked to *The Western Independent,* mulling over her conundrum all the while. She knew that Andy loved her —she really did. But while he said he understood her, she still didn't believe he fully comprehended how integral being an international photojournalist was to her sense of self.

His talk of marriage had been so unexpected, and it had...well, she'd pretty much freaked out. How had conservative Andy Hale, who'd always approached relationships so carefully all his life, thrown this curveball at her?

It was like an alien had taken over his body, except she knew he never said anything he didn't mean. And then there was their mind-blowing lovemaking the other night. That meant something, right?

She schooled her features as she pushed open the front door to the office. A few of the locals who'd worked for Arthur all their lives called out greetings as she made her way across the floor. Everywhere she looked, employees were chatting and talking up the current headlines over coffee, talking with sources on the phone, or hunkered down at the small tables situated in the corners, discussing story ideas.

By the time she passed Meredith and Tanner's offices—which were empty—on her way to Arthur's, she felt calmer.

In many ways it felt like her adult life had started here. Within these walls, she'd been exposed to a world beyond Dare Valley, one that was at once complex and flawed, dangerous and exciting. This place had been her salvation, and Arthur her teacher.

When she stopped in his doorway, he was already looking down his nose at her over his glasses. She couldn't help but grin.

"About time you came to visit this old man," he huffed out, standing up. "If I didn't know you'd been busy with my great-nephew, I would have taken it personally. Now, come and give me a kiss."

To pull his chain, she said, "You never asked me to kiss you when I interned here."

He barked out a laugh. "Good God, no. Who do you think I am? Some sleazy politician?"

She made her way over to him and kissed his weathered cheek. "Not in a million years. Mind if I close the door?"

He arched a brow. "I like when people ask me that. Means they have something good to tell me. Is it a story?"

Sadly, she shook her head. He huffed some more.

"Then it's personal problems," he said, sitting back in his squeaky old chair. "Go ahead and close the door, but I swear, I should start charging you young people money for all the advice I dish out."

She settled into the same scuffed-up wooden chair

that had graced the front of his desk since she was a teenager. Probably earlier even. "Any of it good?" she asked.

He gave her a look. "Still got that sassy mouth on you, I'm glad to hear. When you came home, I thought you might have lost it. You looked pretty done in. Are you going to finally tell me what brought you back to Dare Valley? Tanner said it was your story to tell despite my inducements."

Nodding, she put her hands to her thighs. "I thought I might lead with that and then tell you about my problem."

Waving his hand, he said, "Then get on with it. Who knows how many hours I have left in this world?"

That eased the pressure in her diaphragm, and so she launched into the story about the attack on the village she'd been in, taking him through the events and the subsequent outcome. His face didn't give a thing away, not even when she shared the details about the condition of her right eye.

"Well," she finally burst out. "Aren't you going to say anything?"

He rubbed his cheek. "Journalism isn't without its risks, especially in the places you visit. Do you regret going?"

"To the village?" She shrugged. "Sometimes, but I know it could have happened anywhere."

"Correct," he said in his tough-as-nails tone. "Wrong time, wrong place. It sucks, as you young people say, but that's one of the realities of reporting in high-risk areas. Someone has to do it. You decided it would be you, and for that, me and a whole bunch of other people out there are grateful. Here's another question for you."

It touched her to hear him thank her for putting her life on the line to report world events. Not too many people did that. "Shoot."

"Could you have done anything differently that day

in the village besides being there?" he asked, putting his elbows on the desk.

She'd thought it through plenty of times. Who didn't wonder if an event could have been prevented? "No, there was nothing."

"All right," he said, sitting back again. "So, you have vision problems, and you're a photographer. Double whammy."

Her throat was growing tight. "Double whammy."

"The big question is: do you want to keep taking photographs of world events and writing stories about them?"

She released a deep breath. "Yes."

"Even if you get hurt again?" he asked, his eyes zeroing in on her face.

It took courage to admit how she really felt. "I'm still scared of going back out there. And it's not just because I fear I won't be able to take the same kind of photos again. I don't want to get hurt again or hurt worse."

He tapped his desk emphatically. "That sounds pretty smart to me. Only a moron wanders into a war zone and says he's not afraid. I told you when you went off on your first assignment that fear is only fear. It only has the power you give it."

Right now, she felt like she was battling every shadow inside her while Andy seemed to have finally conquered his. "That's a good transition to my other problem."

She looked down at her hands, feeling suddenly awkward. In all the years she'd known him, she'd never imagined asking her mentor advice about relationships.

"I can already tell your problem concerns my great-nephew," Arthur said in his gravelly voice. "Best spit it out. I'm aging here."

That made her look up. A short smile tugged at her lips. "It might be a little embarrassing."

His head darted back. "If this is about sex, you can

forget it. I might dispense some common sense advice to you young people since you don't seem to have a lick of it, but I am not a sex therapist. For the love of Pete!"

Now she was blushing. "It's not about sex. It's about..."

"Yes? Yes?" he prodded, leaning over his desk.

"Andy wants me to consider having a future with him," she said, clutching her hands. "Here in Dare Valley."

"Mmmm," he mused, rubbing his chin. *"Interesting.* I have to admit I'm impressed."

Now she was confused. "Impressed? I'm not following you."

"I lost my wife after spending fifty-some years with her, and it crushed me." He tapped a finger to the picture of Harriet he kept on his desk. "I've always wondered what I would have done if she'd been taken from me as young as Kim was taken from our dear Andy."

Everything inside Lucy seemed to still, and she leaned forward to listen.

"I've always said a real man realizes the importance of marriage and family," Arthur said, looking back at her. "Seems Andy has found a way to do so twice in his young life, and that takes more courage than most people possess. And let's face it...after losing one woman, it takes big balls to want to forge a life with another whose career could kill her. That impresses the hell out of me."

Shell-shocked, she sat back in her chair. She'd been so focused on her own feelings, she hadn't stopped to think how much courage it must have taken for Andy to visualize a future with her. He'd told her he wasn't afraid anymore, but she hadn't completely gotten it until now.

How many times had he told her he'd struggled with the idea of dating again, let alone remarrying, before

Lucy's return to Dare Valley? Her heart felt constricted in her chest, like it was tugging at bonds of her own making.

"I'm ashamed I freaked out on him, but I'm also confused about what to do. Andy told me my vision shouldn't factor into my decision about our future."

"He's completely right," Arthur said, pounding his desk emphatically. "You either love him or you don't. You either want to be with him forever or you don't. As I told Meredith when she first met Tanner, life is short. Don't dick around."

She blinked at his language, but then extended her hands in exasperation. "But this is Andy we're talking about. He says we'd find a way to make my career work if we had a family, but—"

"You don't believe him," Arthur said. "Ah...I see the problem now."

"He's the settle-down, two-car-garage kind of guy. Heck, I've never even had a garage."

"Do you want to have kids, Lucy?" he asked.

Every time she'd held a child against her breast—be it in an orphanage or a stifling-hot village hut, she'd hoped to have one of her own someday. "Yes. Yes, I do."

Arthur cleared his throat and reached for a water glass on his desk. "All this talk is making me thirsty."

Lucy knew he was only giving himself more time to think, so she gave it to him, all the while fighting the urge to bounce her leg in agitation. Talking about marriage and having kids was raising all sorts of emotions inside her.

"When it comes down to it, Lucy, love is a choice. Sure, there's that warm feeling you get from being around someone you fancy, but it takes more than that for two people to build a happy life together. You have to be willing to hang in there with the person you choose and do your best to support them and let them support you. Andy has already proven he could support one partner."

"She didn't want to travel the globe," she said, thinking of Kim.

"Last I saw, there were still airplanes that could fly you somewhere in a day and vehicles to take you the rest of the way." He pushed his water glass aside. "Maybe you won't be in the field as long as you used to be. Here's a humdinger for you. Did you stay in those countries for all that time because you needed to do your job, or did you stay because you had nowhere else to go between assignments?"

His humdinger, as he'd called it, smacked her right in the face. "Dammit, that hurts."

"But it's true, isn't it?" he said, rolling up his sleeves. "Lucy, you're one of the smartest, most interesting women I've ever known—and I've known a lot. Ever since you were a kid, asking questions about *glasnost,* I knew you were special. You weren't like the rest of the kids around here. Not even Meredith has your global breadth as a journalist."

She remembered discussing the Gulf War and the role of petroleum with Arthur at church picnics. He'd always been willing to listen to her and share his thoughts, making her feel...connected to something bigger, she supposed.

"I don't think you ever knew how grateful that little girl was to you for talking with her."

"I was entertained." He waggled his brows. "Your global interests put you somewhat out of the pack around here, but one thing I always found interesting was how Andy Hale stayed your best friend throughout school. For someone you think is so conservative, he sure picked a pretty unconservative friend."

She'd always found that pretty incredible too. "I still don't completely understand why."

"Because you're a knucklehead." Arthur's mouth twisted. "Harriet used to say she didn't need to accompany me on my trips to communist Russia, for example, because she rather liked hearing about it through my eyes. Perhaps you're Andy's eyes to the bigger world out there."

That might have been the sweetest thing Lucy had ever heard. "I want that to be the case, but I've always had to censor my experiences for him." She ducked her head. "I told him so last night."

"Of course you've censored your stories," Arthur harrumphed. "If you hadn't, he would have sweated out his white doctor's coat worrying about you. Do you think I told Harriet the KGB questioned me for seven hours one time before releasing me in the middle of a snow-covered street in downtown Moscow? Hell, no. But Harriet could have taken it. She was one tough woman."

"She had to be to put up with you," Lucy said, "although you're pretty great."

He plucked a pencil off his desk and shoved it behind his ear. "Are we finished here? I have a newspaper to run. Or are you still unsure about what to do? Lucy, you have a man who's brave enough to want to marry you after a horrible tragedy wrecked his life. That's not the kind of man who'd ever let you down. As I tell all the young people around here, you can dillydally all you want, but you marry people with character. Otherwise you get screwed."

That sparked a laugh out of her. He glared at her.

"I'm sorry, but that was funny."

Arthur waved his hand in the air. "Andy is right. Your vision doesn't matter. You will do what you want to do. If you want to take photos, you'll figure it out. If you want to marry him, you'll figure it out." His eye roll was especially dramatic this time. "Lucy, all of life is about figuring things out. You have a sharp mind and a good heart. Use them. Now, let me get back to work."

She shoved out of the chair and walked around the

side of his desk. Bending over, she kissed him on the cheek and then gave into the urge to hug him.

"Bah!" he protested, putting his arms around her. "You're going to ruin my reputation as a hardass. Get yourself out of here."

She gave him one more squeeze and made her way to the door. "How about I write up an op-ed about how no one really understands or cares what's going on in Congo?"

He pushed the rim of his glasses up his nose. "Make up with the Hale boy, and then send it to me. I've always fancied having you as an official part of the family."

Her mouth dropped. "What?"

"I'm not saying you have to change your name, but you'll be part of the Hale clan, and my blood will flow through your children. Just imagine what kind of journalist we'll get when your DNA mixes with Hale DNA. Just like with Meredith and Tanner. She should be having her baby any day now."

Lucy leaned back against the doorframe. "After everything you said, you end with that?"

He shrugged. "So I buried the lede. Shoot me. Lucy, you'd be the dumbest girl ever to walk away from a life with Andy Hale. And you're not dumb. Get your head out of your butt and go make up with him. You'll figure things out together."

Shaking her head, she tested her balance. "You said all those things, knowing what I'd do the whole time?"

"One thing I'm not is stupid," he said, swiveling around in his chair. "Neither are you."

# Chapter 32

When Andy pulled up to Merry Cottage, he was feeling more than antsy. Lucy had texted him the previous day to say she wanted to talk, but he hadn't been ready. Correction. His plan hadn't been ready, so he'd told her he would see her today for lunch.

Not that he could eat anything, mind you. He picked up his gift for her and exited his car. She was either going to get it or she wouldn't, and there was nothing he could do to change that.

When she opened the door, the brilliant shades of her auburn hair and green eyes seemed all the more dear, all the more lustrous. There was worry between her brows, and when he leaned down to kiss her cheek, he felt like he was wading through raw honey to get close to her.

Things were weird between them again, and part of him wished he'd never opened his big mouth. But he knew better. A person got the kind of love they asked for, and he wasn't going to keep hiding what he wanted from himself or her because it was more comfortable or convenient.

"I'm glad you're here," she said, putting her arms around him suddenly. "When you said you couldn't see me yesterday, I got a little worried. I was the one who supposedly needed more time to think about things."

He edged back and produced the gift he'd hidden behind his back. "One day didn't seem like a lot of time, but I needed it to arrange this. I..." Crap. What should he say? "I hope you like it."

She gave him a puzzled look, but stepped back to let him inside. He closed the door behind him.

"Why don't we sit in your parlor?" he suggested. "You can open it there."

"You didn't have to get me anything," she said, but she went ahead and sat down.

He sat down beside her, putting more space between them than usual to set her at ease.

She unwrapped the orange wrapping paper from the large white box he'd selected to disguise the shape of the gift. When she pulled back the purple tissue paper Moira had thrown into the box, she pressed a hand to her mouth.

But he heard the soft exclamation of air escape from her mouth.

He shifted on the couch. "I couldn't reach you the other day, so I thought I'd try to speak your language. Don't you always say, 'a picture is worth a thousand words'?"

She turned and stared at him.

"Lucy, these photos are my words to you," he told her, wanting to take her hand. "And Danny's. He helped contribute too."

The graceful line of her throat rippled with emotion. "You called it The Calendar of New Beginnings," she said, tears filling her eyes.

He cleared his throat. "I thought it was a pretty great title, and since it's only for you, I knew it would be okay if I used it. Our moms wouldn't care."

"But this is your *house* on the front!" she said, puzzlement washing over her face. "And you and Danny sitting on the front porch? How did you do this? When?"

"I asked Moira to help me. I had some photos, and she took the ones we were missing. There are plenty of online calendar makers in case you didn't know. I couldn't get it finished and printed yesterday, so that's why it had to wait until this morning."

"*Oh.*"

"I'm sorry I put you off, but I...needed to have this ready before we talked. Lucy, I want you to understand what I'm saying about the future."

She touched the cover then and started flipping through the calendar. "I remember this photo of us," she said, tracing the edges of the photo he'd selected for January.

Their teacher had caught them napping together in kindergarten.

"Mom had this one," he said, remembering how moved she'd been by his request to go through the old albums for photos of him and Lucy. "She said Mrs. Hanover thought it was the cutest thing she'd ever seen in all her years of teaching, the way we'd cuddle up together, forehead to forehead, holding hands while we napped on our colored mats."

Her head was nodding as she sniffed. "We really were the best of friends. Even then."

"Yeah," he said, trying to hold it together. They were only on January.

She finally flipped the page. February put the first brush of a smile on her lips. "I always was shoving you up a tree when we were kids."

"It's a medical fact girls have more upper body strength than boys before puberty."

There was a decided snort beside him. "Keep telling yourself that. I liked that you climbed trees with me."

"You liked to, so I had to keep up. It's what friends do."

She sniffed again and turned the page. March showed them doing math homework on her bed when they were in sixth grade. "I think you spent more time with me in my room growing up than I did by myself."

"That's because we hated to be apart," he said, nudging her with his shoulder.

"My mom took this picture," she said, turning and narrowing her eyes at him.

Busted. "I had to go to your mother for some of the photos I had in mind, but I swear we didn't speak. Neither of us wants to get into any more trouble with you."

She leaned her head on his shoulder like she used to when they were kids together. "You're not in trouble. I'm sorry you thought that. I just...had things to work out."

He bit his tongue to keep from asking for more clarification. She turned the next page. April showed them hanging out at a high school football game.

"Personally, I don't know what you were thinking with your hair," he said dryly.

She made an aggrieved sound. "Is that a scrunchie?"

He had sisters. He knew what a scrunchie was. Peering closer, he said, "Yep, hot pink."

"I was making a statement."

"Sure you were," he added, feeling the rhythm of their friendship returning.

When she turned the page to May, she said, "I don't remember seeing this."

"My mom did," he said, feeling his ears burn. "She hid it from me. I found it when I was going through the albums."

"But why? So, we danced at prom. All I remember is you stepping on my toes to 'Candle in the Wind' by Elton John."

He still hated that song. "You don't see it, do you? Look closer. There's a reason my mother took the photo and didn't show it to us."

She lifted the calendar until it was a foot away from her face. *"Oh!"*

"Yeah," he said, clearing his throat. "I might have had a moment. All I remember is dancing with you, and then suddenly all I could think about was how good you smelled, which turned into thinking about how pretty you looked. I lost the beat and stepped on your feet."

"It wasn't a fast song," she said in a dry tone. "You *liked* me."

"Yeah, in that moment," he admitted. "I liked how soft you felt in my arms, and I had some pretty lusty thoughts for my age. It scared me. We were friends. I was sure you'd kill me if you realized what I was thinking."

"I didn't realize it at the moment. My toe was throbbing. Those were open-toed shoes!"

His frustration was rising, for both himself and the boy he'd been. "Would you forget about the shoes? I showed you this because I wanted you to see there was always the promise of something more between us. Now turn the page."

When she looked at him, she blinked a few times. "You're upset."

He strove for patience—like he did when Danny asked for a drink of water for the fourth time at bedtime. "A touch. I'll get over it."

She turned the next page. June showed them together with their respective families and Kim. They were all gathered together at Lucy's parents' house amidst an abundance of Christmas lights. She was sitting between him and Kim, and they were all laughing at one another's holiday sweaters.

"I never fully told you how happy it made me that you and Kim got along so well," he said, his throat thickening as he stared at the woman who had been his wife next to the woman he now hoped to spend the rest of his life with. Choosing this picture had been the most difficult for him, but after changing his mind more than a few times, he'd decided to go with his gut.

"How could I not like the woman you'd fallen in love with?" she asked, and he wondered if it was his imagination, but she seemed to cuddle closer to his side. "Besides, she made you so happy."

Tears popped into his eyes. "Yeah, she did, and I'll always look on our time together with love and joy. But she's not here now. You are."

When she met his gaze, there were tears in her eyes too.

# Chapter 33

Lucy wanted to bundle Andy up in a giant hug. How hard must it have been for him to include a photo of the three of them together?

"You make me so happy, Lucy," he said, wiping at his eyes with his jacket.

Her heart continued to expand in her chest, smarting with every millimeter it gained. "You make me happy too. You always did."

His smile flashed across his serious face. "Okay. Now turn the page."

She was going to say, *yes, sir,* to lighten the mood, but when she saw the photo he'd chosen for June, she pretty much dissolved.

"Where did you get this?" she asked, tracing a photo of herself on assignment in Uganda. "I was working with a local photographer on an AIDS calendar. He took this photo of me at the orphanage where we were taking photos of children whose parents had died from AIDS. Part of my contract with the NGO was to train a leading local photojournalist. Anthony was great. He works for *The London Times* now."

"Moira found this picture by doing a simple Google Images search of your name. Then she copied it and worked her magic to include it in the calendar."

A sense of wonder furled around her still-expanding heart. He'd valued this part of her enough to include it in the calendar.

"Lucy," he said in a deep voice. "I know you still don't believe I understand what your career means to you, but I do. I want you to be who you are. It's who I love. Your work is important."

She was too moved to speak.

"I hoped showing this to you would help you understand that I mean that," he said, taking her hand and putting it on his heart. "I want you to have everything you could ever want. I just hope that will include me."

Hope was shining in his eyes, as bright as the stars over the savannah. She could see he meant it. A surge of emotion pushed through her chest, and for a moment, she couldn't breathe. Everything felt like it was crumbling again, but she wasn't scared.

Arthur had helped her bring the old frame through which she had seen herself and her relationships into full focus. But now it was starting to crack and fall away, like an old camera lens dropped on the ground. She tightened her grip on Andy's hand.

"Andy, I'm not afraid anymore either," she said as soon as she could talk again. "I want it to include you. And Danny and the rest of our family."

His other hand came up and cupped her cheek. "You have no idea how happy that makes me," he said, wiping more tears away from her eyes. "Okay, go ahead and turn the page."

Turn the page? She was almost too lost in the moment to register the words. "I love you."

His face softened. "And I love you. Let's move on to August."

Since he was being so unusually insistent, she went ahead and did as he'd suggested. Then she laughed.

"Oh, I see how it goes."

"I wanted to make sure you understand I have another purpose outside of the home too."

The photo was of him sitting beside an elderly woman, who was hooked up to all sorts of tubes and IVs. Her face was taut with pain, but she was smiling weakly at Andy.

"That's Mrs. Grayer," he told her. "I asked her if Moira could take this picture yesterday when I was doing rounds. She has stage four lung cancer, and she knows she isn't going to make it. I was talking with her about hospice."

Looking at the photo again, she noticed the compassion and sadness on his face. "I'm so sorry."

"Yeah, me too. She's a really nice lady. Has fifteen grandkids, all of whom are decimated at the thought of losing their nana." He took a breath. "I included this photo because I want you to know that sometimes I bring work home with me. Emotionally. I try not to. I didn't always tell Kim about the bad cases. There was this one time the medics brought in a three-year-old who'd been run over by a car…"

She gripped his hand. "I want you to tell me about those days," she said, realizing they were making a pact of sorts.

"And I want you to tell me about hiding from soldiers who are shooting street children," he said in a harsh tone. "I can't guarantee it won't upset me because that's fucking awful, and I love you. I'll worry too, but I'll manage it."

"Deal," she said, giving him an encouraging smile.

"Seems we're making some progress here," he said with an answering smile. "Turn the next page."

She did, and that's when everything inside her exploded anew. September displayed two half-eaten ice cream cones resting on an outdoor table.

"And when we do have bad days or bad moments,"

he said softly, "we're going to share our ice cream cones because that's what partners do."

"I like the sound of that."

"And if you're on assignment, I'm going to send you ice cream emoticons over Skype or something until you come home."

Home. For so long it had been something other people had. She leaned over and kissed him on the mouth. "Thank you for believing I'll be able to return to what I love. I talked to Arthur yesterday, and he helped me see that I may feel differently about my lifestyle than I did before. I won't want to spend as much time in the field as I used to because..."

Oh, this was hard to admit.

"Because I didn't have anything to come home to before," she said, still feeling the barbs of that revelation.

"But you do now," he said, cheering her up like the best friend he was.

"Yeah," she whispered. "I have you, and I'm so grateful, Andy."

"I am too," he said and leaned in to kiss her back.

Their lips met, and everything inside her settled into a new alignment. It was like her heart was a camera lens, and she'd finally found the best setting for her life. It was with him. She could already imagine the photos this new lens would help her take. Ones that involved family time and new babies and quiet strolls through town while one of their parents watched the children.

He broke the kiss, but kept his lips inches away. "I'd like to keep doing that, but you have more months to look at in the calendar. We're only on September."

What were a few more months? She pulled away and flipped the page. "All right, let's see what we have next. Oh, my goodness!"

Danny smiled into the camera. He was wearing his PJs and holding the framed photo she'd taken for him of a baby camel in Egypt.

"He's totally on board with this plan," Andy assured her. "This was his way of letting you know it."

"If your plan was to make me bawl, you've succeeded." She turned to face him. "I need you to know I love him, and I hope you'll let me be a good mother to him. I know Danny's not mine per se, but I'd...want to treat him with the same love and respect I'd give all our other children."

"I'm happy to hear that," he said, his eyes shining with tears. "I'd want you to love him like that. He deserves it. He's a...really special kid."

"Yeah, he is," she said, hugging him again. "And he has a really terrific father."

Perhaps because he'd given her the permission to be Danny's mother, Andy folded up and went to pieces. She held him through the storm.

Once his tears had quieted, he whispered, "I guess that was harder for me than I thought. It's not that I don't know you'll be a great mom to him. It's just... How can I explain? I'm still sad he won't know Kim, you know? It doesn't mean I don't love you."

"I understand that," she said, caressing his back as he shuddered. "It's okay to feel that way. And it will be okay when Danny misses her. It won't hurt me, Andy. Kim was his mother, and she's gone. We'll figure it out." Just like Arthur had said they would.

"Yeah, we'll figure it out."

"Shall I turn the next page?" she asked, sensing he was back to himself.

"By all means. This one's my favorite."

November was a simple portrait of Andy gazing into the camera. His eyes were as soft as the smile on his face.

"Do you remember the photo you took of me thinking about Kim?" he asked.

She nodded, and her heartbeat started to pound

because she already knew what he was going to say. "Yeah."

"This is me thinking about you," he said, reaching for her hand again. "I wanted you to see how much I love you too."

And she did. He'd looked straight into the camera, baring his soul to her. And those smile crinkles around his eyes spoke of joy.

"I love it," she said, hugging it to her heart. "Out of all the photos I've ever seen in my whole life, this one might be my favorite. I take it Moira shot this one yesterday."

"Yeah," he said. "I'm so going to owe her for this."

Lucy decided she was going to do something special to say thank you to his sister—her new friend. Then she realized Moira was going to be family one day, her family. "She wants you to be happy."

"Yeah," he answered easily, "and since she's going to be the director of the Artemis Institute here in Dare Valley, I'm going to have plenty of time to make it up to her."

"Oh, she got the job! That's great news."

"She told all of us last night after she signed the papers. Another Hale returns to Dare Valley. Caroline's a goner. There's no way she'll be able to remain the solo hold-out in Denver."

Lucy wasn't so sure about that, but who knew? She was back in Dare Valley, after all, and this would be home from here on out.

"Shall we look at December?" he asked, running his hand down her hair in the most soothing of caresses.

She flipped the page triumphantly. December was a repeat of the photo on the front—Andy and Danny sitting in white Adirondack chairs on his porch. "I love this photo of you two." They were going to be her guys, she realized.

"You don't get it, do you?" he asked, sighing. "I told

Moira it was too subtle."

"Let me look closer," she said, and brought it closer to her face.

Suddenly everything came into focus.

There was a third chair on the porch, situated right next to Andy's. And on the seat sat a camera.

"You have a space for me," she said, trying to swallow the lump in her throat.

"We bought a third chair for you. When you're on assignment, we'll be home, waiting for you."
Jeez. Did he have to be so freaking sweet? She turned and faced him, the calendar on her lap. "I can't think of a better new beginning."

# EPILOGUE

An extra burst of happiness ran through Arthur Hale's black-ink veins as he watched the festivities around him in Jill's house. Meredith was holding her newborn baby boy, Jared Arthur McBride, in the middle of a crowd of enthusiastic Hales.

It touched him deeply that she and Tanner had given the boy his name, so much so he'd had to drag a worn handkerchief out of his pocket.

Beyond the baby celebration, they were commemorating another Hale's return to Dare Valley. Moira was going to join the ranks of the bright minds shaping a better world at Emmits Merriam University. His old friend, long since passed, who'd founded the university the same year Arthur had returned to town, would have been proud to see a pioneering invention center on the school's beloved grounds. Arthur and Emmits had shared a vision for the world, and in their own ways, they'd laid a foundation for change in Dare Valley.

Another generation was taking the reins now, and soon his time would pass, just like Emmits' had.

Arthur spied another visionary in the crowd—one of the young folks he'd always hoped would return to Dare

Valley. Lucy O'Brien saw a bigger world than almost anyone else he knew, but she found a way to communicate her vision with others using nothing other than a flimsy thing called paper—rather like Arthur did with his newspaper.

A funny thing, paper. He marveled at everything it could capture.

He picked up one of the autographed copies of *The Calendar of New Beginnings* sitting on the table and took a seat in one of the empty chairs in the dining room. April had brought out a bunch of autographed ones to share with the family. Sure, some people in town had gotten their knickers in a wad about the photos, but most of them—Arthur included—had teared up plenty from reading the dedications.

Now those were worth lingering over, especially the one Jill had written about his beloved wife, God rest her soul. *For my grandmother, Harriet Hale, the kind of woman who threw tea parties with champagne glasses filled with orange juice and gave money to her granddaughter to start a business of her own. Her love and vision made her one special lady, and I miss her more than words can express.*

After tearing up over that particular dedication, he'd flipped through the rest of the calendar pretty quickly. He was three feet in the grave and had no desire to see any of the people he knew buck naked, even if they were covered with props like the American flag.

Old Man Jenkins was a class act, and Arthur thought he looked pretty fit for his age. Not that he was comparing himself to that old sack of bones. Joanie liked him just fine, and that was more than he could expect at his age. Of course, he'd stayed on his girlfriend's page a tad longer than most. She'd looked pretty good, draped in all those colorful ribbons, but he'd never tell that to another soul save the woman herself. But if he had to hear another young woman grow breathless while talking about the photo of Chef T hiding his manhood with a meat cleaver, he was going to bash his head into the closest wall.

Some people had no sense.

Of course, he'd heard a few of the men's comments about his granddaughter wearing nothing but a hat of fruit. He'd leveled them a glare designed to shrivel up their man parts.

The chair next to him was yanked back, and he frowned and looked up at the culprit. "I was just looking at your calendar," he told Lucy, who was pretty much beaming like a lighthouse now that she and Young Andy had agreed to hook up for life. Pretty soon, his greatnephew would put a ring on her finger, and Arthur couldn't wait until they tied the knot.

These young people were going to give him a stroke someday.

"I saw that," she said, sitting down and scooting forward until she was beside him. "Why do you think I came over instead of cooing over the new baby? He's only two months old, but he already has more love in the world than he could ever imagine."

"Babies are pure love," Arthur said, and then coughed, realizing he sounded like some greeting card. "What I mean is they're pure. Not messed up yet by this big old world we live in."

She gave him a warm smile. "Not everyone is messed up."

He gave her a pointed look. "You were."

"I'm learning," she said, fighting a smile. "Did you read my dedication in the calendar?"

"Of course I did," he blustered. "I have eyes, don't I?" Then he paused, cataloguing her face. "How is your vision?"

"About the same," she said, putting on a brave face. "But I'm moving forward. I love taking photos and dammit, that's what I'm going to do."

Certainly she'd managed to take good photos for the calendar—although to hear her tell it, she'd sworn a blue streak and relied on Moira's help more than she'd ever imagined.

"Good to hear!" he said, pounding the table for good measure, making some of the adults look over. "Everything is fine."

They resumed their cooing over the baby.

"My new Leica is feeling more natural in my hands," Lucy continued, "and I decided I could try out two approaches when I go on assignment again."

So she was going. "What's that?"

"Aren't you going to ask me about the assignments?"

He harrumphed. "None of my affair." Even if he'd cut his right arm off for details. But he had sources. He didn't have to get all his information directly, especially in his own family.

"I'm making them shorter. Ten days to two weeks and more spread out now. I'm going to places that aren't active war zones for the moment until I get more comfortable with being back in the field."

"That lowers my blood pressure considerably," he said, fingering the calendar.

"I'm going to try taking some photos in black and white to see if that helps any of the color vision issues until my brain learns how to combine the two different images it's seeing into a more cohesive frame. I've talked to a few of the people I've worked for in the past, and they're amenable to working through the issue. And then I'll decide if I need a collaborator to touch things up after I've taken a pass. We'll have to see. As you said, I can figure it out."

"Why does everyone feel the need to repeat me?" he asked, crossing his arms. "But all of that sounds good."

She rose and kissed his cheek, which he only pretended to hate.

"We quote you because you're so wise. Thanks

again, Arthur."

"You have that op-ed on my desk next week," he said, giving her a wink.

She gave a wave and sauntered off. He had plans for her. Ones that included her working at his newspaper. He hadn't figured everything out yet, what with Meredith being away on maternity leave, but he would. *The Western Independent* would continue to report world events long after he was gone. And they could quote him on that!

It was time for the next generation to take over, and Lucy was one of the people he wanted to succeed him. He eyed Meredith and Tanner. Heaven had wrapped up his retirement in a red bow and plopped it in his lap when those two hitched up. And now there was Lucy. She was going to figure out how to take world-class photos again—of that he had no doubt—but she was also going to settle down with his great-nephew and have babies. Arthur had already bought a child's camera for their first born in case he wasn't around.

It was like Lucy had said in the calendar. Death came to everyone, and he'd heard it knocking on his door for some time now. He'd made his peace with it.

His fingers traced the dedication Lucy had written on the back of the calendar. It was so compelling, he found himself reading it again. Raw words filled with power and truth deserved to be memorized.

*This calendar represents a new collage of subjects for me. Every month captures the complexity of what it means to be human. We all die, and that's a fact. And we all suffer loss. How can we not if we love?*

*All of the people photographed in this calendar represent what it means to keep living, to essentially continue being human. Some of them still hold that sense of whimsy from the memory of a loved one. Others are still experiencing the piercing, bone-cutting pain of loss. And then there are those who have reached peace and acceptance and found a way to smile again.*

*All of these emotions matter. All of them are real. All of them deserved to be seen and honored. Regardless of the losses we all endure, they mark a transition point, one we have chosen to call a new beginning. And so life continues in all its majesty and mystery...*

*Dear Reader,*

*Thank you so much for reading Lucy and Andy's story. I used to work in many of the places Lucy did in my old career as a conflict expert, so I understand her journey. It's wonderful she and Andy can have their happy ending after everything they both went through. Hopefully we're all inspired by that message.*

*If you enjoyed this book, please post a review! It helps more readers want to read my story. You can write one at the retailer or on Goodreads. And when you post one, kindly let me know at readavamiles@gmail.com so I can personally thank you.*

*To keep up with all my new releases, please sign up for my newsletter. And join our Dare family fiesta of fun and inspiration by connecting with me on Facebook.*

*So what's next? As you might have guessed, Moira and Chase are our next Dare Valley couple in HOME SWEET LOVE. I'm also releasing a new series called Once Upon a Dare with all of the football stars you met in THE BRIDGE TO A BETTER LIFE. Remember them putting Blake's underwear in a tree? Jordan and Grace are up first in THE GATE TO EVERYTHING. Additionally, the next Dare River book will be out soon as well. Shelby and Vander are primed to discover what happened to her father in THE FOUNTAIN OF INFINITE WISHES.*

*Thank you again for reading and being one of the*

*greatest blessings in my life.*

*Lots of light and joy,*
*Ava*

**To learn more about Moira and Chase's story called HOME SWEET LOVE, sign up for my newsletter.**

**Watch for the next Dare River story, THE FOUNTAIN OF INFINITE WISHES (Shelby & Vander), out later in 2016!**

**And the very first Once Upon a Dare book, THE GATE TO EVERYTHING (Grace & Jordan), will be released in July 2016.**

# About the Author

USA Today Bestselling Author Ava Miles joined the ranks of beloved storytellers after receiving Nora Roberts' blessing for her use of Ms. Roberts' name in her debut novel, the #1 National Bestseller NORA ROBERTS LAND. A mere six months after her debut in 2013, she'd hit the USA Today Bestseller list and released five books. So far, over a million readers have discovered Ava's stories, which have reached the #1 spot at Barnes & Noble and ranked in Amazon and iBooks' Top 10. Ava's books have been chosen as Best Books of the Year and Top Editor's Picks and are being translated into multiple languages.

Made in the USA
Lexington, KY
27 April 2016